by
Cambria Hebert

"The most beautiful stories
always start with wreckage."
—Jack London

#BLUR
gearshark magazine

ISSUE #4

The Past

I'm not going to say I always knew I was different.

We're all different. And at some point in everyone's life, I think we all feel like we don't fit in, like we don't belong or that no one understands us.

We're all human; we're all flesh and bone. But no one is the same.

I think it's just a matter of discovering what it is that makes each of us different. In my case, there was no *ah-ha!* moment. There was no lightbulb to blink on over my head. It would have been easier that way.

Instead, it was a slow realization, a series of moments, sometimes far between, that showed me what made me different.

Sometimes I wish I ignored those signs. Sometimes I wonder where I'd be right now if I had.

Less me.

Happier?

Not here.

Everything I went through led me here. Isn't that the way of the universe? I think I wanted to be here right now. I'm standing at the edge of a precipice; I feel it deep.

I'm not sure if where I go from here is going to be everything I want. Hell, I'm not even sure what that is.

But I do believe something. I have to, because if I don't, misery will be my only companion.

Everything I've gone through, all those far-between moments, the lengthy trips through hell… the abuse.

It was for something.
Something lost is something gained.
It has to be.

Chapter One

Seventeen-year-old Arrow…

A magazine.

Everything changed because of a magazine.

But really, a series of glossy pages filled with half-naked and provocative images stapled together and hidden between my mattress and box spring really shouldn't have so much power.

I guess if I were honest, I would say the changes had been long coming. Inevitable. Undeniable. A magazine couldn't possibly crumble the very foundation on which my life was built. It would take something far more powerful to do that.

However, to a seventeen-year-old who embodied so much innocence and so much… *youth*, well, that kid, he blamed it all on the magazine.

My cherry-red, two-door BMW slid to a stop in the driveway near the double front entry. It wasn't in its assigned spot; it wasn't even parked straight. I wasn't going to be here long. I'd left my gym bag behind this morning and now here I was, rushing home from school so I could grab it, only to head right back.

Coach was going to make me run drills for this. He'd probably even put me at goalie, a position he knew I hated because, frankly, I sucked at it. After I ran drills, I could be pelted with the ball over and over again as I tried to stop it from sailing past me into the net.

I was going to be dirty and grimy. More so than usual. I'd probably have to hit the showers so I didn't get the inside of my Beemer jacked up.

I didn't usually shower after soccer practice. I waited until I got home. It wasn't because I didn't like to shower in the locker room… It was just the opposite, actually.

Maybe you left the bag behind on purpose. Wanted to be late, didn't you? Wanted the punishment… so you could get the reward.

I pushed away my thoughts, took the stairs two at a time, and bounded to my bedroom, which was to the left of the sweeping staircase and at the very end of the hallway. I had a corner room. The windows looked out over the private backyard and pool.

The door swung open the second my hand hit the knob, and I was momentarily surprised. I thought I'd latched it this morning on my way out. I always did. I wasn't the best housekeeper… Okay, fine, I was a slob. Mom told me almost daily I needed to clean up my stuff.

Why bother? I'd just have to get it back out.

I solved the problem by learning to close the door. She didn't have to see the mess, and I didn't have to clean it. Genius.

My feet stumbled a little because I was moving with haste but also because they weren't expecting the door to give the way it did.

My eyes flew up as I faltered over the threshold. I met another pair of surprised eyes.

"Mom?" I straightened away from the door.

"Arrow," she half gasped. "I thought you had soccer practice?"

"I left my gym bag. Can't play without my shoes."

Her gaze strayed across the room to the standard red gym bag with white handles lying haphazardly near my dresser. One of the cleats was poking out of the top, along with a dirty sock. "I hadn't realized," she said, mostly to herself.

'Cause clearly she didn't think I'd be home.

She was perched on the corner of my unmade bed. Neat and put together as always, she was a stark contrast to the twisted navy-blue comforter and white sheets basically piled in the center of the mattress. A few pillows still bore the indent from my head up near the wooden headboard, and my earbuds lay tangled off to the side.

The wooden blinds were open now, letting in sunlight… something this room didn't often see. Again, why open the blinds when I would just close them a few hours later?

I could see small particles of dust floating around lazily in the brightest beam streaking across the room.

Yeah, maybe I should clean up a little in here.

Oddly enough, it wasn't the mess that bothered me. Neither was finding her in here snooping.

She was totally snooping.

It was just easier to focus on the mess in here instead of everything else that was going on.

Like what she'd found.

What she currently gripped in her hands.

My stomach felt as if it had been stabbed with an ice pick. Except the wound was old and aching, not new and fresh. It wasn't a stabbing panic kind of pain. Instead, it was worse. There was a hollow hole carved out inside me, and it never healed. It was doomed to ache and burn, to churn with emptiness and be crowded with scar tissue. Those were the worst kind of wounds, weren't they? They ones that never healed. The ones you knew were chronic and would ache forever.

Along with the overwhelming feeling of sickness came one of urgent flight. As if all the oxygen in this room had been sucked out and panic for air clawed the inside of my windpipe.

Get out!

Run!

Escape!

Trying my best not to stare or even glance at the offending item in her hands, I jolted into motion, swiping the bag off the floor. The sock and cleat went flying, and I scrambled after the shoe. The second my hand closed around it, I vaulted up and lunged at the door.

I was just going to leave. Pretend this didn't happen.

Maybe, hopefully, she would, too.

I'd seen the questions in her eyes in the past. The way she sometimes looked at me like she knew. Mom never said a word. Her questions and suspicions went unvoiced.

Today could be the same.

I made it partway out the bedroom door, not bothering to pull it around behind me as I rushed. Maybe I should have. Perhaps putting the wood between us would have served as an excuse to "not hear" what she spoke after me.

"You're still my arrow. That will never change."

Her words hurt—the stabbing, immediate pain.

I knew why now. I understood the difference between the old hollow ache and this new, more piercing kind.

The hollow ache felt old because it was. A feeling that was always there but mostly went ignored. You'd be amazed what you got used to living with when it became your norm.

I'd been expecting this moment. Dreading it.

I hadn't been expecting her words. The soft way she said them. The acceptance in her voice; I'd never known that, not even within myself. It hurt. God, it cut deep. Piercing, quick, and almost numbing.

When someone gives you something you truly didn't think you'd ever get, it stings. You go through a whole host of fleeting but totally felt emotions in rapid fire.

Shock. *She didn't say that.*

Disbelief. *Is my mind playing tricks on me?*

Desperate want. *Does she know what she's saying? Does she mean it?*

Relief. *Would someone understand?*

After I let the strongest of emotions pummel me, I pivoted and the gym bag fell from my grip to land abandoned in the hall.

I looked up at her from beneath the light-brown wave of hair falling over my forehead, timid, afraid to acknowledge her words.

"From the moment the doctor handed you over to me in the delivery room…" She began. I knew this story. She told it to me all the time. Hell, it was how I got my name. Usually, I rolled my eyes and interrupted her.

I didn't this time.

This time I listened.

This time it was important.

"My love for you was like the strongest, purest arrow shot directly into my heart. I can't explain it to you because you aren't a parent yourself. But something happened the moment I formally met you. The second I wrapped my arms around you, the second I looked into your wide eyes, my world tilted. Not so it was crooked, but so it was straight. I will never love anyone like I do you, son. Never. This changes nothing."

Cautiously, I moved back into the room, crossing the threshold as if she'd cast a line with her words and the hook on the end sank deep. I was reeled in by her. Not just by her words, but by the look on her face.

She was upset, concerned, and even hurt.

I was glad. It made it more real. More honest and somehow a little easier to comprehend.

Total acceptance without any kind of doubt would have been a boldfaced lie, and it would have spoken louder than any words she might have spewed.

I dropped beside her on the bed, my stance mirroring hers as we both perched on the mattress precariously, as if the bed were unstable and we both might fall.

My knees were shaking; my ankles felt weak. I wasn't ready for this. At least I told myself I wasn't.

But here I was. The first chance I was given to perhaps say it, I didn't run. I wanted to, but she made it kind of okay. She made it a little less terrifying, and it made me a little braver.

I avoided her gaze; that much I wasn't ready for. I felt hers on me. It bore into me like the sun on the hottest day of summer. Instead, I glanced down at the magazine in her hand.

It was basically porn.

On the cover was a man with a completely bare chest. His body was defined, but not in a bodybuilder type of way. His shoulders were broad, his chest free of any hair. Water droplets clung to his torso and biceps. His nipples were erect, and in the background was a glass-walled shower.

The only thing that covered his body was a towel. If it dropped just one inch, it would reveal all of his one thousand parts.

He didn't smile at the camera. Instead, he pouted. His full lips pulled into a taunting semi-smile.

The interior of the magazine was pretty much the same, with the exception of the towel. They were naked. Fully erect. Some of them were having sex, and some were getting blowjobs.

It really wasn't all that startling to find porn in your teenage son's room.

The startling part was it featured only men. Guy-on-guy action.

Gay porn.

Usually, I didn't keep it here in this room. For obvious reasons. But not this time. This time I did, and I thought it had been hidden well enough. I knew she suspected, but I didn't think she was ready for the truth. I didn't think she'd go creeping around my room like the fucking FBI.

I wasn't going to call her out on it, though. Secretly, maybe I wanted this to happen. Maybe that's why I kept the magazine instead of getting rid of it like all the others.

Well, that and it was a hot magazine. I liked the pictures. I liked thinking about what it would be like to be on the receiving end of one of the blowjobs.

At first, I started looking at gay porn out of curiosity. Then it became more of a test.

Male-female action didn't do anything for me. The female body just didn't hold my attention like it did for everyone else. Sure, I joined in on titty rating, ass conversation, and I even watched my fair share of M/F porn.

It made me uncomfortable.

Not the sex either. Not the bad porn music or the way some women didn't shave their bush.

Okay, the bush and music were pretty raunchy.

What made me uncomfortable was I was so unaffected by it. Beneath my boxers, my cock stayed limp. Watching some dude get off on a woman was almost boring.

Then I started watching just the guy. The way he'd stroke himself, the way his cock would pulse when he came.

That stirred my desire.

It scared the shit out of me. I tried. I really did.

I got really drunk one night and lost my virginity to a cheerleader. It sucked, and the only way I kept it up was because there was a couple going at it in the room beside us, and the guy was moaning so loud it filtered through the walls.

That was the night I had to stop kind of pretending. I couldn't really ignore all the feelings inside me, but I could hide them until I figured out what to do.

Mom just waited for me to speak. She didn't rush me or even try to pry anything out with a barrage of questions.

I had no idea what to say.

No idea what to feel.

Except suddenly, I wanted to challenge her, what she said. The same way I challenged myself for years.

"It's not a phase," I said, looking again at the magazine.

"I know that."

I lifted my eyes to meet hers. She nodded.

Why wasn't she yelling? Why wasn't she grossed out?

"I'm gay," I said and then pressed my lips together. It was the first time I ever said it out loud. The first time I'd ever admitted it to anyone but myself.

"I wish you weren't," Mom said honestly. "A mother wants the best life possible for her child. Life is hard enough as it is. This is only going to make it harder on you."

I nodded. She was right.

She reached out, laid her hand over mine.

"Why aren't you more surprised? Why aren't you mad?" I asked.

"You never date. You barely even look at girls. I've seen them look at you during your games, when I used to drop you off with friends. There was never any interest on your part. I just… I guess I just slowly realized, probably like you."

"You never said anything."

"You didn't either," she mused.

"I thought you'd hate me."

"I will never hate you. I love you."

I knew my mother loved me, but I hadn't known she loved me enough to accept this. Some of the weight I carried lifted off my shoulders. Some of that hollow pain inside me suddenly seemed a lot less.

She loved me anyway.

Even though I felt relief, even though some of the self-loathing and doubt I held inside didn't seem so fierce… I still felt guarded.

I still had no idea what to say here.

I didn't know how to be myself. Not really.

I never allowed it.

What I had was pieces of who I was. Pieces of who I knew I should be and pieces of the way I felt inside. I never put them all together.

I still couldn't. I wasn't sure I was ready.

"You need to get to practice," she said. "You're already late."

I blinked. How many more times was she going to surprise me today?

"We'll talk when you want to. On your own time. Just know I'll be here when you're ready."

I stood from the bed, relieved to be dismissed from this conversation. Before walking away, I glanced down at the magazine still in her hands. I wanted to grimace.

God, my mother holding a gay porn issue?

My eyes needed bleached.

I might have nightmares.

That magazine was officially the last thing on earth that would ever turn me on again.

With embarrassed haste, I reached for it. "I'll, ah…" I faltered. "Take that."

"Take it with you," Mom said, releasing it. "Probably best not to have that lying around the house."

"It wasn't lying around," I sniped. "It was hidden in my room."

Guess I wasn't totally ready to just let her snooping go. What she did was a total invasion of my space. Of the inside of my head. No wonder I wasn't ready to talk yet. I was completely taken off guard.

"I was worried about you, Arrow. I just wanted to make sure you're okay."

"Whatever," I muttered and tucked the mag beneath my arm.

"I'm just trying to protect you," she said, a different note coming into her voice. Her words were more guarded than before. It was odd.

"Protect me from what?"

She paused. I saw her debating, like she was picking and choosing her words carefully. "I think it may be best if we kept your…" She paused. "Lifestyle choice between me and you right now. Until we've had a chance to talk."

I recoiled for two reasons:

1.) Being gay wasn't a choice. I didn't know a lot, but that I *knew*. It wasn't even a lifestyle. It just was. (That hollow pain inside me, the one I mostly ignored, groaned through me like cold wind on a gusty day).

and

2.) She didn't want me to tell Dad.

"You think he'll hate me." It was a direct accusation even though I said it as more of a statement.

"Of course not," Mom soothed. But I saw it. I saw the doubt in her eyes.

Opposition and anger flared inside me.

He couldn't. He wouldn't… He loved me.

Right?

"Then why don't you want me to tell him?"

"Your father can be very…" There was that pause again while she weighed her words. "Cold at times. Very narrow-minded."

"He is not!" I argued.

"I know you don't see him that way." She agreed. "But he's never showed you that side of himself. Just because you don't see something doesn't mean it isn't there. There's a reason your brother isn't around very much, a reason your father spends so much time at the office."

I was reeling inside. Smacked in the face with the discovery of my deepest secret and now the possibility my father would reject me for it. I couldn't believe it. I wouldn't.

"You said you didn't care," I rebutted.

"And I meant that, but your father and I are different people."

I shook my head. The little boy inside me stomped his feet and shook his fist. Every kid wanted to believe his parents were superheroes. Even when we began to grow up, we still clung to the idea.

If you really believe he'll accept you, why haven't you said anything?

"You're wrong," I argued. Beneath my skin, I was shaking. "Dad won't care."

I'd been afraid of this very thing. Of both my parents and even my brother rejecting me. Of my friends turning their backs and everything I knew in life just slipping away. It's why I never said a word. Why I kept it all inside… So why was I fighting against the truth of it now?

Why was I taking it out on the person who bucked my fears and offered me acceptance?

"I think this is something your father will not be expecting and something that will upset him," she said honestly but gently. "After you and I talk, we can decide on the best way to handle your father."

"As in what…? Never tell him?"

Her stare dropped to the floor. "Possibly."

I laughed, but it was a terrible, rotten sound. "How can you tell me you accept me and then tell me to shut up about it? You can't have it both ways, Mom! You either don't care I'm gay or you do!"

She started to say something, but I made a sound.

"Unbelievable!" I yelled. "You come in here snooping around like you think I'm some serial killer or drug addict. You say you're worried about me, but then when you find something, you want to pretend you didn't! What the fuck, Mom? You should have just pretended to never see this!" I brandished the magazine in front of her like a weapon.

"Don't you take that tone with me." She warned.

"Whatever," I snarled and marched past her into the hall, where I scooped up the gym bag.

"Arrow!" she called out behind me as I stormed down the hallway. "Don't leave like this. Let's talk."

"You've said enough already!" I tossed the words over my shoulder, then disappeared down the wide staircase.

With a heaving chest, I slammed into my Beemer. I turned the stereo up so the bass practically rattled my chest and threw the car into drive. Before I peeled away from the house, I glanced over at the gym bag and magazine I'd thrown on the seat.

Defiance sparked inside me. The need to prove her wrong, to prove the anguish and fear inside *me* wrong was so strong I could barely think straight.

I wasn't ready to talk about this yet, to try and make sense of the way I was made.

But now my thoughts and feelings were muddled and jumbled up. The burning, almost itching need to prove my mother wrong, to have that acceptance from my father, almost overruled everything else.

All these years of logic, of careful thought and deliberate silence, seemed to fly out the window as I tore down the driveway and the wind ripped at my hair and shirt.

Ready or not, here I come.

Chapter Two

My brother wasn't around much.

The older he got, the older I got, the less we saw of him. He was a few years older than me, my brother from another mother. Like literally, we had different moms. But we had the same dad.

Even though my mom raised him since she and dad got married, Jace was always a little distant. Somehow a little more separate from the rest of us. I'd never really thought much about it because I looked up to him no matter what he did. My older brother was cool. He raced cars, lived life on his own terms… Something I'd always been scared to do.

Maybe that's why I never thought about his distance, because I thought it was just him living life on his own terms.

Then I learned the real reason.

If I had only listened, it would have been a lesson I might have been spared.

Jace would say things sometimes. Clues, reinforcements for what my mother tried to warn me about. I thought he was just being his sarcastic, asshole self. He and Dad locked horns a lot over the way Jace chose to spend his time.

Jace never backed down.

I wasn't going to either.

I was scared. So scared it made me sick. More than once, I swallowed back the puke crawling up the back of my throat. The chunks were hot and burned when I forced them back down as I strode through the parking lot and rode the elevator up the huge chrome-and-glass office building.

I considered turning around, aborting this insanity, but then I remembered what Mom said, and the anger I felt. I wanted to disbelieve her so badly it was actually ruling over everything else.

What a mistake it was.

Dad's secretary wasn't at her desk when I stepped off the elevator into the spacious receiving area. I didn't pause as I went right past the large counter and company logo on the wall behind it all. I walked down the hallway, which was quiet toward the end where my father's large office sat, formidably.

I didn't knock. Why should I? I was his son.

I pushed in on the door, but it didn't give. It was locked from the inside.

I heard his muffled voice behind the thick wooden doors. Then more clearly, he called out, "What?" His voice was exasperated and slightly breathless, like he'd been running.

"Dad?" I called. "I wanted to talk to you."

"Just a minute, son," he replied after a brief pause. "I'm wrapping up a meeting."

I stepped back from the doors but didn't bother to go back to the waiting room. I was impatient. Nervous and not thinking clearly.

The conversation I'd just had with my mother still burned between my ears. In fact, my ears felt hot, and there was sweat beaded on my brow.

After hearing some movement and muffled voices, the large double doors to his office opened, but not widely. Just enough so his secretary could slip out.

She was young. I didn't know her name because he got new assistants all the time. Her hair was blond like my mother's. She had large brown eyes and a huge rack that had to be fake.

She cleared her throat when she saw me in the hallway. My stare went right to her face, something that seemed to make her uncomfortable. Her gaze shifted away from me. The red lipstick on her mouth was smeared, as if she'd applied it without a mirror or she'd wiped her mouth on a napkin without thinking.

I shifted, uncomfortable, but unsure why.

"Dylan," she said. I gave her a silent what-up gesture with my chin. I hated when people called me Dylan.

It was my name, but the older I got, the more it seemed Dylan was someone else.

The woman shifted and fussed with her top. The back tail had come out of the waistband of her tight skirt, and I watched her stuff it in quickly. The buttons on her shirt were done up wrong. It afforded me a shot of her lace bra beneath the red silk.

A gross feeling wormed around inside me, and I looked away. Quickly, she lifted the folder of papers in her hands to cover her chest.

"Go ahead in," she said as she rushed off down the hallway.

Without a second thought, I slipped into Dad's office and shut the door behind me.

Dad was behind his desk, sitting in the large, black leather chair. It was a commanding chair, just like him. Over the wide back was his jacket, draped there as if the chair had gotten cold and he'd chivalrously given up his shirt.

The thought was absurd. Chivalrous wasn't a word I would use to describe Sullivan Lorhaven. Ever.

The absurdity sort of brought me back a little from the edge of whatever crazed emotions I was teetering on the edge of.

I cleared my throat and focused on him. He looked as he always did. Steady, impenetrable, and strong.

"Dylan," he said, surprise in his voice. He waved me farther into the room as he spoke. "Come in, son. What brings you by?"

"I wanted to talk to you," I said. Once the door was closed, I went across the carpet to one of the chairs in front of the desk. "There's some things I've been thinking about…" My voice trailed away, and I cleared my throat.

My mother's warning and the tone of her voice filled my head.

Maybe not ever.

Mom wasn't an unreasonable woman. She proved that by her almost easy acceptance of me coming out to her and the fact she found gay porn in my room. It hit me then, as I was sitting here in this giant office that radiated power and money, that maybe I should heed her warning.

"I know why you're here," Dad said, cutting off my inner ramblings. "What you want to talk about."

I felt my eyes widen. "You do?"

"Of course, you're my son. I know what's been on your mind. It has been for a while." He nodded like he was exactly sure.

I relaxed inside. It wasn't a visible change on the outside. In fact, I still sat and behaved the same way. My back was straight, my feet touched the floor, and my hands rested loosely on my thighs. Beneath the exterior, though, relief and smugness whisked away my previous thoughts. The bile rising up my throat settled.

Of course he knew. Just like Mom had suspected.

All this time. All this time I thought I'd been so good at concealing my own inner struggles, my deepest feelings and urges.

They'd both seen. Of course they had. Parents knew their sons more than anyone. We were bound by blood, genetics. Genetics were an almost physic link sometimes… kind of like a secret passkey to the dark web. Except it was to the deepest, most inner place inside their offspring.

He wasn't mad at all. If anything, it was as if he'd expected this talk. He'd been waiting for it.

"I've been nervous to talk to you." I began, and he held up his hand before I could continue.

"I figured as much, which is why I took the liberty of making a few calls."

"What?" I said, a little stunned. *What kind of calls?*

"To the head coach at Syracuse University. And also to the dean."

"You called Syracuse?" I echoed. I was stumbling, trying to keep up.

"You'll be relieved to know the recruiters there have been watching you. The head coach is also interested. He thinks you'll make a great addition to the soccer team."

"He does," I said, again sort of hollow because this was so not what I was expecting.

He's talking about college right now. Soccer. My future.

That was not what I was here for. Not at all.

"And the dean, well, he and I met at a charity event last year. He was also impressed to learn you have applied to his school. I, of course, offered a hefty donation to the school and the sports program upon your admission."

I just stared at him.

Dad went on. "I know your grades aren't quite as stellar as some of the other students, but you're an athlete. Soccer is number one, and Syracuse has one of the best soccer teams in the college league. I have no doubt your application is being fast-tracked as we speak, and you'll be getting an admissions acceptance in the mail any day now."

He thought I was nervous about my college applications, that I was worried I wouldn't get into a top-notch school. I always knew it was important to him that I went somewhere prestigious and that I played soccer at the college level. Me playing soccer was something he was very proud of, even though he'd only been to a handful of my games.

I liked soccer, but it wasn't my dream. I played mainly because it made him proud. And because it was a good way to get out energy, frustration, and it was a good guise.

Playing soccer made me a jock. Jocks were macho… They were womanizers.

They weren't gay.

Truth was I didn't even want to go to college. I didn't know what I wanted to do. I never really thought about it. Honestly, in a lot of ways, it didn't matter. I'd go to Syracuse. I'd play soccer, and I'd make my father proud.

Perhaps doing everything he wanted would make it easier for him to understand how I felt inside.

"That's awesome, Dad," I said, interjecting excitement into my tone. "I'll keep a look out for the admissions letter. Mom is going to be thrilled."

"We're all very proud, Dylan. Keep up the good work, son."

I nodded.

"So don't you worry about a thing. Your tuition will be taken care of, we'll get you a nice apartment right off campus, and all you'll have to focus on is going to class and playing soccer."

"It's definitely a load off my shoulders," I said, even though I hadn't been worried about that shit at all. I barely ever thought about college, but moving to my own place would be nice. More room to be more me.

Dad smiled and pushed back from his desk. "Good talk."

"There was something else," I said before I chickened out.

"Oh?" he asked, mildly surprised. "What is it?"

I watched him walk toward the bar on the other side of the room in his black dress slacks and white button-up. He picked up a decanter of dark liquid and poured some into a clear glass.

While his back was to me, I made a snap decision.

Don't be a pussy.

"I'm gay." The words whooshed out. Just like that. I didn't do a lead up or even try to say it in a roundabout way. Sully Lorhaven was a straightforward businessman. I could be that way, too.

The room went dead silent. My father almost froze in time. Like someone hit stop on a movie screen and everything ceased to move.

He stared straight ahead, the decanter in his hand midair on the way back to the bar top. The muscles in his back bunched together, tense, and stayed that way.

The bile in my gut rose again. I gulped it down. I wasn't sure what else to say. I wasn't sure what to do. Now that the words were out there, all the anger and bravado I felt was rapidly draining away.

I grabbed at it, holding on. This was my father. He'd been proud of me my entire life. He'd never said otherwise. I'd always done everything I thought would make him happy. I played soccer. I got decent grades. I never talked back. I was good… I didn't get into trouble.

This was big, but it wasn't so big it would cancel out all those things. He would love me anyway. Just like Mom.

Because he was my father.

That's what fathers did.

The glass decanter hit the bar with a sharp cracking sound. I sat a little farther upright and stared at his back as he drained the entire contents of his glass in one large swallow, then slapped it down on the top as well.

"What did you just say?" he rasped.

"I've known a long time. I just never wanted to say anything. But Mom knows… and I wanted to be the one to tell you."

He spun, looking at me with hard, cool eyes. They were the eyes of a stranger. Of a businessman with no soul.

I'd never seen him look at me that way.

"You told your mother?"

I nodded. "She sort of figured it out."

"Who else knows?" he asked, his voice cold, void of emotion.

"No one. I don't plan on telling anyone else. I just wanted you to know." *I wanted you to know the real me.*

He turned his head and looked toward the large windows on the other side of the room. They offered a spectacular view of everything around the office building. At night, it was even better, when everything was all lit up against the darkness.

He didn't say anything, just stared off.

I began to fidget. My stomach cramped. My mother's words, the look in her eyes when she said them… It started to haunt me.

I wasn't ready to give up yet. This was my father. The man who raised me. The man who just moments ago talked to me with almost booming pride about Syracuse.

"This doesn't have to change anything," I told him. "I'll still go to Syracuse. I'll play soccer and pick a major. I'll still do everything we planned. Maybe someday I'll come out, but not until I'm ready. Not until—"

My words were cut off, but not by his.

Not by anything he said or even did.

By the bitter, cold draft that blew into the room and brushed around my body like a kiss.

The kiss of death.

This was the moment my life changed forever.

A moment I would forever look back on as the dividing line of then and now.

Dylan died that day.

Well, maybe he didn't die right then. He got sick… with an incurable disease, and it slowly began to eat away at me until there was no more.

The incurable disease wasn't that I was gay.

It was him. The man I looked up to. The man I admired. The man I'd spent almost eighteen years trying to make proud.

After moments of that soul-chilling silence, he turned his head to look at me. He looked *through* me.

"You are *not* gay. You are Dylan Lorhaven, son of Sullivan Lorhaven. A descendent of a long line of strong, powerful men. There is no room for weakness in this family."

"I'm still me. I'm not weak. I'm just not into girls."

His eyes hardened. "You are. Not. Gay. I forbid it."

"You forbid it."

"Whatever silly things you've been telling yourself, stop right now. You are in control of your mind and your body. No son of mine will be flaunting around telling people he's a man lover. It's gross, it's unmanly, and it soils everything our family name stands for." His voice began to rise, and with it, so did my shock.

"Me being gay doesn't ruin the family name." I argued.

"You are *not* gay." All at once, he shot forward, stalking with heavy footsteps to my chair, and planted his palms on the arms, caging me in.

His face, which had turned a flushed shade of pink, leaned down and pushed close to mine. His eyes drilled into mine, his stare intense and dark.

"I forbid you to be gay. I never want to hear this again. We will never speak of this again. You will date women. Only women. You will play soccer, go to college, and when the time comes, you will get married… to a woman.”

"What if I don't want to?" I challenged. The anger and defiance was coming back. It was beginning to take over the shock over his reaction.

My mother was right.

She'd been right. I never should have told him.

He laughed, but it wasn't a pleasant sound. In fact, it was so chilling, goose bumps rose along my arms.

"You don't have a choice. You are my son, and you will do as I say when I say it."

My eyes leveled on his; I sat forward, a bit of challenge in my posture. "Or what?"

In one swift movement, he shoved back and threw out his fist. It came fast and hard. It was so unexpected I had no time to react.

His tight fist plowed right into my nose. White-hot pain exploded behind my eye sockets and radiated across my cheekbones. I flew back in the chair. He punched so hard, I toppled backward. Me and the chair landed in a heap on the rug.

I lay there for one second, stunned.

Then I dabbed at my nose. My fingers came away red.

My brain switched off. I went into autopilot.

My father—a man who had never lain a hand on me before—just decked me in the face.

I scrambled up, dabbed once more at the blood running down over my upper lip.

"Your life is in my hands." He spoke, deadly calm. It didn't even faze him to see my bleed. "Your college tuition, your car, the roof over your head, and the food you eat—that trust fund with all those zeros? It can all disappear. These are privileges; gifts given by me and my good name. If you want them, you will respect my authority. My son is not a fag, and you will never claim to be one ever again. Do I make myself clear?"

"Is this why Jace left? Is this why he's never around? Are you a giant dick to him, too?" I yelled. My voice sounded slightly stuffy, and I knew my nose was swelling.

"Your brother would agree with me right now."

It was another blow. One I allowed to strike. I believed him. I worshipped Jace, looked up to him. Would he also look at me in a cold and angry manner if I told him the way I felt inside?

I don't think I could take it.

"Mom said she loved me anyway," I said, defeated.

He barked a laugh. "Your mother is a weak, stupid woman."

I lunged across the room and grabbed him by the neck. His eyes widened in shock. He wasn't expecting such a move.

"Don't you dare talk about her that way!" I yelled. "That's your wife. My mother!" I spat.

He allowed my hands to close around his neck and squeeze for long moments before he shoved me off.

"Don't touch me again." He warned.

I stared at him. Really looked. I saw the things I'd been to blind to before. As if this short but damning conversation had unmasked the truth. Like a blindfold I didn't even know I'd been wearing was suddenly pulled free.

I saw a lot of things now.

It was an ugly, ugly view.

His shirt was rumpled, especially where it was tucked in. Part of it was coming out, and his zipper was halfway down.

He smelled like perfume… not the kind my mother wore either.

The image of his assistant slipping out of this office with smeared lipstick and her clothes askew passed behind my eyes.

"She was in here blowing you," I said.

His eyes flew to mine.

I shook my head. "You're cheating on Mom with your assistant. Was she under the desk when I knocked, Dad? You're a sick bastard."

"No." He straightened his tie and rose. "I'm a man. A straight, virile man. Men have urges. They like women. They get it everywhere they can. Your damn right I'm putting it to my secretary. She loves it. When you walk out of here, she's going to come back in here and finish what she started."

What the fuck?

I made a sound and lunged at him again. He was ready for me this time, though, and he grabbed me and tossed me aside.

"Be careful," he growled.

Mom and Jace were right about him. How had I never seen it before? How had I never known what a colossal douchebag he was?

"Does Mom know?"

"I keep my affairs to myself," he said. "And you will, too. I provide a very comfortable life for your mother. You wouldn't want to do anything to disrupt that, would you, Dylan?"

I felt my eyes flash. "Is that a threat?"

"Lorhavens don't threaten." He instructed.

"You can't stop me from being gay."

"I can. I will."

I swiped at the blood on my lip and turned to go. This wasn't at all what I thought it would be. Sure, I didn't expect it to be how it was with Mom… But *this?* This was something I hadn't even imagined.

"We have dinner this weekend at seven. A colleague of mine is coming. Bring a date. An attractive one."

I left the room with all the pride I could muster. I admit it felt like the only bit left clung to the bottom of my shoe like used toilet paper abandoned on the bathroom floor.

Once in the hallway, I gave a shuddering breath and leaned against the closed door.

Numb. I was numb. I felt nothing… Shock pressed in on me like frostbite. It took away all my feelings; all that remained was burning pain. I lifted the hem of my shirt and used it to clean up the blood on my face. Then I shoved off the door and walked down the hall. It felt like it took one hundred years until I stepped into the reception area.

The slut secretary who'd had her lips wrapped around my father's dick was sitting behind her desk, acting like an innocent little employee.

She made me sick, and the room tilted a little.

I shoved it back and strode forward, leaned on the top of the counter, and looked down at her. I stared until she hung up the phone and glanced up at me.

Her lips pulled into a pleasant smile.

How she could smile at the son of the woman whose husband she was screwing was beyond me. So messed up… Everything was much more convoluted than I ever let myself see.

I fished my lip balm out of my jeans as I stood there and smirked. Carefully, I stood the small tube on its end right there on the counter in front of her.

"What's that for?" she asked.

"You'll probably need it once you're finished blowing your boss," I said.

Her eyes widened.

I leaned in and whispered, "Might wanna get checked for STDs. According to the old man, he gets around."

She made a sound.

I pushed off the counter. "See ya later, slut," I called over my shoulder and strolled to the elevator.

Once inside, I leaned against the paneled walls and took a deep breath.

I realized something.

When I first arrived, he hadn't noticed. He didn't ask why I wasn't at practice. It was the first thing Mom noted. He hadn't even known I was supposed to be at practice.

He didn't know anything about me at all.

He didn't care who I really was.

All my father cared about was that I turn out to be the man he wanted me to be.

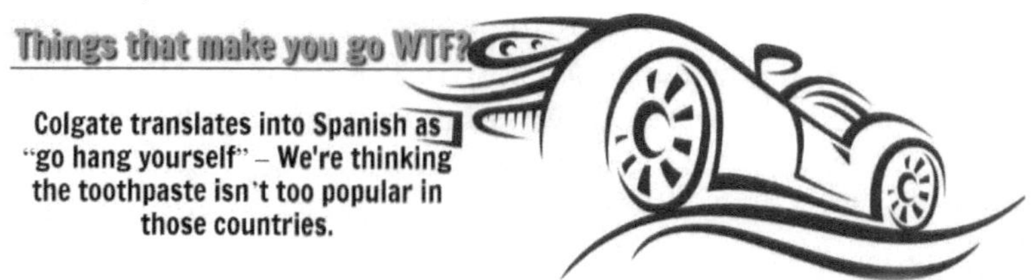

Chapter Three

I didn't bring a date to dinner.

The asshole seemed to know I wouldn't, even though I never told him I wasn't.

Remember that physic-type link I said parents must have had with their offspring? Yeah, I hated it. I wished I could somehow sever it. I would search for ways until one day I could.

Until then, I was stuck.

I showed up for dinner in a suit and combed my messy brown hair so it looked groomed and neat. I hadn't brought a date, but there was one there for me, waiting. Sully had made sure of that. It was the daughter of his colleague. She was tall and thin, her dress tight and short, her hair long and sleek.

She was pretty, but even if I were straight, she wouldn't be my type. Not that I knew what my type was.

But it wasn't her.

I thought about throwing a fit and leaving just then. Showing him I wasn't going to bend to his rule or be his puppet.

The thing was I didn't want to piss off my father.

I played along. She groped me under the dinner table the entire night, and I sat there with food lodged in my throat while my father gave me knowing looks all throughout the meal, like he knew she had her hand on my crotch and was trying to get me to cum in my dress pants.

He probably paid her to do it. A thought I never would have had in the past, but now I knew it was the truth. It was just one more way he could prove I wasn't gay.

Because you know, some girl with her hand on my dick made me hetero.

When dinner was over, I did my "duty" and escorted her out of the room so they could talk business. Mom retreated to her suite, and I was treated to a blowjob by my date.

I let her blow me. It felt good to get off. I closed my eyes and pretended I was somewhere else, with someone else, and gave myself the escape for a few.

When the night was over, Dad slapped me on the back like he was proud.

It made me feel sick.

I was pissed off with him. Hurt. So incredibly hurt I still felt numb. I lay in bed at night and stared at the ceiling. I replayed the day in his office over and over again.

I replayed the look in his eyes, the way his words cut deep, and I heard the sound of his fist plowing into my face.

Jace came by once. I hid in my room, pretending not to be home. I didn't want to see him. I was too afraid he'd disappoint me like our father had.

Part of me knew Jace wouldn't be like that. The logical side to me knew the reason Jace was never around was because he knew who our father really was.

Now I did, too.

Then there was the illogical side of me. The emotional one. The one that'd just been pummeled by a man I'd foolishly thought would love me when I told him my deepest secret.

What if I told my brother and he rejected me, too? Then what?

How could I be myself if it cost me everything? What would I have left? My ideals? My feelings?

Sure, I'd have my mother, but c'mon. I might be gay, but I wasn't a momma's boy.

Don't get me wrong. I loved my mother. I always had. In fact, I probably did more now. She earned my respect. Something I hadn't realized until recently parents had to earn.

It was because I loved her I couldn't lean too heavily on her for this. She'd seen my face when I walked in the door that day. She'd seen my puffy nose and the dried blood on the hem of my shirt.

She knew.

She knew without me saying a word or confirming he was the one who did this.

I didn't tell her he was cheating. I should have, but I couldn't. My life was blown apart enough already, it seemed cruel to blow hers apart too.

Besides, I'd already sort of done that. I heard them fighting that night. I heard her yelling at him, something I'd not heard very often my entire life. My father yelled too, but she didn't back down. I stood in my room, in the dark listening with muscles so tense they ached the next morning.

If he dared raise one hand to her… he'd see just how much of a man he didn't think I was.

They just argued and fought. He worked so late the next night and the night after, I'd fallen asleep before I even heard him come home.

Mom never asked me what he said that day, she didn't tell me "I told you so" either. She just hugged me and whispered she loved me.

I knew my parents' marriage wasn't great. Hell, even a guy with his head in the sand couldn't miss that. But it was much worse now. Because of me. Because of who I was.

I tried not to be gay. For years. Even now, I sometimes tried. *Especially now.*

It was like telling the sun not to come out. Even when it was behind a cloud, it was still there; the sun was still the sun.

It had been a mistake, a naïve thought that I could come out to my parents and still live my life the way I had. It was too hard to process, the ramifications of this, the reason I insisted on outing myself when I hadn't had to.

Being gay was so easy perhaps that's where I went wrong. It was so easy inside me, so natural of a thing, realizing others would hate it so fiercely was almost impossible to fathom.

I walked around in a state of perpetual shock, everything just moving on autopilot. I smiled at the dinner, spoke when spoken to, and went to soccer practice and school. I watched "normal" porn on my laptop and tried to like it.

One night, my father came home early, though it was already dark outside. I was lying across my bed, playing some mindless game on my phone when the bedroom door swung in and he filled the doorway.

"Dylan," he said.

I winced. I hated that name more than ever now.

"Your date will be here in five minutes."

I whipped around. "My date?"

"A client's daughter. I told him you would show her a good time on the town tonight."

I turned away. "Gonna be hard to do that considering I don't have a car anymore."

He'd taken it right after the night I showed up with no date and got a shitty blowjob from the whore he'd paid.

He was having it "serviced." New tires, the works. And he was sending it away for the work because he only wanted the best. It was a lie he told to placate my mother. He really did think she was stupid.

He took my BMW as another way to prove he was in control. Another way to make me not be gay.

Almost eighteen years I lived with him, and never in all that time had I thought he was capable of treating me this way.

Joke was on me, I guess. But really, what did that say about him… and about me?

"You can take the Jag," he said. A set of keys landed on the mattress beside me. I didn't spare them a glance.

"I'm busy."

"It wasn't a request."

"Arrow, honey…" My mother's voice came down the hallway.

"What did I tell you about calling him that?" my father snapped. I glanced up to see him scowling in the direction from which her voice had come. "His name is

Dylan. Quit coddling him, Donna. It's probably the thing that put the fag thought in his head."

There was a beat of electrified silence following his declaration. Order. Or maybe it was just a plain asshole slur. I couldn't tell with him anymore. I was used to him telling me certain things I was doing were "making me gay."

It was the first time I'd heard him tell Mom not to call me Arrow. She'd been calling me that from the day I was born. She wanted to put it on my birth certificate, but—big surprise—Sullivan wanted something "less weird and hippie."

"How dare you?" Mom gasped. "Don't ever talk to him like that again."

"Do not tell me what to do," he intoned, then turned away from her, dismissing her words.

I felt my stare narrow in challenge.

He met my gaze full on, but I didn't back down. He smirked, as if my challenge gave him pleasure, as if it made me more a man.

It just made me more like him. More of an asshole.

Downstairs, the sound of the doorbell rang through the house.

"She's here," he said.

"If you're so interested in her, you take her out. It's what men do after all."

I sensed Mom's presence and immediately felt contrite. I glanced at her, standing just behind my father. She didn't seem to catch my double meaning.

"I look forward to hearing about how your date went tomorrow," Dad said, disregarding me and striding down the hall.

Mom came in the room, closing the door softly behind her.

Her eyes were sympathetic, and oddly, it just pissed me off. In that moment, it seemed both she and I were weak. Pawns on my father's chessboard. Nothing more than pieces he played.

"I know this has been hard, Arrow." She sat on the bed beside me, cupping my jaw with one hand. "Just play along a few more months. Then you'll be out on your own."

Between us, she held out a large envelope. The seal for Syracuse was in the upper corner. Butterflies hit my stomach. I glanced between her and the envelope.

"It just came a little while ago." She smiled.

I took it and ripped it open, reading the cover letter on the stack of papers. "I got in," I said, somewhat surprised.

She grinned wide and flung her arms around me. "I'm so proud of you."

I hugged her back as a sense of accomplishment filled me.

It was a nice moment.

Until I remembered…

My father basically bribed the dean with a donation to get me in. He called in a favor with the head coach, too. I had no way of knowing if I got into this college because I earned it or because my father manipulated the situation.

"I don't want to go here," I said, tossing the papers onto the bed.

"What?"

"It's what *he* wants, not me."

Her eyes softened. "Maybe it could be what you want, too?" she said gently. "Not because of him, though, but because it's a fresh start."

I glanced up.

"You like soccer, right?"

I nodded.

"And New York is just beautiful. You like it there, too. We'll get you a nice apartment where you won't be under his thumb. You'll have freedom. Sports, classes, and a new place. It won't be so hard." She paused. "To be happier."

I noticed she didn't say to be who I really was. I was starting to wonder if maybe she was hoping I'd decide I wasn't gay after all.

Like it or not, Mom had a point. Moving to New York would be fucking bomb. I could get away from my father, which I would do almost anything for at this point, including enrolling in college.

"Yeah, it sounds like a good idea." I agreed.

Mom beamed. The relief in her face was obvious. I wasn't sure what that relief was for, but I let myself believe it was because she just wanted me to be happy.

"Just stick it out until after graduation. We'll get you moved up to New York this summer. Until then, maybe just play along with what he wants."

"Is that what you do, Mom?" I asked. "Play along with what he wants?"

Her face paled slightly. I felt bad, but not bad enough. I stood from the bed and snatched up the keys. "I have a date," I said, bitter, and walked away without looking back.

My date was a wild child dressed in conservative clothes. The second I pulled the Jag out of the driveway, she started pulling off layers and tossing them into her bag.

I glanced at her once, not because I wanted to check out her skin, but because I thought it was fucking amusing. Clearly, I wasn't the only one playing along with what our parents thought we should be.

"Not as wholesome as you'd like them all to believe I see," I mused.

"If you rat on me, I'll deny it." She informed me as she applied a thick coat of something shiny to her lips. When I didn't say anything, she glanced over. "I can always add in you touched me in places you weren't supposed to."

I rolled my eyes at the way she made her voice sound wispy and innocent. Then I made a rude sound. "Are you kidding? My father would be proud of that macho behavior."

"I see we have the same kind of parents." She relaxed back into the seat, as if my admission upped her impression of me.

"I don't think there's anyone quite like my father," I said, dark.

"There's a party across town. I want to go."

"Is it loud, and do they have beer?" I asked.

"Duh."

"Tell me the way."

I followed her directions to some big party in an abandoned building on the other side of town. There was graffiti on the walls and broken bottles in the parking lot. The music was loud, so loud I wondered why the hell the cops weren't there, and so many people milled about they were spilling out of the building onto the sidewalk.

I parked the Jag somewhere my father would probably have a coronary about and enjoyed every second of it. I thought about leaving it unlocked and hoped it got lifted. Hell, it would serve him right.

But he'd punish me later.

So I locked it, pocketed the keys, and told myself if it got damaged or stolen while it was parked, it was his fault for letting me drive it and taking away my BMW in the first place.

My scantily-clothed date, who said her name was Giselle, flipped her long brown hair. "So hey, how about you go your way and I go mine?" she yelled in my ear when we got close to the entrance.

"Find me if you need a ride home," I yelled back.

She nodded. "Oh, and I'll be sure to tell the 'rents what a great time I had and what a gentleman you were."

I rolled my eyes.

She grinned.

I stepped toward the door, toward the flashing lights and pounding bass, but she caught my wrist. I turned around and glanced down into her stare.

She leaned up next to my ear to say, "The gay crowd hangs near the back."

I jerked back and stared down at her. I knew I looked astonished.

She laughed and patted my T-shirt-covered chest. "No worries. I won't tell, especially your father."

My eyes bounced between hers, searching for something. Anything. All I saw was she honestly didn't give a shit.

How the fuck did she know? Was there something about me that screamed gay?

"Feel free to tell your father you screwed my brains out and I was hot for your cock," she whispered in my ear before kissing me on the cheek and disappearing into the suddenly foggy doorway.

Literal fog. Someone turned on a fog machine.

I stared into the vapor and the strobing light. I could just leave right now. Drive around until enough time passed for my date.

Or…

I could hang at this party… maybe wander toward the back.

It called to me, the so-called "gay crowd." It was so stupid, the fact there was a crowd of any type of person. I wasn't any type of guy. I was just me. All these people were just… people.

Likely, most of them were pretending to be someone they weren't, just like me and Giselle.

I stayed. I went inside, found the keg, and downed a beer. Then I downed another. The music was loud and drowned out the thoughts in my head. It was hot in here, bodies were everywhere, and the room was dark except for flashing lights and glowing people brought out of the shadows by black light paint.

A killer song came on, and I started to dance. Some chick beside me grabbed my hand and pulled me around, and we started grinding together while the music thumped. It was good to let loose. Good to just be.

After a while, she moved off, and I danced through the crowd, stopping every once in a while to dance with someone new.

Eventually, I made it toward the back. People were still dancing here, too. Funny, I expected it to look different, like there would be a giant lit-up sign or something.

I was a fucking moron.

It looked exactly like the rest of the party. In fact, as I danced and finished off my beer, I was beginning to think Giselle had just been messing with me. There probably wasn't a gay crowd that hung here at all.

I crunched my cup in my grip and dropped it on the concrete floor. It disappeared almost immediately into the crowd of gyrating bodies. I turned to go, but something wrapped around my wrist.

I glanced over my shoulder.

Then my whole body followed.

He had dark hair, so dark it blended in with the night. It was cut short, and he was dressed in a pair of ripped-up jeans, a big white T-shirt, and a pair of Nikes. I guessed he was around my age, maybe a year or two older. Another thing my attention seemed to zero in on were his lips. They were full and tilted into a smile as he looked at me.

"Wanna dance?" he yelled out.

I nodded.

I let him pull me a little closer, and we started moving to a new song that just blasted over the speakers. The undertones of this one spoke sex; the beat was heavy and it made you want to move your hips.

When my partner palmed my waist and pulled me in so he could fit his knee between my legs, I froze for a second. I'd never had much contact with another guy.

Not much = none.

I'd been with a few girls; none of it was enjoyable.

All my "experience" with other men was through magazines and videos online.

"Relax," he said, and one of his hands slid down to my hip.

The center of his body rotated toward me, thrust out, and I felt his jeans brush against mine. I liked it. I liked it more than I thought I would. We were barely touching, yet my heart hammered, my balls tingled, and my fingers itched with the need to touch him.

I glanced up again, and he gave me a flirtatious smile.

I'm dancing and flirting with a guy.

I smiled back, suddenly bold, and grabbed his hips, pulling him right up against my body.

We danced and grinded to the music. Feeling his body so close to mine, feeling his hands run down my back and over my arms, turned me on in ways I didn't know were possible.

If this were an experiment, I would call it a success.

But maybe it was too soon; maybe I was drunk. Dancing and somewhat groping a guy I'd just met wasn't confirmation I was gay.

I already know I'm gay. Why do I need to prove it?

But I did.

Suddenly, there was this overwhelming urge to prove to myself once and for all that I was gay. That it didn't matter what my father said.

After about five songs, we were both sweating and grinding against each other pretty hard. I was rocking a hard-on I wasn't even embarrassed about.

"Let's get a beer," the guy called over the music, and I nodded.

He took my hand like it was a natural, no-big-deal thing and led me off the dance floor and out of the crowd. Instead of heading over to the beer, he headed for a side door I hadn't noticed before and into a stairwell that went up and down.

He went down into the darkness. Just one flight below, he stopped on the bottom step and pushed me against the wall.

With my back against the cold concrete, he came forward, aligning his body with mine until we touched feet to chest. I grabbed handfuls of his shirt at his side and held on as his lips swooped in.

It was the first kiss I'd ever had with a man.

It was a lot like kissing a girl.

Except better.

He fit against me in a way no girl could. His mouth seemed braver, his kiss deeper. Our tongues twisted together, and he moaned, his hips thrusting forward. Boldly, I reached around and cupped his ass, deepening the kiss as my heart galloped in my chest.

He tasted like beer and sweat. His chest was solid against mine, and I liked the way his weight felt pinning me against the wall.

After several minutes of us making out, he ripped his lips off mine and kissed down my neck. I cupped the back of his head so he wouldn't stop. My body hummed. I felt alive. I felt… like me.

His fingers brushed the buckle of my jeans. My eyes sprang open in the dark as he sucked my neck. Without any thought, I thrust my hips forward, inviting more. He pulled back, and in seconds, my jeans were down around my knees.

My boxers molded to my body; my dick was hard and jutted out the fabric so it looked like a tent. The guy—I still didn't know his name—lifted the hem of my shirt and dragged his fingers across my abs.

"Definition," he murmured, tracing the lines of the muscle.

I was skinny, but I was muscular. It was all the soccer I played.

The guy dropped onto his knees, and I spread my legs a little as my dick jumped anxiously beneath the fabric. He was gonna fucking suck me off. Right here. Right now.

Hell yes.

I wanted him to. I'd never wanted a blowjob so badly before. I didn't have to pretend I was somewhere else or with someone else. I didn't have to picture the porn I watched online or even stroke myself.

All I had to do was feel the air brush over the smooth skin of my cock when it was freed of the confines of my clothing.

"Nice rod," the guy said, giving it a stroke. I shuddered, my abs contracting.

I made a sound; I was incapable of speaking. My knees were shaking and so were my hands. I tucked them between my ass and the wall, thrusting out so he would have better access.

The first contact of his mouth made me moan. It echoed in the stairwell, but I didn't care. I wasn't going to hold back right now. Everything inside me was screaming, *Yes!*

His lips were silky smooth and warm. His mouth was wet, and he applied the perfect amount of pressure as he moved his head back and forth. I looked down, watching his dark head bob at the center of my body, and rocked into his mouth.

He took me deep, as deep as he could. I wanted deeper, so I thrust just a little more.

He pulled back, licked up the rod, and circled his tongue around my head. I shuddered.

I wasn't going to last much longer. This was too fucking good.

He felt me trembling. He grabbed my sack, felt how tight it was drawn against my body, and then sucked my head into his mouth.

He licked and sucked like and expert until I went rigid and gave a shout. His fingertips gripped my hips, and I started to move. I pumped into him, fucking his lips as an orgasm ripped through my body.

I yelled and moaned, the sound of it bouncing around and filling my ears.

When at last he pulled back and my cock fell against my body, completely satiated and spent, my legs felt like Jell-O, and I was glad to be leaning against the wall.

"I like a guy who yells," the guy said, standing.

"You yell, too?" I asked. My voice sounded drunk and heavy.

"Maybe you should find out," he suggested and reached for his buckle.

I reached for his fly and guided it over his already hard length.

He sank down on the steps, sitting in the center and spreading his knees wide. I sat down between them and freed his dick.

So the first night I got head from another man was also the first night I gave it.

I did make him yell, which awakened some kind of lion inside me. I liked hearing him moan and feeling him buck beneath my mouth.

I even liked the salty flavor of his orgasm as it shot across my tongue.

It was the best sexual encounter I'd had yet. It was with another man.

No, I didn't have to prove I was gay.

But if I did… this would have done it.

Chapter Four

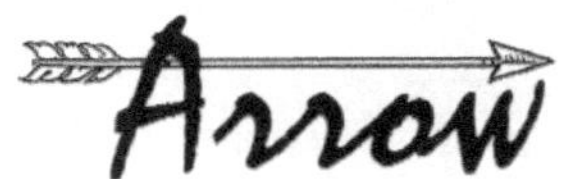

Conversion therapy.

Something I'd never heard of until I heard my parents fighting. Again.

My father knew his "tough love" and demands that I be straight weren't working. I didn't give him any reason to think it wasn't, except for the fact I wasn't dating or being caught with girls racing out of my room at all hours of the night.

I thought about doing it. I thought about playing his game.

Fuck that.

Fuck him.

I didn't want to pretend. I didn't even want to be "all out" and waving it in his face that I preferred men.

If anything, I'd just become more withdrawn. I stayed out late, avoided him when I knew he'd be home, and when he'd arrive when we weren't expecting, I'd hide in the house or bury my nose in "homework" and pretend I didn't know he was there.

I snuck out a couple times, too. I went back to that party place. Faces were becoming more familiar there.

People would what-up me when I walked through the fog.

I hooked up with the same guy a few more times. We never exchanged names. It didn't matter. I went for the blowjobs and making out. I had a feeling it was the same for him. Maybe he couldn't be himself when he wasn't there either. Maybe those nights were all he had, just like me.

The admission papers for Syracuse were filled out and ready to mail in. All they needed was a signature from my father and a check for tuition. I was anxious to get the hell out, to not feel like I was unwanted in my own house.

He hadn't signed them yet. I wasn't sure why he was waiting.

It felt like everything hinged on something, some test I wasn't aware of.

Maybe he didn't know what it was either. Maybe that's why the words "conversion therapy" floated along the hall at night when everyone was supposed to be in bed.

Bedtime now consisted of us going to our rooms, my parents fighting, and me sitting in the center of my room, listening.

It was odd because Mom never wanted to make him angry. She tended to just go along with what he wanted. I hated to say it, but now that I was seeing things more clearly and had a lot of time to think and reflect…

My mother was a doormat.

My father stepped on her constantly.

I had to wonder if she knew about all his affairs and just turned a blind eye.

I didn't want to think she would. I hoped she knew she was worth more than that. But just because I didn't want to think it didn't mean it was true.

I learned that lesson the hard way.

Doormat or not, it seemed the one thing my mom refused to back down on was me. She hated the way he treated me, something she told him almost every night. They fought about the name she called me, about the color of my clothes, my car, my dating… They fought about everything.

And then the subject of conversion therapy came up.

I didn't know what it was. I Googled it.

I wished I hadn't.

It was basically abuse disguised as "therapy" to make someone not be homosexual (or anything other than straight). The suicide rate related to something like this was off the charts. The practices involved made me sick. And the examples….

Electric shock.

Snapping a rubber band on the wrist every time a person got hard at homoerotic images.

Institutionalization.

Shame.

Orgasmic reconditioning. (I was afraid to look up what the fuck that even was.)

Forced hetero dating.

Hypnosis.

The list went on and on. The horror stories on the web were shocking. The fact that parents did this kind of thing to a child they claimed they loved was something I didn't think I'd ever understand.

That wasn't love. Was it?

Dad brought it up. Mom had a fit. They fought about it so long I fell asleep in the center of my bed. The resounding theme about conversion therapy (according to the internet, which of course is law) was it didn't work. So basically, you torture someone who is already confused, and the only thing you manage is to break them.

Maybe waiting it out until Syracuse was a bad idea. Maybe it would be better if I just left now.

My parents were fighting, tension was high, and the way he looked at me…

It would be better if I just left.

Maybe I could find Jace. Maybe he would understand. He was basically my last hope.

My eighteenth birthday came. In the eyes of the law, I was an adult. In the eyes of the law, I could finally walk out of this house and not be considered a runaway.

I was already planning my escape, planning on calling Jace as soon as I could slip up to my room the second I got home. It was already dark out. I'd gone to school like any other ordinary day, gone to practice, and then some of us went out for pizza and women to celebrate my birthday.

I just had pizza… I left the women to all my friends.

They were planning a big party this weekend. Beer, more beer, and probably some weed. One of the guys' parents were going out of town, and my birthday was the perfect excuse to throw a rager. Of course I said I'd be there; it was for me.

But I wouldn't. I'd be gone. I had no idea where… just not here.

I had no earthly idea what my life would be like tomorrow, but I knew it wouldn't be the same. I hoped my brother would know what to do, because in all honesty, I didn't.

Here I was eighteen years old, a man, but still a kid. The shock I felt that first day I'd boldly told my father I was gay hadn't worn off. I was still surprised, still slightly numb from the way everything had shifted.

He wasn't at all who I thought. It was almost like I'd been living a lie up until recent months, but the lie hadn't been my sexuality.

It had been everything else.

I bounded in the door and stopped dead in my tracks. He was the last person I expected to see. The last one I *wanted* to see. Something went flat inside me, like soda that suddenly lost all its fizz. The numbness I'd just mentioned, I grabbed it, tugged it around me like a thick blanket. Like armor one dressed in before a battle.

He'd yet to say one word. Not a single syllable. But I knew what he was doing.

Waiting for me.

"Dylan!" he said, almost jovial. I didn't know how he did it. How one minute he sounded like the father I always thought he was, and the next, he was some complete stranger. It was like two people lived inside one skin.

I hadn't seen this side of him since that day in his office. The father I thought he was. He smiled at me like the past few months had never happened, like I was still the son who made him proud.

"What are you doing here?" I asked, cautious.

"It's my son's eighteenth birthday. Where else would I be?"

"Work," I deadpanned. *With your trashy ho-bag of a secretary.*

"Work can wait. This is a big day! I have plans for us."

"I already have plans." I shook my head and started past him. There was no way in hell I was going to celebrate turning into a legal adult with him. I wanted to celebrate by getting as far away as I could.

"Cancel them," he replied. That fatherly tone I hadn't heard in so long vanished, replaced by one I was all too familiar with.

Even though I'd heard it less than the previous, I understood this was the real Sullivan Lorhaven. The man I thought he was all these years?

A lie. A fabrication. A wish.

I think that hurt worse than anything he'd said or done. I longed for that man who didn't exist. I missed the lie I so comfortably lived. I guess I could understand why my mother always just went with what he wanted, how she just kept the peace.

She lived a lie, too.

Sometimes lies were easier than the truth.

Why did I open my mouth that day? Why couldn't I just have said nothing at all?

A question I'd asked myself a million times. I didn't think I'd ever know the answer.

My feet reached the bottom of the staircase before he spoke again. "I have your birthday gift."

I stopped, looking over my shoulder. "I don't want anything."

"I think you want this." He held up a familiar packet of papers enclosed in a crisp envelope with the address already neatly applied to the front.

The admission to Syracuse. My escape. My way out.

But it wasn't anymore. Was it? I planned on throwing it all away tonight when I walked out the door.

"I signed the papers and transferred the money and wrote out a check for the whole first year's tuition," he said, still holding up the envelope. "All that's left is to mail it."

Did he want a thank-you? I wasn't going to give him one.

"I'll drop it in the mail tomorrow." I lied.

It was a painful lie. Soccer wasn't my life, I didn't really want to go to college, and Syracuse was his choice, not mine… But it was still something to me.

A way out. A fresh start. A chance to be something other than what he wanted.

"I'll make sure it's mailed," he said, taking it over and dropping it on a nearby table. The centerpiece was a large bouquet of blue and black balloons with two silver Mylar balloons in the in the shape of a one and eight. They were from my mother.

She'd gotten me up early this morning, ushered me into the kitchen where the balloons, a latte from the café I loved, and a wrapped gift sat on the table. While I drank my coffee, she made homemade blueberry pancakes and we talked just like we used to.

"I made us a reservation," he said, giving the balloons a distasteful stare.

He probably blamed those for making me gay, too.

"Go change," he said, glancing at my soccer pants, T-shirt and letterman jacket. "Put on something nice."

"And if I don't?" I challenged.

He looked up at the ceiling, slid his hands in the pocket of his dress pants, and waited a few heartbeats before he spoke carefully into the room. "Be smart here, Dylan." He warned. "You're a man now. I'll treat you as one, but I need to see you're ready to be who I raised you to be."

You didn't raise me. Mom did.

"Prove to me you're ready to be a man, and everything goes back the way it was. Your car, your college career, your life."

So this is a test.

A final exam. If I passed, I could go back to that comfortable lie I was living. I could go on like all of this had just been a bad dream.

I wouldn't have to move out. I wouldn't have to tell Jace I was gay and risk losing my big brother. My mother could have her world back… I wouldn't hear them fighting anymore. I could go to college, get some distance, and then maybe I could start to make sense of things.

My father didn't wait for me to answer. He picked up his keys. The way the metal jangled together made a distinct sound. "I'll pull the car around. Meet me out front. Don't keep me waiting."

With that, he was gone, out into the night, the front door not completely latched.

I went up and changed. I put on a pair of navy dress pants, a white button-up shirt, and added a blue striped tie.

I had no idea where we were going. Did it really even matter?

As I slid into the leather passenger seat, I glanced over, the interior lights lighting up his face. He didn't look at me; he didn't smile. I used to think maybe my old man had a resting bitch face. You know that look where you just always appeared pissed off even when you aren't?

Sullivan Lorhaven didn't have a resting bitch face.

He was just an asshole.

And by getting in this car, it felt I was selling my soul to the devil, succumbing to the pressure to be who he wanted me to be.

A moment of panic hit me hard in the chest, and my breath shuddered. I groped for the handle. I wanted to eject myself from this car, from this situation.

He hit the gas, and the car accelerated forward. My back hit the seat with the force of the acceleration. He'd known what I was about to do.

He wasn't about to allow it.

I was in his clutches, and it appeared it was where I was going to stay.

The last place on earth I would have expected…

That's where I was.

Brought here by my father, the last person on this earth who should have brought me here.

I could just consider this another those unexpected blows robbing me of pieces. Pieces of who I thought I was, of who I always believed myself to be.

How ironic really, how very… humbling to realize that in the desire to be accepted for who I was—to become more of the man I felt like on the inside—was actually the very thing that took more away.

Did that make sense?

In my convoluted mind, it did. There was a cost to everything, wasn't there?

A cost to being a person, to being accepted. Maybe acceptance wasn't something any of us had. Perhaps it had been nothing but a juvenile pipe dream, something my innocence thought I deserved.

Perhaps acceptance was just a perception. An overall herd of people who acted the same, who portrayed something they weren't in order to appear like everyone else. Who decided what that something was? Who declared what it was that made each of us "acceptable?"

The thing was we all wanted to be accepted. I hadn't realized how much pretending was required.

And so here I was, sitting in the passenger seat of my father's Jaguar, staring through the windshield at a place I never imagined I'd be.

Clearly, I needed to expand my perception of the potential of those around me. This shit just got weirder by the day.

"Seriously?" I said, glancing at the neon sign in the window. "A strip club?"

What kind of father took his son to a strip club?

He shut off the engine and pocketed the keys. "You're a man now. It's time you enjoy the privileges that come with it."

So was it privilege by age or by dick that I was able to come watch women shake their skin?

"I'm pretty sure you have to be twenty-one to get into this place," I said. It was my last effort at getting out of this.

It was fucking gross. Who the hell went to a titty bar with their dad?

"I called ahead. We have a private room."

Money. That's all it took to break the rules. It's all it took for him to get what he wanted.

What do you want? To not be here.

"Happy birthday, son." He clapped me on the shoulder.

The second we approached the solid black door, it opened and a large bouncer stepped out and held it open. He nodded at us on the way in, and I felt his eyes bore into the back of my head.

The inside was just what TV and movies portrayed. Oh, and porn flicks, too. Yep, this joint looked like the perfect setting for some bad porno.

There was a huge stage with a runway that stretched out into the center of the tables. A silver pole ran from floor to the ceiling at the end, with two more farther back on the stage.

The lights were dim, all of them focused on the stage and the girl. She was naked. Completely. The men all hollered and whistled as she worked the pole, spinning around and spreading her legs wide, showing everyone exactly what she had between them.

Her tits were fake. They literally looked like globes positioned under her skin.

Dollar bills floated onto the platform as she gyrated and sexy music pumped through the air. It smelled like smoke and alcohol with a hint of sex. As far as I knew, most strip clubs were for only stripping; usually you weren't allowed to touch the dancers. Maybe it only smelled like sex in here because the women were all naked and the men were turned on.

I wasn't.

Not in the least.

In fact, as I looked at her on the stage, I couldn't help but feel kinda sorry for her. I wondered what led her here, what kind of life she must live to be willing to let perverts ogle her on a nightly basis.

Her long legs wrapped around the pole. She leaned backward so her head was below her feet and she was totally on display upside down. The long length of her blond hair fell like a curtain toward the floor, and body glitter glistened across her stomach.

I was staring, and she must have felt it because our eyes locked.

A mutual understanding tethered us. I had a lot in common with that girl. Neither of us wanted to be there. And whatever it was that led her to that stage, something equally as shitty had me standing in front of it.

"This way." A woman appeared with a small, round tray in her hands and a tiny pink G-string on her bottom. Her top was bare, her chest glistening with oil or something.

My father's eyes went right to her rack and then locked on her ass as she sashayed ahead. She stopped in front of a velvet curtain and motioned for us to go ahead.

Dad went first. Then I ducked in right after. The heavy fabric fell immediately back into place, closing in the private room.

There was a single table, two chairs, and several drinks already waiting. Looked like several shots of an amber-colored liquid and a few mixed drinks with small straws bobbing at the top.

There was also an ashtray in the center and a stack of what looked like dollar bills.

My stomach rolled. Instead of being excited or turned on by any of this, I felt embarrassed, humiliated, and honestly… bullied.

This was my test.

Be a man. Get drunk. Grope naked women. Do it all right here in front of a man who should have wanted better for me.

Why didn't he want better?

And if I succeeded in being enough of a pig, I would get my future, a future that came with a whole lot of strings.

But freedom, too.

"Have a seat," Dad said, already pulling out a chair. He took off his suit jacket, hung it over the back of the seat, and then loosened his tie and the buttons around his neck.

I pulled out the chair and sank into it, and he handed me a shot.

"Bottoms up," he said, lifting an identical-looking glass into the air.

I emulated his action, and then we both tossed back the tequila. Mine had the worm in it. I fought back a gag and hoped it didn't get stuck on its way down.

Dad laughed and slapped me on the back. "That'll put some hair on your chest."

He picked up another shot and glanced at me. Quickly, I reached for the mixed drink and took a swig of it. He seemed placated as he tossed back his second shot.

I'd only ever seen him drink expensive shit. I'd never seen him do shots.

After he slammed the glass down, two cigars appeared out of his jacket. One for me and one for him. We lit them up, and the distinct scent of tobacco filled the small room.

"Drink up, enjoy," Dad instructed, settling back in the seat and motioning to someone I didn't see.

I took another drink because, frankly, being drunk for this seemed like a pretty fucking brilliant idea.

A dim red light came on across the room, and three women dressed in what looked like lingerie appeared. One of them already had her chest completely bared, like her bra was missing all the fabric that actually offered some modesty. Instead, all she had was the band that wrapped around her ribcage and the lacey straps around her shoulders. Her panties were also lace, and her thigh-highs were white.

Both her nipples were erect, and I wondered if she'd been fondling them before she entered the room.

The other girl was wearing a tiny see-through dress, a pair of thongs, and nothing else. The third stripper had on leather chaps, leather crotchless panties, and a black leather vest that showed a lot of cleavage. Her heels were probably five inches high, and she carried a long black feather in her hand.

Music started playing through speakers I couldn't see, and the women converged on the table.

Their hands were everywhere. In my hair, on my shirt. Fingers trailed across my lips, dipped into my ears, and slid beneath the collar of my shirt to scrape their nails over my chest.

I reclined in the seat, forced my body into a lazy, relaxed position, and stared at one of the women's chest as she straddled my legs.

My father made a grunting sound, and I glanced over. He had one hand wrapped around a boob and the other was stuffing a wad of dollar bills in the tiny string that held up her panties. He was taking his sweet time with the money, too, shoving it between her legs way farther than it needed to go.

She giggled and purred like she liked it a lot and ran her hands through his thick hair.

He noted me watching, and our eyes locked.

The look he gave me was a direct order. A challenge. I was supposed to act like him, to be like him.

My eyes tore away from his, and my palm slapped onto the table as I grabbed some money. I went into autopilot, shoving the dollars wherever I could. At one point, I leaned forward and shoved my face between her tits, and she laughed and gyrated against my face.

"Lap dances," my father called out a little while later and leaned back in his chair with the cigar between his lips.

The girl with the no-bra bra crooked a finger at me in the center of the room. I stood, dragged the chair with me, and when it was in the center of the room, I sank into it.

She basically dry-humped me in the seat. I grabbed her tits, and when she rubbed them across my lips, I licked them. I grabbed her ass and squeezed, and I tilted my hips up when she dry-humped my lap.

In truth, my stomach was churning. The shot and half a drink did nothing to make this enjoyable; it did nothing to distort what I was doing or seeing.

The sound of my father grunting had me looking around the woman. The girl with the see-through nightie was in his lap. His hands were on her hips as she ground down on top of him. His head was bobbing as he sucked at her chest.

I started to get up. This was just too much. Hands grabbed me from behind, pushing me back into the chair. The next thing I knew, I was being serviced by two dancers.

My tie disappeared. My shirt was ripped open, and the belt on my dress pants was abandoned to the floor. I squirmed in the chair. Disgust and humiliation warred inside me. I just wanted this to be over. I wanted to get through it.

In frustration, I made a sound, grabbed the girl straddling my lap, and squeezed her hips and ass. She gave a squeak, and I knew she'd likely have fingerprints on her ass, but I was beyond caring.

"I think it's time he gets his gift," my father said, the girl still in his lap.

You mean, this isn't it?

Fuck.

All three girls assembled in a line in front of me.

I stared at them, wondering what the fuck was happening now.

"Pick one," my father all but demanded.

I gave him a look.

"Pick one, or I'll choose one for you."

My temper flared. All my shock and numbness was starting to boil.

"You." I flung a hand at the girl in leather. She looked the roughest of the three. It's who he'd want me to pick, a test within the test.

"Exactly who I would have chosen," he mused. "Have fun."

She grabbed my hand and pulled me through a curtain in the back. The room here was much smaller, like a small box. There was a small bed with a mountain of pillows and a chair in the center of the room.

The light in here was red, giving everything a warm cast. She shoved me down in the chair and then straddled my lap. Her hips began to rotate, and then her lips descended upon mine. I kissed her back while she rocked in my lap, until my heart felt like it was going to explode and my fingers shook with anger.

Abruptly, I grabbed her face and pulled her back. Holding her jaw, I stared up at her. "How much did he pay you to have sex with me?"

"Ten thousand."

Wow. It was impressive and insulting all at once.

"I'm not having sex with you," I declared. "Would you want to have sex with your father in the next room?"

"I'm here to get paid," she replied, rocked in my lap again, and started kissing my neck. Her hand was large, her nails long as she held my head back so she could scrape her teeth down my throat.

"Yeah, well, I won't tell him we didn't actually do it. You'll still get your paycheck."

She sat up, her eyes mildly surprised. She didn't climb off me, though. Instead, she ripped open the leather vest and flung it away. Her large breasts spilled out. She took my hands and placed them on the flesh.

"Doesn't work that way. Not tonight," she said, grinding some more and pushing her tits into my hands.

"Why's that?"

"There's a camera behind me. No sex, no money."

"Are you fucking kidding me?" I gasped.

She smirked, unbuttoned my pants, and shoved her fingers into the waistband of my boxers. "You got one fucked-up relationship with your father. I've seen a lot of crazy shit in here, but a father wanting to watch his son have sex? That's a first."

"He's watching?"

She didn't answer. Instead, she slid between my legs, landed on her knees, and pulled my pants and boxers down to bare my totally soft dick.

She looked at it and then glanced up at me. "I don't turn you on at all?"

"Not in the least," I spat.

She shifted in a way that made me think she was using her body to block the fact I wasn't rocking a raging boner.

"Look, I'll make it good and quick, okay? I know what I'm doing." She picked my cock up and started massaging it in her hands.

I wondered how many other dicks she'd touched this week. Tonight.

"I'll put on a show for your old man. I'll get paid. Then you can go."

Her lips wrapped around my cock, her head began to bob up and down. I fisted a hand in her hair, giving it a tug. She made a sound like she liked it, so I pulled her hair again. Her nails dug into my inner thigh. I figured it was payback, but I didn't care. I leaned back and let my head tilt up toward the ceiling like I was enjoying myself.

My father wanted to watch me have sex. He was so desperate to prove to me I wasn't gay he was willing to set up dates, get me drunk, bribe me with my future… and pay some ho ten grand to screw me so he could watch.

This was beyond sick. It was demoralizing. Humiliating.

Did he really think this made me a better man? Was this the person he truly wanted me to be?

He would rather I be some depraved womanizer than be gay?

No.

No, no, no.

It was wrong to come here. Wrong to allow myself to be led by him once again. I was stupid to believe if I just passed his test, my life would be mine again.

It wouldn't.

Not ever again.

There would always be another test.

Another stripper. Another blowjob. Someday he'd expect a wife. Grandkids he'd never actually want to see. He expected me to be absolutely fucking miserable… just so *he* could look good.

"Get off me!" I growled and shoved the woman off.

She stumbled and fell back onto her ass as I stood.

Quickly, I tucked my junk into my pants and fastened the buttons. My shirt was still hanging open, the tie on the floor. Inside my chest, my heart raced, my stomach lurched, and the numbness…

It lifted like the fog on a rainy Sunday morning.

I'd rather be someone he hated than someone I didn't recognize when I looked in the mirror every day.

"You're gonna have to get your paycheck somewhere else tonight," I spat, wiping my mouth with the back of my hand. Wiping away the stench of her kiss. "Go sleep with my father since he's so hard up for some action."

Beyond the curtain, I heard a curse. I barged out, the curtain swinging wide with my deft movements. My father was at the table, a tablet in front of him. There was a cigar in one hand and a drink in the other.

The son of a bitch was kicked back watching the feed of me about to nail a slut. He was enjoying this.

Our eyes locked. My temper flared.

Get back in there, he silently demanded.

"You are a sick fucking pervert," I spat. I was impressed because I didn't yell. In fact, my tone was similar to his.

Guess I learned something from him after all.

"If you think I'm going to stick my dick in some girl you paid and let you watch just to prove to you I'm a real man, then you're the one who needs fucking therapy."

He tossed down the cigar and the drink to stand. "Don't you talk to me that way."

"Or what?" I spat. "You'll take my car? My bank account? My college education?"

His eyes narrowed.

"You already did." I spread my arms wide. "I'm still here. And I'm still gay. Nothing you do is going to change that."

He lunged forward and punched me in the face. I was ready this time. One free surprise punch, that's all this man would ever get from me. My head snapped back, and then I swung, catching him right in the jaw.

He looked at me with shock rippling over his features.

I enjoyed the look.

"Keep your money, your cars, and your fancy school. I don't want any of it. It's dirty money. Blood money. From here on out, I'm going to live life the way *I* want to, not the way you declare."

"Dylan!" he roared as I headed for the curtain.

I stopped. Turned back.

"My name is Arrow."

"You little son of a bitch!" he growled and lunged at me again. His hand wrapped around my throat and squeezed. Oxygen stopped flowing down my windpipe;

my airway seized. I stared at him with wide eyes, scared but refusing to struggle.

If he wanted to kill me, I'd let him. Hell, it might be easier that way.

"Get out of my house. Out of my life. Get out, you faggot, and don't you ever come back."

Tears burned the backs of my eyes. I told myself it was because I couldn't breathe, not because he just disowned me.

My body was tossed back, and I stumbled, falling into the thick, heavy folds of the velvet door. I gasped and wheezed. I was absolutely reeling. Beyond shock. Beyond disappointment.

I pulled up to my full height and gave him one last look, searching, desperately searching for the man I'd always thought he was. I wanted just a glimpse, even just a nanosecond of confirmation he ever existed.

His upper lip curled as he stared back. Disgust was the only thing I saw.

I stopped searching. He wasn't there.

Out in the main room, I felt the stares of a thousand eyes. I kept moving. I didn't look back. The bouncer opened the door before I even got there, and I ejected myself into the night like an emergency flotation device.

The night air was cold. Clear. Brisk.

I inhaled deep, sharp lungfuls, letting the stinging cold bring back some feeling. I stood there for long moments, still stunned, not knowing what to do.

I had nothing. No car. No money. No place to live.

I could call my mother. She'd come get me. She'd find me somewhere to stay.

In that moment, I blamed her as well. This was her fault, too. I was here because… because she wasn't strong enough. Because she married that asshole and made him my father.

Something whispered in the back of my mind she wasn't really to blame, but I didn't hear those whispers just then. All I heard were the loud screams of rejection and anger.

I pulled out my phone and dialed my brother. His voicemail picked up.

"Hey, um, Lorhaven?" I said, realizing I sounded like the wreck I was. *Pull it together.* "You were right about Dad. He's a world-class asshole. I, uh, need somewhere to stay. If you could call me back… Yeah, thanks."

I disconnected the call. He was probably driving tonight. He drove every night. I'd go to him. He'd know what to do.

Unless he rejected me, too.

The thought was sobering. Like a kick to my nads.

It didn't matter. I didn't have a choice. Jace was my last option. My last hope.

He was all I had left.

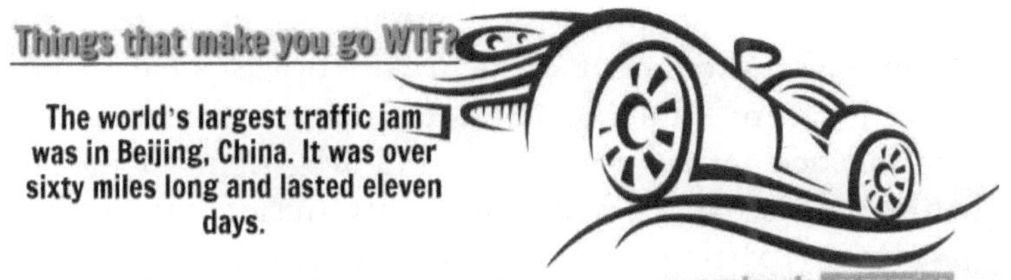

Chapter Five

They say your life flashes before your eyes when you die. Like a mirage or images, a slideshow of the highlights and even the lows of your existence.

As I walked, as I put distance between me and that strip club, a movie played in my mind.

It seemed stupid and silly. Melodramatic and even kinda corny, but the images stayed. They replayed on a loop that didn't have an off button. I watched them because I didn't have any choice. My brain was a TV without an off switch.

I saw myself running across a bright-green soccer field. I felt the wind rush through my hair and the way my jersey molded against my body as I ran. I recalled the joy and endorphins rushing through me as I worked with my team as the crowd cheered. Soccer was never my favorite thing in life, but I would miss it. I would miss the comradery. The sense of normalcy it gave.

The images faded out, and a new one took its place. My mother and me and Lorhaven sitting in the living room on a large fur blanket. The sound of muted Christmas carols played in the background and a crackling fire popping and hissing as heat from the flames brushed over my cheeks. I was smaller. My hands were chubby, and I still remembered the innocence in the way I felt. All was right then. The three of us spent a lot of nights during the holiday seasons roasting marshmallows in front of the large fireplace in the living room.

The picture of my cherry-red BMW broke into the Christmas scene. What a sweet ride it had been. A sixteen-year-old's dream.

Then I was walking down the hallway at school. The bright-blue lockers lined the walls, and people stood around in groups, laughing. I was smiling, smirking at something my friends said, and people would call out my name, slap me high-fives, and wave from the other end of the hall.

People liked me. I was never the one who wasn't liked. Even when I felt like the kid on the outside looking in, I wasn't, not to everyone else. I seemed to fit in with every crowd, something I'd always taken for granted—probably because I didn't realize just how much of a blessing it was.

I didn't know why the inside of my mind was like a reel of home movies that refused to shut down. It served as a distraction from the scene I'd just lived through back at the club, but it also brought me further down, almost as if the memories were taunting me with things that would never be again.

I walked for several miles, toward the turf Lorhaven drove on. He had a reputation there; he was well known. All I'd have to do was say his name. Someone would find him. I was anxious to see his face. I wanted to hear him say it would all be okay, and I wanted him to sympathize with me about the total douche our father was.

I pulled out my cell and checked the time. It was getting late, but not so late he was probably done driving. By the time I got there, maybe he would be. Maybe I'd catch the end of his race. I always liked watching him drive. I liked sitting shotgun, too. It was a rush and something I envied.

Hell, now that I seemed to have a hella lot of time on my hands, maybe I'd take up driving, too. If I was half as good as my brother, it would be an accomplishment.

The sound of a purring engine cut through the dark and the loudest places in my head. Headlights bounced on the pavement around me, stretching past and down the road. I glanced around, squinting into the bright light.

I couldn't tell who it was, only that it wasn't Lorhaven because his car wasn't blue.

I expected them to drive right by. Instead, the car downshifted and slowed so it was right beside me. I kept walking but glanced over.

The Mazda's dark-tinted window rolled down, and the passenger looked out at me. "Yo!"

"Hey, man," I said, still walking.

"You lost?"

"No," I said. "Going to meet my brother."

"Oh yeah? Who's your brother?"

I glanced over again. "Lorhaven."

I heard some voices inside the car, but not what they were saying. Between the engine and the music they had thumping, it was impossible.

The car stopped. The door popped open. "Get in!"

My steps faltered. "What?"

"Get in. We'll give you a ride."

"You know where he is?" I asked.

"Won't be hard to find him. There's a big race not far from here."

So they did know him. Enough to know he was a driver.

"Cool, thanks," I said, accepting the ride and sliding into the backseat.

There were four guys in the car, two in the front and two in the back. It was a tight fit, but I managed to squish in next to the window.

Once I was in, the car tore down the street, and I felt eyes on me. I glanced over to the guys beside me. There was something familiar about them, something I couldn't quite place.

"Hey, thanks for the lift," I called up to the driver.

He glanced over his shoulder at me. He was a bigger guy with a black beanie on his head. He looked familiar, too.

"So you're Lorhaven's brother? Like no shit?" the driver said.

"No shit," I replied, still feeling the stare of one of the guys in the backseat. I glanced at him again.

"That guy is a piece of work," the passenger up front said.

"You know him?" I asked, gruff. I didn't take too kindly to people insulting my brother, and that sounded like an indirect insult.

"Hey, aren't you that guy from the parties over in the old Bleaker building?" the guy in the back said.

It dawned on me where I'd seen him before. In the crowd at the parties I started going to after my "date" with Giselle. I'd seen both guys in the backseat, and I was pretty sure the driver, too. It was possible I'd seen them all, but I hadn't gotten a good enough look at the other guy in the front.

"Yeah, I've been to a few. You guys go much?"

"Every weekend," the guy beside me drawled. "That's our turf."

I nodded, and an uncomfortable sort of feeling prickled the back of my neck. Of course that building was on someone's turf. I'd never really thought about it before. In this part of town, everywhere was part of someone's "turf." I had no idea how many there were, only that there was more than one.

And usually all the different groups hated each other.

I swallowed. This was Lorhaven's turf I was on… wasn't it?

"You're the one who hangs out in the back," the other guy on the end said. "Ain't that right?"

"I hang out by the keg," I replied, trying to keep it light.

Had he seen me with the guy I met up with there?

He shook his head. "No, you're always there dancing with that guy. I've seen you disappear with him a few times."

I swallowed.

"You a flamer?" the driver asked, suddenly not so friendly.

"A what?" I asked, playing dumb.

"A twink, a sausage jockey…" He looked over his shoulder, and I just stared.

"Are you a fucking fag!" he yelled.

"Fuck no." I lied. It turned my stomach to lie about myself that way. However, it turned it more to actually admit it.

"No way," the guy beside me said. "I've seen him, G," he told the driver, whose name I could now assume was G. "He's always grinding on the same guy, they're always in the back, and they always disappear into the stairwell."

"You don't know what the fuck you're talking about," I spat. "You wanna spew shit, you go ahead and do it, but I'm not gonna step in it." I hit the back of the driver's seat. "Let me the fuck out."

"So you're saying you ain't a fag, but my boy here says you are."

"You know how Johny feels about butt pirates on his turf," the guy in the front said.

Oh shit, I *was* on the wrong turf. That meant they likely didn't like my brother, and judging from their very colorful terms, they weren't so fond of me either.

I let out a sigh. I really wasn't in the goddamn mood for this. Putting up with my father had been more than enough for a lifetime.

"Who do you think I should believe, kid? You or my boy?"

"I don't give a fuck who you believe." I tossed the words out. "My ride ends here."

The driver kept driving, picked up his cell, hit a button, and held it to his ear.

"Picked up some trash on the property tonight, Johny," he said after a few. "Seems he belongs to the west. Says he's Lorhaven's brother."

G listened a few, then whistled and tossed me a look.

"Another thing. He's a fag. My boy has seen it with his own eyes."

A beat of silence.

"Oh yeah, right here on your property, wandering around like he owned the place."

I didn't say anything, though I was sorely tempted to unleash a bunch of colorful words of my own.

"Will do," he said, and then the phone disappeared.

Seconds later, the car pulled over, screeched to a stop, and I almost flattened against the back of the seat in front of me with the force of the halt. Both doors opened, and the second the guy in front was out, I shoved the seat up and got out.

I started walking without looking back. These guys were bad news, and I was outnumbered.

The sound of rushing feet behind me clenched my muscles, and I swung around so I wasn't taken off guard.

Four guys stood in front of me, all looking at me with dark expressions on their faces.

"You a fag?" one of them asked.

"No." I denied.

"So what are you doing in that stairwell? Baking cookies?"

I didn't say anything. What the fuck was I supposed to say? Of course, I figured people saw us dancing, maybe even touching, but it never occurred to me someone might actually recognize me, would actually know the reason I went to those parties.

What a blow it was to have something else taken from me. Those parties had become a refuge. A place where I could learn about myself, a place where I had some firsts and no one seemed to care.

Just one more thing to add to the long list of losses tonight.

"Got nothing to say?" One of the guys, the bigger one, the one who'd been driving, took a step forward. "All out of denials?"

"What do you want me to say?" I asked. "I already said I wasn't gay. You don't believe me."

"Guys like you make me sick," he spat. "You're a fucking abomination to everything the male gender stands for. What the fuck is the point of having a dick if you don't know what to do with it?"

"Don't worry," I said, having heard enough. "Your dick doesn't hold my interest. I prefer ones with size."

One of his buddies made a sound.

His eyes about fell out of his head. "What the fuck did you just say?"

"I said the only reason guys like you worry about other guys' dicks is because the one you got is lacking."

The rude sound he let loose floated behind him when he lurched forward. He threw a punch, but I dodged it, and when he spun to throw another, I lifted my leg and kneed him in the face like he was a soccer ball and I was aiming for a goal.

His nose gushed blood, and he made a sound of distress. He straightened, dabbed it with his hand, and then looked at me with fury in his eyes.

"Hold him!" he roared.

The next thing I knew, I was being pinned by two guys who were bigger than me, older than me, and were a lot more experienced in street fighting.

They dragged me into a nearby alley that was dark, damp, and smelled like foul trash from the giant dumpster nearby.

I fought and struggled. I kicked and squirmed. I got in a couple kicks, but then the third guy grabbed my legs, and I was physically lifted off the ground and carried the rest of the way.

The second my shoes hit the pavement, the fist caught me in the nose.

My head snapped back, and as it flung forward, he hit me again.

Pain exploded behind my eyes, splintering across my jaw, and a burning sensation filled my lower lip. The warm ooze of blood coated my chin, and I felt the splatter of more across my forehead when he hit me again.

I don't know how many times he hit me before I sagged, unable to hold my weight. I was still held prone, a guy on each side and one at my back. They let me hang, dangling from their grasp.

He kicked me in the side once, twice, a third time. I sank onto the ground, and they dumped my body there as I coughed and wheezed.

I thought maybe they would leave then, that getting my ass beat was the worst they would do.

I was so, so terribly wrong.

One of the other guys (the one I didn't knee in the face) leaned down, grabbed a handful of my hair, and slammed my face into the pavement. "I'm gonna ask you a question," he said. "If you lie, I'll know and I'll bash your head on the ground until your nose falls off your face."

His words were muddled in my brain a little. The pain made it hard to focus.

I squinted up at him through a swollen eye.

He spit in my face.

"You a fag?" he demanded.

Somewhere from the side, the toe of a shoe buried in my ribs. I wrenched to the side and fell onto my back, four angry faces peering down at me.

"Are you?" he demanded.

I nodded. Maybe if I told them, they would just go away.

I started coughing, the copper, metallic flavor of blood splashing over my tongue. I rolled onto my side, pain nearly cracking me in half. I spit it onto the pavement, seeing the dark splatters beside my head.

"I told you!" a voice yelled. "I fucking knew it was that gay boy."

"I hate fags," a low voice growled. "I think he broke my nose."

"You worked him over good, G. He learned his lesson."

"Not good enough," he said.

I pushed to my hands and knees. I was leaving. I just wanted to go home, wherever that was.

"What are you going to do?" one of the guys questioned.

"Where the fuck do you think you're going?" he yelled and kicked me in the side.

I fell onto my stomach, groaning. Another punch clipped me in the back of my head, and I felt my ear scrape open on the road.

I glanced up, blinking at the dumpster, wondering if there was something nearby I could brandish as a weapon.

I was shoved roughly onto my back. G thrust his broken, bloody face into mine. "You like men, huh? You like taking it in the ass?"

I didn't say anything.

He grabbed my jaw and squeezed my face.

"You think I have a tiny dick? I don't know what to do with it? Well, fuck-boy, do I have a treat for you."

My brain was sluggish. I didn't quite understand what he was saying…

Until he reached for my pants.

I started fighting then, like a hellcat with renewed energy. I kicked and screamed. I punched the side of his head.

He cursed and came back, unbuttoning my pants.

His fist buried in my stomach, and all the air whooshed out of me. As I hunched in on myself in the fetal position there in the dark alley, he stood over me. The distinct rattle of his zipper caused a horror of which I'd never known to rise inside me.

"What are you doing, man?" one of his buddies yelled.

"Hold him," he said.

"Fuck no," someone replied. I heard a pair of retreating footsteps.

I started to get up. I was getting the fuck out of there.

"I said hold him!" he roared.

I made it to my feet, wobbled, and took a step. Suddenly, I was surrounded. Two guys grabbed my arms and dragged me farther behind the dumpster. I started yelling, fighting, cussing.

It didn't matter.

I was given another blow to the head, and everything went fuzzy.

It all became clear again when the worst pain I'd ever felt in my entire life ripped me in two. That's what it felt like…

As if I were being sawed in two.

The pain was excruciating. So bad I almost passed out.

I wished I had.

Instead, I was painfully aware of what was happening to me. Pinned by two men, beaten until I almost blacked out. And the sounds—the slapping of skin, the grunting—and the feel of his fingers digging into my hips from behind.

Tears fell from my eyes, mixing with the blood already on my face.

I stopped yelling out. My voice had already gone hoarse.

"You like that, fag?" his voice grunted as he shoved himself inside my body.

My knees buckled.

"C'mon, man, that's enough," someone else said.

He didn't stop. The arms that held me let go. I sagged, would have fallen if he didn't hold me up and shove me against a wall for added support.

I don't know how long it went on. How long I was raped by a hater in the alleyway… It didn't matter really.

One second or an hour… I was never going to be the same again.

I now knew why my life had flashed before my eyes. I was dying.

I died that night. Again.

Somewhere between the stripper and being raped, Dylan Lorhaven died.

Arrow Ambrose was born. Arrow, a shattered, jaded, and untrusting soul who sometimes wanted to be dead so badly he often fantasized about it. Maybe once, he tried.

But just like his father, death didn't want him either.

All he could do was exist: bleach his hair, shave half his head, and get a dozen tattoos—all to cover up the boy he was forced to bury.

And though Dylan was gone and dead, his ghost still occasionally rattled beneath my skin. He haunted me just like an insidious demon. The kind there was no exorcism for.

Sometimes when I looked in the mirror, it wasn't Arrow I saw at all, but the boy who just wanted to be accepted.

To the extreme.

That explains a lot of things in my life. It explains me.

When I do something, I'm borderline obsessive-compulsive about it. Attractive character trait, isn't it?

No.

Well, it's who I am.

If I've learned one thing in my twenty-six years on this planet, it's I am who I am and it isn't going to change. Like it or not.

In fact, one might argue the more time goes on, the more me I become.

I guess I'm pretty good at talking in tongues, too, because sometimes the shit that swirls around my own brain marauding as thoughts confuses even me.

Regardless, I'm trying to learn to accept myself, maybe even give myself a break. Currently, it isn't something I'm excelling at.

That's the thing about being OCD. It isn't just for the world around me, but also for me and the expectations I hold myself to.

It's those extreme expectations that are my ultimate downfall.

And the downfall of someone who was my infinity.

Chapter Six

Five years ago…

Complacency gets you nowhere. Actually, no. You know where it gets you? The same place you've always been.

To improve, to make headway in anything in life—like racing—you needed to push the envelope (or the throttle, if you want to make a racing pun). You must be comfortable with being uncomfortable.

Being uncomfortable was the new black.

Okay, I don't know what the fuck that means, but it sounds good. Right?

No?

Whatever.

Change wasn't easy. It never would be. But nothing worth having ever came easy, and I wanted this. I wanted this so goddamn bad I could actually taste it.

The flavor? Hopes and dreams.

Not.

It tasted a lot like exhaust and felt more like road rash.

I was obsessed with pushing myself. Insistent on being better than I was the day before. Racing was a high, but success, that was an addiction.

I'd been on the pro moto circuit for two years now. I'd debuted with good numbers and fought my way into the top ten motorcycle racers in North America.

It all came down to this moment.

This race.

This bike and this track.

I was dressed in my typical one-piece leathers, which wasn't as fashionable as it sounded. It wasn't as comfortable either. It wasn't like the supple leather pants every rocker wore in the eighties. This kind of leather was thicker, tougher, and didn't give as much when you moved.

I was used to it, though. In fact, sometimes when I was off the track, I still moved like I had it on.

My leathers were red and white. They molded to my body like a glove because I'd worn them often enough. The elbows, spine, and shoulder areas were heavily guarded—you know, in case I ate the pavement.

My knees were also well protected, something I learned to ensure because I was the kind of racer who liked to get low. So low my knee dragged the pavement as I turned.

I had permanent scars on my kneecaps. I considered them trophies.

The Kevlar gloves I wore, the specially made helmet and boots, it was all part of me. It kept me safe, but it also helped me stay in the zone. Like the way a uniform gave someone an air of authority.

Except leather was more badass.

In my humble opinion, of course.

My body folded over my Ducati exactly as it should, and my legs vibrated with the purr of the engine. I drove at such a high speed, everything around me was blurry. I didn't focus on it anyway; all I saw were my markers. Markers were reference points drivers used to keep their driving in check, to keep the track from swallowing them whole.

If a driver lost track of his markers, he'd end up like Alice in Wonderland, falling down a deep, endless hole, trying to find his way out.

I used markers for everything. When to brake, when to open the throttle, when to turn. They were my map on the course.

I was pushing myself today, as I did every race, but more so today. It was a calculated risk on my part really, one that most drivers probably would save for a day when everything they wanted wasn't riding on their success.

It was just me and one other driver on this track.

We were battling it out. Man to man. Bike to bike. This was a match of skill. A match of endurance, and to me, a match of who was willing to take enough risk to get just a quarter of a second faster.

Because winning by even a fraction of a second was still winning.

"Back off just a little," the familiar voice in my ear instructed.

My next marker was coming, a final turn in the course, and then hopefully I would be able to punch it right through the finish line. If I could push it now, I'd have the advantage around that curve.

"Jay, back off," the voice growled again. I heard impatience and a sense of anxiety in his tone.

I backed off… just a smidge.

If he was getting worried, then I was pushing it too hard.

I wanted this win; I needed it. But I didn't want it at the expense of everything else.

I took the turn, leaning so far to the side I was practically parallel to the ground. I let my knee kiss the pavement for brief moments, and when my marker came up, I punched it a little early.

It took a lot of strength to keep the bike in a solid line, but I managed, and once I straightened completely, the engine revved, the loud sound of acceleration piercing through the air and vibrating my thighs.

I shot over the line. The other racer was right beside me.

We both kept going, driving all the way through without hesitation. I let up a little and glanced over. He was already peeling away. A wake of smoke rose from his tire burning with the forced U-turn.

I grinned and punched my fist in the air.

He might have been beside me, but he was pissed off. I knew what that meant.

I managed to get that half second advantage.

I was going international! And not just smalltime international; this was top level. I'd just earned the single spot left in my division to invigorate the American motosport with an international spotlight. The next time my tires touched down, it would be in an entirely different country.

I would be racing the best of the best. A gathering of top-notch motoheads all from different countries in the granddaddy of all races.

MotoIntercontinental, here I come.

After my engine cooled a little, I looped around and buzzed over where everyone gathered. I grinned wide, even though they couldn't see it through my helmet. The second the bike stopped, I ripped it off and vaulted off.

Matt leapt forward with the biggest grin I'd ever seen on his face and smacked me in the middle with his clipboard, his headset still around his neck.

"Fucking yeah!" he yelled.

I felt a little wobbly since I'd just been on a vibrating speed machine, but I shook it off and whooped with pleasure.

Matt came in fast, wrapping his arms around my shoulders for a quick, congratulatory hug. "When I get you alone, I'll congratulate you properly," he whispered, then backed up.

Heat suffused the back of my neck, and I tucked away that little promise so I could pull it back out when we were indeed alone.

Even though everyone pretty much knew Matt and I were together, we still didn't shove it down people's throats. It made me uncomfortable. Him uncomfortable... And honestly, everyone else, too.

Roger Epps, the big man in my division, came striding over, a large smile on his face. I wiped at the sweat on my forehead and straightened as he reached me.

"Congratulations, Jayson. That was some damn fine driving. You've earned your spot at MotoIntercontinental."

I shook his hand, giving his entire arm a full, hard shake. "Thank you. I'll definitely show them all what America has."

Roger chuckled. "I have no doubt you will."

I grinned, barely able to contain my glee but needing to remain professional.

"Paperwork and everything will be done by Monday. You can sit down with your team, review it all, and then travel arrangements, training, etc. will be arranged," he added.

"Yes, sir." I nodded, eager. Adrenaline still pumped through my veins. I was hungry to succeed, to push my career on a multinational level.

"Make us here in North America proud. Show the world just how serious we take our moto." Epps encouraged.

I smiled, lightning fast. "Consider it done."

Matt slapped me on the back, and I glanced at him and grinned.

"If you want to show the rest of the world what our country is made of, you picked the wrong racer." A bitter, yet self-assured voice injected itself into our private conversation.

Private = it didn't include him.

Blaine was my opponent in this race. He was the best of the best, but I had beat him. Was it wrong to basically pit two fellow drivers against the other for the high-stakes prize of worldwide glory?

Hell yes.

But that was what this sport was made of.

It would only be wrong if they didn't give the top drivers in this division a final chance to battle it out.

Epps turned so he was angled toward me and Matt but also Blaine, who approached. He was dressed like me, in leathers and boots. His helmet and gloves were gone, and sweat beaded his hairline.

He was pissed off, sour. I could tell by the look in his eyes he wasn't going to give up that easily. I couldn't really blame the guy. This was a huge deal.

However, I wasn't giving it up.

"You were given an audition," Epps told him. "You're a damn fine moto racer, but Jayson was a little better today."

"Today." He scoffed. "But what about all the other days?"

"I'm up for the challenge," I replied, tossing him a look.

"I believe it." Epps held out his hand one last time, and I shook it. "Bring us home a trophy." On his way past, he offered Blaine a hand, and as they shook, he congratulated him on his kickass driving as well.

When he was gone, the crews were off doing whatever they had to do, and I was left standing there with Blaine.

"We both know I deserve this spot more than you," he deadpanned. It was like he expected me to bow down and agree.

What-the-fuck-ever.

"Why's that?" I scoffed. "Because you've been racing longer? Because you feel like you're due? Or maybe because you know your days in the moto world are numbered and this might be your last shot at Intercontinental?" The words were harsh, but they were reality.

He was older than me, more experienced. It pissed him off that I was better. In his eyes, he should have had that half second because he was the more seasoned of us.

It didn't work that way. Not on the track.

Pretty soon, his body wouldn't be able to keep up with the demands of racing, not because he was so terribly old, because he wasn't. However, in this world, you burned out fast.

I was younger, more able-bodied. Maybe that was why I was able to push it more today.

Or maybe I was just better.

Either way, it was no secret Blaine was on his way out. Guess he was feeling the burn.

"You self-righteous little prick," he ground out. Blaine lunged at me, barreling into my body like a truck.

I stumbled but didn't go down. Matt shouted and was at my back instantly.

His body steadied mine, and I stood back up, planting my feet into the pavement.

With a hard shove, I delivered Blaine back into his own personal space. "Cool down!" I insisted.

"That should be *my* name on that paperwork, *my* plane tickets being booked! I don't know how you pulled it off today or what you did to your bike…" He eyed my Ducati suspiciously, as if he possessed X-ray vision that would somehow point out an obvious illegal alteration. "But that was a lucky win. A one-time success you just happened to achieve on the right day."

It pissed me off. It pissed me off more than him openly telling everyone I wasn't good enough. To suggest I had to resort to cheating to win? Or I just got lucky, that my hard work and dedication over the last few years had nothing to do with it?

Unacceptable.

"We both know I'm not a cheat," I spat. "And as for luck… I'll beat you anytime, anyplace."

"Care to put that to the test?" He dared.

Matt made a sound. "You seriously want to race again? You must like losing."

Blaine gave him a harsh stare. "Maybe your boy here is afraid I'm right."

"Fine," I spat. "You want a rematch? I'm down. Name your time, your place. Stack the odds against me. When I beat you anyway, you will shut the fuck up about me not deserving the spot I earned."

Blaine shrugged. "Fine. And when I win, you'll go to Epps and withdraw, tell him to give your spot to me."

"Are you high?" Matt scoffed.

Blaine crossed his arms and stared at us, challenge glittering in his eyes.

I sighed. "Fine." I held out my hand. "You got yourself a deal."

"Tomorrow. Noon. Pinnacle Ridge."

"You want to street race… on Pinnacle Ridge," I deadpanned.

What the fuck. He was that pissed? Pinnacle Ridge wasn't just a road. It wasn't just a flat surface. It was a challenging maze of curves and twists over hilly terrain.

He nodded decisively. "If you can win there, you can win anywhere."

I stuck out my hand again.

As we shook, he said, "A no-show is a forfeit, so don't even think about playing sick."

"I don't play," I responded, the urge to put this guy into his place once and for all strong.

It was the handshake that signaled the beginning of my end.

Chapter Seven

Hopper
infinity

The fresh scent of pine clung to the sheets and lingered in my nose as daylight broke into my sleep-drunk mind. It wasn't Christmastime; it wasn't even winter. But to me, pine wasn't regulated to just that time of year.

It was Matt's signature.

The woodsy, earthy aroma embodied the guy I loved.

I inhaled deep before I even opened my eyes. My fingers came up empty when they reached for him, so they fisted in his pillow and pulled it against my face.

My body felt languid, lazy, and in no hurry to remove itself from the warm, delicious confines of this bed. His scent lingered all around me, and the touch of his hands and lips from last night still echoed in my body.

Even though I'd been beyond hyped after the race yesterday, and then after the challenge from Blaine, the second we walked into our place, those things took a backseat.

We ordered Thai food, ate on the couch, and made out like we used to when we first started dating. Matt was my perspective in life, the brake to the drive inside me. He didn't slow me down; he balanced me out. He helped me appreciate there was more to life than just motorcycles.

He also taught me about love, about generosity, and that sometimes even in the face of defiance, love really could win.

We'd only lived together about six months, but I already couldn't remember what it was like to be alone.

Sure, we dated a lot longer than six months. The first year no one knew about us at all. But then we came out, not as a couple, but one at a time when each of us was ready.

Eventually, people would pair us naturally. I'd get asked if maybe I was into him. I told myself it wasn't because people saw a shit ton of chemistry between us. It was just because when you were gay, it wasn't always easy to meet someone.

But still, the chemistry between us was pretty fiery. We just kept it private, sort of like a secret only the pair of us knew.

The sound of water falling interrupted my thoughts, and I glanced out the window, thinking first about rain. Rain wasn't a stranger here in the Seattle climate, but today, I couldn't have the rain. I wanted this challenge over and done with. I had better things to do.

Rain wasn't falling; there were no wet streaks on the window. It was the shower. I stretched and thought about going to join Matt beneath the spray. Just as I was about to move, it shut off and I heard the shower door open and close.

I rolled so I had the best view of the bathroom door, so when he opened it, I would be greeted with his sexy body.

Matt appeared, rubbing a towel over his head, completely naked.

My skin heated just looking at him, and I made sure my eyes ate their fill.

"Like something you see?" Matt asked, tossing the towel on the floor and climbing onto the bed. I rolled so he could come over me.

Water droplets from his hair fell on my forehead as he gazed down.

"I like *everything* I see," I replied, staring into his eyes.

His teeth caught my lower lip and tugged. As he sucked, I reached around behind him to cup his ass.

My morning wood was like a spear between us, and he rocked against it as I squeezed his ass and made out with his lips.

He pulled back when I started to pant, then dove beneath the blankets and finished me off. I admit it didn't take very long because all his humping had brought me to the edge.

After he swallowed me down, Matt slid up my body once more, and his tongue delved between my lips. I tasted myself on him, and I smiled.

"Your turn," I murmured against his mouth.

He made a sound. "I'm gonna have to wait. We have a race to get to."

I groaned and seriously considered blowing it off, and my fingertips caressed the base of his spine. He smiled like he knew exactly what I was contemplating and pressed his forehead to mine.

"I'll make you some French toast." He bribed.

He made stellar French toast. Actually, everything he made was bomb, which was a definite bonus, because the extent of my kitchen know-how was how to open a beer.

I raked a hand through his soft brown hair and smiled. "I could eat."

He laughed. "What else is new?"

"Nothing, because I still love you," I replied.

The side of his mouth turned up. "I still love you, too."

Matt sat up, his long, lean torso towering above me as his legs straddled my hips. The pad of his finger met my chest, and he traced a symbol over my skin.

"For always," I vowed.

He nodded. "Infinity."

We stared at each other a moment longer, but then he was slipping into a pair of boxers and running a hand through his still damp hair. "Meet you in the kitchen?"

"Clothing optional?" I yelled after him.

His chuckle floated in from the hall. "Sure, but if you actually want to make it out of the house this morning, I would suggest pants."

Pants were totally overrated. Even so, after I tossed the blankets back, I picked up a pair of shorts and tugged them on.

Staying in all day had a definite appeal. But that would have to wait until tomorrow. Today was my race with Blaine. Our final showdown.

Hopefully after I smoked him this last time, he'd move on with himself and leave me the fuck alone.

Chapter Eight

Hopper

Show up early.

Be energetic with your competitive nature, especially if you're the one who was challenged. Sometimes winning started with the mind.

The mind was a very powerful thing, and if channeled properly, it could be an even more powerful weapon.

I was scheduled to race at noon, so we planned to be the first at Pinnacle Ridge. I planned to be dressed in my leathers, helmet on, and ass on the bike when Blaine pulled up.

It would throw him off. It would give him even a nanosecond of doubt that he wasn't as sure to win as he expected. Why?

Because losers didn't show up early. They didn't sit at the start line, waiting for their humiliation.

Blaine issued the challenge, but I was the one who would rule it.

We pulled up an hour early, the road kicking up a cloud of dust when Matt pressed the breaks and parked on the side.

Pinnacle Ridge was paved, but it was done so long ago some of the gravel was loose from road repairs that were less than professional. The landscaping at the road's edges was unkempt, mostly because this ridge, while known by all the locals, wasn't used excessively. It wasn't a main road or even a shortcut to anywhere in town.

Mostly used by people who lived up the hill in the Peaks (which, by the way, had views that would give a man a hard-on). Or by the postal workers and other locals.

And of course, this was a hot spot for racing. Even though it was forbidden.

This wasn't exactly a safe road to race on. The blind spots, the hills and sharp curves… there was even a drop-off on one side that plummeted down to where the road wound below.

Large pine trees, maple, and other mature landscape grew in tune with the road, almost like it shielded it from too much commercialism.

It was actually a pretty cool place. People had been known to walk it as well, and I knew from experience there were a lot of four-wheeler trails that branched off away from the road and into the woods that separated this ridge from the nearby neighborhood.

It was a tepid morning, nothing unexpected for the outskirts of Seattle. It didn't really get hot here, even in the summer. It rained a lot, but today was clear and bright. Almost like the motogods in the sky blessed this clash of racers.

Matt cut the engine, and his palm curved around the back of my neck. My head swiveled in his direction, and we locked eyes. His eyes were deep and dark. Some people called them secret eyes because they seemed so dark they had to be hiding something.

I knew better, but I could see the reasoning behind the term.

The thick pads of his fingers rubbed over the back of my neck and base of my skull. He liked the way my buzzed hair tickled his rough hands. Once, he told me it was like a light massage for his senses.

Gooseflesh broke out over my scalp, and I closed my eyes.

"You're going to own this," he said, not speaking loud. He didn't have to shout. We were in our own little universe inside the car.

"Once I do, we can check international travel off our bucket list," I mused.

I was hyped for MotoIntercontinental, but I was also looking forward to traveling the world with Matt. A lot of the countries we would be visiting were a lot more relaxed about men in relationships. I didn't know if it would make it easier to hold hands with him on the street or let my hand rest on his thigh in plain sight at a restaurant or even go in for his lips at a café, but I sure as hell wanted to find out.

"I'm proud of you," he told me.

My chest swelled. Praise from him was like getting it from the highest order. "Couldn't have gotten this far without you."

He scoffed.

I grabbed his jaw and forced his head around. "Seriously, Matt. You are just as good a racer as me, but you've put so much into my career, I think it maybe hampered your own."

His hand wrapped around my wrist, giving it a gentle squeeze, and I dislodged my hold. He kissed the inside of my palm, the scruff on his jaw an added layer of sensation.

"My career is where I want it to be. I'm happy, and I win enough. Besides, if we were both racing gods, how the hell would we ever see each other?"

He was pretty incredible. He made a choice, one I honestly wasn't sure I could have made. When it came down to it, between our relationship and our careers, he decided for us to have both, a sacrifice had to be made.

And he made it.

For me.

For us.

"I love you," I told him.

He smirked. "I know. You screamed it last night when I was sucking your dick."

I made a sound of appreciation. That was good fucking blowjob.

But not quite as good as feeling him fill me with his length, which he did right after I exploded.

With our hands linked, he leaned over the stick shift and connected our mouths. The kiss was leisurely, slow, and full contact.

Matt's tongue was wide and thick. He knew how to wield it so my mouth was completely owned. My full lips rubbed over his, refusing to separate even as my lungs lurched for oxygen.

It was him who broke away first, slowly, languidly, but enough so I could breathe once more.

"I love you, too," he whispered, pressing one last kiss against my lips before pulling away completely.

"You know what?" I said, grabbing his forearm as he turned to get out of the driver's seat.

He glanced back around, an expectant look on his features.

"I think we should use this tour at Intercontinental to learn inside secrets, tips, and tricks,"

He tilted his head as if to say, *What for?*

"That way when the North American circuit starts back up next season, you'll have a ton of advantage to get there yourself."

His eyes lit up deep in their depths. I smiled, satisfied. That was the look I wanted to see. It proved that even though he wanted us, he wanted to race just as much as me.

I didn't want to be the only one fulfilling that dream. Sure, Matt was an awesome racer. He had good sponsorship deals, trophies, and a high placement in the division. But he was held back by us. By *me*.

This season had been mine, and now Intercontinental would be, too.

Next year? That was going to be for Matt.

"I like it," he mused.

"I know." I wagged my eyebrows, and he laughed.

We got out of the truck and walked around to the trailer hitched to the back.

Both Ducatis were enclosed inside. We always traveled with our bikes this way to keep them protected. And to give us a little more anonymity. These were expensive pieces of equipment, and they caught attention. Matt's was in the back as well, even though he wasn't racing—you know, in case we wanted to do some touring after I beat Blaine.

I waited while he undid the lock on the back doors, perusing the street, trying to get the "lay of the land."

I'd driven this road numerous times. It wasn't something I was used to racing on, but I wasn't starting out blind.

I heard the lock give, metal scrape metal, and I glanced back around as Matt removed the padlock. He grabbed the handle and tugged, but the door didn't open.

We needed a new trailer; this one was a piece of shit. For as much as I paid for it, you'd think it would have lasted a little longer.

The damn doors always stuck. They never wanted to open.

Shit, we probably didn't even need to bother with the lock. It practically took an act of God to get the damn things open regardless.

I made a mental note to start shopping for a new one.

He tugged again. The doors rumbled under his strength, but didn't budge. He cursed, and I chuckled.

"Here, let me mess with them. Don't get the boxers molded perfectly to your fine ass in a bunch."

Matt barked a laugh but continued to fight with the stubborn metal doors. I moved up behind him, ready to step in, when the doors popped open like they'd released a ton of pressure.

"Whoa," Matt yelled, surprised as they burst open. He lunged back to catch them but only succeeded in catching one.

I caught the other one.

With my face.

"Ugh." The sound oozed out of me when the edge of the thick metal smacked me in the side of the head. It swung with such force it knocked me onto my ass.

Pain exploded on the side of my head the second I fell back. The pavement was cold even through my hoodie, but I barely noticed. I lay there stunned for long moments as sharp, piercing shocks of pain electrified my head.

"Jayson!" Matt worried, leaning over me, his hands hovering nearby without touching. "Shit, I'm sorry."

"It's not your fault those doors are assholes," I muttered and pushed myself up.

"Easy," Matt urged, putting his arm around my back and helping me sit up.

"That fucking hurt," I cursed. I pressed a palm to my temple.

"You're bleeding," he said softly, taking my hand to stop me from smearing the blood.

"Shit," I muttered, reaching for the hem of my hoodie to wipe it away. I didn't have time for this shit.

Behind us, the metal doors rattled as the wind blew, banging around like the bunch of peckers they were.

"Stop," Matt ordered, but there was no bite in his voice. There hardly ever was when he spoke to me.

I'd probably do a double take and think he needed an exorcism if he ever yelled at me.

"I got this." He grinned and ripped his own hoodie off his body. There was a flash of his solid abs when he moved before the T-shirt (with a black peace sign in the center) fell back into place. His hoodie was light gray with the motocross symbol on it.

Gingerly, he blotted at the cut. There was more blood than I originally realized. I felt it trickle down my head, near my eye. "It got ya good," he murmured, still blotting and wiping at the wound. I think you might need stitches."

"No," I growled. "I don't have time for that."

"Well, the bleeding says otherwise," Matt refuted.

"I'm fine," I grumped and moved to get up.

I swayed a little, feeling woozy. Refusing to let it get me, I pushed on.

Matt wrapped his arms around me and lifted, helping me up.

His arm stayed around me while he held the hoodie to my head. "You don't look so good, Jay."

"I said I'm fine." I tried to push him away so I could stand on my own.

He dropped his arm but kept the other against my head. My stomach rolled, and I blinked. Sucking in a sharp breath between my lips, I swayed again.

"You could have a concussion," Matt noted, lifting the hoodie to look. He grunted. "Still bleeding." He pressed the shirt back down.

"I have a race to win."

"You can't get on a bike, man. You know it, and I know it."

"I know if I don't, I'll forfeit that damn race and I'll lose Intercontinental."

We locked eyes. His jaw hardened. He knew it as well as I did. I couldn't back down from this. What we had wasn't a legal agreement, but I gave my word.

My word was more binding than any document that would hold up in court.

"Yeah," he snapped. "I know."

I pressed my head a little farther into the hoodie, willing the bleeding to stop and my world to right itself.

Matt brought up his other hand, pulling me against him. His hug was hard and full.

"I'll drive for you."

I jerked back. "What? No!"

It wasn't that I thought he couldn't win. He could. I knew it. It was this was *my* challenge. *My* reputation on the line. I was the one who accepted the dare, and I was the one who needed to finish it.

"You aren't driving, Jayson," Matt said, his tone firm.

My eyes flashed up to his. Was that some steel I heard?

The corner of his mouth kicked up. "Don't make me get all alpha on you."

I grinned. "*You* get alpha on me?"

"You know I'm capable of it. I just don't because I love you."

"You can't drive for me, Matt."

He glanced toward the trailer. "Sure I can. We're about the same size. With your leathers, helmet, and the rest of your gear on, plus me sitting on your bike… no one will even question the driver isn't you."

He was right, but I didn't like it.

"Blaine is an asshole." I bitched.

"No shit. That's nothing new. I've raced with him plenty of times."

He had, and I knew he could handle this. But I wanted to be the one to do it. I wanted to earn every single victory I got.

Matt's hand fell to my shoulder and squeezed. "I know. But I'm not letting you drive, Jay. Your eyes are foggy-looking and your head is still fucking bleeding."

I sighed. "Fuck!"

Matt's lips pressed against my forehead, and he chuckled. "After I win, you're going to the hospital and getting stitches. Maybe a CT scan."

I gave him a *hell no* look, and he grinned.

"Hold this," he ordered. I pressed my hand over his hoodie. "Good thing we got here early. It'll give me time to suit up so no one sees us play an old switcheroo."

I made a rude sound, but my voice was fond. "You've probably been saving that in your back pocket, just waiting for a time to bring it out and say it."

"It's a good saying." He tossed a smile over his shoulder before disappearing inside the trailer where all my gear was.

I stood in the doorway (the doors were tied open now so no one else got hammered) and watched with a brooding stare as he suited up in my red-and-white leathers.

When he was almost done, I moved to unlatch the binds holding up the bike, but a wave of dizziness pressed in on me.

"Hey," Matt murmured, wrapping his arms around me from behind and gently pulling me away. "Sit. I got this."

I sat in the trailer as he did all the heavy lifting, moved the bike out into the sunshine, and then slid my helmet over his head.

He had a pair of dimples that charmed everyone. They made him look younger than he was. They were basically a permanent fountain of youth built right into his olive-toned skin.

His high cheekbones and pair of dark eyes stared out a me from the helmet. I knew he was smiling even though his mouth was covered. I saw it in his stare.

I smiled back, though I felt like shit and was livid I wasn't driving. Still, he was right. My head was foggy and my hands felt unsteady. Driving like this was basically handing over my win yesterday.

Not going to happen.

I trusted Matt. I knew he'd win this. For me. For him. For us.

"Just stay in the trailer." He crouched between my open legs. "That way no one sees you. They won't even think to question I'm not you. If anyone asks, I'll tell them I stayed home."

I nodded miserably. The helmet was thick enough that it muffled his voice. If they weren't expecting it, they wouldn't even know it wasn't me talking.

"Thanks for doing this, man."

"Anything for you," he replied. The smile was back in his eyes again.

He leaned down, pressing the forehead of the helmet gently to mine. "Don't pass out while I'm racing. If you do, I'll kick your ass."

I laughed. "I'll be fine."

"You better be. I need you around."

I smiled. Our eyes connected. As he watched, I kissed the tips of two of my fingers and pressed them through the opening of the helmet to touch his skin.

"Love you, Jay," he said, muffled, but I still heard it loud and clear.

"Love you, too."

The sound of another car pulling up and slowing had our attention turning to the outside world.

He held his fist out between us. I hit mine against his.

"See you in a few," he said, then left me there, letting the doors close (but not latch) behind him.

I leaned my head against the metal wall and stared up at the ceiling. This fucking blew.

A short while went by, and then the sound of a bike firing up filled the air. With a deep breath, I shoved up off my ass. I swayed a little, blinked against the blurriness in my sight, and went to a small window in the side of the trailer.

The window was tinted and small; it was also at angle where I didn't think anyone would notice me standing there watching.

Matt was on my bike, looking ready in all my gear. Blaine's bike was right beside him, but he wasn't on it. I glanced around, noting him standing beside his trailer a few yards away. His buddy, Rockford, who was also a racer, was in front of him.

They were talking, and it appeared somewhat intense. Obviously, there was no way to know what they were saying. When I tried to concentrate on Blaine's moving lips, all I got was extra shooting pain in my head.

I pressed the hoodie harder against the gash and observed them. I couldn't tell if they were arguing or just having a heated conversation.

Finally, Blaine ripped the helmet out of Rockford's hands and jabbed it at him in the space between them. Rockford nodded as if he were conceding.

He jammed the helmet on and went to his bike, starting it up, and not much later, they both signaled each other and took off.

I watched Matt until I couldn't see him anymore, but I stayed at the window, not feeling inclined to move. My stomach rolled still, and the arm holding the hoodie in place was beginning to get tired.

I pulled it down, looked at the deep-red stains on the fabric, and shook my head. Of all the stupid shit to happen right now.

They hadn't been gone barely long enough to worry, but I was anxious. I should have been the one out there. I should've been the one whipping over the road and rubbing my knee on the pavement. I hoped Matt was enjoying himself and that Blaine wasn't riding his ass too hard.

An uncomfortable feeling wormed inside me, and I knew it was something apart from the shit going on with my head.

Call it intuition maybe. Or even just a bad omen.

I glanced back out the window, and my suspicions only intensified.

Rockford was moving around at the back of their trailer. The doors were propped open, so I couldn't see what he was doing. Of course, that trailer didn't have loose, piece-of-shit doors.

A few minutes later, his bike came down a ramp. When he appeared around the side of the door, pushing the bike beside him, he was completely dressed in leathers.

And a helmet.

What. The. Fuck?

Why would he be dressed to race? This was a man-to-man rematch. There was no need for other drivers.

He gazed off in the direction Matt and Blaine had gone and then checked a thick watch on his wrist.

It was almost as if he were expected to be somewhere. Or he was timing something…

They weren't planning on what it looked like they were planning. Were they?

I thought about yesterday, about the look in Blaine's eyes when he lunged at me. I'd hit a nerve when I boldly spoke aloud that his racing days were likely numbered.

I watched Rockford glance around like he was suddenly worried about being seen.

Sabotage.

Blaine was totally planning to sabotage my driving today, and Rockford was going to help him.

Except I wasn't the one driving. Matt was.

He was out there right now, taking the brunt of anger and aggression meant for me.

Not only that, but Rockford was about to join in and make it worse.

Son of a bitch!

We weren't wearing any kind of communication or headsets. Matt was out there on his own on the ridge. Two against one.

Adrenaline and worry for Matt was stronger than the concussion I likely had. My body shoved away from the window, and the bike started up. The nausea and fogginess that clung to me was disregarded.

I didn't have time for this.

Matt needed me.

What the fuck had I been thinking? I should have known Blaine was going to pull something.

I moved fast, able to do so because these tasks had been done by my hands thousands of times. The second Matt's Ducati was unhooked, I shoved it toward the doors and kicked them open. They banged and wobbled under the force of my boot, and I rushed to roll the bike down the ramp.

Rockford had taken off seconds before. I glanced up to see him disappear around a turn.

Without hesitation, I jumped on the bike and started the engine. I revved her as hard as I could, not milking it at all today. I needed results, and I needed them now.

The bike shot forward, and I blinked against the wind and the sudden pressure I felt in my skull. I wasn't wearing any kind of protective gear—gloves, a helmet, or even leather. All I had on was a pair of well-loved jeans, boots that weren't made for driving, and my hoodie.

The gash on my head felt weird, numb, but not so numb I could forget it was there. It almost felt like it was bleeding again, but I pushed away the thought.

Beneath my hands, the bike fishtailed a little, and I righted it. I could do this. I could operate this machine in my sleep. I could certainly do it even if I wasn't firing on all cylinders.

I raced after Rockford and the other two, flying around the curves and up the ridge as my eyes sought out any of the others.

The knee in my jeans ripped out. Gravel and pavement burned my skin, and I gritted my teeth against the pain as I navigated a sharp turn and then gradually came out the other side. As I drove, I caught sight of them up ahead.

What I saw made my blood run cold. I was right.

Rockford and Blaine were trying to make "me" lose. Why bother asking for a rematch if you know you can't win fair?

It was pretty fucking stupid of me to not think about the fact that people didn't often care about fair; they only cared about getting what they wanted.

The two bikes were boxing in Matt. He was holding his own. He didn't seem rattled.

But I was.

Fuck, this could go so bad. Matt wasn't as strong on the inside as I was. And right now, he was boxed in on the inside.

I wanted to scream. In fact, I did. But of course, the wind whipped away that sound, sending my voice trailing behind me.

I blinked, my vision slightly blurry, and my stomach lurched, but I swallowed it all back.

Get to Matt.

Rockford squeezed in farther; Blaine tightened the gap between them.

I raced forward, pushing the bike as hard as I could until I was close enough I could feel the way their bikes disrupted the wind and energy around us all. My bike was doing the same, but there was no one behind me to notice.

Rockford glanced around, then did a double take.

I gave him the finger and then pointed at the side of the road—the opposite side from where Matt was racing.

His bike wavered. The speed dipped a little. But then he sped back up, still glancing at me every couple seconds.

Blaine noticed Rockford change speed and placement, and his head swiveled around as well.

I knew the moment he saw me, the moment he realized he was chasing the wrong guy. I felt his shock, then his anger.

He swerved toward Matt. I screamed. Matt swerved with him, avoiding contact. His bike went off the road for just a second before he righted it.

That second changed everything.

He hit a patch of gravel. The tire jolted and slid out from beneath him.

"No!" I screamed.

I watched his arms fight. I watched his body struggle to keep the bike upright. Fear clogged my throat; pain filled my head and my eyes. Surely they played tricks on me.

Even as I flew closer, I saw Blaine, who now knew it wasn't me on that bike, nudge Matt's Ducati, giving it just that little last push.

Everything happened at once, then, so fast.

The Ducati flipped. Matt was slammed into the ground, then flung into the air, discharged off the bike, and hit the side of the road with such force I felt it. But he didn't stop there. His body skidded over a hill, disappearing from sight.

"Matt!" I roared.

I was on Blaine now, and I used my bike to ram him. I didn't slow down. I didn't even hesitate. This motherfucker deserved to die, and if I had to take myself out to make sure he got his just rewards, then I would.

Our tires locked up, the bikes went spinning, and then everything was nothing but darkness filled with the sounds of crunching metal. I came to I don't know how much later, severe pain radiating throughout my entire body.

My fingers dug into the dirt where I lay, and I shoved my head up, blinking through the dirt and wetness, seeking out Matt.

I saw him yards away, off to the side, just over the hill. He was lying still, not moving, not calling for help.

I pushed up to run to him, but my body refused to obey. "Matt," I called out. My voice was weak and my throat scratched, but I yelled anyway.

He didn't reply. He acted as if he didn't even hear.

I heard other sounds, shouts behind me somewhere nearby, but I blocked it all out.

I gave one last valiant attempt to rush to Matt's side, but there would be no rushing today. My body failed me, refusing to walk.

I clenched my hands and flexed my fingers. They still worked, so I used them. I pulled myself in a half crawl, half drag toward Matt, the entire time trying to remain focused and call his name.

It seemed it took forever to get to him. The entire time, I prayed to God he was going to be okay.

Please, please, God, I begged. *Don't let the death that was meant for me claim him. He is too good for death.*

I reached him, my hand closing around his boot. "Matty," I sobbed. "I'm here. Oh fuck, I'm sorry."

He still didn't reply, so I crawled up his body, partly sprawled over his chest.

The helmet was shattered. Blood covered what I could see of his face. "Matt." I tried again, gripping the helmet with barely any strength.

I tugged and pulled, but I couldn't get it off.

A sob broke in my chest, and the sound catapulted out of my throat like a high keen or a howl at a full moon.

I shook his shoulders, grabbed his hand, and hit his chest. "Wake up!" I demanded.

But he didn't.

"Call 9-1-1!" I yelled, but I don't know who I spoke to.

"Hang in there," I told him, all my energy seeping away, leaving me feeling strangely void. Wetness leaked out of my eyes as my head fell onto his chest. I tried to hang on to consciousness. I struggled to stay there in the moment with Matt. "Everything's going to be fine," I told him.

But everything wasn't fine. I knew it deep inside me. Even the blow to my head, the wreck, and then literally crawling to his body wasn't enough to block out the fact that this was all my fault.

Sirens in the distance were a welcome sound. Help for Matt was on the way.

The beckoning darkness swallowed me whole.

Chapter Nine

Hopper
infinity

We all know we don't have enough time.

It's common knowledge. So common it's often overlooked. Kind of like the heat in the dead of summer in the south. It's easy to forget how brutal the humidity is, how intense the sun can be, when we're able to close the door to it and revel in air-conditioning. Or sit in a restaurant, impervious to the heat, sipping a cold beer with a frosty-to-the-touch mug.

The thing is with heat, with time, there are always reminders.

Like when you first climb into your car after exiting an efficiently cooled place and nearly melting off half your skin. Or when you tell yourself "tomorrow," then…

Tomorrow never comes.

Infinity is just an illusion. Something we tell ourselves we have, because truly realizing just how fragile time is would be close to crippling.

The silence around me was absolute. So soundless there was this static energy about it that almost fooled me into thinking I wasn't actually waking.

But I was. Slowly, my eyelids fluttered. Pricks of light filtered beneath the dark curtain of my vision. I blinked against the bright haziness, trying to get everything to come into focus.

Urgency, I could feel it in the way my heart rate accelerated despite the fact my body was at rest. Imperative terror, the kind that gripped your chest and made it hard to think, rose inside me.

My body bolted upright, lips parting to gasp for air. Beside my hips, my hands fisted into the fabric nearby as I tried to make sense of my surroundings and everything my mind and body was trying to tell me.

It was so much. So much so fast.

The annoying sound of beeping barely registered, only enough to make me wish it would stop because I had more important things to think about.

The walls were white; the window was large and boasted drawn generic blinds. This wasn't my apartment, my bed… my home.

This room was empty except for me, this bed, and a few other no-nonsense pieces of furniture I couldn't care less about.

I tugged at the covers, trying to get free because there was somewhere I had to be. Someone who needed me.

Matt.

Just the whisper of his name in the back of my consciousness alarmed me. My breathing became desperate, coming in short gasps, almost as if I were hyperventilating, but not quite.

"Sir." A woman in a pair of scrubs rushed into the room. "Jayson? You're doing just fine." She hurried over to my side as I struggled with the blankets and tried to calm me by putting a hand to the center of my chest, gently pushing me back.

The beeping silenced. I realized it was coming from the machine beside the bed. There was also an IV stand. I followed the cord all the way to where it stuck out of the back of my hand, the needle concealed by about three pounds of medical tape.

"Where is he?" I gasped, struggling against her hold. "Where's Matt?"

I was confused, my mind muddled. I searched desperately for the answers I needed, begging the knowledge to burst through the fog.

"You were in a serious accident. You have serious injuries. You need to lie back and rest. You don't want to rip out any stitches."

I grabbed her arm, my eyes fastened on her face. "*Matt*," I implored.

Suddenly, everything around me turned inward. I heard metal scraping over the ground, parts scattering, and a sick engine sputtering out as the smell of burning rubber filled my senses. The sight of a tire that spun even though it was no longer on the road completed the horrible memory.

"Sir," the nurse said again, calling me back.

"Matt!" I hollered, sounding raspy and old. "Where the hell is Matt?"

The beeping of the machines started up again, but I blocked it out.

The vision of a prone body, a body I knew as well as my own, lying near the wreckage stole over me. I let out a strangled sound. His helmet was shattered, his leg awkwardly bent, and there was blood…

Too much blood.

"I'm so terribly sorry." The nurse began.

My voice broke. A sob caught in the back of my throat. "No."

Her voice was gentle and swift. "Your friend that was also in the accident… he didn't make it."

"No," I keened, finally collapsing against the pillow. I rolled onto my side. Pain seared me everywhere, and a breath hissed between my teeth.

Visions of the man I loved in various states of our relationship flashed through my mind. Smiling, laughing… wet in the shower.

He was gone.

All those visions were now memories. Memories of what would never be again.

"Are you in pain?" The nurse hovered. "I need to get the doctor."

I was crying. I felt the wetness on my cheeks. Utter despair tightened my chest.

After a second of hesitation, the nurse laid her hand on my shoulder. Hers wasn't the touch I drew comfort from. Hers wasn't the hand that knew me.

"I'm so sorry for your loss," she whispered.

She bustled from the room, saying something about a doctor. I heard the door close behind her.

The silence that pressed on me when I first awoke… it was back. I was alone in this room.

Matt was dead.

Because of me.

I killed the one person I loved most in this world.

Solitude was now my permanent and only companion.

It was more than I deserved.

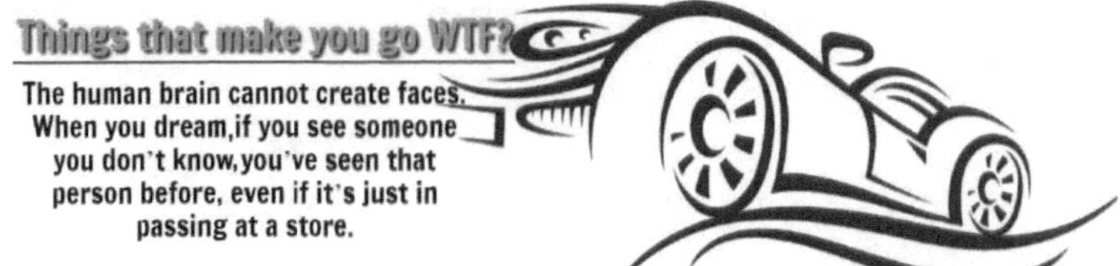

Chapter Ten

Hopper

I went to the morgue. To identify the body.

He wasn't just a body.

He wasn't just lifeless flesh, broken and torn in an unfortunate accident, that just needed to be labeled correctly.

My feet were bare. They slapped along the cold, hard hospital corridor as I walked unsteadily toward the wing where Matt's shell lay. The IV stand I leaned on had a squeaky, crooked wheel that echoed around us as we went. I was dressed in a hospital gown, one I didn't even bother to make sure was closed. The cold air in the hall brushed against the small of my back and the backs of my thighs as I walked, but it didn't matter.

My bare feet, unclothed state… even the pain radiating in my body was of no importance.

He was gone.

I was here.

Left behind. Living… but dead.

My heart still beat, my lungs still took in air, but it was all details now because life as I knew it was shattered.

I limped, leaned a little farther against the pole as I trudged on. They'd wanted to wait. The nurses, the doctors, the police, even my managers.

Waiting wouldn't make it any easier. I wanted to see Matt. The thought of him lying on some sterile, cold table beneath a scratchy white sheet surrounded by other lifeless bodies made me so incredibly sad.

And so incredibly angry.

He deserved better than this. How could a man with so much life inside him be drained and reduced to this in only fleeting moments?

A swinging door was held open for me. I pushed inside a square room with a single table that looked like a slab of steel.

The white sheet was exactly as I imagined. Exactly as it was portrayed on movies and TV.

The coroner was standing nearby. A white lab coat covered his body, a pair of blue latex gloves on his hands.

My stomach lurched and churned. I knew I wouldn't throw up; there was nothing inside me. Absolutely nothing.

I stopped beside the body, near his head.

The coroner moved up, grabbed the edge of the sheets, and glanced at me.

I nodded once, then fixed my eyes downward.

Matt's face and upper body was revealed to me.

He was still. Eerily so.

His lips were blue, his skin was white, and the dark hair that always fell over his forehead was shoved back off his face. I wanted to reach out and ruffle it, to put it back in its rightful place. Maybe then he wouldn't appear so inert. There was no fixing his hair, putting it back the way it should be, because it was matted and stiff with dried blood.

I stared at him. I stared so long my legs fell asleep and my hand trembled with weakness where I gripped the pole at my side.

All the injuries he incurred from the race that should have killed *me* marred his body, making him appear even more garish. It was unsettling to see so much violence on such a still being.

"Can you give us confirmation?" the coroner asked, his voice low.

I glanced up, then immediately back down.

"Is this Matthew Lewis?" He pressed.

"Matt." My voice scratched out. "He liked to be called Matt."

I felt rather than saw the coroner motion to someone, and then he began raising the sheet.

My arm shot out and gripped his, squeezing so hard my fingers ached. I was weak, far weaker than I'd ever been.

Weak in body. Weak in spirit. Weak in mind.

He didn't even wince at the way I grabbed him, even though I gave it everything I had.

"No," I begged. "Not yet."

"You should get back to bed." The nurse spoke softly from the door.

"I'm never going to see him again!" I raged. "This is the last moment I will ever have with him. I don't give a damn about bed!"

The coroner cleared his throat, smoothed the sheet back, and stepped away. "We'll give you a few moments."

The door closed audibly.

I sucked in a shuddering breath.

Tears blurred my vision as I clung to the image of my lover's face.

I stepped forward until my body hit the side of the table. I smoothed a shaking hand over his bare shoulder.

I knew he wasn't here. Not really.

But this was all I had left.

"I'm sorry, Matt," I told him, my voice shattering. "I'm so fucking sorry."

It didn't matter that he was broken, bloody, and just an empty shell. He was still everything to me. I leaned forward, wrapped my arms around his cold, stiff shoulders, and pressed my face into the side of his neck.

He wasn't warm like usual. He didn't smell of pine and dirt.

It was then I truly realized just how quickly infinity can be ripped away.

In many respects, it left me crippled.

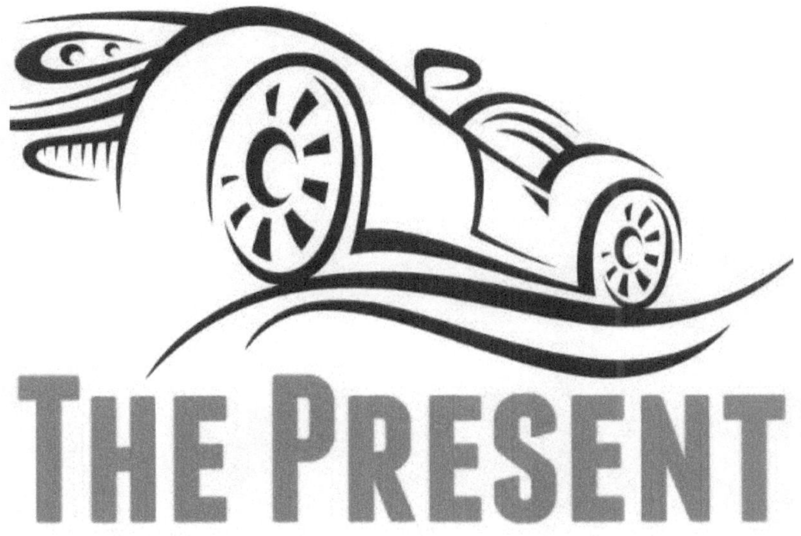

The Present

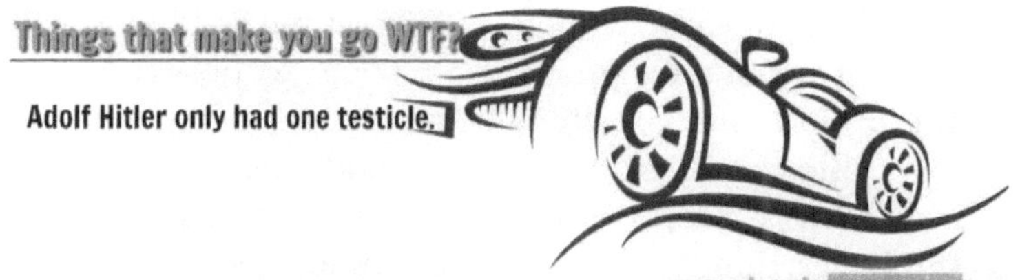

Chapter Eleven

I found myself caught between two different worlds.

How did I end up here again?

I told myself the last time there would never be another. I would always remain true to who I was, no matter the cost.

After all, I'd already paid so heavy a price. There couldn't possibly be anything worse.

Regardless, choices were heavy.

Perhaps that was why so many of us lived in limbo. Sometimes the discomfort of indecision was preferable to the pain of choice. Especially when so many of the decisions we made in a moment could alter the rest of our lives.

I knew that better than most.

Maybe life was a series of crossroads, and it seemed I was doomed to stayed at the junction and debate which way to go so long it was almost crippling.

Maybe that's why I was always alone.

Left behind.

Everyone else was whizzing past me as I stood still, waiting for some sign I wasn't going to do something that would cause a belly full of regret.

Thing was I didn't want to stand still.

I was a racer, destined for speed. Destined to go until everything around me was a blur.

What a giant juxtaposition I'd become. Wanting badly to drive fast, but always, always hitting the brakes.

My life didn't turn out the way I expected. Hell, where I was now wasn't even something I'd ever imagined.

However…

Where I was, it wasn't a bad place to be.

I found myself in a unique situation. With a unique opportunity. Not one, actually, but two.

Indie or pro.

To some, maybe this was a no-brainer. Not for me. The decision to drive in the NRR with my brother, my new sister, and my best friend Drew or take a spot up for grabs with NASCAR with a heavyweight sponsor was something I'd been sitting on for months.

Months.

The clock on patience was running down with everyone involved. Pretty soon, I was going to have to put up or shut up.

I couldn't shut up. This was my chance, an opportunity to break free of where I was and start over. I was no stranger to starting over.

Or was I?

Maybe that's why this choice was so hard. Maybe it was why the call to take a spot right next to my family wasn't such a no-brainer.

Perhaps all this time, I'd only been in limbo.

I'd jumped in the car, sped away from what use to be, but the engine stalled on the side of an empty road. There I'd sat.

Lorhaven tried to tow me. In fact, he did.

But a man can only be carried so far until he must stand on his own two feet.

The clock was ticking. Days rolled by on the calendar. I felt a season of change in the air, something inside me unsettling more every day.

My phone taunted me with the voicemail.

Ron Gamble had called. He wanted to see me.

He wanted a decision.

Only problem?

I was scared.

Chapter Twelve

I couldn't sleep.

I had an early morning meeting, but that wasn't why.

Insomnia was my best friend. Sometimes my only companion.

When sleep eluded me, I wasn't the type to lie in bed and stare at the ceiling. Instead, I got up, got dressed, and left.

Throughout the years, I'd become a connoisseur of the night, more familiar with downtown in the midnight and early hours than I was at any other time.

I liked darkness. It shrouded a lot of things. It was also quiet, which lent itself to lots of thought.

I avoided it as much as possible, but you couldn't run from what was in your own head very easily. It always came out one way or another.

The thump of my black boots echoed off the pavement as I walked across the newly dampened street. The rain had stopped, but the air was still thick with the kind of cold drizzle that possessed the ability to seep past your skin and deep into your bones.

The red neon COFFEE sign hanging off the building cast a red glow on nearby puddles and neon stripes over the rusty-red brick. My leather jacket was broken in, a little shabby, but it was thick and kept out the worst bite in the air. Beneath it, I wore a plain black hoodie, the hood pulled up, concealing my hair and face. I walked hunched in on myself, my shoulders drawn up beneath my ears and both hands shoved deep into the pockets of my jeans.

The large glass window at the front of the coffee shop was lit up from inside. Why the place stayed open practically all night was something I never bothered to ask. I was just glad it did. I ended up here more often than not—me and a few other night refugees who never spoke to one another.

No one was there to talk, but in a way, it was a support group all the same. After all, whatever had these people downtown in a coffee shop in the middle of the night probably wasn't good.

The deep scent of strong coffee hit me the second the door opened. Next, a brush of warmth against my cheeks. I pulled my hands out of my pockets and pulled off the hood concealing my head. At the same time, I nodded to the woman behind the counter and took up my customary seat near the window in the corner.

Here I could look out on the street, stare out into the night, but it was harder to look back at me because of my position.

A white mug filled with black brew appeared in front of me. Steam wafted upward toward my lips.

"Thanks," I said, gruff.

She dropped a few packs of creamer on the brown tabletop beside the cup and shuffled away. Her feet never seemed to leave the ground. I don't know why she always left the creamer packs. I never used them. Not once.

Sometimes I thought it was her way of acknowledging the anonymity I wore like a cloak. As if she'd never seen me before, I'd never sat in this corner booth, and she had no idea how I took my coffee.

Or maybe she was lazy and didn't want to take the chance I'd ask for it the one time she didn't bring it over.

It was probably that. Surely she didn't spend that much time thinking about the guy who sat in the corner and never spoke.

The brew was scalding to the touch when I wrapped a single hand around the body of the mug, tucking a few fingers beneath the thick, white handle. The coffee was always fresh here. Always hot. A detail that was never lost on me. It bespoke of unspoken care. Like the woman behind the counter was thoughtful enough to make sure the beverage was digestible.

This brought back my previous musing about the creamer and the real reason she always brought it.

This was how I spent most of my nights, those hours when the previous day died and the new day had yet to be born. Pondering creamer and the actions of a woman I didn't know. I drank cup after cup of near-boiling coffee, maintaining a permanent burn on my tongue.

Those quiet, dark hours were lonely and sometimes threatened to swallow me whole. Regret seared worse than any coffee ever could, and some nights I sat there and longed for the break sleep offered but never granted.

That was my punishment, though.

No peace. No break from reality or the life I created.

Instead, I wandered the night like a ghost doomed to never cross over, haunted with unfinished business.

My empty mug made a hollow sound when I placed it once last time against the table. The caffeine I consumed never affected me, never made me wired. Sometimes I thought it calmed me down. With steady hands, I fished into the pocket of my faded jeans, pulled out some cash, and tossed it by the cup and unused creamer.

Everyone else still sat in their designated seats. Sort of like they were all part of the mannequin challenge, but no one was taking a picture.

The night air was brisk and bit at my cheeks. The sound of an engine a few streets over rumbled through the night, and the low whistling sound of the wind brushed against my ears. I pulled my hood back up and shuffled off down the street.

The sun would be up soon. Another day gone. A new day arrived.

I would pound the pavement tonight, barely notice the window displays or passing cars. Just when the sky began to brighten, I would drive back home, shower and change, and head into work.

My head was down when a familiar sound cut through the night. Just like that, a million memories washed over me like a rainstorm.

A tidal wave of homesickness and guilt threatened to drown me, and I was left gasping for breath.

Then I remembered.

I wouldn't drown. Not tonight. Not ever.
Apparently, I could breathe underwater.
Another cruel joke, another punishment.
I didn't live anymore. I merely survived.

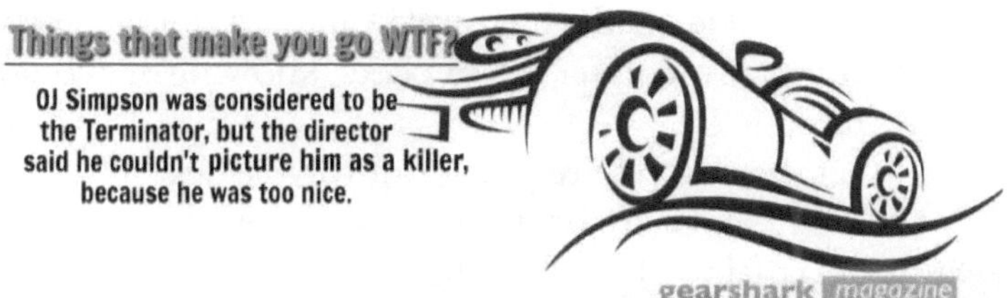

Chapter Thirteen

Someone was breathing over me.

The tiny hairs on the back of my neck rose, and I lay there with closed eyes and listened to the in-and-out of air. Right. Over. My. Head.

"Don't you ever knock?" I groaned, whipping the pillow from beneath my head and throwing it toward the annoying sound.

"I don't knock," Lorhaven intoned, sounding like the ass he wanted everyone to think he was.

I cracked open an eye to see him towering over me, my pillow in his clutches.

"You're being creepy."

"You're being lazy."

I rubbed a hand over my face. "What time is it?"

He grunted. "Nine."

My hand fell onto the bed. "It's still the middle of the night!"

"Get up, asshole," he muttered and threw the pillow at my face.

"I missed you, Lor!" I yelled from beneath the white fluff.

His chuckle made me smile, and I sat up. "You didn't bring me coffee?" I bitched, knowing it would annoy him.

"Get dressed. We're going out for waffles."

I didn't have to be told twice. I loved me some waffles. Actually, I loved any food.

I rushed into the bathroom, did everything I needed to do, then threw on a pair of jeans and a long-sleeved black shirt.

His white Lotus was spotless, even with all the wintry weather, salty roads, and snow.

"Where's Joey?" I asked as he sped down the street toward our favorite breakfast place, The Waffle Shack.

"Home. I'm driving down there after we eat. We have to go out of town. Work shit."

"How long you gonna be gone?" I asked, my mood darkening a little knowing he was leaving.

"Few days, a week tops."

I digested that as he pulled into a front parking spot by The Shack. The parking lot was pretty vacant, as usual. I didn't know why more people didn't come here. Their waffles were the bomb.

We got out of the car and headed toward the door. I grimaced. I guess I kinda understood why people didn't come here. It wasn't called a shack for nothing.

But I didn't care. I didn't need fancy. Hell, I wouldn't know what to do with it.

I liked this place. I liked its dilapidated exterior and old, sort of rundown interior. It didn't try to be anything it wasn't. It never claimed to be some five-star dining experience. All they claimed to have was waffles, which happened to be the best in town.

Rough on the outside, kinda sketchy on the inside, but deep at their center was a warm, fluffy concoction that made a man's mouth water.

Maybe I identified with the place. Except of course for making a man's mouth water. That thought made my stomach twist.

We slid into a booth near a window, and a waitress appeared wearing a pair of jeans and a shirt that read WAFFLES across it. That was one way—no, the only way—to get me to stare at a woman's rack.

"Haven't seen you boys in a while," she said, snapping her gum.

"Looking good, Shirley," Lorhaven said with a smile.

"Charmer," she crooned. "Coffee?"

Lor nodded. "Waffles, too."

Shirley glanced at me, and I nodded.

"Coming right up!" she called as she walked away. "Frank, get off your ass and turn off that TV. We got customers!"

"Why do we come here?" Jace muttered.

"Because it's cheap?" I suggested.

He rolled his eyes.

I glanced out the window at the Lotus, and Jace knocked on the table in front of me. "Hey, you wanna come with?"

"Out of town with you and Joey?"

He nodded and sat back. "Sure. It's NRR shit. It'll be good for you. I'll introduce you around so when the season starts, you'll have an edge over all the new drivers."

Even though the thought of being here alone for a week was less than desirable, going with my brother wasn't an option.

"Nah, but thanks."

His eyes narrowed. "You sign the contract yet?"

I averted my gaze.

"Arrow," he growled.

Shirley appeared with two white mugs filled with coffee that kinda looked like oil and set them in front of us. "Waffles are coming up."

"Thanks," Lorhaven said, and then his stare returned to me.

I pushed away the mug. Coffee wasn't my favorite to begin with, but having to chew it?

Gross.

"Why the hell haven't you signed? The sooner you sign, the sooner we can get your name out there."

I shrugged. "I still haven't decided."

"What's to decide? I get NASCAR is a big deal, but the NRR is almost just as big. Give it another year or two and we'll be giving the pros a run for their money. Besides, the NRR is family."

"I know." He was right. It was completely logical for me to sign with the NRR. Shit, I'd been driving with most of the drivers for the division for months and months now. I did some qualifying races, hung out in Lorhaven's pit. My name had been building, getting out there, and it was because of the NRR, Lor, Joey, Trent, and Drew.

Yet I still hesitated.

Why?

"Arrow," Lorhaven demanded, and I glanced up. His face softened. Lorhaven disappeared and Jace took front and center. "What's going on in your head? You need to talk?"

Shirley appeared and slid two huge plates, piled high with golden-brown, steaming waffles in front of us. Butter melted over them, trickling into every groove and soaking into the fluffy pastry. A jar of maple syrup appeared, and I snatched it up and poured it generously all over the plate.

When I was done, I slid it across the table to my brother, who was still staring at me.

"I don't need to talk." I relented. "I'm fine." *As fine as I normally am.* "It's just a big decision. When I make it, a lot of shit is going to change."

"I know," he said. "I understand it's hard. I'm not trying to push you."

I gave him a look.

He chuckled. "Well, maybe I am. But only because I want what's best for you. This is a huge opportunity for you. A chance to start all over, make a name for yourself."

"Yeah," I agreed. "I know."

"I just don't want you to not make a decision because you're scared. I don't want you to look back and regret this. Those contracts won't wait forever."

"You're right," I muttered and stabbed the side of the waffle with my fork. "I'm gonna make a decision."

"This week." Jace pressed. "When I get back, we'll drive down to Gamble's and you can sign."

I nodded. "I'll decide this week. I promise."

Lorhaven grinned. "Fuck yeah."

One week. I had one week to make a decision that would likely affect the rest of my life.

I wasn't good at making decisions, but really, I already knew what everyone wanted me to do. It wasn't as if a single week was going to change anything.

"Eat your waffles," Jace said as he dug in.

As I chewed the delectable concoction, I couldn't help but wonder why I suddenly had a twisty feeling that everything in my life was about to change.

Chapter Fourteen

Early morning meetings weren't unusual.

Being summoned to the boss' mansion for said meeting?

A little unorthodox.

Especially lately.

Ron Gamble and I had more than a business relationship. At least that's what I'd always believed up until a few months ago. For the past several months, our meetings had been at headquarters only. I hadn't been to any family dinners or any other social or family events that Gamble hosted.

In all honesty? The blackout stung.

But I understood it. Hell, I expected worse.

Joey suffered at the hands of men I'd been managing. Men I was basically in charge of. When I say suffered, I mean she was bullied, harassed, and physically assaulted.

I probably should have been fired. I had my shit packed when it all hit the fan and Ron called me for a meeting.

He didn't fire me, though.

I did get punished. Being on the receiving end of the ire of a powerful man like Gamble wasn't something I enjoyed. Especially when the powerful man was someone you looked up to, someone you considered a friend, and someone who was basically your savior.

I deserved the punishment I got, welcomed it as much as I hated it.

I guess I was a glutton for punishment.

The truth was I didn't realize Joey was being hazed the way she was. It was the lamest, likely most unbelievable truth I'd ever tell.

Didn't make it any less so.

I was selfish. The obsessive-compulsive way I sometimes got wasn't a strength, but a major weakness. Matt was the first victim.

Joey was the second.

I was grateful to Ron Gamble for so many reasons. I loved my job because it allowed me to still connect to the racing world I had walked away from, but it also allowed some distance and anonymity.

I was a good manager—on the track that is. I knew racing, I knew cars, and I understood sometimes it was about more than the time you put in on the asphalt. I was also solely dedicated, with almost single-minded precision. It was the *almost* that got me in the most trouble.

Not to mention I was loyal as a Labrador. Ron Gamble earned my loyalty when he basically pulled me out of a ditch and helped me reconstruct some kind of life.

It was because of Ron and Joey I began putting one foot in front of the other, the reason I didn't fall into the bottom of a bottle and never found my way out.

And this was how I repaid them. By allowing Joey—Ron's only child—to be tortured on my watch.

As I said, I was selfish.

Sometimes I got lost in my own head. Sometimes I didn't see things that were right in front of me because I chose not to look. I avoided conflict, avoided pain.

I avoided a lot of shit.

I focused on the cars, the racing, and driver performance.

Of course, I knew about the early hazing. I caught the bastards. I put the hammer down, too. Or so I thought.

I restricted driving time, made them pay a fine, and set them up on cleaning duty in the garage, community bathrooms, and the cars.

I watched them closely, and I thought I made it clear that kind of asshole behavior was a no-go. So when Joey told me everything was okay, I believed her.

Maybe if I looked deeper, paid better attention, I would have seen she was lying.

I took the punishment I was served. No more managing Joey (my favorite driver), and that meant I wasn't crossing over into the NRR indie division with her. I'd wanted to go there. It was exciting, faster paced…

Maybe a little of the energy reminded me of the kind of racing I used to do.

It was the past, though, not my future.

I was staying on with NASCAR and cleaning up the mess the scandal with Joey left behind. We fired all the drivers but one. There was a strict no-tolerance policy when it came to hazing, and Gamble saw to it personally that anyone who even breathed in a way he found offensive was escorted off property.

Building a new NASCAR team for Gamble was no easy feat. But I was doing it. The guys were coming along. Come spring, our drivers would be ready.

Unless, of course, I was still living with blinders on, still too focused internally that I missed more crucial information.

Perhaps I was being summoned to Gamble Mansion because I was getting the axe.

I parked my matte-black Audi R8 near the large front doors, pocketed the keys, and strode toward the house like I wasn't wondering if that was the last time I'd drive that car.

It was my car. I'd been driving it a while, but technically, it belonged to Gamble Enterprises. It was a company car I was given to drive.

NASCAR managers had images to uphold, you know.

It was a sweet-ass car, but my preference would always be a large pickup. However, even if my Audi were confiscated today, I wouldn't get a pickup.

It was too much of who I once was. Not enough of who I was now.

You don't even know who that is.

I was dressed in a pair of very dark jeans, tan suede loafers, a grey crewneck sweater with a checked dress shirt beneath it, and a matching tie. After I showered this morning, I combed my hair back so it looked like I attempted to control the unruliness, even though I hadn't.

The front door opened before I knocked. I was ushered inside to Gamble's study, which was basically an old-school version of an office.

Old-school = no foosball table or anything else entertaining.

He was already behind his desk, dressed in a full suit with a tie and a cup of coffee at his elbow.

"Hopper," Gamble said by way of greeting. "Thanks for meeting me here this morning. Coffee?" He gestured toward a polished cart that had all the fixings for the perfect cup. He legit had kitchen help that wheeled in coffee service to him in the morning.

"Thank you," I said, going to the cart and pouring myself some of the liquid crack. Once it was in hand, I carried it to the chair directly across from his desk and sat down.

"Are you firing me?" I asked, direct. I didn't want to sit here and wonder. I liked to know what I was dealing with.

Gamble looked up, surprised. "Firing you? Why would you think that?"

I glanced at him dryly. "Because I'm here and not at the office. Last time I was here, I was interrogated about Joey and put on probation."

"You're not being fired," Gamble answered, just as direct.

"How is Joey?" I asked, taking a sip of the coffee. I hadn't seen her in several months.

"My daughter is doing just fine. She's happier than I've ever seen her. The NRR agrees with her."

"I imagine Lorhaven has something to do with it as well," I added. Bringing up her boyfriend didn't feel out of line because at one time I considered her a friend.

"I wouldn't disagree."

"So why the meeting at home?" I went right for it. This conversation felt slightly awkward, and that alone was making me uncomfortable. I was used to an easy dialogue, not something slightly stiff and almost polite.

"I wanted to speak to you without the listening ears of all the other staff members at headquarters."

I waited.

He picked up his coffee, sipping at it while staring at me over the rim of the mug. Gamble was a formidable man; his presence alone exuded power.

I wasn't intimidated by him, though. I wasn't intimidated by much these days. When you go through hell and survive, there isn't much that can inspire such a feeling.

"I've been keeping a close eye on the new team you're building, and I'm impressed. I want your input on how it's going."

He called me here for a report? The staff could have heard this.

"It's going well," I said, going into a few details about the drivers, the cars, and getting ready for this spring.

"And how are they getting along? Any issues?"

"None," I said, decisive. "I've made it abundantly clear no form of bullying, hazing, or discrimination will be tolerated. Plus, the fact they were all hired to replace those who didn't heed that warning carries a heavy weight." I paused, clearing my throat. "I've been making sure to pay closer attention. I'm focused on what's going on around me." *Instead of what's going on inside me. At least I think I am.*

Sometimes when you wake up to reality, it's a sharp slap in the face. Here you'd been going along, living life, and thinking you were handling everything— then *BAM!* You realize you'd been living in some fog, and all the things you thought you knew you didn't know at all.

Except even waking up from the fog wasn't enough to shake it completely. It was still a daily fight, still something I had to remind myself to be careful of.

My insomnia was worse lately. The fog was relentless. The more I fought it during the day, the thicker it became at night.

Gamble nodded as if he expected everything I said. "I'm glad to hear it because there's something I want you to do."

"Which is?"

"You're aware I'm recruiting Arrow Ambrose, Lorhaven's brother, to drive for me."

Something in my stomach dipped. My attention sharpened tenfold. Not much had the ability to blow away the relentless fog over my brain, but he did.

It was something I didn't like to acknowledge. In fact, I never did, except of course internally when just the mention of his name (or the sight of him yards away) made it impossible to ignore.

"Yes," I hedged, wondering where this was going. "Pretty rare for you to offer someone a spot of their choosing on either your NRR team or your NASCAR team."

Gamble made a sound. "So imagine my surprise when I can't get the kid on the phone."

I felt my eyebrows shoot up. "He's not answering your calls?"

"He's yet to return the couple I've made."

Interesting.

"It's been several months since he first auditioned for me. As you know, he's been racing in a few minor races, building his name, getting more experience. He's also driven in a few NRR classifiers."

"He's a good driver. He'll only get better." I agreed.

"I want you to find him, meet with him face to face. Figure out where his head is and which team he's going to drive. I need his signature on a contract, the ink dry." As he spoke, he pulled out two yellow envelopes, both sealed, and laid them across the desk in front of me.

Okay, whoa.

Back that ass up.

Slam the brakes.

Whiplash.

What the fuck was happening here?

A.) Ron Gamble want me to drive to the other side of the state. (And yes, I knew the town in which Arrow lived… because Joey spent a lot of time there. At least that's the lie I told myself.)

B.) I was being tasked as an errand boy to get a signature on one of *two* contracts. Contracts any other driver would chew off their own arm to obtain.

C.) Clearly, Arrow was not "any other driver." (That totally intrigued me)

And…

D.) There were butterflies in my stomach.

Not to mention the obvious. "I have to say," I observed coolly, not letting on that the inside of my brain was suddenly humming with thought, "the fact that Ron Gamble would chase after anyone to get an answer is surprising."

"Some people are worth a little more effort." He stared at me meaningfully, and I couldn't help but wonder if it was me or Arrow he was talking about.

"So why not just have Joey or Lorhaven bring him down here?" I asked.

"This is business. You're my business manager. You handle my drivers. You train them."

"If he signs with the NRR, I won't be." Yeah, maybe it still pissed me off the NRR was a club I wasn't allowed to join.

"I want him in NASCAR. I think he's a good fit. We need new, young, up-and-coming drivers on our team."

"You want me to convince him." I surmised. "You know it won't be easy. Lorhaven disapproves of NASCAR, and after the big shakeup…"

"Which is why you're going to convince him that being gay in NASCAR will not be an issue like being a girl was for my daughter." His voice left no room for argument. Gamble was a businessman first, and he knew how to get results.

"And his brother?" I asked again.

"Lorhaven and Joey are out of town right now, handling their own careers."

That means I'll be alone with him.

"Lorhaven will of course be notified I'm sending someone to present contracts. I don't do underhanded business dealings," he added when I didn't immediately respond. Maybe he thought I was worried what Lorhaven would do when he found out I was within feet of his bro.

I wasn't worried about that.

"Of course," I murmured, still mulling over the fact I would actually be face to face with the blond-haired, tattooed driver.

"I want you to leave today," Gamble announced.

I snapped out of my own head. "Today?"

Gamble nodded once. "Arrow has an interview with *GearShark* in two weeks to announce who he's signed with."

He pulled out a piece of paper and laid it on top of the contracts. "Here's his address."

I stood and picked up the envelopes and address. "And if he doesn't want to sign anything?"

"He will."

Gamble was more confident than I was on that. Of course, I'd never actually had a conversation with Arrow Ambrose; I'd only seen him from afar. So it seemed logical Gamble would know him a lot better than I would.

Yet logic had nothing on emotion, and something deep inside me (past the butterflies) whispered that perhaps I knew him better.

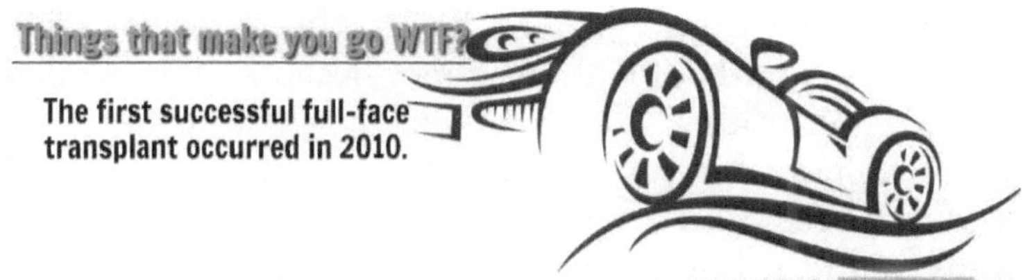

Chapter Fifteen

Darkness claimed the sky early. Winter was known for short days and long cold spells. It felt late, likely because the sky said it was, though it wasn't much past five.

Outside, the wind howled, occasionally shaking the metal walls of the hangar. A sharp whistling sound accompanied the rattle of tools against metal as I worked because the hangar door was open a few inches near the pavement.

I liked the airflow, and truth be told, I liked the bite of the cold wind.

Because I had the door open enough for the cold to slip in, I also had a large space heater on. I liked a chill in the air, but I didn't want to freeze.

It was a quiet machine, and it put out a pretty strong blast of heat—more than the one I originally had, which was a small box that sounded like a broken-down engine and I had to stand within two feet in order to get any of the warmth it provided.

The second Lor saw the thing, he gave me a lecture and smacked me in the back of the head. After he sped off in his Corvette (which he later totaled protecting me), he came back with this fancy heater and demanded I use it instead.

I had a lot once. It taught me a valuable lesson: I didn't need much.

In fact, I preferred not having a lot attached to my name. That way there would never be any kind of pain if I lost it. It was easier to walk away when you didn't have a lot to drag behind you.

The Camaro was my prized possession, a car. I'd only recently come to think of as mine. Lorhaven bought it for me, and though I drove it from almost day one, it had been hard to accept the fact that he intended it as a gift.

We had a lot of cars at this airstrip. An entire hangar full of them and a couple others in a few other hangars. I worked on them all.

Cars were my hobby, my salvation. In some ways, they represented my revenge.

Revenge that had yet to be exacted, though. The truth was revenge took a lot of energy, and I was weary. I heard something once that didn't apply to me, not really, yet I adopted it, and it was a phrase that sometimes echoed in the back of my mind.

The Usage Principal.

When your energy stores are limited, you have to use them wisely. It may not always be on things you want most, but instead on the things you *need* the most.

Like survival.

For a few years, that's all I did. Survived.

The wind shuddered the slightly open door, and I refocused on what I was doing beneath the hood of my black vintage Camaro. It was a classic, full of muscle, and needed a lot of babying under the hood.

There was a lightbulb with a plastic cage around it clipped to the underside of the propped-open hood, acting as a spotlight on the engine as I worked.

Beside me was a rolling tool chest with greasy fingerprints all over the top and metal parts lying there at the ready.

My phone was docked in a set of speakers, rock music competing with the wind.

My nose was cold, and my fingers, but I kept working, bent over the engine. My jeans were loose, halfway falling down, and over my black T-shirt, I wore an oversized black zip-up hoodie.

I don't know how long I'd been working, long enough my fingers were covered in grease, but something in the air around me changed. I cocked my head to the side, pausing in the middle of what I was doing to listen.

The sound of wobbling metal, wind, and music pressed in.

I straightened, tossed down the tools, and then lowered the volume of the music so it was almost silent.

The sound of an engine purring replaced the music, and then the not-too-faraway blare of a horn. And not just one or two quick beeps.

Long, deliberate ones.

Suspicion bunched the muscles in the back of my neck, but I hit the button to lift the large hangar door. As it opened, light from inside spilled out across the pavement, and cold wintry air rushed in.

From the doorway, my eyes went right to the bright spot in the darkness.

There was a car at the gate. The driver must have seen me; his headlights flickered once, then twice.

I didn't recognize the car, but I was curiously drawn to it.

No one ever just "dropped by" here. Except for Lorhaven, Joey, Trent, and Drew. They didn't count anyway.

Instantly, my stomach cramped. I thought about some of the missed calls on my phone, even went as far as glancing back at the device where it was still docked.

Was it my father?

Lorhaven told me he wanted to talk to me. I was pretty sure a few missed calls were from him.

Would he just show up like this?

Yes. Yes, he would.

He probably thought of this airstrip as his property, even though it was Lor who owned the title.

The lights flickered again. A gust of wind whipped through the long strands of my hair. I tugged the hood over my head and tucked my hands deep into the pockets. There was no hurry in my pace.

Whoever this was could wait. Showing up unannounced like this, in the dark? They were lucky I wasn't greeting them with a crowbar or a gun.

As I drew closer, I made out the Audi, which was a matte black. I'd seen it before around Gamble Speedway.

It's not your father.

The realization removed some of the dread from my stomach, but it didn't necessarily make me feel better.

At the large security fence, I stopped and threaded my fingers through the chain-link and looked out. The headlights were killed, which my eyes were grateful for, and the driver's door popped open.

The back of my neck prickled with anticipation, my fingers tightening on the freezing-cold metal of the fence.

A man with a backward red hat stood up, stepping around the door. His hips rotated with ease as one foot moved in front of the other.

I stared, like I always did, and a flush of awareness rushed up my spine.

"Arrow? I'm Hopper, Ron—"

"I know who you are." I cut him off.

He stopped midsentence, both hands falling at his sides. In the darkness, through the security of the fence, our eyes locked.

For a second, I actually wondered when the fence became electrified. Volts of power sizzled beneath my hands and crackled up my forearms.

But it wasn't the fence.

It was me.

It was him.

It was the product of our eyes meeting for the first time.

It was the feeling that always seemed to charge the air when we were nearby that we never acknowledged.

His chest rose and fell with enough force I could see it from yards away. One hand flexed at his side, but his feet remained planted in the same spot.

I was hyperaware of him, of the fact my breathing had turned slightly shallow.

I stared at him longer than I'd ever allowed myself, for two reasons:

1.) The fence between us was like a security blanket; it allowed me to look without the danger of touch.

And…

2.) There was no one else around to notice the way my eyes begged to linger on just about every detail of this man's face.

Even in the dark night, I saw him as if I'd done more than just glance his way, as if the sky were fully lit by the bright beams of a full summer sun that shone on him like a spotlight. He was tall and broad, but not bulky. His body had strength that wasn't portrayed by muscle mass. His lean waist tapered down into narrow hips, but his legs were thick, his thighs strong, as if they had more potency than any other part of his body.

The boots on his feet were so dark they blended in with the road. His jeans fit his body a lot better than mine; they showed a lot more of his form.

But most of all, my eyes lingered on his, as if they were two magnets and the pull was undeniable. His were icy blue, piercing just like the cold air. They cut right through me, holding me hostage even as I squirmed to run away.

Alarm bells rang in the back of my mind.

An uneasy feeling blossomed in my gut, but I didn't tear my gaze away. Looking from danger was a mistake. Looking away gave it a distinct advantage.

Instead, I took in the dark shadow on his jaw, his mouth, and the way it was relaxed yet I knew he wasn't. The red hat turned backward slashed over his forehead, seeming to frame the rest of his facial features.

I like the way he looks.

His face, his body, and even the invisible vibes that floated around him attracted me. I wished it didn't. But wishing something didn't make it true.

"What are you doing here?" I asked, still gripping the fence with my fingers but straightening to my full height.

"Gamble sent me. You haven't been returning his phone calls."

I digested that, didn't have a reply.

"This where you live?" he asked, those icy eyes sweeping around behind me, across the airstrip.

I nodded once.

"What's it going to be, Arrow?" he asked, tilting his head to the side as crystal irises returned to my face. "You going to let me in?"

A simple, seemingly innocent question. Charged with so much meaning.

I stared at him longer without saying a word. Waiting didn't seem to bother him. In fact, he acted as if he expected as much.

You have no idea.

His eyes locked on mine. *Try me.*

My hands dropped from the fence. I stepped back, then once more. My fingers stung from the cold, so I tucked them in my pockets.

A lot of things blew in with the winter winds at night.

Thoughts, memories, regrets… sometimes snow.

But the wind had never blown in a man before. A man who challenged me and scared me at the same time.

In that moment, I felt I'd been playing a giant game of hide-and-seek. I was hiding, all this time, just waiting for someone to find me.

The way Hopper watched me right now… I felt unspoken words drift through my chest.

Ready or not, here I come.

I began walking backward, my eyes never left the man watching, waiting. Distance intruded. The only reaction he gave was to flex his hands. Still walking backward, my steps curved, veering right toward a small booth. I reached inside and hit a button.

The definitive sound of a lock unlatching and the sight of a red light on the gate changing to green. Slowly, the gate began to roll open as I stood there and stared.

Hopper retreated into the matte-black Audi and pulled through the second there was enough space.

He didn't stop to offer me a ride the short distance back to my hangar.

I wouldn't have taken it anyway.

Instead, I stood and watched the gate close.

When the lock was fully engaged, I started toward the hangar. Toward the man I least expected to see tonight (*or ever*). Toward a man I wasn't supposed to like.

I didn't, not really. I couldn't like someone I didn't know.

And I couldn't dislike him either.

Chapter Sixteen

Hopper
infinity

We were like two sharks circling, drawn by the scent of blood.

Whose blood? I wasn't yet sure.

I watched him for months the way a predator eyes potential game. Sharks never go straight in. They circle, measure.

Almost always, they take an exploratory bite. You know, to see if what they're stalking is worth the fight.

Arrow was going to be a fight. No. Not a fight. Not a battle.

A war.

Everything about him was so contained, right down to the fence he literally lived behind. It made me wonder… Was the fence to keep him in or keep people out?

What would he be like uncontained? How would freedom look on him?

I'd known deep down this moment was coming, even though I avoided it. Eventually, we'd come face to face. Eventually, I wouldn't be able to ignore the gravitational pull. I wasn't sure I was ready—if I'd ever be.

Now I knew he watched me, too.

Sure, I guess I'd known he noticed me. When I would glance his way at races, his eyes would quickly skirt away. Just now was different, though; just now he didn't hide the fact he saw me.

I felt it. All I could do was stand there and let him study me. Maybe that made me the prey.

His stare was heavy, like it weighed a thousand pounds.

Or saw a thousand lives.

He seemed too young to be so old; however, his age was undeniable. I wasn't talking about the year on his birth certificate or the number of years that marked his life.

I meant the hundreds of pieces he was broken into.

I had no idea what broke him. I wasn't sure I was ready to find out.

But I recognized him.

I *saw* him.

Past the blond hair, baggy clothes, and the wall he'd built up and only peeked around.

Like recognized like.

We were strangers but intimately so, in the most basic way. What was his favorite color, food, and how did he take his coffee? Did he sleep on the left side or the right? What was the scent unique to only him?

I didn't know anything about Arrow, but I knew him completely.

Never in my twenty-six years did I react to someone this way. It scared me. It excited me. It brought on a tidal wave of guilt.

Before I could totally get myself together, Arrow appeared. The dark clothes he wore concealed him as he approached. One minute I was alone, and the next he was crowding all the space around me.

"Nice car," he remarked as he passed the Audi. His knuckles rapped against the hood. "Handles well?"

"It's a smooth ride." I agreed, watching him.

The jeans he wore were baggy. If I had to guess, they weren't pulled up either. Strangely, I didn't mind that fact. It made me wonder what kind of underwear I'd see if he lifted his oversized shirt.

The shoes on his feet were high-tops, all white, and looked a little funny because his jeans were tight around his calves and ankles. He was thin, not to the point he looked skinny, but almost like he just needed to fill out so his big feet would match the rest of him.

Arrow stepped into the garage and pushed the hood off his head. Very blond strands of hair appeared, which he reached up to shove over to one side.

He almost had a baby face, with smooth skin and no trace of facial hair. What kept him from looking like jailbait was his bone structure. Sharp cheekbones, a strong jawline and brow. And his mouth… dear God, his mouth.

I want to suck on those lips.

He had a permanent pout. The perfect amount of flesh to latch onto and press against my own.

He glanced at me where I stood beside his Camaro, and I didn't bother to hide the fact I was checking him out. He'd just done the same.

He glanced away, moving past and beneath the hood, where he picked up a tool and leaned down to do whatever it was he'd been doing before I showed up.

I didn't jump right into business. Suddenly, business was the very last thing on my mind. I was in his space, closer than ever.

I glanced around, wandered to the tool setup, and checked it out. There were awards and car titles on the metal walls. Vintage car parts and shelves of oil.

Music played in the background, a song I had on my playlist as well.

I was nervous, an emotion I wasn't familiar with. I felt I was seeing inside his world, a place not many people got to visit. I'd basically challenged him to let me in, and when the lock on the gate slid open, I'd found victory.

After I glanced around the tools, I turned toward where he worked. I moved up to the side of the Camaro and stared down at him.

Arrow paused for a brief second, just barely tilting his head toward me, then resumed working. I watched him; I couldn't not.

He wasn't my type.

Not in the least.

But I had a sinking feeling no one else would ever be again.

An image of Matt swam through my head, and I closed my eyes, clinging to it for a few seconds. A wash of calm loneliness moved over me. Once I felt slightly less rocked, I reopened my eyes.

Arrow was watching me, the tool in his hand suspended over the engine. The chocolate color of his eyes seemed bottomless.

That calm peace I'd searched for was pulled out from beneath me like a rug.

I shoved my hands deep in the pockets of my jeans.

"You okay?" Arrow asked.

The sound of his voice made my fingers curl into my palms. I answered his question with one of my own. "Is your real name Arrow?"

"Yep." He straightened, tossed the tool down, and it made a clanging noise. On the edge of the Camaro was a rag. He snagged it up and began wiping his hands.

"Your real name Hopper?"

I met his eyes, looking away. "No."

We were still doing it. Still circling. Still sizing each other up.

I wanted more.

The wind blew, rattling the sides of the hangar and bringing a blast of frigid air around us. I wondered where his place was, the personal space where he slept and lived.

He tossed the rag down and moved around me to hit a button so the hangar door would lower. He glanced back around and shrugged. "It will be a bitch to heat back up if I let it get too cold in here."

I shrugged like I didn't care. But I did. I cared so much, so fast it fucking terrified me.

"So Gamble sent you." Arrow tilted his head to the side, exposing his neck. There was a tattoo of an arrow. The point faced down, toward the hollow behind his collarbone, that soft, vulnerable spot…

Just asking for a kiss.

I cleared my throat, told myself to get my damn head out of the gutter. "I've never met anyone who's never called him back."

Arrow shrugged. "He pissed?" He tried to sound nonchalant, but he cared; that much was obvious.

"Not yet." I smiled.

Arrow's lips pulled up, and we both stood there for a moment, smiling at each other.

The smile fell off Arrow's face, the broody look he wore so well returning. "Why did Gamble send you?"

"I manage his drivers."

"Not Joey. Not any of them in the NRR," he pointed out.

"You saying you're signing with the NRR?" I crossed my arms over my chest, slightly miffed. I didn't want him to sign in the NRR. I wanted him in NASCAR. Where I was.

"That's not what I'm saying."

"Then what *are* you saying?" I challenged.

"My brother would shit a brick if he knew you were here. He hates you, you know."

"You gonna stand in your brother's shadow forever?"

His body went rigid. The muscles in his jaw jumped. I hit a nerve, just like I knew I would. "I'm not in his shadow."

"I think we both know you are," I remarked. "It's a safe place to be. But it isn't where you belong."

An angry glint flashed in his eyes. "You don't know shit about me."

I stepped closer. His nostrils flared and the dark pools of his eyes deepened, watching me. I spoke low, like I was imparting a secret. "You know that isn't true, and it scares the piss out of you, doesn't it?"

"You let my sister be tortured." He accused, as if he could turn the tables on me.

It worked, at least for a few minutes. What happened to Joey was a deep regret of mine, second on a very long list.

"Yeah, I did," I admitted. I wasn't going to make excuses for myself. "She's my best friend. Well, she was. The shit she went through shouldn't have happened. I'll live with it forever."

He'd expected a fight, and I didn't step up. Arrow's eyes softened. "She's not mad at you, you know."

That surprised me. "She's not?" We'd barely spoken since the shakeup. I honestly thought ours was one more lost relationship in my life.

"Nah. I hear her and Lor sometimes. He's still pretty pissed, and that pisses her off." Arrow smiled ruefully, like he enjoyed watching his big brother have his ass handed to him by a girl.

I made a sound between a groan and a laugh. That was Joey; she never backed down.

I felt him watching me, studying all my movements and facial expressions.

"She likes you."

I rubbed a hand over my face and took a breath. I didn't realize that was something I wanted to hear until he said it.

I glanced up, and my stomach dipped. He'd somehow known, as if he felt the hurt I carried over the loss of my best friend. "I like her, too."

He stepped away from me, went over to a space heater sitting nearby, and fidgeted with the buttons.

Arrow was very guarded, but his walls came down during a moment when he saw I was hurting. And even though he fought to protect himself, that slipped so he could give me something to ease the turmoil inside me.

It was too much. It hit me in all the softest spots I'd worked so hard to toughen. Panic punched me in the stomach. It felt as though the wind had been knocked right out of me.

"That lead outside?" I asked, gesturing to a nearby door.

Arrow nodded.

"I'll be right back," I said, then fled the hangar.

Outside, the cold slapped me. I breathed it in with deep, gulping pants. It smelled like snow out here, and my breath puffed out in front of me in a giant white cloud.

I took my time grabbing the contracts out of my car, but I couldn't linger forever. Back inside, my eyes sought him out instantly. I couldn't decide which was more alarming: the fact I wanted to see him more than anything or the anxiety that tried to choke me when he was nowhere to be seen.

"Arrow?" I called out.

He appeared from out of the back of the hangar, stepped around the heater with two mugs in his hands.

"Coffee?" he asked, extending one.

"Thanks." I reached for the mug, and our hands brushed as he transferred it into mine.

Our eyes locked. His Adam's apple bobbed, and then he stepped back swiftly.

I took a drink of the brew. It was strong and hot, just the way I liked it.

"You need cream?" he asked.

"I drink it black."

"Me, too."

I held up the two envelopes. "Here's the contracts."

He didn't move to take them.

"I need you to sign one. He's already lined up a *GearShark* interview for you in two weeks. You're supposed to announce where you're going."

He took the envelopes, making sure not to touch me, and set them on a nearby workbench.

"Seems like it would be a pretty easy choice." I observed.

"Seems like," he echoed.

"You know what you want. You're just afraid of it."

"What the fuck do you know about it?" Arrow swung around, angry.

"I know your entire family is with the NRR. It's a no-brainer. So the fact you haven't put pen to paper makes me think you'd rather sign with NASCAR. You're just afraid of what your brother will do when you tell him."

"I'm not scared of my brother," he snapped.

"You're close with him, huh?" I changed direction.

"He's all I have."

Ah, the honesty in that tone I recognized well. "Don't you want more?"

His eyes flashed, swept over my entire body, and then he turned and walked away. I pursued him, not ready to let this go.

I stepped deeper into the hangar, following his steps past the heater, the work benches, and into another type of space.

There was a bed. It looked like a twin, and though he was thin, he wasn't small. I wondered how the fuck he slept there comfortably.

He couldn't possibly.

The blankets were twisted like someone had slept there and not bothered to make it up when they awoke.

There was an oval multicolored rug in front of the bed, a pair of headphones, and a pair of high-tops beside the bed.

I glanced at the high-tops on Arrow's feet and then back at the blue ones.

A hollow, sick feeling burst inside me.

Arrow's back was still turned to me. The coffee he'd been holding made a low thud when he set it on a wooden dresser. There was a hoodie and a T-shirt tossed on top. Beside the bed was a metal rolling toolbox. On top was a clock with glowing red numbers.

No.

No, no. no.

Something about this setup churned up a bunch of feelings, a bunch of anger.

That predatory way I'd been feeling—you know, a shark circling—it was back. But I wasn't going to circle anymore.

"You *live* here?" I snapped.

He spun. Whatever he heard in my voice surprised him. "I already told you I did."

"You live *in* this garage?" I ground out. "In a fucking garage?"

Arrow's eyes widened. "You thought I had an apartment on the airstrip?"

It was cold in here. Not just in temperature, but in every way. It was almost utilitarian. He had nothing. Why did he have nothing?

He deserves so much more.

"I thought your brother loved you," I spat.

Lorhaven hated me, but I never hated him… until right this minute. He let his brother live like this. A guy who was clearly already broken—he let him live *here*.

"He does," Arrow argued.

"Fuck he does!" I spat. "If he loved you, you wouldn't be homeless!"

Arrow jerked. "I'm not homeless!"

I flung my arms wide, gesturing to this place. "This ain't a home."

He crossed his arms over his chest and glared. "It's where I want to be."

I laughed. It was bitter and angry. "No. You don't want to be here. You think this is where you belong. You're too scared to reach for anything else, just like you're too scared to sign the contract you really want."

Arrow lunged across the room. "Fuck you," he growled.

"Man up," I growled back.

With an angry yell, his hands shot out, grabbed handfuls of my shirt, and yanked me forward with some force. My muscles tensed, but I didn't fight back. I wasn't even threatened.

My pulse hammered against my temples; beneath my ribs, my heart beat fierce.

Arrow's eyes burned with anger, the deep-brown shade glowing with an amber fire. His chest heaved. I felt his fingers slightly tremble where he fisted my clothes. His eyes bounced between mine with something more.

He's attracted to me, even in anger, even in fear.

I held still but didn't back down. I stared back, right into the amber flames, and dared him to do something about it all.

"Stop hiding." I challenged.

With a grunt, he pulled me forward a little bit more. His head came down and those pouty, angry lips crashed over mine.

You know that expository bite I mentioned before?

He was taking it.

I was surrendering.

Hell, I was offering.

He sucked in a deep breath through his nose as our mouths latched together. My hands shot out, grabbing his elbows, and my fingertips dug into his arms.

He kissed angrily, like he didn't want to kiss me at all, but he couldn't help himself. I kissed him back with the same amount of ire, diving into his mouth, his emotion, and drinking it all in.

After a few strokes of his lips, something changed. It was like the angry haze that had suddenly taken over vanished and reality crashed back in.

Arrow's grip on my shirt went lax, his lips stopped, and I felt the stare of his chocolate eyes.

I opened up to stare back. Our lips still touched even though they didn't move. He stared at me, shock in his eyes. Shock, loneliness, and want.

Carefully, I disengaged my grip on his elbows, reached up, and cupped the sides of his face.

Arrow's eyes flared when my palms cupped his jaws. His lips twitched.

He had his bite.

Now he was digesting. Maybe seeing if I was worth the fight.

Waiting wasn't my strong suit. In fact, every second that went by was like a red-hot poker scalding my skin.

I moved, his hands tightening in my shirt again. I bit back a satisfied smile. He wasn't ready to let go.

That was good. Wasn't it?

I kept my eyes trained on his. Slowly, I licked across his lips. They were just as soft and full as they looked from across the room.

He sighed in the back of his throat, and his mouth opened, covered mine, and we sank into a long and languid kiss.

His tongue met mine halfway, and they tangled together with lazy abandon.

Alarm bells went off in my mind, but in that moment, it was just music. My stomach flipped and flopped, but all I felt were his trembling fingers in my shirt.

Too soon.

He pulled back too soon.

The second he lifted his head, his fingers peeled away from my clothes, and he all but jumped back. His face was pale, dark eyes wide.

He was shocked.

So was I.

"Get out," he ordered, taking another step back.

"A—" I started.

"Leave!" he roared.

I glanced around his "home." Some of my anger came back, but it was overshadowed with sadness.

And guilt.

I went to the door. He didn't follow.

When I glanced back, I couldn't see him.

"I'm staying at the DoubleTree," I said. I knew he was listening. "I'll be there when you're ready to sign."

I waited for the sound of his voice. It never came. It was better this way. We were both too broken. We'd end up cut by each other's jagged edges.

I let myself out of his cage, but I wasn't being set free.

Chapter Seventeen

My mom's favorite movie is *Beauty and the Beast*.

I spent many nights watching it as a kid. As I stood in this empty, rattling hangar with the winter winds whipping around outside, I was reminded of that movie.

I felt some kind of kinship to the beast.

I was alone and miserable, most of which was my own doing.

I was angry and closed off. I blamed everything around me for all the damage inside.

There was a clock ticking; it just wasn't in the shape of a rose.

I didn't exactly remember what turned the man into a beast, but I knew precisely what turned me into what I was today.

He saw.

He couldn't possibly know, but somehow, impossibly, he understood.

That kind of understanding only came from experience, from the kind of pain strong enough to bring a man to his knees.

I saw it in him, too.

What were the odds? The odds that two men so shattered would meet? The odds that all our broken pieces would somehow fit together to create something whole?

A million to one? More?

It didn't matter. The odds weren't in my favor; they never were.

It made me furious he would just drive right up, brandishing some contracts and a set of icy-blue eyes that saw past my exterior, past my angry wall.

He called me out.

Man up.

What was worse? He was right.

I was hiding here behind the fence around this airstrip. Licking my wounds? Maybe at first—okay, definitely at first. But those wounds weren't open anymore.

They didn't bleed.

What was left were scars and echoes of pain that would likely never go away. What happened to me altered everything I was and thought. There was no going back.

But perhaps there was a chance at moving forward.

I was standing in place now. Looking in the rearview mirror. Gazing in a direction I couldn't or wouldn't go.

I did all that fighting, went through all that excruciating pain.

I lost my home. My family. My entire life.

For what?

To end up here? To spend my days in a perpetual frozen state? To always be looking over my shoulder instead of ahead? I was in Lorhaven's shadow, not because he's forced me there, but because that's where I felt safest.

He protected me. Shielded me. It was with him I was able to get to this point of internal reflection. I looked down on myself for a lot of things. At one point, I didn't even think I was worthy of life.

I would always have an internal battle. There would likely always be days when my self-worth was reduced to what happened to me in that alley that night.

But I wanted to live.

I wanted more.

Those feelings had been stirring in me for months now. They were the reason I auditioned for Gamble, the reason I started coming out of my shell with Drew.

Those things turned out okay. Even when they weren't what I expected. Originally, I was attracted to Drew. I'd been brave enough to feel him out. We didn't end up dating, but instead, I found a friend.

Life was happening around me. Sometimes I participated and sometimes I hid in my cage like a beast in a castle—lonely and afraid.

It was time for more. No more longing. No more standing on a precipice, too afraid to jump.

Hopper ignited something in me. His anger lit my fire.

Our kiss… it lit desire. (A kiss *I* initiated.)

I sat on the edge of my bed, as if the revelations in my mind exhausted my limbs. My head was spinning. My lips were tingling.

All the sudden I was invigorated. Scared but willing.

Ten minutes with Hopper, mere minutes with someone I'd just met, but somehow it opened my eyes.

Everything I wanted was in my grasp. I wasn't so naïve to think it would be so easy as to just reach. It was worth the struggle. I'd come this far.

I'd fought for life. The least I could was live it instead of merely existing.

Shoving my hand through my hair, I jumped up, grabbed the keys off a nearby table, and slammed the hood on the Camaro.

The door to the hangar slowly slid upward. White flurries of snow drifted in, flailing about in the winter wind. The smooth purr of the engine elicited a satisfied smile as I backed out into the dark and flipped on the headlights.

A light dusting of white coated everything around me. The momentum of the car sent the light drifts rushing away as I drove to the gate and then through. As I cruised along the streets, I noticed the dusting of snow more clearly, as in it had been lazily falling for a while now. The streets were empty; there were no bodies walking down the sidewalks and no cars sharing the road. It was even colder now than before.

I glanced at the clock on the dash, then did a double take.

It was late, almost the middle of the night.

I'd sat for hours, pondering what had happened. Some realizations took longer to accept. Some kisses took longer to wake from.

At the end of the block was the DoubleTree where Hopper said he was staying. I turned in and pulled through a parking spot but let the engine idle.

It was the middle of the night. He was probably in bed. Banging on his door now was insanity. Yet the thought of waiting 'til morning caused my hands to shake like an addict who needed a fix.

"You're being a stupid fuck," I told myself out loud. "Come back tomorrow. With an actual contract, signed."

I backed out of the parking spot, gave one last look to the hotel and drove away. Before pulling onto the road, I looked for oncoming traffic—as all responsible drivers do—but it wasn't any car my eyes focused on.

About halfway down the block, there was a lone man walking, hunched in a little on himself against the cold. Awareness shot through my body. The pulse in my veins doubled.

Even though I knew it was him, I still sat and stared, dumbfounded. Surely my eyes were playing tricks on me.

The man walked under a streetlight. Golden light shone down over hair so dark it was nearly black. It was slightly wild and kinda curly. The leather coat he wore took on a sheen.

What the fuck was he doing outside in the middle of the night? Alone on the street?

Didn't he know what happened to men who wandered around town alone in the dark?

I know.

I know too well.

My blood ran cold.

The tires of my Camaro made a squealing sound when I peeled around the corner and muscled the car down the street. Hopper stopped and glanced around, no longer beneath the light. I couldn't see his expression too clear, but I knew he knew my car.

His body swiveled toward the street, bending forward when I stopped beside him at the curb.

"What the fuck are you doing wandering around this late?" I bitched out the lowered window.

"I'm not wandering. I'm going to the all-night diner at the end of the block."

"Their pancakes taste like shit," I told him. "I'm hungry."

His mouth tilted up at one side, but his eyes held a note of wariness. "I'm just getting coffee."

"You can watch me eat." I leaned across the front seat and popped the passenger door open.

He hesitated a moment before sliding into the Camaro. He glanced at me as the interior lights blinked off. "What are you doing here?"

"I told you. I'm hungry."

"You're hungry, huh?" he repeated like he wasn't sure he believed me.

"Starved actually," I replied and pulled back into the street. He didn't say anything. I glanced in his direction, but he was staring out his window. I couldn't see his face.

I cleared my throat. Nerves bundled up inside me, coiled tight. "And, uh…" I began. "Maybe I wanted to see you."

"I wasn't expecting you," he replied, still gazing out his window.

Something about his tone whispered this was about way more than me yelling at him earlier. This was about whatever it was that broke him.

"It's okay," I whispered, wanting to help him, but not very confident I could. "I wasn't expecting you either."

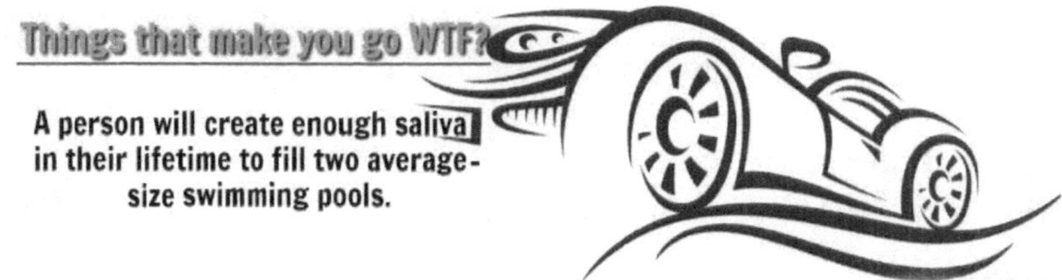

Chapter Eighteen

Hopper

Insomnia came with chronic solitude.

Tonight, it spontaneously came with pancakes.

And a blond-haired guy that looked a lot like Justin Bieber.

The pancakes must have really tasted like shit at the diner I was heading to, because he drove right by. Two blocks over, he pulled into another place. It looked like an old caboose from a train. The building was long and had the look of red-painted iron. The entire front had a stripe of windows down the middle, allowing a clear view inside. All along the top of the windows was a stripe of hot-pink neon light. Above that, the body of the place gave way to the roof and the giant oblong sign perched on top.

The perimeter of the sign was trimmed in more of the hot-pink rope light, and the name of the place was lit up with gold—literally DINER.

No originality awards for that.

In the window on the front door was a sign that advertised the place being open twenty-four hours.

Inside, it smelled like coffee and breakfast food. Mostly bacon.

It wasn't a bad scent.

It was empty except for a man sitting at the counter, eating a piece of pie that was completely covered in whipped cream.

Arrow slid into a booth by the door, so I scooted into the seat across from him.

I wasn't used to talking during my late-night strolls. I was used to staring off into the street, coffee in hand, not saying a word. My mind was loud enough; words were never needed.

The waitress came over. She wasn't in a uniform. Instead, she had on a pair of jeans and a hot-pink T-shirt with the word DINER on it.

Seriously, who came up with that?

"Coffee," I said, slightly gruff and out of practice. "No cream."

Arrow nodded. "Me, too." He began. "But I also want a stack of hotcakes, some bacon, and a couple eggs, over easy."

When the waitress was gone, I glanced at him. My stare slid over his honed features and dark eyes. I liked his hair, even if it was an unnatural color. I liked the way it showed off the side of his head where it was cut close. I don't know why, but it reminded me of someone who was wearing a shirt that slid off one shoulder.

Kind of exposing, yet not really.

Clearly, I was overly tired. I was comparing his hair to a shirt.

I should have forced my tired ass to stay in bed. I should have forced myself to vie for anything more than two hours of shuteye. Now I was just delirious.

Still, I'd rather be delirious than lying in that bed and staring at the ceiling while thoughts marauded around my head, taunting me… confusing me.

"You really gonna eat all that in the middle of the night?" I mused.

"Don't worry." He smiled. "I'll share."

I blinked. It was the second time since he appeared at the curb that I could have sworn he was flirting. Or at the very least, teasing.

It was a side of him I really hadn't expected.

I didn't know how to take it. I didn't know how to react.

Part of me wanted to pull him close. The other part? Wanted to shove him away.

We settled into this awkward state of silence. I found it interesting how we had moments of perfect ease with each other, but others we struggled to interact.

I didn't know what to say to him. I felt I'd already said it all. I pushed him, and I had no idea why. My only excuse was seeing where he lived turned me inside out. It wasn't even about the contracts, not really. But about so much more.

Thing was I had no right to any opinion. I had no right to any say.

I didn't even want any.

Telling yourself that doesn't make it true.

Yes. Mind over matter.

The coffee came and with it, the waitress slid two plates of food in front of Arrow. His eyes lit up like a child on Christmas, and I smothered a grin when he grabbed the clear jug of syrup at the back of the table and poured about half of it over the tall, butter-drenched stack of hotcakes.

"Can we get another fork?" he asked, giving the waitress a shy smile.

She smiled back, completely charmed, and returned with another set of silverware wrapped in a napkin. "Here ya go, hon."

"Thanks." He took it and slid it across the table at me.

He dove in like he was for real starving. I watched as he shoved a huge bite into his mouth and nodded, pleased. Did he always eat like this?

It annoyed me that I didn't know.

All those little things I didn't know about him, that paled in comparison to the way I recognized him.

Absentmindedly, I reached for my coffee, wrapping my hands around it, but not lifting it to my lips. I watched him eat, like I usually watched the night through the diner windows. And as he licked syrup off a generic silver fork, his eyes flashed up to mine, and I had a piercing thought.

I wasn't lonely. Not just then.

Instant guilt crashed down on me. My fingers tightened around the mug, and I forced my eyes away from him, sipping the dark liquid and staring out the window into the parking lot.

"What were you doing out in the middle of the night?" he asked, breaking the silence between us.

"I could ask the same of you." I countered.

"I went to the hotel… to see you."

I looked away from the window, back at him. The fork was gripped in his hand, paused in consuming his sugar stack. "You went to the hotel?"

Arrow nodded. "Then I saw what time it was and figured I'd just come back tomorrow. When I was driving out of the lot, I saw you."

I nodded slow. "I don't sleep much."

He glanced up. The solemn way he stared at me was like a knife in my chest. "You shouldn't walk the streets at night. Not around here."

I tilted my head to the side. "I can take care of myself."

"That's what I thought, too." He said it so softly I almost didn't hear. Haunted. That's how he sounded.

He sounded the way I felt.

He cleared his throat, gesturing to the still-wrapped silverware. "You gonna help me eat all this?"

"Something tells me you could put it away all by yourself."

He pushed the silverware at me.

Once my fork was unwrapped, he pushed the plate of half-eaten pancakes across the table in front of me. Then he grabbed a piece of bacon and shoved it in his mouth.

"You were right," he said, glancing toward the window.

"I don't hear that very often." I cracked.

"I've been scared to make a decision." His voice turned sincere, more serious than when he'd been talking about pancakes.

I tried not to react so much because I knew he wasn't done. I wanted him to talk. I wanted the sound of his voice, and I wanted to know just a little more about all his jagged little pieces.

So I just nodded. I took the fork and turned it on its side to cut through the thick layers of pancakes.

"Sometimes it's hard to step out of a place you've become accustomed to. A place that makes you feel…" His words trailed off. He abandoned the food, reaching for his mug.

"Safe." I finished for him.

He nodded. "I think you know something about that."

"Oh yeah," I murmured. Syrup dripped off the bite, so I pushed it in my mouth. Buttery sweetness exploded across my tongue, and I sighed.

Arrow made a sound. "See? Good shit."

I went in for another bite.

"Gamble sent you here to talk to me about NASCAR, didn't he? He wants you to promise I won't get hazed for being gay."

"He thinks that's why you haven't signed." I hedged, reaching for a piece of bacon.

"That's not why I haven't signed."

"I know." I dropped the fork and leaned back in the booth. "If that was the reason, you'd have just signed with the NRR. You're almost guaranteed no trouble there because of your brother, Joey, and because Trent and Drew are the hot romance of that division."

His head bobbed slowly. "My entire family is there."

"But you want to sign with NASCAR." That was the bottom line.

"It's like you said. If I stay with the NRR, I'll always be in my brother's shadow. It's comfortable there. I'll be successful, but in the back of my head, I'll always wonder if it's because of him."

"But?" I drank some coffee, glancing again out the window at the snow floating down to coat the parking lot. Matt had loved the snow.

"I care what Lor thinks. He's my family, but he's more than that. In a lot of ways, he saved my life. I can't turn my back on that."

Just as I couldn't turn my back on the life I didn't save.

"Loyalty is a tricky thing, isn't it?" I mused, still watching the snow fall. "It never changes, even when everything else around you does."

He didn't reply. In fact, the silence I coveted so much at this hour suddenly seemed suffocating. I glanced across the table. He was watching me. Measuring me. Reading me.

I tried to slam my pages shut, but it didn't work that way, not with someone like Arrow.

"Time is the ultimate test of loyalty." He agreed. Then in a much softer tone, almost a whisper, he asked, "What broke you?"

I sucked in a breath. It was so real between us, so real and raw. It was everything, or it was nothing. There was no in between with Arrow. That's why the way we interacted with each other was hot or cold. Awkward or playful.

We didn't have a lukewarm state; there was no middle ground.

All or nothing.

"I can't do this." The words ripped out of the deepest part of me. I shot out of the booth and rushed out of the diner.

Outside, I heaved a deep breath, rushed down the small ramp that led to the door, around the rails, and leaned against the red iron wall. I lowered so my head was below the window and my body disappeared in the shadows.

It hurt. No matter what I did, there was pain.

From the second Matt flipped off that bike to this very moment, there was some degree of pain in every day.

It hurt to be without him. It ached to remember him. It ached to try and forget.

I was the reason he was dead. It should have been me in the ground right now, not him. The least I could do was remain loyal and true.

The back of my head hit the side of the diner. I stared up at the inky sky. Snowflakes fell against my cheeks, melting instantly but spreading their chill across my skin.

Arrow made me want things.

Lots of things.

Things I never thought I'd want again. Things I told myself I didn't deserve. The life I had died when Matt took his last breath.

The universe didn't seem to care, because here it was. Here *he* was.

The way Arrow looked at me, how he spoke with such honesty. The way his lips felt over mine. Even the damn way he ate pancakes like he hadn't eaten in days.

Holy shit. What if he really hasn't eaten in days?

The thought thrust me into action. I shoved off the wall, leapt over the railing, and raced toward the door. I saw him too late. We collided before I could stop my momentum.

We knocked together, chest to chest, and bounced back.

"Whoa." Arrow cautioned.

Both our hands came out at the same time, grabbing to steady each other as if we thought the collision would knock the other down. Our faces were mere inches apart, our lips so close I could smell the syrup and coffee on his breath. I jerked back, shoving my hands into the pockets of my leather jacket.

"I was just coming in to pay the tab," I told him, feeling like a complete ass for running out before. I didn't know what his financial situation was, but he lived in a garage for fuck's sake. And he was hungry.

How can you walk away from him?

Because if I didn't, it was stark betrayal. Matt deserved better.

So did Arrow.

"No worries." He shrugged. "I paid it."

"You didn't have to do that," I growled.

"I'm the one who ate," he pointed out.

"I'm sorry I ran out like that," I said, not even bothering to hide the misery in my voice.

"I get it," he replied, fished the car keys out of his jeans, and started ahead. "C'mon. It's gonna take my sack three days to thaw if we stand out here any longer."

I blinked. Watched him walk away.

I wished his jeans were tighter, 'cause even though they shouldn't, my eyes searched for a glimpse of his ass.

No questions. No demands. No explanations needed.

Hell, most men would be counting their lucky stars to have a guy (or girl) not want to pick apart their words and actions with a fine-tooth comb.

The rumble of the Camaro cut through the night. The subtle squeak of the windshield wipers brushing away the falling snow was distinct. I started forward, toward the car, toward my ride back to the hotel.

I wasn't counting my lucky stars tonight.

In fact, I stewed about it the short ride back.

I didn't want to explain what happened back there. I was relieved he understood enough to just let it go.

Still, at the same time, part of me wanted to explain.

It's all or nothing. I had to remember that.

If I gave him just a little, he'd end up taking it all.

Chapter Nineteen

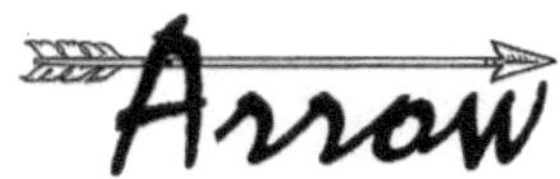

Pen to paper.

Sign my name.

It wasn't that easy. Not even when it was something I wanted.

Old habits were hard to break, even harder when those habits were born out of survival. I lay in bed, staring at the ceiling of the hangar, my eyes roaming over the dips and peaks in the metal as if they held the secrets of life.

The T-shirt under my hoodie carried the scent of pancakes and coffee. I left it on, exchanged my jeans for a pair of pajama pants, and tossed the hoodie on the end of the bed. Every time I shifted against the mattress, a burst of butter and rich carbs mingled beneath my nose. Sometimes I shifted on purpose just so I could inhale the scent again.

I couldn't get him out of my head. The look on Hopper's face at the diner when I asked him what broke him or the look in his eyes when I first pulled up to the curb.

He said he didn't sleep much. I wondered why. When he smiled at me, I wondered when he would do it again, and when he told me he couldn't do this, I wondered what *this* was.

Truth was I wasn't even sure I could do it.

Any of it.

NASCAR, reaching for an actual life, and seeing Hopper without wanting to know everything about him.

Wanting him.

I hadn't wanted anyone in a very long time. My inexperience was almost crippling. The experience I did have?

Traumatic.

And something more—no one had ever wanted me.

Ever.

Not even my own father.

How could I expect someone to want me now? When I was broken. Used.

Who would choose that? Who would choose half a man when there was an option of someone better, someone whole?

I dozed off eventually. When I woke, the hangar was still dark, but that didn't mean anything, because it was always dark when the lights weren't on. There were no windows.

I didn't bother to glance at the clock. I closed my eyes and wondered what he was doing. If he was wondering what I was doing.

Disgusted with my thoughts, I tossed off the blankets and was slapped with a rush of frigid air.

"Fuck," I muttered. Once I jammed my feet into my sneakers, I turned on the extra heater and turned up the other one. Then I put on a pot of coffee and grabbed my shit so I could take a quick shower.

There was a small bathroom in this hangar, which was why I stayed in this one. It wasn't fancy. In fact, it was so basic it was almost a half bath. The shower was small, basically just a corner of the tiny rectangular room, with a plastic shower curtain that drew around to help keep the water contained.

The toilet and sink were rudimentary, and the mirror above the sink was very small.

I didn't mind it. It might have been nice to have more space, specifically counter space so I could leave my toothbrush and shit out instead of having to keep it in a tote, but whatever.

The water was hot, and that was all that really mattered.

Beneath the spray, I thought again about the contracts in the other room. Once I was dressed, I would sit down and read them. I would make a decision.

You already know what you want.

I grabbed the soap to wash my body. As I scrubbed, the palm of my hand rubbed over some raised scars on my arm. I glanced down. I knew they were there; they always would be. Sometimes I barely noticed them, and other days, they were all I saw. I shoved my arm beneath the spray, watching the suds rinse away to reveal them clearly.

They were a reminder.

Of a dark time.

But also of something else.

Of last night. Of everything Hopper said to me. Of the decision I made to stop hiding, to live instead of merely exist.

What would Lorhaven say? He wasn't going to be happy, and I wasn't sure that was something I could ignore.

Once I was completely clean, I shut off the water and dried quickly. After running a comb through my wet hair and doing all the other shit a guy does in the bathroom, I pulled on some clean boxers and the pajama bottoms I had on earlier.

They were thick and soft, kind of like a blanket, a Christmas gift from Joey. They were black with a bunch of yellow emojis all over them. She liked to give me goofy shit. She had told me she liked when I smiled, something I did a lot when she was around.

I kinda liked having a sister. Especially one who liked me for me. I never had to work to impress her or be someone I wasn't because it was who she expected. In some ways, she and I had a lot in common. We were underdogs. Except she fought against it, but me?

I succumbed to it.

I glanced in the mirror before leaving the bathroom. All I could see was my head in the small square. My hair was a little darker because it was wet, less blond, less wild because I'd combed it down. It didn't equate to a new me, but maybe someone more improved?

Not anymore, I told myself. *No more succumbing.*

I pushed my feet into my high-tops (the hard floor was way too cold to just wear socks), grabbed my shit, and walked out of the bathroom.

Cool air brushed over my bare chest, and my nipples tightened. It was warm out here, but not as warm as the bathroom had been.

I dropped my stuff onto the dresser, stepping around to open a drawer to grab a shirt. Movement out of the corner of my eye stopped me.

All the muscles in my body went rigid, adrenaline spiked in my blood, and my entire being went into fight mode. I rotated immediately, my hands ready to strike.

"Whoa," Drew said, holding up his hands. "I come in peace."

"Jesus," I muttered, my arms relaxing. "Don't you knock?"

Trent moved up beside Drew, both of them dressed casually in jeans and hoodies, but Drew was wearing his signature leather jacket. Trent had on a gray knit cap, pulled low over his ears.

"I thought you giving us the code meant we didn't have to," Trent explained.

Drew gave him a sidelong glance and smiled. Trent turned his face toward Drew and winked.

I wasn't used to seeing such ease in couples. It was like these guys were a TV movie come to life. Like seriously? Did other people actually get along like them?

Yes. They had a whole family of people who were all in love.

It was like the damn Twilight Zone over there. Oddly, I liked it.

"For the record, we honked. And called you. When you didn't answer—" Drew said, but Trent cut him off to finish the sentence.

"We thought you'd fallen and you couldn't get up."

I gave him the finger.

"Seriously. You should get Life Alert. You live here all alone," Trent said sagely.

Drew guffawed. "You'd be the youngest dude in history to have it."

Something in the background of the Trent and Drew Show shifted. My body stiffened again and my eyes sharpened.

Hopper stepped forward from beside the Camaro, where the heater wasn't blocking him.

My eyesight condensed, almost like tunnel vision, and he was the center of the tunnel. I was surprised to see him. No, actually, I was shocked.

After last night and the way he'd bolted out of the diner and said barely two words on the short drive to his hotel, I thought I wouldn't see him again until I had a contract to hand him.

But he was here. Now. And he looked good. So good.

No red hat today. Instead, his overly long hair was wild around his head. The dark strands curled out from his neck, flipped out around his ears, and fell over his forehead in waves. There was a shadow on his jawline, and all the dark hair on his head and face only made the lightness of his eyes more startling.

The grey cargo pants looked good on him, accentuating his lower half, not too tight, but not baggy either. With the pants, he wore a white waffle-knit, long-sleeved shirt. It molded against his wide shoulders and draped over his narrow waist. The leather bracelet he always wore on his right wrist was there, thick and dark brown.

I'd never seen him without it (and I looked at him a lot). I wondered if it had some kind of significance.

This unsteady feeling tingled my stomach, and he returned my stare. I watched him swallow, shoving his hands deep into his pockets as his gaze dropped, roaming over my bare chest and farther down my stomach to my lower half.

"Nice pants," he drawled. His voice was joking, but his eyes were anything but.

I fidgeted under the heat in his gaze. I never knew such icy eyes could produce such warmth. His stare was like a touch, intimate and personal, and it made me hungry for more.

"He was at the gate when we pulled up," Drew said.

I forced my eyes off of Hopper and back to Drew.

"Thought he was gonna climb the fence," Trent drawled. "He thought you'd fallen and couldn't get up, too."

"I did not," Hopper muttered.

Trent glanced around at him. "So you were just scaling the giant-ass fence because you planned on robbing the place?"

Hopper muttered something I couldn't hear, and Trent and Drew laughed.

I watched the three of them like they were aliens and they spoke an entirely different language.

"I honked, several times." Hopper's eyes came back to me. A dark cloud passed behind them. "You didn't answer."

He'd been worried.

"I was in the shower."

He nodded, glancing away.

My eyes bounced between Drew and Trent. After a moment, I shook my head and poured some coffee into a mug.

I gestured toward the pot as I took a sip. "Help yourself." My eyes went back to Hopper, lingering there.

"We came to get you," Drew announced. "We got plans."

"Plans?" I echoed, lowering the cup.

"Man stuff." Trent nodded.

Drew glanced between me and Hopper. "Unless you two are already busy."

Trent wagged his eyebrows at me.

I wasn't amused.

"You busy with Arrow?" Drew turned his back to me to fully face Hopper.

"We're going over contracts."

"Boring," Drew declared.

"C'mon. We have shit to do."

Trent made a sound of agreement. "Dude, put on some clothes, not pants that look like something my granny sent in a text message."

"Your granny texts you?" I wondered.

"In all emojis. It's like trying to decode directions in Arabic."

"Granny's my favorite person ever." Drew smiled.

"Dress warm," Trent ordered. "We're gonna be outside."

I glanced back at Hopper. He was watching us all like he was on the outside looking in. I didn't like it. In fact, I hated it. There was no way I was walking away from him right now. I was shocked he was here, and yeah, he probably did just want to go over the contracts, but I'd take it.

"You busy today?" Drew asked him before I could decline their order to dress.

He shook his head.

"When do you have to be back at headquarters?" Trent asked.

He glanced at me. "When I have a signed contract."

"So you got time," Drew said. "You can come, too."

"Come where?" he asked, suspicious.

"To have fun." Drew pulled his keys out of his pants and walked toward the door. "We'll wait outside."

Trent followed along behind Drew but stopped by Hopper. "Might wanna borrow a shirt or two from Arrow. It's cold as hell outside."

"Five minutes!" Drew called, and then the pair were gone.

I was still standing there in my pajamas with no shirt, wondering what the fuck was going on.

"I, ah, hope it's okay they let me in," Hopper said, slightly awkward.

"It's cool," I said, turning toward my dresser. My stomach was bunching up beneath my ribs. Suddenly, the garage felt twice as small with the two of us standing in it.

"I'll be at the hotel. You can come by when you're done with them if you want to go over the papers."

"Aren't you coming?" I asked, glancing up.

"I'm pretty sure that was a polite invite."

I made a sound. "Trent and Drew aren't polite. If they invited you, it's because you're welcome."

He hesitated like he wasn't sure what to say. I felt the war inside him. He wanted to come, but at the same time he didn't.

I cocked my head to the side. "Were you really gonna climb the fence?"

His eyes flashed. "You didn't come out. I waited and waited. I don't have your number. I thought something might be wrong."

He was worried. Worried enough to consider breaking into this place. I set down the coffee, closing the distance between us until I could touch him if I wanted.

"Let me see your phone." I held out my hand.

He pulled it out of his pocket and handed it to me, screen up. I pulled up the contacts and added in my cell. When I was done, I handed it back. "Here. Now you have my number."

It took him a minute to take the phone. His gaze lazily perused the sleeve of tattoos down my arm, caressing my chest and my still-tight nipples. But I wasn't cold, not anymore. Now they were hard because of him.

No one had ever wound me up like this before. No one had ever been able to make me forget all the reasons I didn't like to be touched with just a look.

His eyes still on me, Hopper took the phone. Our fingers brushed together, something I thought might have been intentional.

"So you're here until I sign?" I asked, moving back across the room.

"Yeah."

I opened my dresser drawers and pulled out some jeans, a long-sleeved T-shirt, a thick hoodie, and a knit hat.

I glanced back at Hopper. He was watching me. I found a blue hoodie and tossed it his way. "Here."

He snagged it out of the air and looked between me and the shirt. I smiled and quickly dressed, pulled on the hat, and then reached for the waistband of the pajamas. "You mind?"

He shook his head.

In one quick movement, the pants were gone. You could have heard a pin drop in the room when I tossed them aside and picked up my jeans.

My heart was beating rapidly; a fine tremor shook my hands. I wanted to turn and glance at Hopper. God knew I could feel his stare.

But I was afraid to look. Afraid of what I'd see.

Instead, I ignored the desire in my veins and hurried to dress.

Once the jeans were on, I busied myself turning off the coffee pot and the two heaters. After that, I found a pair of gloves, shoved my phone in my pocket, and picked up the blue coat on a nearby workbench.

"C'mon. You can ride with me," I said, still avoiding his stare as I moved toward the door.

He caught my wrist. His strong hand pulled me around. "Hey."

I glanced down to where he held me. He didn't let go.

"You sure you want me to come?"

"No."

He didn't seem surprised or even offended. I knew he wouldn't. I could see the same feelings reflected in his eyes.

Beneath his grip, my wrist rotated. I lifted my hand and wrapped it around his, long enough to give it a gentle squeeze. "Let's go."

He pulled back and slid my hoodie over his body. It fit him a little more snugly than it did me, but just about all my clothes were baggy on me. I liked it. It made me feel possessive, sort of like a part of me claimed him.

"Where the hell are we going?" he wondered as the garage door slid up. Inch by inch, the winter's day view revealed itself to me.

More snow had fallen since last night. Even though the sun was high in the sky, it just wasn't hot enough to melt any of it. There were several inches now. It created an undisturbed white blanket over the entire airstrip. Off in the distance, it glistened where the sun hit it, making it reflect light like an expensive diamond.

Trent and Drew sat in Trent's steel-colored Mustang, and they gestured for me to follow them. I waved and slid into the driver's seat of the Camaro.

Hopper climbed in beside me. I didn't resist the urge to look at him.

"I have no idea," I answered his previous question. "With Drew and Trent, it's hard to say."

In all honesty, I didn't care where we were going, not when Hopper was riding shotgun.

Chapter Twenty

Hopper

Yes, I debated scaling a large fence.

Yes, I got caught by two bigmouths.

No, I didn't want to talk about it.

And now?

Now here I was on a huge piece of private property, standing in front of four snowmobiles.

My stomach was churning. The cramps twisting my guts were uncomfortable as hell. In fact, they made it near impossible to stand still.

Sure, for most anyone—especially four guys in the racing business—a day spent zooming over freshly fallen snow on top-of-the-line snowmobiles sounded like hella fun.

I wasn't most anyone.

In fact, most days I felt I was the only one of my kind on the entire planet.

I hadn't been on a motorcycle, dirt bike, jet ski, hell, not even a moped since that day with Matt.

Basically, anything with a motor besides a car, anything that went fast, I disavowed.

How could I? How could I get on something like that and not be totally transported back to the day I'd lost Matt?

It seemed ironic I was still in the racing business. Especially given my aversion to speed and actual racing. But I didn't race. Not anymore. I managed, I instructed, and I gave tips.

I tried to make my drivers safe and prepared so maybe, just maybe, something like what happened to Matt didn't happen to anyone else.

Because honestly? I wouldn't wish that shit on anyone. Not even my worst enemy.

Death is more than a punishment. It's more than revenge.

It's permanent.

It's unforgiving.

It was now my fear.

I wasn't afraid of dying. In fact, there were lots of times I sort of wished for it. Why wouldn't I? I could be with Matt again. The fear I had about death was someone else close to me would be taken.

That's why I was alone.

Death couldn't rip my life apart again if there was no one I cared about to be taken from me.

Are you thinking, *Well then, why would he be afraid to get on the snowmobile?*

Two reasons:

1.) Those snowmobiles were a stark reminder of what I lost, something that cut me so deep I hadn't been on anything like a Ducati since.

And

2.) Arrow was getting on one.

What was even worse?

The second reason was outweighing the first. My God, he wasn't anything to me. He was an acquaintance. A work assignment.

He liked pancakes, drank his coffee the same way I did, and had never once looked at me with an ounce of pity or judgement in his eyes.

Arrow wasn't anything to me—except the potential to be everything.

So here I stood in the center of a snowy driveway, in front of a machine I knew was powerful enough to steal everything away.

A cold sweat beaded between my shoulder blades and beneath the beanie I wore, right at my hairline. I was thankful for the sunglasses wrapped over my eyes because I was worried they would show my panic.

I couldn't exactly get out of this. Not without looking like a giant pussy.

Yeah, sorry, I can't ride this, uh, sweet snowmobile because, well, my boyfriend died in a crash. I gave up my entire life and basically became a hermit… And, well, if I drive this today, I may have a massive panic attack.

Dude, no.

Just no.

No one knew about my past. Except Joey and Gamble. I put it behind me because reminders made it worse. Because seeing the pity deep in someone's eyes every single time they looked at me was unbearable.

"What's better than freshly fallen snow? Tearing it up with a speed machine!" Drew said, gazing out over his toys.

"Hells yeah." Trent agreed.

We were on their family compound, which consisted of a giant-ass house and then a more manageable-size house where they lived, along with their giant garage filled with toys. It was a sweet setup. Maybe something like I'd always wanted to have one day.

Until my life shattered into a million pieces.

"These are sweet," Arrow said, stepping up to one and grabbing the handle. My stomach revolted, and I turned away, pretending I was checking out the view.

"We got four because we figured our brothers would want to tear it up with us sometimes, too. But they're busy today." Drew went on.

"Diaper duty, ya know." Trent supplied.

"So we thought we'd come get you, A, because you know these beasts gotta be driven so the batteries don't sit and die." Drew finished.

"Thanks for thinking of me," Arrow said. I didn't know if anyone else heard it in his voice, the sincerity, the shy surprise someone thought of him.

Sweat ran down my spine. My knees felt like Jell-O.

"Lucky for us Hopper was there. Now we have a fourth driver."

"Let me just grab all the keys and we'll head out," Drew announced. He and Trent went into the garage.

I took a deep breath of the crisp air, hoping it would shock my lungs into working properly again.

A hand settled on my shoulder, and I tensed, swinging sideways. Arrow's hand slid off with my movement. His brown eyes studied me, looked *into* me. "This is no good for you."

So perceptive. Almost scarily so.

It was proof—irrefutable proof—that he got me just like I did him.

I swallowed. "I'm not sure I can get on that." I tossed a look toward the toy.

"Let's go, then."

I blinked. It took a second for my brain to process his offer. "You would do that?"

"Without a second thought," he replied instantly. "I can feel how tense you are. How freaked out. We'll leave, find something else to do."

Oh shit. He was offering to give something up for me. Offering to be there for me.

"Why?" I said abruptly. So abrupt it sounded more like a barked demand.

He didn't even flinch. "Because it's what you need."

I didn't want to need him.

I didn't say anything. I couldn't. Words failed me.

Arrow shifted, uncomfortable, as if he thought what he said was somehow wrong instead of so incredibly right.

"I mean, it's not trying to scale a giant fence or anything, but…"

He was joking. Trying to make light of what he just offered because he thought I was rejecting it. I couldn't let that happen. "It's better." The words rushed out.

His lips pressed together. His stare asked if it was true.

"Yo!" Drew called out. "Let's do this!"

Arrow swung to face the guys. "Actually, we—"

I grabbed his arm, speaking low. "No. Let's do it."

"I can feel your fingers shaking." He glanced down to where I held him.

"I can do it." I insisted. Maybe this was something I needed to do. For closure.

Or maybe I was afraid if we made an excuse and left, my time with Arrow would be over for the day. I guess the thought of that was worse than the thought of a fiery snowmobile crash.

I had more issues than the house of *GearShark*.

"Are you sure?" Arrow murmured, studying me, penetrating me with his eyes.

No. "Yes."

I glanced up at Trent and Drew. They were watching us with interest. Those two were way too perceptive. I'd noticed that since the moment we'd been introduced. Especially Trent. That guy was good at reading people.

"Take 'em out. Let's all try to stay in the same vicinity, but let's stay away from the main house." Drew pointed off in the direction of the giant house.

I nodded and moved toward the vehicle. Arrow wasn't far behind. My legs were shaking when I straddled it. My breathing was shallow, and an image of the Ducati wreckage was stapled to my brain.

The sounds of engines starting up nearby made me want to flee. I told myself to shut the hell up, and I fired up mine. It was a smooth-running engine, loud but nothing over the top. The seat was comfortable, and I knew by looking at it and feeling it purr between my legs it was well taken care of.

This was just a friendly drive. Fun. No competition, no anger about who was getting what deal. It was going to be fun. No drama.

I glanced over at Arrow, wanting to reassure myself he was okay. He was scowling at the vehicle, and I noticed then the engine wouldn't turn over.

All three of us watched him do everything he could to start it up. It was a no-go.

"Shit," Drew swore over the engines. "That fucking sled."

Arrow nodded like he was disgusted. "Battery's dead."

Trent nodded. "That one's been giving us some trouble. Thought I had it fixed." He glanced over at Drew. "We're gonna have to get a new battery. Maybe some new plugs."

A sense of giddy glee overcame me. The urge to grin was shoved down, but I was relieved. So fucking relieved he wasn't going to be driving that thing.

"You guys go without me," Arrow said, climbing off the vehicle and tugging the edges of his black hat down over his ears.

"You can take mine," Trent offered, moving like he might get up. "I can ride with Drew."

All that glee inside me drained away. As if he knew it, Arrow glanced at me, then back at Trent. "Nah, these are your toys. You should enjoy them. Besides, you two are too big to fit on one."

Drew spoke up, hitching a thumb in my direction. "Ride with Hopper."

My belly dipped.

Trent agreed. "Yeah, good call, Forrester. They fit better on one sled."

I felt Arrow's stare.

If Drew and Trent picked up on any of the vibes between Arrow and me, they acted like they hadn't a clue.

Fuckers.

"C'mon!" Drew yelled and took off. Snow flung up behind him, spraying in Trent's direction, who took off behind him.

Arrow looked at me. I hitched my chin, gesturing for him to come on. His eyes widened with surprise. His boots crunched over the snow, a sound I probably shouldn't have heard over the engine, but I did. I heard everything connected to him.

"You sure?" he asked.

I nodded. At least with him on the back, I had some control over our speed, over the route we traveled. I could protect him better. The thought made this a little more bearable.

Arrow straddled the sled. His body fit behind me, but not up against me. He held himself back a little, keeping some air between us.

I thought about the way he looked when I first saw him today. Bare chested and in those fucking emoji pants.

He wasn't as skinny as he appeared in all those baggy clothes. He was lean for sure; the guy had almost no body fat. His skin clung expertly to all the sinewy muscle corded beneath the surface. He had solid, flat abs, smooth skin, and his nipples… They were erect.

My mouth ran dry when I noticed. My tongue practically scraped the roof of my mouth when I tried to swallow. And the pants? They were loose but showed off more of his ass than anything else I'd seen on him.

I resisted the urge to shove back just a little, to bring that upper body against my back to see if it felt as good as it looked.

I glanced over my shoulder. My chin brushed the leather collar on my coat I'd put over his hoodie. "You ready?"

"Whenever you are," he answered, his knees brushing the outside of my hips.

I turned back around, glancing down at the machine.

It had been so long, yet it felt like yesterday.

The throttle on this sled was the same as a motorcycle. My right hand gripped the handle and twisted. The sled responded immediately, and we shot forward.

The sudden movement jerked us both, and Arrow's hand shot out, steadying himself on my side. It was the ultimate distraction from the nerves suffusing my brain.

Cold wind whipped against my face, pushing at the layers of clothes I wore. Some of the cold cut through my pants, penetrating through to my legs. I ignored it as snow sprayed out around us and pointed the nose in the direction Drew and Trent had disappeared.

I wasn't going terribly fast. In fact, back in the day, I'd have compared my speed to that of a turtle. Or a granny. But it was all I could manage right now. I was trying to push past the memories and feelings assaulting my chest.

It was the achingly familiar feelings that got me the most. How something so simple could remind me of so much was overwhelming. I could almost taste the memories that assaulted me. God, I used to love this so fucking much.

It was freedom.

The air. The speed. Being in control of the craft.

There was nothing quite like being on a motorcycle and flying over the ground.

The sound of crunching metal, shattering glass, ruined my reminiscing. My brain was intruded upon by flashes of Matt lying on the ground, unmoving and unresponsive.

I remembered the morgue, his dead body.

The sled jerked violently beneath my hands, swerving toward the right.

"Whoa." Arrow's voice rumbled against my ear.

His body surrounded mine. Long arms reached around, his hands covered mine, and smoothly he guided us back into a straight line.

"How about you stay here in the moment with me for a while?" His voice was low. It mixed in with the rumble of the engine. So I told myself my limbs vibrated because of the machine between my legs, not because of the whispered words over my shoulder.

I glanced back briefly, just long enough for our gazes to connect, before I turned back ahead. Beneath his hands, mine flexed. He gave them a gentle squeeze.

I wanted to. I wanted to stay in the moment with him.

"I got this," I called back.

His hands lifted off mine. His body began to pull back. With my left hand, I caught his retreating arm, tucking it around my middle. He paused briefly. I felt the stiff surprise in his muscles. Still, he allowed me to hold his hand there, pressed against my chest. After a moment, I released him so I could drive and held my breath and waited to see if he would pull away.

He didn't.

Arrow's other arm followed suit and wrapped around my middle. His chest pressed closer against my back, his thighs tightening on either side of my hips.

I was overwhelmed, almost frozen in the moment of feeling him wrap around me. It was sort of like a jumper cable to a completely dead battery. I didn't start up, but the sparks of life were there. I felt them. It was like all I needed were a few more jolts, and then impossibly, this completely dead battery might sputter to life.

The warmth and brilliance of that feeling, of being touched after so many years…

Five. Long. Years.

It was indescribable.

I hitched a breath. Sucked in another.

"You gonna drive like a granny all day?" Arrow teased in my ear.

I felt one eyebrow shoot up beneath the brim of my beanie.

"Is this the best you got, Hopp?" He challenged, still teasing.

Before I could even think twice or second-guess myself, my hand twisted the throttle as if it were the most natural thing in the world. The sled tore over the snow, bounced on a slight dip in the landscape, and I turned sharply, creating a curtain of high-flying powder.

Instead of stopping there, I tore off in the new direction, completely losing myself in the ride, and the joy I suddenly remembered overcame everything else.

We moved so fast the wind felt like sharp blades against my cheeks, and my eyes scanned the white-capped trees, the sparkling white blanket, and the way the blue sky dropped to meet it.

We caught up to Trent and Drew. The three of us buzzed around, and at one point, I saw an opportunity, a slight bank of white fluff. Still caught up in the moment, still feeling startlingly secure with Arrow wrapped around my back, I took off, giving the throttle exactly what it needed, and hit the bank.

We were airborne a few seconds, flying over the white blanket not very far below.

Arrow screamed in my ear, a loud, *"Whoop!"* that likely echoed half a mile. It was a joyous sound, and for a blissful second, it gave me the same joy, but then it brought me crashing back.

The sled hit the snow and slid across the ground. I turned sharply and hit the brake. The vehicle did a full turn so we were facing the way we'd just come, and I stopped.

I could hear my heart thundering in my ears. Felt my breath squeezing my lungs as I wheezed, trying to draw in more.

What the fuck had I been doing?

I'd been flying. I fucking took a jump.

With Arrow on the back.

Jesus Christ, I hadn't driven in years. What if I'd lost control?

My hands dropped off the handles. The snowmobile shut off, and the only sounds around us were the two sleds in the distance and the thundering of my erratic heartbeat in my ears.

I slumped forward a little. The crashing guilt, a wave of regret, and all of reality came like an avalanche I had no hope of outrunning.

"Where the fuck did you learn to drive like that?" Arrow said, amazed excitement in his voice. It barely registered. Even he was muffled by the avalanche.

"Another lifetime ago." I wasn't sure if it was a thought or something spoken.

The trembles came back, but they were more like quakes now.

It was embarrassing to lose it like this. Here. Now. But I had no hope of controlling it.

Arrow slid off the sled. The wind hit me in the back like a snowball to the face. It made me quake more.

"My turn to drive," he announced.

I glanced up, then numbly slid back, giving him the driver's seat. I was glad he wanted to drive. I was done. No more. I loved it just then, but I couldn't do this again.

Arrow's jean-clad leg swung over the seat. His body lowered in front of me. I looked up, startled, right into his brown eyes.

Our knees knocked together. His hands fell onto the tops of my thighs and stayed.

"I thought you wanted to drive," I remarked.

"I do, but not until you're ready to hang on."

Our stares bounced between each other. Again, I saw no pity or even that he had the need to ask.

"You stayed for a while," he said. The sound of his voice calmed me, and so did the shy way he said the words.

"I'm still here." My voice was scratchy as if it were out of practice. In many ways, it was.

He made a sound of disagreement. "No. You're slipping away again."

"I don't want to." The words ripped out as if they knew if they waited, I would shove them down.

Arrow glanced between us, and I followed his stare.

I'd grabbed his hand, clutched it like a lifeline.

Both our stares lifted, connected.

"Make me stay," I whispered.

The minimal distance separating us disappeared. Arrow swooped in at the same time his hands came up. The soft, scratchy material of the gloves molded to his hands brushed over my jaws, pulling a little in my stubble when he cupped my face.

Those pouty lips I coveted so much fused with mine, full on, without hesitation. It wasn't like the last time; this was different. Better.

He wasn't angry or defiant. He wasn't trying to prove something to anyone.

He kissed me purely out of desire. Out of want. I tasted it on his tongue. I lapped it off his lips. Holy shit, the passion in him. The deep way he kissed shot another jolt of life right into my chest.

With a moan, I grabbed the front of his coat and pulled him closer. Our skin was cold, the total opposite of our mouths. It was sort of like sitting in a hot tub in the center of a snowstorm. Neither of us lifted our head. Our lips stayed fused the entire time we kissed. He turned his head one way and then the other, but he did so without completely pulling away.

"Breathe," he spoke, his lips still against mine.

I sucked in a breath. Then we were kissing again. I forgot where I was, who I was. It didn't matter, either. Arrow's lips were smooth, gliding over mine like they knew exactly where they were going.

His fingertips tightened on my face. My tongue swept past his lips and over the roof of his mouth.

He groaned.

I wanted closer. I wanted more. I wanted it with infinite desperation.

I slid forward. The way we sat made it hard to get in a position so more of us touched. I lifted my legs, threw them over his, and pulled him close so I was still between his legs, but because mine pinned his down, we were nearly chest to chest.

The kiss changed. Arrow started slipping away, and suddenly, I knew exactly how he'd felt when I did the same.

I started grappling, searching for a way to pull him back. My hands fisted in his coat so he couldn't physically pull back. The physical wasn't all I wanted, though. Actually, it wasn't as important as the other. I wanted him present mentally. I wanted all those shards of glass that made up his insides to all be focused on me.

It didn't work. Instead of moving closer, as my hands demanded, he broke the kiss. His chin dipped; his entire body leaned back and away, rigid and trembling.

I searched him, tried to understand what I'd done wrong.

Everything was exactly right, and then it was exactly wrong.

I released his coat, tipping his chin up with one hand.

The look on his face was a cold, hard slap. I held back the wince, but fuck me, I felt it. Arrow was haunted, scared… cornered.

That was it.

He looked cornered. Trapped.

I glanced down to where my body pinned his. Realization dawned.

So did horror.

What. The. Fuck?

I didn't move fast. I was afraid I'd freak him out. Instead, I lifted my legs, carefully sliding my body back so he was no longer held down. I let my arms fall to the sides, not touching or restraining him.

He swallowed thickly. A shuddering breath moved through him.

He'd asked me before what broke me. Now it was me who wondered what broke him. I had a very, very bad feeling whatever it was might break me, too. The idea of him in any kind of agony was almost more than I could bear.

What the fuck were we doing?

Two broken shards, two drained batteries, two men who were merely shells.

What could we offer each other?

"I, ah…" He started, regret and embarrassment in his voice. "Sorry."

The need to protect him flooded through me. The questions I'd just been pondering ceased to exist. All I wanted was to make that look on his face disappear.

"How about this?" I suggested, starting forward with deliberate movements.

He watched with hooded eyes, wariness filling the air around him.

I reached down, hooked my hands beneath his knees, and tugged. His ass slid across the seat toward me, and I positioned his legs like mine had been on his just moments ago.

Now he was the one pinning me down; now my legs were beneath his.

Before I pulled my hands away, my palms rubbed down his thighs in a simple caress.

I sat back, waiting to see what he would do.

Arrow looked up. The emotion in his eyes was unidentifiable. Relief but something else, something more profound.

He dove forward, kissed me swiftly, then pulled back enough to look into my eyes.

I held up my hands in surrender, and he half growled and dove at my mouth again. Like he was starved, like we hadn't just made out.

I welcome him, opened wide and twisted our tongues together until I was afraid they'd never come apart. He shifted on me, pulled himself up as if he wanted even closer.

I slid my hands beneath him, holding him up, and he slid fully into my lap.

Both of us moaned and kissed with renewed passion.

All the blood drained from my head and went south, swelling my dick and making me ache to rock against him. But I held back. I didn't want to scare him again.

Here we were treading carefully, worried we might step on the other's landmines.

But then there were these moments of unbridled restraint, when the landmines were momentarily shut off and all that existed between us was everything we felt for each other.

We made out until the distant sounds of engines rumbled closer. Even then, I didn't want to disengage, but I did. Something told me being found in my lap was something that might thoroughly embarrass Arrow.

Our lips made a smacking sound when I pulled away. Immediately, he sucked his lower lip into his mouth while large brown eyes stared into me with apprehension.

Such innocence. Such youth.

How did that still live inside him when I knew the complete opposite was also there?

How would I compete with that? How would I resist?

Just that kiss and now the way he sucked his lip… I was slayed.

"As much as I kinda like having you in my lap…" I began, resisting the urge to pull his lip out of his mouth so I could suck it myself. "Company's coming."

The look that brightened the chocolate depths when I first spoke changed to alarm. He slid back, nearly falling off the damn sled as he glanced around for Trent and Drew.

I chuckled, watching him scramble and then plant himself in front of me so he could drive. Slyly, I adjusted my hard-on before settling a little closer and reaching for his waist.

He fired up the snowmobile, and I tentatively wrapped my arms around him. "This okay?" I asked in his ear.

He nodded once, then took off across the snow just as our friends appeared ahead.

The rest of the afternoon, I couldn't turn off my thoughts. However, this time I wasn't lost in my own little world. I wasn't reliving the past or freaking over the ride.

I thought about the few times Arrow reached in and pulled me back, of the times he was patient and just sat there with me wherever I seemed to disappear. Arrow was willing. I saw him try more than once to connect with me.

Perhaps… Maybe… Yeah.

It was time I did the same.

Chapter Twenty-*One*

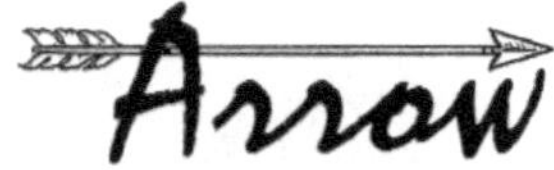

Arrow

Triggers. Life was filled with tiny little triggers.

It was almost impossible to know where they would appear and in what form. But I always knew they were there, sort of like a stalker who shadowed my every move.

Perhaps that was one of the reasons I stayed locked up behind the fence.

It was a controlled environment. A place where the triggers couldn't really reach, a place I wouldn't have to face them.

It caught me off guard today. I wasn't prepared. 'Course, when could anyone ever be?

I'd been focused on Hopper. On whatever triggered him. I knew it was happening I think before he did. I could almost smell it on him, as if the fact that I also sometimes emitted the scent gave me some sort of unique ability to detect it.

Damn, could he drive.

Good drivers weren't really something unusual for me, but he surprised me. Obviously, Hopper had skill with speed. His job practically required it.

This was different.

There was some kind of magic in the way he steered the sled. Almost as if he'd become part of the vehicle, like he sensed the way it would react to every move he made.

And the way he twisted the throttle?

Pure instinct.

If I hadn't seen the way he reacted when we were first presented with the snowmobiles, I would have suspected he drove one all the time.

We had a moment, maybe more, out there in the center of the field where the sky stretched overhead and the snow underfoot.

He wanted me to make him stay. Truth was I had no idea how to pull a man back from the shadows of his past, but I really wanted to kiss him.

Since that first night when I'd attacked his mouth with angry defiance, I wanted more.

A do-over.

A first kiss the way it should have been.

This was that. It was the best fucking kiss I'd ever had.

Until it wasn't.

Until he all but climbed on my lap and everything inside me seized.

The trigger. I craved physical contact, but I also shied away from it. Collateral damage from that night in the alley. Something I thought might fade with time. Hell, it had already been three years.

Three years of barely any contact at all, and what contact there was had been from family.

It was lonely. It played with my mind. It made me want.

I'd never been tempted to act on that want, though, until Hopper showed up on the other side of my fence.

I guess three years hadn't been enough.

I was beginning to wonder if any amount of time would ever assuage the panic I felt when the weight of someone else settled against me.

It was a double-edged sword.

Know why?

Because it reminded me, of course, of the dangers of being too close. Yet it also created an even stronger desire.

But only with Hopper.

The way he reacted floored me. I expected him to be angry, to maybe even call me a freak. He'd pulled back, held up his hands in surrender.

It was the closest thing to a white flag I'd ever seen. Acceptance… that even though he had not one fucking clue I was freaking the piss out, he tried to understand.

Then he reacted. He put me in charge.

It shifted everything inside me. The panic taking over my limbs, the memories of searing pain and being held down.

I kissed him again. Not only because kissing him was something I could survive on for the rest of my life, but because I was so fucking grateful.

And now we were here.

Sitting inside Drew and Trent's house, a place that pretty much fell out of the pages of some magazine.

Ivy, Drew's sister, decorated the place. She was pretty cool, in a bossy way. She tried to give me style tips every time she saw me, and her husband, Braeden, only ever referred to me as the Biebs.

He wasn't the only one.

It was practically a running joke.

When I dyed my hair platinum, the comparisons never ended. Whatever. When people focused on how I looked like someone else, they focused less on who I really was.

The sports channel was on the giant-ass TV hanging above the fireplace. I was sitting in a black leather chair near the gray couch Trent and Drew filled.

Hopper was across from me, on the other side of the coffee table, in a chair of his own.

I chose this chair, not something where anyone else could sit beside me. I needed a little personal space, a little distance after our make-out session.

I was jolted. But I also craved more. And I was afraid of more. So, so afraid.

I knew Hopper was attracted to me. I hadn't the faintest clue why. No one else had ever been. But he was. I felt it—attraction crackled around us.

It wouldn't if he knew.

I knew it was the fastest, most effective way to get rid of him. Sort of like a nuclear weapon when shit became too real.

All I'd need to do was deploy the truth that I was used, damaged goods. And beyond that damage, I was utterly a virgin.

A victim at eighteen. A virgin at twenty-one. Unwanted always.

I was developing an… attachment.

Feelings.

It was beyond dangerous, and I knew it would only end in pain.

I should tell him now, get it over with, and drive him away. But with the intense urge I had to protect him, to shield him from whatever it was that broke him, I couldn't.

How could I protect someone else when I couldn't even protect myself?

But I *could* protect him. By sending him away. Letting him in would only damage him worse.

I was brooding, stewing, becoming more agitated by the minute.

Hell, we'd ordered pizza, and I'd only been able to eat five slices. I held it together, though. I was pretty sure no one else knew the underlying earthquake shaking up my brain.

"I need another beer," Drew announced. "Fratboy?"

Trent grinned up at him from the couch and shook his empty bottle.

Drew snagged it out of his hand, picked up his own empty longneck, and glanced at Hopper.

"I'm good, thanks," he said, holding up his still half-full bottle.

"C'mon, kid." Drew slapped me on the shoulder. "You need a soda."

"I told you not to call me that," I bitched but followed him into the kitchen. It was an open-concept house, so we could still see the TV and part of the living room.

"I know," he quipped as he helped himself to a beer and then set another on the counter for Trent.

He held up a soda, and I shook my head. He held up a water, and I again declined.

"Better do something to dilute that beer in your bloodstream. You can't be driving home until you piss water."

I rolled my eyes. "It was one beer an hour and a half and five slices of pizza ago."

"What's up with that?" Drew closed the fridge and leaned back against the stainless steel. "You usually eat double that."

I shrugged. "Not hungry."

"You're always hungry."

I gave him a look. He returned it.

I held, stubborn. I didn't feel like talking.

"Lorhaven called me," Drew said, watching me.

I made a rude sound. "Of course he did. Is that why I'm here?" I couldn't help it. I doubted everyone's motives, including those of my own friends sometimes. My self-esteem didn't always make it easy to believe people might actually want to hang with me unless my brother ordered them to.

Just like your father used to pay women to blow you.

"Like I'd do anything Lorhaven told me to do." Drew scoffed, pushing off the fridge and stepping up to the stone-topped island.

"So he didn't ask you to talk to me?"

Drew met my eyes. "He said Hopper was bringing some contracts. He was worried about you. Trent and me wanted to hang out. We planned on coming over anyway. Hell, I wasn't even going to mention the contracts, but you've been brooding since you got here."

I believed him. Drew and Trent had proven their friendship on more than one occasion. It was stupid to doubt their motives. It was stupid to look for reasons they were around instead of accepting the fact they really were just friends.

"How'd Lor sound?" I asked. He'd called, but I hadn't called him back yet.

Guess I was avoiding him, too.

"Pissed off you haven't called him back."

"I have a life," I muttered.

"How's it going?" Drew asked. "Two contracts, huh? That's pretty impressive shit."

"Says the man with the first NRR championship under his belt." I scoffed.

Drew smirked. "That makes me an expert on impressive shit."

I grinned.

"Have you made a decision?" Drew cut right to it.

"Still deciding," I answered.

"So you know what you want to do." He pressed.

I shrugged.

"You and Hopper seem to be getting along."

I glanced back into the living room where Hopper sat. "Yeah."

Drew made a noise. "I've had better conversations with a rock."

"How do you know what the right thing to do is?" I asked. If he wanted to talk, I could talk. Hell, I respected Drew. I considered him a friend.

"You don't really," he replied, honest. "But in my experience, the right thing is the one that scares you the most."

"Everything scares me," I whispered.

"Trent scared me the most." Drew confided, his voice low. "Some days he still scares the shit out of me."

I gaped at him. "Seriously?"

His mouth tilted up on one side. "Hells yeah. But if I had listened to the fear when I first realized we were more than just friends, I'd have missed out on a lot of really good shit."

"Your father disowned you, didn't he?" I asked. I probably shouldn't have asked, but it was on my mind, apparently a lot more than I realized.

His blue eyes darkened. They were a much deeper shade than Hopper's. I preferred the crystal shade to Drew's.

"Yeah, he did. The day I told him about me and T." Obviously, this was still something that wounded him.

In a sick way, knowing someone as together as Drew, someone who had so much, wasn't immune to the same pain as everyone else gave me a little bit of hope.

I swallowed. "My father disowned me, too."

He nodded. "Some people have small minds. They can't accept anything they don't understand. It doesn't make it any easier knowing that, but it's something."

I nodded once. "It's something."

Drew stepped a little closer, until his middle hit the counter between us. One of his palms pressed against the sleek top. "It's why when you find people who care about you anyway, you have to hold on. Even when whatever you're reaching for has the power to destroy you."

"I can't go against Lor," I said.

"Lorhaven is a lot of things. Specifically, a giant ass."

I narrowed my eyes because he was insulting my brother, but Drew held up his hand and yawned.

Clearly, I was very threatening.

That pissed me off. I needed to work on that.

"But." Drew went on. "He's a good brother, and he just wants you to be happy."

"I want to sign with NASCAR," I whispered quickly. It was the first time I'd said it out loud.

Drew smiled. "Then sign with NASCAR. I can't wait to watch you smoke them all."

I scoffed. "I think I need some more practice for that."

"We'll make sure you get it."

Something warm bloomed in my stomach, but I pushed it back. "Do you think it's a mistake? After everything that happened with Joey?"

He considered my words, then slowly shook his head. "I think it's an opportunity. Shit's changing over there. It's a good time to step in. Besides, you'll have people watching your back." His eyes slid toward the living room.

"He was watching Joey's back, too," I pointed out, not wanting to totally disregard the elephant in the room.

Drew made a dismissive sound. "That was different, and you and I both know it."

I nodded. I did know. I didn't blame Hopper for what happened with Joey. I didn't blame him even a little.

"Look," Drew said, looking a little like he swallowed a marshmallow whole and he was trying not to choke. "I know shit is stirring between you and Hopper. Even a blind man would see it. Hell, you two have been staring at each other for months and months when you thought no one else was looking."

Embarrassment crawled up the back of my neck. I thought I'd been sly about that. I didn't think anyone noticed.

"Take it from someone who's been there. Fighting against it only makes it harder."

I nodded, really taking in what he was saying. I wasn't necessarily fighting against the feelings I had for Hopper, though. They were there; the fight was already lost.

But I was trying to keep myself from getting hurt.

"You're going to hurt either way, man. Might as well reach for something that makes the pain more bearable."

It was like a punch to the gut, like a sack in the middle, and all the air was stolen from my lungs. He was right.

Drew came around the counter and slapped me on the back. "Enough of this talking shit. I think you're catching what I'm throwing down."

"Don't say that ever again," I told him. I shook my head sadly. So lame.

He laughed. "Seriously, though, anytime you want to talk, no judgement, no expectations, I'm here for you. Trent is, too. You're always welcome here, Arrow, and we'll always have your back."

Well, shit.

Between the kiss with Hopper and this damn near Nicholas Sparks movie in Drew's kitchen, I was feeling pretty fucking see-through.

On one hand, it was good. I knew I didn't need Drew's permission for any of the decisions I would make, but his understanding gave me a boost of confidence.

On the other, I felt more vulnerable than ever.

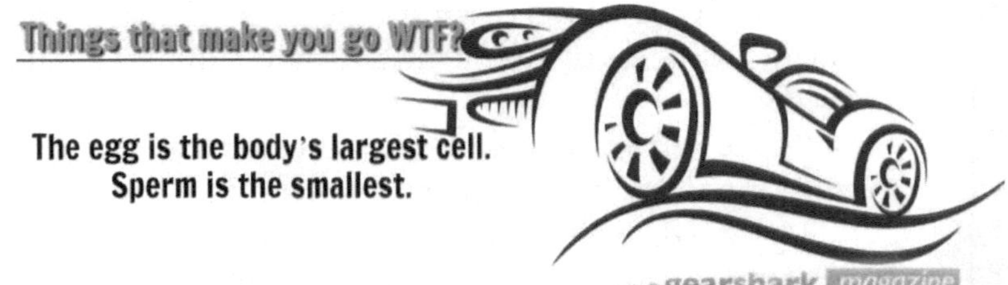

Chapter Twenty-Two

Hopper

I wondered what was taking so long.

I glanced toward the kitchen for the millionth time since Arrow disappeared around the corner with Drew.

It was sort of driving me crazy.

It also drove me crazy he was on the other side of the room all this time. All I could think about was having him against me on the sled. And, of course, the way he'd reacted when I got really close.

Trent made a sound, a sort of muffled laugh. I glanced over to where he was sprawled on the couch. He was watching me like he knew what was going on inside my head. It was disconcerting.

It was one thing when Arrow read me. I liked it. But Trent? Dude needed to stay the hell out of my head.

"You know no one in this house blames you for what went down with Joey," he said, point blank.

My head tilted. "I thought everyone blamed me."

He smirked. "Just Lorhaven."

"Seriously? Here I thought he was my biggest fan." I cracked.

Trent snorted. Like for real snorted.

Where the fuck did he learn that?

"Thanks for telling me," I said sincerely. It actually meant something to me, and I wanted him to know it. I'd been isolated a long time since Matt, but even more so since what happened with Joey.

"I had fun today," he responded, glancing at me before turning back to the TV. "We'll have to do it again."

The thought of that pretty much made me want to hurl. Instead of readily agreeing, I just nodded.

"He really likes you," Trent said after a moment, his voice lower than before.

My gaze drifted back toward the kitchen. I heard lowered voices but couldn't make out what they said.

I glanced back at Trent. He had a strong profile and an even stronger-looking body. "I like him, too," I admitted. Even as I did, guilt threatened to strangle me.

"Good," Trent answered. I felt his stare, so I met it directly. "Because if you hurt him," Trent vowed, "I'll fucking break your neck."

"I'll let you," I replied.

We went back to watching TV.

Chapter Twenty-Three

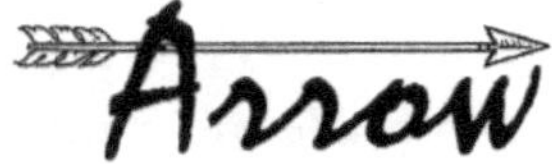

Arrow

Open the gate.

It took me a second to read the text because my vision was blurry and my brain was still partly asleep. What the hell time was it?

Too fucking early to get out of bed. Hell, I was surprised I even heard my phone go off. It chimed again.

I have coffee. And food.

Ooh. Well, that was enticing. With a groan, I rolled out of bed and winced when the cold concrete hit my bare feet, but I kept going, found the remote, and hit it so the gate would swing open. Then I dove back in bed to claim a few last moments of sleep.

'Course, sleep was long gone.

Hopper was here. I anticipated him walking through the door like a plant anticipated the rain on a cloudy day.

Outside, I heard the purr of his engine. I could tell he'd parked it beside the hangar this time, near the side door, because the large garage wasn't open.

I yawned and rubbed a hand over my face, pushing the long strands of hair out of my eyes.

The side door opened, the metal around it groaning. Heavy footfalls echoed from out near the Camaro. Then he stepped around the heater. His icy stare came right to the bed.

He looked good dressed in an army-green jacket and the same color hat. This time he wore it the regular way, not backward, so the brim shaded his eyes.

"It's ten in the morning," he said, gruff, still staring. I couldn't see the look in his eyes because of the hat. However, clearly he thought I shouldn't still be sleeping.

I wondered what he would say if I told him my exhaustion was his fault. After I'd gotten back from Trent and Drew's, I lay in bed and stewed for hours about the stuff Drew said, about Hopper… and about the way I reacted when he got really close.

I yawned.

He chuckled (a sound I liked) and came forward to hold out a brown paper sack and a large box of donuts. "Figured you were hungry."

I sat up so the blankets fell around my waist and grabbed the bag out of his hand. "Starved." I stuck my face in the bag and inhaled the scent of ham, egg, and melted cheese. "Thank you." My voice was muffled because my face was still in the bag.

"Anytime."

Without waiting, I yanked the sandwich out of the bag, unwrapped it, and took a huge bite. It was heaven.

He was watching me. I felt very… visible. I paused in chewing. "You want some?"

He shook his head. "I ate." Then he held out the box of donuts and the drink carrier with two coffees perched on top.

I yanked the rolling toolbox I used as a nightstand from around the head of the bed and parked it in front of me. Hopper set down the box, then moved the coffees off the top.

"Have a seat," I offered, gesturing to the end of the bed.

He glanced around quickly, looking for another chair, but there wasn't one.

I took another bite of the sandwich while he debated. After a moment, he lowered himself, bringing his coffee with him.

I polished off the sandwich and went for the box of donuts, flinging open the lid. I snagged a blueberry cake and welcomed it into my mouth.

"You always eat like this?" he asked, amused.

"Like what?" I asked, shoving in another bite.

"Like you might never eat again."

I shrugged and finished the donut, going in for a glazed. "I didn't eat much last night."

"You had five pieces of pizza." He countered.

I glanced up. "You counted?"

His eyes averted. Suddenly, he was very interested in his coffee.

I let it go, even though secretly I was kinda pleased he was so aware of me. No one really ever paid attention to my details before. "I have a high metabolism."

"You're young," he said, still not looking my way.

I lowered the donut. "Not as young as you might think."

"I've got a good five years on you. Maybe a little more."

"Think our age difference matters?" I asked honestly. I swore if he told me I was a kid, I'd nut punch him right there.

The thought totally distracted me. Thinking about touching his sack kinda turned me on.

I felt his gaze from beneath the brim of his hat. I wanted to rip it off so I could see the icy depths of his eyes. It helped me read him. His eyes were like a compass for me, pointing me in the direction I needed to go.

"No, I don't."

Good news. I went back to eating. When the donut was gone, I reached for my coffee, taking a sip of the strong, dark brew. I felt his eyes again, hotter than the drink. I peeked up, over the rim of the cup. He was still staring, but not at my face.

He was studying my tattoos, glancing over the sleeve and staring at my chest. The last time I was shirtless in front of him, he looked at the tattoos, too. I wondered if he hated them. Or if maybe they turned him on.

"You have any tattoos?" I asked.

"One." He cleared his throat. "They look good on you."

My stomach dipped. "Thanks."

"You know," he said after a minute and when I was halfway done with my third donut. "The NASCAR contract comes with an apartment."

I paused in chewing. "It does?"

He nodded. "At headquarters, right there by the track."

"It really bothers you that I live here, doesn't it?"

His eyes met mine. "Honestly?"

I nodded.

"I fucking hate it."

"Why?"

"You deserve better," he growled.

I set aside my coffee. "Maybe I don't."

An impatient, angry sound ripped from his throat. Hopper leaned forward so he could set his coffee beside mine. Instead of pulling all the way back, his hands fell to the mattress on either side of my hips.

I felt his stare, but it was too shadowed to see.

Bravely, I reached up and pulled the hat off his head. Dark, wavy strands sprang free over his forehead.

The look in his eyes was intense. It didn't waver. I drew back slightly. He was crowding my space, looking at me with so much intensity. I liked it, but it also made me uncomfortable.

He shook his head once. "Don't," he whispered.

"What?"

"Pull away."

"I'm not," I argued.

"You are."

He leaned forward more, closing the small amount of distance I'd gained. My hands started to shake a little; the muscles in my back tensed. I fought it, though, because beyond the panic, beyond the nerves, there was intense desire.

He was coming for me, or at least that's the way it felt in that moment.

"I'm not real good with closeness," I murmured.

"Felt pretty fucking good yesterday." He countered.

My eyes shot up.

He watched me watch him as he slowly lifted his hand and pushed his fingers through my hair. "You gonna let me kiss you right now?" he murmured.

My voice shook. "If I say no?"

He backed away, still watching me without any kind of anger or disgust on his face.

I caught his wrist. "Yes."

The space between us became nonexistent when he dove in swiftly but connected our lips gently. He was kissing me. *Kissing me.* It wasn't the first time we kissed, but that's how it felt because he was the one who made the move.

Maybe it didn't seem like that big of a deal, but for me it was everything.

It meant he wanted *me*. I was wanted.

My chest hitched as our lips caressed. He pulled back just enough to look at me with an unspoken question in his eyes.

"Don't stop," I whispered.

His hand curled around the back of my neck and tugged me close again. I let him take the lead, even though I felt vulnerable as fuck. I hoped he couldn't feel the way my lips trembled. I didn't want him to think I was weak.

The tip of his tongue stroked my lower lip, tentatively asking to be let in. It was scary to let someone in. In your heart. In your mind. In your body.

I did it anyway. My lips parted to make room for his silky tongue. He felt so good, so natural, and like something I'd never tasted before. His hand was on the back of my head now, in my hair, and small goose bumps raced down my arms and over my chest. I felt my nipples harden, and I wanted so badly to just succumb.

Desire enclosed me, so did a sense of security I wholly wanted to embrace.

Maybe that was why my body trembled, because it was fighting against my brain. My head was telling me to slow my roll, to back up and beware of danger. My skin, though, it hummed for more.

Hopper's tongue stroked slowly over mine. Then he pulled back and sucked my lower lip into his mouth. He groaned as he sucked, the sound and gentle pressure a double assault.

When at last he released my lip, he tipped his head and went for the upper. It slid between his lips just as easily as the other, and I scooted a little closer on the mattress.

The hand in my hair slid down, his fingers dragging over my arm and down to my wrist. So far I'd barely moved, other than my lips and tongue of course. My hands hadn't roamed his body, though I was tempted.

I wasn't exactly rigid; kissing Hopper made me feel too languid for that.

His fingers threaded through mine; our hands linked together.

I jerked back, unlocked our lips, and glanced down to where our hands were threaded.

I stared at the difference between our skin while the very tip of my tongue darted out to get another taste of him off my lips. His hand was thicker than mine, the skin rougher. My hands weren't exactly baby soft—I spent too much time under the hood of a car— but they did seem smoother, longer, and leaner.

The nails at the tips of his fingers were short and blunt, while some of mine were slightly jagged from being bitten.

My hands weren't as pretty as his. I'd never tell him out loud I thought they were pretty. I guess they really weren't, not in the eyes of the world. He had man hands, working hands. Complete with some hair on the back.

To me, though, they were pretty. Because his was holding mine.

"A?" he asked. I watched the pad of his thumb stroke the back of my hand.

I shivered.

"I'm sorry," I whispered, embarrassed yet unable to tear my eyes away from our physical connection.

"Don't ever be sorry, not to me," he said passionately. "Whatever you are is okay."

I lifted my eyes, seeing truth in the depths of his.

"No one's ever held my hand before." It was the truth but also a challenge. He might say whatever I am was okay… until he found out what exactly the whatever was.

He reacted, though I knew he tried not to. The dark lashes that lined his eyes widened, shock filling his stare. He banked the expression almost as soon as it arrived, but even still, I watched him process, trying to understand.

"Ever?" he asked.

"Ever." I confirmed. The back of my neck burned with shame, but even that wasn't enough to force me to reclaim my hand.

Such a simple thing, contact most people took for granted.

Hopper pushed up off the hand he leaned on, sitting back a little. His free hand reached for mine, and our fingers entwined.

"Think we could entwine our toes?" he asked, a playful smile turning his features bright.

"Why would we want to?" I made a face, but he got to me.

Oh, he was getting to me. Deeper than ever before.

His eyes sparkled with laughter, and I realized there was a dimple beneath the stubble on his jaw. He made a sound, the laughter in his eyes faded away, and I watched, partly stricken, as he lifted our entwined hands and kissed the back of my fingers.

After he lifted his lips, he used his unshaven chin to graze over the spot he kissed, like he was making sure to rub it in.

My heartbeat tripped and rolled beneath my ribs.

Still holding both my hands, he leaned back in. This time I met him halfway. Our lips collided again in a searing, too-short kiss.

"You taste like a donut." He half smiled.

You taste like a second chance.

I didn't say anything for fear my thought would tumble out. We sat there for a while, holding hands, nothing more. Eventually, he pulled one hand free and swiped his thumb over my lower lip.

It was sensory overload. It felt too good, his touch… His *affection* was too wanted.

I pulled back, tugging my hands free of his. He let them go, and I regretted it almost instantly. I shoved back the blankets and stood. My emoji pajama bottoms brushed the tops of my bare feet.

I needed a minute to breathe, a second to get myself together.

"I gotta piss," I grumbled and took off for the bathroom without looking back.

I stared at myself in the tiny mirror. I still looked the same as yesterday and the day before that.

But I felt different.

More alive. More excited about life.

It was scary, and maybe just a few days ago, more specifically before Hopper appeared on the other side of that fence, I would have snuffed out that spark of life. I would have run scared.

Part of me still really, really wanted to do that. My fingers still trembled with need.

But they didn't tremble when Hopper held them.

That was something. More than something.

I stepped away from the mirror and took a piss. As I did, I glanced around the tiny bathroom with no real mirror, no counter space, and a poor excuse for a shower.

I needed more than this.

I needed to let myself out of this cage.

Maybe an apartment at headquarters was a good start.

Resolve solidified inside me. As I washed my hands, anticipation curled my toes. Or maybe it was the cold-ass floor against my bare feet.

Nah. It was anticipation.

I was going to sign with NASCAR.

For so many years now, I literally thought life would amount to nothing and that was exactly what I deserved.

Gradually, over the past several months, changes started to bloom inside me. Small at first. I found a friend in Drew. Then in Trent. I saw two men in love make it work, and there was no abuse, no fear… just love.

Lorhaven fell in love—something I thought was impossible. Joey accepted me without pause, and I gained a sister. Lorhaven started driving for the NRR and encouraged me to try out for Gamble.

All this time, I'd been building a life. A life just waiting for me to take a chance and join it. Without realizing it, I was healing. I would never be the way I was back when I was Dylan.

I didn't want to be him.

But I didn't want to be who I was now either.

I wanted to be a hybrid. Me now… just happy.

I didn't think I'd ever be whole, but a little less broken might be nice.

I shut off the water and dried my hands. The sound of muffled voices came through the bathroom door. My nose wrinkled, and I tilted my head to the side to listen.

Was Hopp talking to himself out there?

All of a sudden, a yell cut through the garage, followed by a grunt and then the definite sound of a struggle.

Panic sliced through me. It was sharp and reminiscent of the past. Something new rose to match it, though.

Resolve to protect something I loved.

I ripped open the bathroom door and charged out into the fight.

Someone was messing with Hopper, and that someone was going to pay.

Chapter Twenty-*Four*

His nerves calmed mine.

The tremble in his hands made mine more steady.

Arrow brought out something in me I thought was long gone. Well, okay, he brought out more than one thing, but the most surprising was compassion.

I cared about him despite trying not to.

I told myself I came here this morning to talk contracts, to get a signature. Gamble was waiting to hear the word. He called and reminded me at the ass crack of dawn.

As I swung through a drive-thru for coffee and copious amounts of food, it became harder to lie to myself.

I wasn't just coming over here for business.

It was pleasure, too.

When I walked in the garage and saw him sprawled out in the too-small bed, yet again without a shirt, his sleeve of ink on full display, the lie I still clung to laughed right in my face.

I'd come here to see him. If the contract was already signed, I'd have found another excuse.

I hated whatever made him think he wasn't good enough. I hated the fact he lived in this dump. I hated the scars I felt on his wrist.

So careful... I had to be so careful with him.

Sitting next to Arrow, going in for a kiss, was sort of like walking across a floor covered with shattered glass. The shards would absolutely pierce me; they would even draw blood.

I kept walking anyway.

I knew what it felt like to be cut deep, and I knew without a doubt, every time he stepped close to me, he walked over the same broken glass.

God, the way he responded when I kissed him. Timid but eager. Entranced but guarded. He felt so much, more than quite possibly anyone I'd ever known. The way he'd looked at me when I held his hands. Awe. He'd been in awe of me for doing barely anything at all.

It inspired me. It challenged me to give him so much more.

He'd become overwhelmed quickly, though, an expression I knew well because I'd worn it so many times myself. I watched his bare back retreat, and the second he disappeared behind the bathroom door, I shot up from the bed and paced away.

The guilt was instantaneous. It was never far, but sometimes, especially when Arrow was close enough to touch, it didn't swallow me whole.

He wasn't beside me right now, and though I still wanted him, the guilt was taking over.

I felt as though I'd betrayed Matt today. No. Not just today. Every day since I got here. I made a promise to him and a vow to myself.

Infinity.

My heart. My loyalty and the memories of us were forever. Why should I get to move on when he was frozen in time?

By a death that had been meant for me.

Holy shit, if I'd only been on the Ducati that day. If only I hadn't hit my head.

I wouldn't be here right now. Maybe I'd be in Matt's place, or maybe I'd have kept control and walked away. Maybe I'd be an international Motocross star. Maybe Matt would be, too. Maybe we'd still be together. Maybe we'd be happy.

Maybe.

What a cruel fucking word. It was torment wondering what would have been.

I asked myself why every single day.

I never had an answer, and I likely never would.

Perhaps between yesterday with the snowmobiles and then this morning with the intimacy (Because that's what it was. It hadn't been just a kiss this morning; it had been so much more.), it was too much, not just for me, but also for him. I should have left and come back in a couple days when the world tilted back again, tilted back to the way it was supposed to be.

Lonely and cold.

I could make an excuse to Gamble, spin it in a way that didn't make it look like Arrow was stalling. I didn't want to hurt his career because there were things between us neither of us knew what to do with.

The sound of a door opening and closing brought me around. When Arrow didn't fill my line of sight, I frowned at the bathroom door.

Heavy, quick footfalls rushed in behind me, and I swung around just as Lorhaven barreled around the heater toward the back of the garage. "Who the fuck's car is—" He stopped when he saw me. His eyes narrowed into slits. "What the fuck are you doing here?"

It was the world's worst secret that Arrow's brother hated me. Honestly, I didn't really blame him. The woman he loved got hurt, and it was my fault.

I couldn't be mad at him for hating me, not when I hated myself.

I'd never harbored any ill will toward Lorhaven, not even when he hurled harsh words at me on behalf of Joey. Sure, he was rough around the edges (read that as: he was an asshole), but life likely made him that way, just as life made me the way I was.

However…

Looking at him now, standing in the middle of an airplane hangar where he allowed his brother to live?

Fury ignited. I no longer saw just an asshole life made. I saw a man who had the ability to protect Arrow and did a piss poor job.

"What the fuck business is it of yours?" I snapped back.

Lorhaven's narrowed eyes widened. "Excuse me?"

"I didn't stutter."

He took a step toward me. "If it concerns my brother, then it's my fucking business."

"You mean the brother you let live in this fucking hellhole?" I growled, all the muscles in my back tensing.

Lorhaven's face darkened. His eyes swung around, pausing on the bed, which clearly had just been vacated. I shifted a little so he could take in the two coffees and the breakfast right beside the mattress.

He made a strangled sound. "You better not have touched him."

I smirked.

He rushed me, but I was ready. Hell, I was primed for a fight. All the pent-up aggression inside me roared to get out, and seeing him here, in the middle of this space, well… He lit the fuse.

I ducked under his fist when he threw it out, hooking my arms around his middle, and ran until we collided with a stack of tires near the wall. The top one fell off, and both of us tumbled but didn't fall.

Lorhaven shoved me backward, and before I could right myself, he caught me with a right hook. My head snapped back, pain exploded, but I ignored it and delivered a punch of my own to his middle.

The sound of breath whooshing out of him was pretty satisfactory, so I buried my fist again.

I swung a third time, but he blocked the hit and came in with a low punch of his own, right into my side.

Blows started flying rapidly then. Some connected; some didn't. We went at each other like two caged tigers who'd been starved and the winner got a steak.

As we fought, we knocked into a table. Tools scattered all over the floor, and someone behind me shouted my name.

"Hopper!" Arrow roared, but beneath the anger, I heard his panic. I felt his anxiety.

I stopped battling Lorhaven instantly, swinging around to assure him everything was fine. Lorhaven didn't stop, though. He swept out his leg and knocked my feet out from under me. I fell back, hitting the concrete with a considerable, *"Oomph."*

Adrenaline pumped through my limbs; retaliation sang in my veins. Lorhaven lunged toward me like he thought he had the upper hand now that I was down.

Stupid fucker. I knew how to fight better than most when I was down.

In a blur of movement, Arrow appeared. He literally jumped in front of me and shoved his brother with both hands. "Back off!" he growled in a tone I'd never heard from him before.

I forgot about Lorhaven, the fight, and everything in between. All I saw was Arrow, all six feet one inch of him planted in front of me in a fighter's stance. All the muscles in his back were bunched, his hands were fisted, and the muscles beneath the sleeve of tattoos down his arm rippled.

He was fucking sexy.

He was about to throw down with his own brother to protect me.

He was still wearing pants covered with emojis.

And that right there explained Arrow to a T. Innocent enough to sleep in emoji pants, but beneath it all was a man made of steel who, when push came to shove, would come out swinging.

"Arrow…" Lorhaven gasped, partially out of breath from our rumble but also from shock. Clearly, he'd never been challenged by his brother before.

"Don't fucking touch him again, Jace!" Arrow warned.

I definitely didn't need him to protect me. But the fact that he intended to?

Realization hit me like a gallon of frigid water.

That question I thought I'd never have an answer to? *Why?*

I had one.

It was him.

It was Arrow.

Chapter Twenty-*Five*

There was a look on my brother's face I hadn't seen before.

Well, not directed at me anyway.

The second I heard the struggle, I barged out of the bathroom, and by then it had turn into a full-blown fight.

Tools scattered, fists were flying, and the sound of flesh against flesh turned my stomach. It reminded me of the past, of something I didn't even witness, but it didn't matter because that unwitnessed event reminded me of greater shit that went down that night.

Shit I was all too present for.

I loved Lorhaven. I really did. More than anyone else on this planet. But the second I saw his fist connect with Hopper's face, something inside me screamed.

I raced across the room, forgoing the sick feeling and pushing past the memories. Hopper hit the floor, and I panicked. Lorhaven was a beast. I knew exactly what he was capable of.

I lunged between them, planting myself right in front of Hopp. "Back off!" I intoned. No way was this fight going to happen. No way would I stand by and watch.

Lorhaven's eyes flicked to me with surprise, but then he looked over my shoulder at the man behind me.

"Don't fucking touch him again, Jace!" I yelled, bringing his focus back to me.

That's when the shock took over his face. The genuine confusion that I would challenge him. I never had before. I let him fight my battles.

Not today.

Not ever again.

My battles were now my own.

Beyond the surprise, I saw a pinch of hurt. As if he felt betrayed. I didn't want that. It was the last fucking thing I wanted.

Well, second to last, because the very last thing I wanted was Hopper getting pounded by my unrelenting brother.

"What the fuck is he doing here?" Lor asked, his breath heavy. As he stared at me, he swiped his mouth with the back of his hand.

I caught his stare wandering accusingly toward the man I was guarding. I stepped over a little farther, just to send the message I wasn't fucking around.

I'd never win in a fight against my brother. No way in hell. In fact, if it came down to it, I probably wouldn't fight him. But he wouldn't fight me either.

I trusted him, more than anyone else, and he trusted me.

But I'd deck him if I had to.

He raised an eyebrow, regarding me with some derision. "Are you protecting him?"

"Yes," I replied, unflinching.

"I don't need protection." Hopper inserted.

I didn't turn to look at him. Lor acted like he wasn't there.

Lorhaven looked over at my bed, then back at me. He literally appeared as if he swallowed an entire lemon.

"I thought you weren't coming home for a few more days?" I asked, trying to distract him.

"Yeah, well, when some asshole comes sniffing around, trying to take advantage of my brother, I cut my business short."

"So you can boss him around, but not make sure he has fucking heat in the winter?" Hopper spat.

"He has heat," Lorhaven growled.

Hopper made a disgusted sound. "Yeah, from a box that plugs into the wall!"

"You accusing me of something?" Lor challenged, taking a threatening step forward.

Behind me, Hopper's body heat connected with mine. "I don't have to accuse. The evidence is right in front of your face." His chest bumped into my shoulder when he spoke.

I turned sideways so my back wasn't to either man. I pressed my palm to the center of Hopper's chest and was momentarily distracted by the feel of his heart thumping beneath my skin.

I glanced down to where I touched him. I wished he wasn't wearing a shirt.

I wished I could see him, just once, without it.

"Arrow," Lorhaven growled, like me standing there touching Hopper was going to send him through the roof.

I tore my eyes from his chest and up to his face. "Calm down," I murmured. "I live here because I want to. Jace doesn't like it either."

Hopper turned his head and glanced away from me. He wasn't buying what I was selling.

There was blood smeared on the side of his lip. It streaked into his stubble from where he obviously tried to brush it away.

I made a sound, grabbed his chin, and squeezed. "You're bleeding," I spat. Then I whipped around to Jace. "He's fucking bleeding!"

"It's barely a scratch." Jace scoffed.

I loathed the sight of blood on his face. It physically hurt. The sight of blood at all wasn't something I enjoyed. Ever since that night… and then the one later…

Blood stood for too much in my mind, and none of it was good.

"He split your lip," I told Hopper, fully turning to face him again. I reached for the hem of my shirt to dab away the red, but I wasn't wearing one.

He grunted. "It's fine. I got in a few punches of my own."

I didn't say anything. Instead, I used my thumb to swipe at the blood. My finger came away red, and for a moment I stared at the smear, dumbstruck. Transported back in time. To another place.

Hopper's hand wrapped around my wrist. "Arrow."

"Don't fucking touch him!" Lorhaven roared and jumped forward, wrapping his arm around my waist and towing me back.

Hopper's hand fell away.

It snapped me out of it.

I jerked away from my brother and spun, advancing on him. "What the fuck is your problem, Jace?"

"He's taking advantage of you."

"You know why I'm here," Hopper said without heat. "I know Gamble called you."

"So you came to check up on me?" I asked, angry. "You came to make sure I wasn't making the wrong decision with *my* life?"

Lorhaven drew back like I'd decked him. "I came because I thought you needed me."

That took the anger right out of me. What the fuck was I doing yelling at my brother? The only person who'd been there for me through everything.

Caught in the middle. That was me right now.

I didn't much care for it.

"I do," I told Jace. Then with a sigh, I turned toward Hopper.

"I'll, ah, go. Give you guys some room."

"I don't want you to go," I said instantly.

Behind me, I heard Lorhaven's indrawn breath.

Hopper's light eyes widened.

"Maybe just give us a few?" I asked, hoping he would understand. I didn't want him to feel like I was choosing.

But I also wanted to smooth things out with my brother without the pair of them snarling at each other over every other word.

Hopper's eyes bounced between mine. Then he relented. "Sure." He produced the keys to his Audi from his pocket. "I'll go sit in my car. Handle a few calls I need to make."

I followed him to the door and then out. Instantly, my nipples hardened against the frigid air.

"What the fuck are you doing?" Hopper bitched. "It's below freezing out here."

"You're not leaving, are you?" I asked, feeling stupid and vulnerable.

"Leave you here with that asshole? No way."

"He's not that bad." I scoffed. I reached up to wipe at the blood still on his lip.

Our eyes connected. "You're close to him," he stated.

I nodded, rubbing my thumb over the prickly yet soft stubble lining his jaw.

"You got between us, though, went up against him." He shifted a little closer, his body blocking the coldest of the wind.

"Yeah, I did."

"Do you regret it?" he asked.

Was that vulnerability in his voice?

"I'd do it again."

The icy quality to his eyes warmed. He leaned closer, palmed the back of my head, and pressed his lips to my hairline. My eyes closed. Affection wasn't something I was used to. I took it straight to my heart because I didn't know where else to put it.

"Go back inside. Your sack is gonna freeze." With every word he spoke, his lips brushed over my forehead.

I grinned.

Hopper pulled away, a half smile tugging his lips. He gestured toward the door with his chin. "I'll still be here when you're done."

When I was at the door, he called to me. "Hey, A?"

I glanced around.

"Put on a shirt, would you? You're driving me crazy."

I was smiling when I stepped inside.

Lorhaven stood there, just feet from the door, scowling. "What. The. Actual. Fuck?"

"Where's Joey?" I asked, moving farther into the room, toward my dresser for some clothes. Following Hopper out into the freezing weather seemed like a good idea at the time.

Now I was just going to low-key freeze to death.

"She's still out of town, doing interviews. I took the jet. I gotta be back later today. Grab some shit. You can come with."

I glanced up from the open drawer. "No."

Jace raised an eyebrow. "No?"

"I have shit here to do."

"You better not be talking about that douche."

I pulled out a black T-shirt and tugged it over my head. "He's not a douche." Then I rummaged around for a red-and-black flannel, which was well worn and well loved. It was also warm.

"Need I remind you what he did to Josie?" Lor asked, smug.

Both my arms slid into the flannel at the same time, and the fabric fell around my body. I left it unbuttoned and reached in for a pair of black jeans.

I shoved my hair out of my face and made a sound. "What happened to Joey wasn't his fault."

Lor scoffed. "Is that what he's saying?"

"No. He didn't say anything," I rebutted. Sure, we talked about Joey briefly, but it wasn't even anything worth mentioning. If anything, Hopper agreed with my brother about his guilt.

"Because he's fucking guilty." Lor persisted.

"He is not," I snapped. "He ain't the first person to make a mistake either."

Jace stalked in the room and stared down at the two Styrofoam cups and box of donuts. "Why are you defending him?"

I finished dressing, pulled on some socks, then reached for my black high-tops. "I like him."

He sucked in a breath. "You don't know him."

I shook my head. "I know more than you think. We have an… understanding of each other."

"I know he's got some kind of past." Lorhaven began emphatically. "Joey eluded to that much. But, A… What you went through, not many people can understand that."

"But you do?" I challenged.

"I was here," he shot out. "I found you that night, right over there." His voice cracked when he swung and pointed to the farthest corner in the room. "Bloody. Beaten so bad I wondered if your face would ever be the same. Your clothes were ripped, some even missing. And your fingertips." His voice went hoarse. "They were rubbed raw, like you'd been clawing at something, like you fought so long it literally ripped off your skin."

The brick wall. They pinned me behind the dumpster right by the brick wall.

The putrid smells from the dumpster still wafted up my nose sometimes. I could smell it right then, the spoiled food, animal waste, and week-old garbage. I clawed at the bricks. I tried to get away. I tried to run. I couldn't get away.

"You were damn near catatonic." Jace continued, jolting me out of the horrid memory. "You couldn't walk, and when I tried to help you, clean you up…"

It was the first time he'd ever gone into detail or so much as hinted at the way he perceived the night he found me. I'd never asked because, honestly, just trying to handle my version of that night was more than enough.

I waited for the pain to slice me. For the mind-numbing panic to wipe out the rest of my thought.

Neither came.

"I what?" I pressed.

"You flinched away." It seemed that was the worst for him. It made me feel incredibly guilty for my own desires. Lorhaven had given up a lot for me. It seemed disloyal to want things I knew he wouldn't approve of.

It was wrong of me to act like Lorhaven couldn't understand. He didn't, at least not from my perspective or at the physical level of what I endured. But he *was* haunted as well; that was evident in the vivid way he spoke of that night and the hollow tone in his voice.

"If only I'd answered my phone," he groaned. "If only I'd been there."

"What happened to me wasn't your fault, Jace," I said, using the name very few did. I hoped it made my words sincerer. "And you've been there for me since. I wouldn't have survived without you."

His eyes flashed up, stark pain and fear echoing through his dark stare. I knew he was remembering that night. The other night that came months after my rape.

We never talked about it, but it was always in the room with us.

It was time to put it to rest.

"I've put you through a lot." I began. Jace stiffened and opened his trap to argue. I held up my hand. "Listen," I demanded.

He relented.

"Not only did you find me that night, but you found me again, the night I tried to kill myself."

"You don't have to talk about it."

"Yes, I do." I insisted. "It's brought us here. And it's holding us back, holding *me* back."

Jace went over to a large tool chest and leaned against it. "All right."

"I hit rock bottom. And I stayed there for a long time. As lousy as it was, it was better than where I'd been, you know?"

He nodded.

"I let you take responsibility for me. I let you take over my life." He stiffened, and I rushed on to say, "I'm grateful you did. I'm grateful for you."

The confrontational look in his face drained away. Left was just my brother, the one I knew best. The one who in recent years had become more like a dad to me than anything else.

Yes. A dad. Not a father.

There was a difference.

"I needed it. I lost everything." My voice went hoarse. Emotion, memories, and feelings that haunted me still rose up. But I kept going. I couldn't shove this shit down anymore. It was leaking out of my pores, out in my behavior (or lack thereof), and holding me down.

"My future. My home. My family. Hell, even my past. It was like Dad just completely erased me. Dylan died. Arrow was born." I paused, sucking in a breath. "But I still had you. You stuck by my side. Not only did you accept me for who I was, but you shared your money with me. You gave me a place to live. You taught me about driving, about cars."

"You're my brother," he said simply, like that trumped everything.

"Yeah, but Dad taught me blood isn't always everything."

"Dad is a giant dick," Lorhaven announced.

We both snickered.

"You loved me when no one else did."

"Donna loves you," Lorhaven insisted. "Hell, she left Dad because of the bullshit he pulled."

My mother did love me, and I loved her. I still saw her to this day. I spent holidays and birthdays at her house.

But it was different.

Mom loved me, but it was Lorhaven I depended on. She just wasn't as strong as him.

"I love you," I told him. I wasn't sure how many times I'd told him. I could count them on one hand. I didn't recall ever coming right out and stating it so bluntly.

My father would tell me saying that made me weak. He'd tell me I was being "gay" because I admitted how I felt.

Screw him.

"Thank you. Thank you for being more of a dad to me than our own father ever was."

Jace shifted from foot to foot. He sniffed, and I hid a smile. I'd gotten to him.

"Why does it feel like you're breaking up with me?"

I laughed.

"It's not you; it's me." I joked.

He rolled his eyes. But then his lips twitched. "Of course it's not me. I'm fucking perfect."

"I need to take responsibility for myself now. For my own life. I can't do that when I'm hiding in your shadow."

"You were never hiding," he rebutted softly.

"I was. I am. And it's okay because I needed that time. You gave it to me. But now I need to make choices and take risks. That's what life is. It's not locking myself behind a fence and only taking opportunities that are the safest."

"I don't think you're ready," he admitted, but not unkindly.

"I'm not or you're not?"

His tongue slid over the front of his teeth, and he smiled. "Both."

"I want more," I replied, stark. The words startled me because I realized I meant them. The way I was living right now, it just wasn't enough anymore.

"So I guess all this stepping out of my shadow talk means you're signing with NASCAR and not the NRR." Jace surmised. I couldn't read him just then; I couldn't tell what he was thinking. He was digesting everything I was saying.

He was listening, though. I had his ear, so I forged on.

"NASCAR is something I have to do. It's a way for me to stare into the face of something I've been rejected for, something I've been abused for, and smile. Signing that contract is like giving the middle finger to everyone who ever hated me for being gay. I know it will be harder than the NRR, but I've been through worse. I need to stop letting being gay define me and instead define being gay."

Silence fell around us, around my words. I didn't realize how right those words felt until I gave them a voice, until I let them out of the prison inside me.

Was I healed?

I didn't know what that even meant. I would always have those reminders. The triggers. I would be defined forever by everything that happened to me. I was tired, though, tired of fighting against it. Tired of trying to push it away.

There was no pushing it away. I could no more push away my past than I could live with a still heart.

I couldn't embrace it either.

Acceptance. It was my only option. I could accept what happened to me. I didn't have to like it; I just had to acknowledge it was there.

I could be a work in progress. Better that than frozen in place.

I waited for Jace to answer. To say something. Anything. My foot tapped anxiously on the floor. For all my self-talk, all my newfound confidence, I still needed my brother. I always would.

His approval was vital.

He sighed deeply. I glanced up as he pushed away from where he was leaning. I held my ground when Jace stepped in front of me. His dark eyes searched mine, and then he did something.

He stuck his hand out between our bodies.

I glanced down at his waiting palm, then slid mine into it. We shook like two men who were being formally introduced.

"I'm really fucking impressed," he said as he pumped my arm. He cleared his throat. "I'm also really fucking proud of you, Arrow."

Jace tightened his grip and pulled my arm. I came forward, and he wrapped both arms around me in a hug. My face was pressed into the top of his shoulder, and against his shirt, I smiled.

Emotion overcame me, but the good kind.

My arms slipped around him, and we hugged it out for more than a few seconds.

When he finally pulled back, he wiped at his eyes with the back of his hand.

"Are you crying?" I ribbed. I had to. This was fucking classic.

"No," he demanded. "You fucking stink. It's making my eyes water. Take a shower!"

I did not stink. He was a liar.

But I pretended like I believed him.

"My little brother, a NASCAR driver." He mused.

"I haven't signed yet." I cautioned.

He waved his hand dismissively. "Details."

"So…" I began. "You're really okay with it?"

"Obviously, I'd rather you be in the NRR with me and Joey. But yeah, I'm okay with it."

Being with Joey was making him soft.

Shh, don't tell him I said that. He'd kick my ass.

Relief like no other lightened my body. Knowing Lor wasn't disappointed or feeling betrayed by me was a huge weight lifted.

"You're sure NASCAR has nothing to do with the douche canoe sitting out there in the Audi?" Lorhaven asked. Then he went on to mutter, "What the fuck kind of car is an Audi anyway."

"You like Audis," I pointed out.

"Not anymore," he grumped.

I bit back a smile. "My decision to sign has nothing to do with him and everything to do with me," I said, decisive. "I am looking forward to working with him, though."

My brother crossed his arms over his chest, and his chin jutted out stubbornly. "I don't like him."

"You didn't like Joey either," I retorted.

His arms dropped to his sides. He opened his mouth, then closed it. I had him, and he knew it. Lor didn't like Joey at first, but now he and I both knew he wouldn't be able to live without her.

"You're an asshole!"

I laughed. That meant I was right.

"He's too old for you." He argued.

"Five years isn't that bad." I countered.

"It's five more years of experience than you have." He spoke meaningfully.

He meant sex. Physical closeness.

I had no answer for that because he was right. Hell, just hearing him bring it up had doubt and fear crashing through me all at once.

For all my bravado, for all my motivation to forge ahead with life, I was still damaged goods. Hopper didn't know the baggage chained to my ankle. And though I knew we grew closer every minute we spent together, at my core, I understood something.

He wasn't going to want me when he found out exactly how far my inexperience went.

"Yeah." I agreed, quiet. "I know."

"I just don't want you to get hurt. Having a life and going after the career you want, getting a new apartment, it's all awesome. I understand it. Adding in a relationship? That's heavy territory."

"It's not a relationship." I corrected him. "Hopper isn't interested in that. Not with me."

Lorhaven made a rude noise. "Who are you lying to right now, little bro? Me or yourself?"

I was dumbfounded. "What?"

"Hopper is into you. Has been for months and months. Joey called it. She was right."

"Joey called what?"

"You two." He shook his head. "She knew before either of you."

I shook my head, bewildered. "I don't think so."

"You think any guy who came at me swinging because he's pissed about where you live is just here for a contract?" Lorhaven started, then flung his arm toward the door. "That he would sit outside in the freezing cold so you could have time to talk to the guy he just got into a fight with? I know you have some innocence under all that experience, bro, but you aren't *that* innocent."

I glanced at the door. Thoughts of the way Hopper kissed me before, the way he kissed my forehead just outside… Butterflies fluttered beneath my ribs and my heart skipped a beat. We were both flirting with something beyond just business.

But we were both also very shattered.

"He doesn't know." My voice dropped. Most of the boldness and conviction I felt and portrayed disappeared.

This was what I meant by me being a work in progress. I still wanted all these things, but I was still scared of them.

"I figured," Jace said, quiet. "It's why I flew in. I didn't come here to stop you from signing a contract. I came here because when Gamble told me he sent Hopper here, I knew what was going to happen."

I tilted my head to the side. "How?"

"Vibes don't lie. Neither do the curious, longing glances you both throw at each other when you think no one else is paying attention."

"So you came here to stop me from getting involved with him," I deadpanned.

His shoulders moved beneath the weight of his sigh. "I came because I want you to be happy. Hopper ain't my choice for you, but no one ever will be. No one will ever be good enough."

"How do you tell someone something like that?" I whispered. How did you tell someone you were abused by a parent, rejected, beaten, and then… raped?

Men were supposed to be stronger than that. They were supposed to not be vulnerable in certain ways. The fact that I was made me somehow less than in the eyes of everyone. Except for maybe my brother.

"I don't fucking know, A."

"You told Joey, right?" I asked, not in the least mad about it. Joey was my family now, and she looked at me with acceptance in her eyes, always.

He made a sound. "I told Joey from my point of view, from the way I experienced it. There's a lot more to your side."

There was. More than I could really expect anyone to handle.

"He's gonna run," I murmured.

"I'm definitely not taking up for the guy. I'm sure as hell not on his side," Lorhaven spoke up. "But after today? After he came at me over something as small as where you sleep, then promised to wait outside? I saw the way he looked at you." He shook his head. "It's the same way I look at Josie."

Hope bloomed inside me. It was a foreign emotion, and I wasn't quite sure what to do with it, so I tried to fight it back. Hope was dangerous, especially for a guy like me.

Hope could be crushing, especially when the thing you hoped for didn't show up. Sometimes it was better to live with nothing than to live with the disappointment of hope unfulfilled.

"What are you saying, Jace?" I asked, still beating it back and hoping my usually pessimistic asshole brother would help me.

"I'm saying I've never seen this side of you before. There's a fire in your eyes that hasn't been there ever. I feel like I'm literally watching you come into your own." He smirked, and I knew something smartass-ish was about to come out. "Your balls tripled in size, bro. Why don't you give 'em a grab? See for yourself."

"I'm not grabbing my balls," I deadpanned.

I'd do it later. When he wasn't watching.

Jace smiled widely, thoroughly amused. "You're sure you won't come with me?" he asked.

"No, I have a contract to sign. And, uh, apparently, it comes with a place at headquarters. An apartment."

He nodded. "It's a nice building. Good security. I made sure."

"You already checked up on it?"

"Of course."

I shook my head, bewildered.

"I'm always gonna look out for you, Arrow. That's never going to change."

"It goes both ways, you know?" I said. "I'm here for you, too. I know in the past I was more of a… responsibility, but I'd like to level the playing field a little. You can count on me."

"Good. You can help me and Josie move."

"Move!" I echoed, surprised. "You're moving?"

"Now that you're going to be living across the state at headquarters? Hell yes, I'm making the move, too. No more of this driving back and forth shit. Josie and I have been looking at places near Gamble Speedway."

"You've been commuting all this time because of me?"

Lorhaven and Joey lived together. They had a townhouse not far from her father's estate, but Lor also still had his place here. I thought it was because he was still running his turf on the other side of town."

"No shit," He quipped. "Like I'd give up my place when you were still here. Hey, maybe you could tell Hopper you have a room at my apartment, that you aren't *actually* homeless."

I couldn't help it. I grinned. "He got in a few good hits, did he?"

Lorhaven grunted.

"I have to be across the state soon. I have a *GearShark* interview."

Lorhaven grinned. "Fucking right! Just send me all the info. I'll be there. Josie, too."

I nodded. "I, ah, may just stay down there when I get there."

The thought of moving, of leaving this garage permanently, made me a little panicked. This place was my safe zone.

He nodded. Then, as if he knew, he said, "This place will always be ours. You can come here whenever you want."

"Thanks, Jace."

He slapped me on the back. "Well, as long as everything's okay here, I'm gonna jet. Duty calls. But if you need me, just holler. I'll see you when you get to town. You still have the key to our place there, right?"

I nodded.

"Use it. You can stay there until you get the keys to your apartment."

I nodded again. He was staring at me, and it made me self-conscious. But then he laughed beneath this breath and pulled me in for another hug. "I love you," he said. "I'm proud of you, no matter what."

I hugged him tighter.

"I can't believe I'm saying this," Lor said and pulled back. "But tell him. Give Hopper the chance to see all of you. He just might surprise you."

"I'll think about it." I promised.

Jace turned and walked toward the door. Then he stopped, pivoting back around. "Hey, A? You talk to Dad?"

My stomach dropped. "He's called. I've ignored him."

He nodded, relieved. "That's good."

Jace didn't want me to talk to our father. He was dead set against it. He might be willing to give Hopper a chance, but our father? Never. According to what he told Jace months ago when they saw each other, my father felt bad about the things that happened between us.

Between us = shit he did to me.

He wanted a chance to talk to me. He'd been hoping to find an ally in Jace.

Jace told him to go fuck himself.

Since then, I hadn't reached out. I hadn't answered his calls. I'd been hiding from that, too. Part of me wanted to talk to my father—that part of Dylan that still lived inside me. Maybe it was that innocence Jace liked to tell me I had.

The other part of me? I was so hurt and angry by what he'd done. I blamed him for a lot of shit that went wrong in my life. I didn't want to give him any kind of opening to do that again.

Just like everything else in my life, I couldn't hide forever. I was going to have to face him eventually. I wanted to move on. I couldn't do that by forever ignoring his attempts at contacting me.

He made me feel powerless, something I hated.

Maybe it was time.

Time to take that power back.

Chapter Twenty-Six

I didn't really have calls to make.

I just said that to give him some time.

To give *me* some time.

Fuck, I felt like hitting the gas, speeding away, and not coming back.

I couldn't. I promised Arrow I'd be here. Keeping that promise, being here for him, was way more important to me than the way I felt.

Fuuuck.

I sat in the driver's seat of the Audi, heat pumping into the cold car, and stared out the windshield, seeing nothing at all.

He defended me. Put his body in front of mine. Just minutes before, he'd been trembling when I got close, slightly unsure, yet he protected me.

What was I supposed to do with that?

I didn't think I could walk away (or speed away in my car).

But—

Bam! Bam! Bam!

I jerked toward the sudden knocking, surprised to see someone standing right there at the window. I didn't even see him approach.

I hit a button, and the glass lowered. Wintry air carrying the fresh, distinct scent of snow swirled in and mixed with the heat.

"What?" I intoned.

Lorhaven braced his palm on the roof of my Audi and leaned in. We locked eyes. I wasn't about to back down. If he wanted to go another round, I'd take him on.

The look on Arrow's face when he'd seen us fighting flashed in my mind. That look before he went all fierce on Lorhaven.

Fearful. Haunted. Freaked out.

My stomach twisted. I didn't like seeing that look. I understood it all too well.

"I'm out," Lorhaven told me. "But I'm watching you. Every move you make, I'm gonna see."

He was leaving? "Where's Arrow?" I asked, suspicious.

"Inside."

"He okay?" I asked, a little accusatory. Lorhaven better not have upset him.

He made an impatient sound. "Of course he's okay."

So he was leaving without his brother, knowing I was still here. Kinda made me wish I'd stood outside the door and eavesdropped. I wondered what Arrow said about me.

"Look, I'm not gonna pretend I'm happy about you being here. But it's what he wants. And Josie likes you. Even when I tell her not to."

I made an amused sound. I missed her.

"So I'm gonna give you another shot. Don't fuck it up. Don't fuck with my brother. He's been through way more than anyone should."

I felt my brows crease. His posturing didn't concern me. What concerned me was what I didn't know about A. "Care to elaborate?"

He gave me a look like I should know better than to ask. I did, but I asked anyway.

"That's for him to share. And when he does…" The muscles in his jaw clenched. His eyes darkened.

I waited for him to finish, anxious.

He tapped the roof of my car, looking away and then back. "Bottom line? If you hurt him in any way, I'll kill you."

I could have made a million responses.

Get in line.

I've heard that before.

Kill me? I'd like to see you try.

Go ahead. Put me out of my misery.

I didn't voice any of the best replies I had. Instead, I came out with something neither of us was expecting.

"What if he hurts me?"

Lorhaven pulled back, straightening out of the window. I could tell my answer caught him off guard.

Good.

"I'll be seeing you," he murmured and walked away.

I rolled up the window and shut off the engine.

I glanced up at the door leading into the hangar. Arrow was in there. With a heavy exhale, I leaned my head against the seat and closed my eyes.

Am I ready for this?

I want to be.

I'm not sure I'll ever be ready.

Even though my eyes were closed and I was sitting here alone in my car, I felt his presence. It was unsettling as much as it was welcome.

I opened my eyes, stared up at the ceiling of the Audi for a brief pause, then cautiously lowered my chin. Arrow was there, just as I knew he would be. Beyond the matte-black hood, he seemed to tower, eyes affixed on where I sat.

He was dressed in a red-and-black flannel. It didn't look very "woodsy" or mountain man-ish on him. Instead, it appeared slightly grungy, metro. The black T-shirt beneath it only made it seem edgier.

His hair was tamer than when he first got out of bed, but it still ruffled around on the side of his head in the wind. My gaze swept over his facial features, checking to make sure he wasn't upset or even hurt. If he was, I knew I'd fling myself out of this car and chase down Lorhaven before he stepped back on the jet he landed in.

How had we not even heard him land?

Because we were too involved with each other to hear or notice anything else.

Arrow seemed fine, perhaps a little cautious as he watched me, but that wasn't out of the ordinary. His hands were buried deep in the pockets of his jeans, and even though he hid it in his stare, I still heard the question he was silently asking.

Are you staying?

My fingers curled around the door handle before I even noticed I'd moved. The door popped open, and the thick scent of winter rushed in. It was fucking cold as shit out here. The temperature woke me up, slapped me out of whatever trance I was in, and I hustled around to where Arrow waited.

His eyes. Whoever said they were windows to the soul must have known someone like Arrow. I'd never really thought much about that statement, but now… now there were no truer words.

What I saw when he looked at me like that, like he was naked and insecure but wanting so badly to trust me—it wrapped around my chest like a vise, and the longer I looked, the tighter the vise became.

"You left your hat backward," he noted.

I nodded slowly. "In case you might wanna kiss me again."

"Oh, I want to," he murmured, so low I almost didn't hear.

My stomach burned like the butterflies had fluttered so fiercely beneath my ribs their wings caught fire.

I slid my arm between his and his side, slipping it around his back. Both his hands came out of his pockets, and he shifted a little closer. I pulled him tighter into my side.

We walked inside, and I was once again struck by how intensely I hated this hangar. Not because it wasn't a nice place for cars. Hell, it was.

But it was no place for Arrow.

"We should talk," I said.

Slowly, as if he didn't want to, Arrow pulled away from my arm. I watched him retreat to a nearby tool bench and pick up an envelope. "Go over this with me? I want to sign it now."

I swallowed. Something lodged in my throat, and I had the sudden urge to race out after Lorhaven to get in a few more solid punches.

Arrow hadn't been this sure about signing a contract until his brother walked out of here.

Obviously, the guy had a ton of pull over his brother. Obviously, he told him to sign with NRR.

I didn't want Arrow in the NRR. I wanted him in NASCAR. With me.

"Maybe you should give it some more thought," I told him.

His head tilted to the side. "I thought you wanted me to decide ASAP because of the *GearShark* interview and the beginning of NASCAR season."

"I want you to be sure of what you're doing."

"I am sure. More sure than I've ever been." He sounded sure, confident. I loved the look on him, but I hated it was taking him away from me.

He's not yours to be taken. Sure as hell didn't feel like it in the moment.

I cleared my throat. "So I guess Lorhaven helped you decide."

Arrow nodded.

I made a sound and turned away. This was hard. Harder than I thought it would be. I wanted to call Gamble and tell him to go fuck himself for sending me up here. Then I wanted to speed away, go somewhere else, and start all over again.

I'd done it once.

It wasn't fun then. It would be worse now.

"Hopp." Arrow's voice was so close. Then I felt his hand, his fingers wrapping around my wrist.

I glanced over at him. He was so close yet so very far away.

"Not gonna lie," I said, gruff. "I was hoping you'd pick NASCAR."

"I did."

I blinked. Blinked again. It was like my brain did a double take, but the rest of me didn't move. Then suddenly, once I realized what he'd said, I jerked around to face him. "You chose NASCAR?"

He half smiled, nodding. "You're surprised?"

"Well, yeah." I scoffed.

A look came over his features, cautious yearning. Slowly, he reached up and brushed the backs of his knuckles over the stubble on my jaw. "Shouldn't have been that big of a surprise," he whispered.

My heart seized. "Everything about you is a surprise," I murmured.

I moved forward abruptly, tilted my face, and affixed my lips to his. I had to kiss him just then. There was no other course of action. I breathed in as our lips locked, as if kissing him wasn't enough, as if I had to fill my lungs with the very air that caressed his skin.

He was surprised, but then all the stiffness drained from his body and we melted together. One of my arms wrapped around his shoulders and pulled him closer. Arrow was tall, but I was wider than him, maybe once inch taller.

He fit inside my hold perfectly. He filled in all the hollow places so even though it was me who surrounded him, he made me feel full.

Arrow's fingers flexed at the small of my back, bunched in my shirt, then released. I hunched in a little closer as our lips tasted one another over and over again. I licked at his tongue, that pouty lower lip I loved so much, and even glided over his teeth.

My blood hammered with need, and I went in a little bit deeper. He moaned, and I swallowed it. The taste was something I wanted never to end.

His chest was pressed right against mine. Our bodies rubbed together as we kissed and fought to get closer. I couldn't tell if it was my heart or his pounding so forcefully. I hadn't felt this way in so long. I hadn't felt all reason fly away and pure instinct take over.

I stepped forward, grabbed him even closer, and started walking. His steps shuffled over the ground as we continued to kiss, and I practically bulldozed him across the floor until his back hit a large storage locker.

I reached up, cradled the back of his head with my palm, and then dove into his mouth with renewed ferocity. His fingers dug into my sides, anchoring his body close, and he kissed me back with all the passion I thought I'd never know again.

I ripped my mouth free, and we both gasped. Then I kept kissing. Across his jaw and down his neck. He tilted up his head, giving me access, and I licked and nipped in the direction the arrow tattoo on his neck pointed.

I wanted to sink my teeth into that spot. I wanted to suck the flesh and leave an *I was here mark* so the arrow pointed to it like a lit sign pointing to things that needed extra attention.

Just the thought, just the intention of doing it, made me growl like a predator. With the sound, I thrust my hips forward and pinned Arrow even farther against the locker. My fingers curled in the edges of the flannel and T-shirt, yanking the fabric away from that spot.

Something changed in the air. It took a second to break through the haze of fucking need, but it did. Arrow's body was rigid now, and instead of just being pinned between me and the locker, he was plastered against it as if he were trying to get away.

The hands against my sides were vibrating they shook so much. I even felt a slight tremor in his knees.

I lifted my head, mere inches from the spot I was dying to own. His lips were pink, glossed, and slightly swollen from the way we'd gone at each other.

But instead of the hazy, horny look in his eyes I expected, there was panic…

Fear.

I backed up instantly, even though it felt like prying a tongue off a frozen pole. I couldn't bring myself to let him go completely, so one hand remained pressed against his abs.

"What did I do?" I asked, my voice rough.

He glanced at me, then looked away. His head shook once in the negative.

"Tell me," I demanded.

"I… I can't." His voice was shaky.

I felt compelled to say something, to understand. The vibe in the air was unmistakable, but I didn't comprehend it. "You know I'm not going to hurt you, right?"

Arrow didn't say anything. Instead, his gaze remained averted. His quaking hands fell away from my sides, and it felt I was losing something, something I fiercely wanted.

"Hey," I said a little more forcefully, a little angrier than I intended. My hand caught his chin, forcing his face toward mine. "Who hurt you?"

His eyes searched mine. The fear went away, but left in its wake was obvious misery. "I'm sorry," he whispered.

"For what?" I demanded.

"It's always there." He went on as if he were speaking to himself and not me. The dark eyes that were so much like a vise to my chest swung to me, piercing with desolation. "I can't do this."

I dropped his chin, caging his body with my arms, pressing my palms against the locker. "Do what?"

He gestured between us, his tongue darting out to wet his lips. "This. I thought I could. I want to." His voice cracked. His eyes begged me to understand. "God, I want to. But just now—" He stopped, shaking his head. "I'm afraid I'll just bring you down with me. The only thing worse than what I'm saying now is to someday have you look at me and realize you made a mistake."

He was rejecting me.

It hurt.

It hurt worse than just pain.

It was nothing short of total annihilation.

I'd finally started opening up. I'd finally started to maybe feel again, only to be served a cold dish.

I shoved off the locker, paced away from him, and stared at the cold floor.

What the fuck was I thinking? I knew better than this! Opening myself up to this again was nothing short of suicide.

"I have to go," I said, brisk.

I didn't look back. I didn't say another word.

I high-tailed it the fuck out of there, my tires leaving tracks in the newly falling snow.

Chapter Twenty-Seven

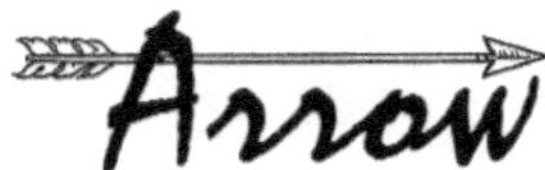

God, he felt so fucking good against me.

One second I was drowning in him. The next? The next I had water in my lungs and drowning took on a different meaning.

So much for taking my power back.

I was beginning to think the only kind of life for me was a lonely, solitary existence.

Chapter Twenty-*Eight*

It was dark, and I was roaming the streets.

Not an unfamiliar place for me, though it wasn't the middle of the night.

My insomnia started early tonight. The fog hung low over all my thoughts with no sign of settling anytime soon.

I was back. Back where I'd been for five long years.

How odd yet entirely eye-opening these past few days had been.

You never quite realize how much you hurt, how much of a fog you live in until you're granted a reprieve.

My reprieve was short. Hell, it wasn't even total.

But it had been enough.

Enough to make the way I felt now far worse than it was before.

It was like being sick for so long you forgot what it was like to be well. Being chronically exhausted only to have a few days of infinite energy.

Going back should be easy, right?

Oh, hell no, it wasn't.

It was like being given a few bites of rich chocolate cake only to have it swiped away and a Brussel sprout put in its place.

Now I knew what I was missing. Just that brief taste made going back to nothing so painful it was shocking. So here I was. Out walking already. Out drowning in thoughts, letting them blow me around like a piece of paper in the wind.

It was just past dinnertime. Night claimed the sky and the temperature dropped. Snow continued to fall lazily, but it was random, so it likely wouldn't amount to much more than the inch that coated the ground earlier that afternoon.

The pockets of my cargo pants were weighed down with my phone, keys, and the money clip that held all my cards and cash. I approached the coffee shop up the block from my hotel. I stopped and stared at the welcoming lights in the windows and knew the entire place was likely scented with brewing coffee.

But I kept walking.

Arrow didn't like that place. And now I didn't like it either.

I don't know how long or far I walked. Hell, I didn't even pay attention. I couldn't tell you how many people were out in the streets, how the traffic was, or anything else about my surroundings.

I was lost in my own head, replaying the scene with Arrow over and over and over again.

All the fighting I'd done inside myself. All the tug and pull, the guilt. Somehow, surprisingly, it started to be overcome. Overcome by Arrow and the way I felt when I was near him. How the look in his eyes was like two hands reaching into my chest and taking my heart.

The way he pulled me back from the edge of the fog so many times.

The way he boldly kissed me when now I knew physical contact wasn't something he was used to.

Hell, he'd even leapt between me and his brother. He challenged Lorhaven, something I was sure not many people did.

For me.

He'd done that for me.

He also looked at me with panic in his face. With dread and even terror. His eyes, which I loved when they focused on me, glazed over. His lips, which were pouty and juicy, the perfect place for my own to rest, whispered words that felt like a knife stabbing straight into my heart.

It wasn't the first time Arrow trembled when I touched him, but this was the first time he let it overcome the moment. Not just the moment; it overshadowed everything between us.

I ran.

Without looking back.

I had to protect myself. I had to guard what was left of me.

Who will protect him?

He'd been protecting himself just as I had done.

Except he didn't run away. He'd stood there, albeit trembling and clearly feeling threatened. He apologized, and he tried to explain.

I'm afraid I'll just bring you down with me. The only thing worse than what I'm saying now is to someday have you look at me and realize you made a mistake.

He wasn't rejecting me to hurt me. He'd been trying to *protect* me. Again.

And I ran.

My footsteps halted over the stone-cold concrete. A great gust of wind slammed me in the face from out of nowhere, like the universe itself was smacking me in the face.

I deserved it.

I was selfish. Self-absorbed. I'd thought only of myself back there instead of trying to stand and deal like Arrow.

The memory of the day on the snowmobile flickered in my mind like a home movie. The texture was grainy and slightly lagging, but I saw it all so clear.

I'd been panicked that day. I'd been insecure and downright fucking scared. He didn't get mad when I retreated into my own world. Arrow offered to leave with me. When I refused, he stuck it out. I asked him to pull me back. I asked him to help me stay there with him.

He'd done it.

He kissed me. He kept me close. It was as if I'd been learning to walk again, and he'd held my hand to give me balance.

I stopped walking again, bent at the waist, and put my hands on my thighs.

What the fuck have I done?

It wasn't the first time he'd responded with apprehension when things between us got heated. The first time I'd stuck it out with him, adjusted what I was doing, and it turned out okay.

Why hadn't I done that this time?

Why hadn't I pulled him back the way he had for me, more than once?

It was a missed opportunity. A chance to draw him out of his shell, maybe understand a little more about what shattered him into those million tiny jagged edges.

Something Lorhaven said to me echoed through my head.

That's for him to share. And when he does…

He didn't say if he does. He said when. His words implied Arrow planned to talk to me. He wanted me to know.

Arrow stayed. He sent his brother back to his plane and stayed. He'd chosen NASCAR. The way he looked when he said it? It felt like he'd chosen me just as much as NASCAR.

I'd been so fucking euphoric I'd practically jumped him. Kissed him so fiercely I'd felt like I was burning up. He'd been right there with me. I knew he liked it. I felt the electricity and hunger in his lips.

And then I'd put him up against the wall and ripped at his shirt…

Fuck.

The more the scene replayed in my head, the more I heard the words that had been spoken…

The more I knew.

I fucked up so bad.

I should have thought about him. I should have looked past my own hurt and paranoia about being slaughtered by loss again and seen him. I shouldn't have focused on what he was saying.

Fuck, what he must be thinking right now. He was probably beating himself up, feeling like he wasn't enough.

He was.

Arrow was more than enough.

I had to see him, to go to him. Like that night he'd shoved me away and then pulled up to the curb. He'd come to me. He'd talked to me. I'd shoved him away that night, too. I told him I couldn't do it. The same thing he'd said tonight.

He understood. He drove me back to the hotel. He didn't run.

I started running. Snow was falling more steadily now. The icy, wet flakes pelted my cheeks and pierced my eyes as I ran. I felt blind, numb, but I had to get there.

A little bit of reality rushed in, and I searched around my cargo pocket for my keys. Once I had them, I glanced up, noticing my surroundings for the first time in a while. I scanned the street for my car, for the hotel sign. *I need to get to Arrow.*

More snow blew into my eyes, and I blinked furiously to get it out. Once it was melted, my vision cleared. This place was familiar to me.

I turned slowly, glancing across the wide street.

The airstrip was there.

Seeing the airport was an even bigger wakeup call than my thoughts had been.

Even drowning in brain fog, even overcome with regret… I'd led myself here.

To Arrow.

I rushed across the street, closing in on the large fenced-in area.

My footsteps slowed as I looked at the gate. It was open, something I knew was unusual.

I glanced through toward the hangars. Everything looked okay.

But I knew better than most that didn't mean a thing.

Chapter Twenty-Nine

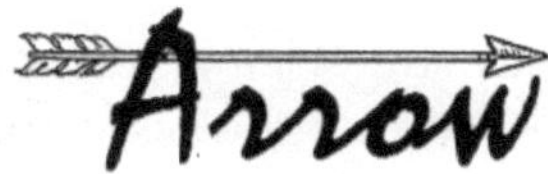

I didn't notice the cold.

If anything, it helped numb the pain. But it wasn't enough to stop my brain.

The look on his face before he left—I hurt him. It was the last thing I wanted, but it would be worse for him later.

Like the kind of worse I was experiencing right now.

Snow fell from the sky, the white flakes streaking the darkness with sprinkles of light. I hoped it kept coming. I hoped it covered the mere inch that fell earlier and blanketed everything with the kind of cold stillness only snow could bring.

My feet were propped on the old, useless dash, my head resting against the cold pleather of the chair. I remained unmoving, stared out through the three-sixty-degree window, and tried to reconcile myself to the fact I did the best thing.

It wasn't what I wanted.

A foreign sound disturbed the silence, but I didn't move. Normally, any kind of sound would have put me on alert, but not tonight. Tonight, I just didn't care.

Behind me, in the direction of the open doorway, the noise came to a stop.

"The gate is open," Hopper said. His voice was low but breathless, like he'd been running.

My chest clenched. The melancholy wrapping around this entire space pressed in at the sound of his voice. I loved the way it sounded.

"Forgot to close it," I replied, still staring out the wide windows of the old control tower. I always came here when I needed somewhere to just be, when working in the hangar wasn't enough. I liked the feeling of being suspended in the air, high off the ground. The only thing in my line of vision was the sky, the vast horizon, and landscape below.

One might think it would make a guy like me lonelier, but in fact, it was just the opposite.

"How did you know I was up here?" No one knew I sat up here, not even Lorhaven.

"It's where I'd be."

I didn't know why he was here. Part of me was relieved he was; the other whispered it would only make it worse.

"My real name is Jayson Hamilton." His voice filled the circular, window-encased room. It was quiet and steady, kind of like the snow I stared at.

He cleared his throat. "Do you, uh, know that name?"

"Should I?"

"Five years ago, when I was right around your age, I was at the top of my game. I raced in Motocross, specifically for Ducati."

His past. He was telling me about his past. My interest was piqued, and though I didn't turn to look at him, my head tilted a bit, my ear ready to capture all his words.

"I was in the top ten racers in North America. I fucking loved it, the thrill speed gave me, the way I could make a bike respond to my every command. I was chosen to go international, to race overseas, go on tour, and basically kick my career into worldwide success."

I could tell by the sound of his voice, by the rawness of his words, he didn't speak of this often. Hell, if ever. He literally went by another name now, and I'd never seen him on a bike.

The day on the snowmobiles flashed into my memory. How panicked he'd been, how nervous and unprepared. It also explained how he handled it so well. He was practically a racing superstar.

"What happened?" I asked, invested.

He didn't answer at first, not for a few minutes. I didn't push him because I knew whatever he was telling me was likely what broke him. I continued to watch the snow blow around beyond the glass, just waiting… hoping.

The pain I carried up to this control tower tonight was muted now. The second his cautious, heavy voice floated through the room, pain became second.

"I was involved with someone five years ago," he said, and my heart deflated. My teeth sank into my lower lip with the news. Picturing him with someone else made the pain reappear. "In a relationship. I met Matt when I was eighteen… He was a Ducati driver, too."

I swallowed, closing my eyes.

"I loved him," Hopper said, stark, and it pierced my heart. "We lived together, drove together… He was basically my life."

My feet dropped off the old control counter, my high-tops making a heavy thud when they hit the floor. "Hopper." His name ripped from my throat. I couldn't hear this. I didn't want to.

"He died," he rushed to say. I didn't know if it was because it was beyond painful to recall or if it was because he knew I was getting ready to bolt.

I stayed in the old chair, my back ramrod straight and my feet flat on the floor. My fingers ached from the cold, but they squeezed my knees as I sat there.

"He died because he took my place in a stupid challenge, one I never should have agreed to. I had hit my head, and he drove for me. The guy I was racing… he was pissed. He'd planned on taking me out so he could take my international spot. He *did* take me out that day…" His voice went hoarse, then fell away for a moment. "But it was Matt who died."

I couldn't think. All I could do was feel. I knew how much it cut him because it still echoed in his voice. Whoever Matt was, he'd been everything to Hopper. And he died.

"He died on the side of the road because of me." Hopper's voice was anguished. "I tried to stop them from running him off the road, but I was too late… I saw it all. The way his bike flipped, the way his body shuddered on impact… *I was too late.*"

I wanted to get up and go to him, but I held myself back. He was grieving still. Maybe he always would be. I couldn't compete with that. I didn't even want to try. His pain hurt me, too. Not because he'd been in love either, but because he'd lost it.

"Afterward…" I could hear him swallow from across the room. "I sort of went into a freefall. My life fell apart. I quit racing, cut off my friends and family. I drank too much. I walk the streets at night because sleep never gives me any peace. Gamble found me about eight months after Matt." I heard his feet shuffle. "He offered me a job, a place to live, and a fresh start."

"You took it," I said, impressed.

"Ron Gamble isn't someone who takes no for an answer. So I moved across the country, from Seattle to Maryland, into an apartment here at headquarters and changed my name."

"The press?" I questioned, thinking of the way they fed on Trent and Drew, my brother and his woman.

"Were ruthless," he spat. "Matt dying, the wreck, and my crash and burn was the hottest story of the year. Gamble helped me bury it, gave me a place to start over."

"I'm sorry," I said. Two stupid words. But I meant them. I meant them infinitely.

"I grew my hair, a beard, and fell off the map."

And that's what broke Hopper, aka Jayson. It was bad. I understood now why he was so careful not to get close, why the first sign of hurt when I pushed him away sent him running. He couldn't go through it again.

I understood.

"And so I can't give you my body, and you can't give me your heart." I surmised, depression threatening to swallow me whole.

It was us in a nutshell. Broken beyond repair. Tethered together by understanding; kept apart by experience.

"What about your heart?" he whispered as if he hadn't heard what I said. Only what I didn't.

"My heart isn't mine to give."

Footsteps echoed behind me. I sat back when Hopper stepped around the chair to stand before me. I didn't look up. I was a chicken shit and I was afraid if I looked in his eyes, I'd crumble.

He was still in the same clothes from hours before. He still looked just as good.

"Your heart isn't yours?" he intoned.

I shook my head.

Hopper dropped, squatting in front of my chair. His thighs were spread so me and the chair were between them. I avoided his stare, though I felt the penetrating gaze.

The gruff quality to his words caught me off guard. "Whose is it?"

I didn't reply.

His hands shot out, gripped the edge of the seat, and pulled. The wheels the crappy office chair perched on squeaked and creaked as it moved closer. So close my knees bumped his chest.

"Arrow," he commanded.

I lifted my eyes.

We stared *into* each other. I don't know what I was looking for, but it seemed he was searching out the same.

"Who?" he demanded.

He was jealous. When I said my heart was unavailable, suddenly it didn't seem to matter his was, too.

There was a difference, though. A huge, gaping difference.

His heart belonged to Matt.

And mine?

"You," I practically growled. "My heart is already yours."

The icy quality in his eyes flared; the color turned brilliant, like a sapphire on fire.

"I tried to stop it." I went on miserably. "I kept it behind all these walls, the locks, the fences… but it got out anyway."

The pleather where he gripped the edge of seat groaned under the pressure of his hands.

I shouldn't have told him. It wasn't as if it would change anything. It merely made me look weak, made my inexperience shine through, my loneliness. My heart had been ripe for the picking—I saw that now—but even if I had known before, nothing would have changed.

Hopper was it for me. I felt too deep. I knew too much.

My first love would be my only, and it would cut the way only a first love could.

"Why can't you give me your body?" Hopper's question caught me off guard and titled my thoughts.

I sucked in a breath. He told me about his past. It was time for me to do the same.

Could I?

I thought I was ready. I'd said as much to Jace.

I'd never said it out loud before. *Never.* I barely even thought it. No one knew. I never even admitted it to my brother, even though I knew he knew just by looking at me that night.

Hopper was watching, and I knew he was resolved to wait me out.

I met his eyes, though I desperately wanted to look away.

"I was raped."

Chapter Thirty

I thought I kind of knew.

I definitely suspected something in the way he tensed when we got close.

But this… *this* was worse. This was so bad I hadn't even let my own mind go that far.

I just… I just sat there and stared at him. Horrified was an understatement. Rage? Also a massive understatement.

I felt him looking at me, the weight of his confession. I knew it required some kind of response, but what the fuck did a man say to that?

"Arrow…" I began, shock lacing my voice.

"My name was Dylan Lorhaven." He cut off the words I couldn't produce. "I always knew I was gay." He looked up at me. The hollow, ghostly expression deep in his eyes turned my stomach. "But I didn't really *know it* until high school."

I nodded, giving him the support he so desperately needed. "I get it. I always knew, too."

"I didn't tell anyone. I was afraid to. But my mom found out. Found a stupid porn magazine in my room."

I chuckled, and he glanced up, his lips tilted and a little bit of warmth melting his eyes. *I'd die to see just a little bit more of that, to take away any of his trauma.*

"She told me not to tell my father. She knew what I was too stupid to see."

I nodded, sinking back from my squatting position and onto my ass. I brought my knees in a little so my feet were flat on the floor, resting my elbows on my knees to let my hands and forearms dangle between my legs.

"The floor's cold." He frowned.

"I'm fine." I promised, even though the inside of my chest lurched. Even after that confession, he still cared enough about me to worry about my comfort.

He said his heart is mine. Holy fuck, he meant it.

My own heart beat rapidly, as if I'd just run five miles in record time.

"I didn't listen to her. I was stupid and young. Thought I knew better. I marched right into my father's office and told him I was gay."

"What did he say?"

"He punched me in the face."

My body stiffened. What the fuck kind of father punches his own kid in the face? I knew what it was like to "come out" to family and friends. I knew the kind of gut-wrenching worry and fear that kind of tell brought on inside a man. People weren't as accepting and open minded as they'd like you to believe.

Me? I got lucky. My family stood by me. They embraced Matt the first time I brought him home, and that was that. Until I shoved them all away.

Some people, though, wear masks. Some pretend, and some just never show their true colors until they're forced out.

This pained me, knowing he was once entirely innocent. He was likely more endearing than he was even now.

That kid, he walked into his father's office, confident he would be accepted, trusting the man he thought loved him... and ended up with a fist in his face.

I never met Arrow's father. I didn't know him.

I hated him anyway.

"Basically, he told me I wasn't *allowed* to be gay." Arrow continued. "He took away my car, my trust fund. He set me up on dates. He even paid a few girls to blow me or have sex with me."

I rubbed a hand over the back of my neck. "Are you fucking kidding me?"

"Wouldn't be a very good joke," he replied, his voice even and emotionless.

I made a sound, ripped my hat off my head, and threw it across the room.

"On my eighteenth birthday, he took me to a strip club. It was a test. He dangled everything I wanted in front of me. Full tuition to a college away from home, my car, my trust fund. All I had to do was prove to him I was 'cured' of being gay."

I didn't look up. I was afraid if I did, he'd see the murderous look in my eyes and stop talking. This was excruciating to hear, but I wanted to all the same.

"He got us a private room, hired strippers... You know, the usual." I nodded, and he went on. "I was taken to another private room where the stripper started blowing me. She said my father paid her ten grand to have sex with me. I told her I'd just lie and say we did it, she could collect her money, and I wouldn't have to try and get it up."

I made a sound, a cross between a growl and moan. This was sick. *Sick.* I didn't want to think of him with anyone, let alone with some stripper in the back of some seedy club.

"She told me we had to actually do it because there were cameras. He was watching."

I shot up. My fists clenched at my sides, and I paced to stand in front of one of the windows, away from Arrow. The sky was pitch black out, the perfect color to match my mood.

"I snapped," Arrow said. "I told him to keep his college, his money, and everything else. I told him it didn't matter what he did. I would still be gay."

"He disowned you."

"On the spot." Arrow confirmed. "I left the club, went in search of my brother. He didn't know I was gay, but he was my last hope."

I felt my loathe for Lorhaven begin to soften. He was an asshole, but he didn't turn away his brother.

"Some guys saw me, said they knew my brother, and offered me a ride." His voice turned weaker, shakier, and I knew. "I thought I was on his turf, you know?"

"Just tell me what happened." The words came out harsher than I intended.

"They recognized me from this club, a place I'd gone to party a few times. I… uh, I hooked up with a guy there sometimes, so they knew I was gay."

My eyes closed. Not only was he abused and disowned by his father, but he was the victim of a heinous hate crime. I was so angry, so disgusted, tears actually moistened the back of my eyes. I bit them back because A deserved better than my stray tears.

"They pulled me into an alleyway, beat me up pretty bad," he admitted. "I tried to fight back, but there were four of them and only one of me."

"This wasn't your fault," I whispered. Above anything, I wanted him to know that.

"I guess beating me wasn't enough, because they dragged me behind the dumpster... I still smell the putrid trash tainting the air."

He was getting lost in the memory, sucked into that terrible time.

I shot across the room and sank before him once before, taking both his hands in mine. "Stay here, A," I murmured. "Stay here with me."

His eyes appeared even darker here where there was no light. I fell into their depths. I felt the chains of his hell shackle my wrists.

But I wasn't scared. I wasn't scared because he was here with me.

"Two of them held me, and the other... he, uh, did it."

I made a sound, lifted a hand, and cupped his face. He pushed farther into my hand.

I thought I was completely shattered. I didn't think there was anything left of me to break.

I was wrong.

I felt the splinter, and then it spidered out... The sound of another piece of me breaking was like a shotgun going off right beside my ear.

"I came here, to the hangar. I don't even remember how I made it. Lorhaven found me." Arrow's eyes met mine. "He almost killed all four of them. A couple are permanently fucked up because of what he did."

"I wish they were dead." I vowed.

"Me, too." Arrow nodded. "Jace almost went to jail for attempted murder, but our father made the charges go away."

"He's been protecting you," I said. "I accused you of hiding behind him, but you weren't. Not really." I felt like shit for saying that. For telling him to man up. I had no right.

The side of his mouth curved up, and the hand cupping his cheek moved with it. "You were right. I was hiding. Jace is really good at protecting people, and I got comfortable."

I shook my head, pulling back.

"It was three years ago," Arrow said. "I can't live in the past forever. I've been trying to move forward. I thought I was gaining."

"And then I ran out of here like a pussy," I deadpanned.

He laughed, and my heart rate sped again. "If you were a pussy, I wouldn't have cared you ran."

I grinned.

"I didn't mean to hurt you. I was trying to avoid that." Sincere sorrow saturated his voice.

My hand slashed through the air. "You have nothing to apologize for. I'm the one who owes you the apology."

Arrow started to protest, but I cut him off.

"I'm sorry. I came at you too much, too fast. I shoved you against the locker. I ripped at your clothes." *Holy fuck, what it must have triggered inside him.* "Then I ran off when you tensed up. I should have stayed. I should have pulled you back."

"I don't blame you," he said.

How? How could he not be completely bitter and untrusting of everyone he ever encountered? Even me? Especially me, who was rough and hard to reach.

"How in the hell could you have given me your heart?" I wondered aloud.

"Because you're the one who taught it to beat again."

This time I fell back onto my ass, once again in front of his chair. Breath whooshed out of me, and those words, those beautiful words, filled me.

It was the single most significant thing ever said to me. Ever. And yes, it hurt because that included Matt, but I couldn't deny the truth. I couldn't deny the way that one sentence slayed me.

Arrow credited me. It was as if I brought him back to life. In a sense, *I* saved him, something I'd desperately wanted to do for Matt but couldn't.

He was offering me a second chance.

This man who was both innocent and jaded, closed off but open, and so very easy on my eyes was my second chance.

A chance to love again. To live again.

"We don't work, though, do we? Two halves. Both too broken," Arrow whispered.

I was still reeling from his previous words. Words that reminded me what it was to love and be loved.

My God, how I missed being part of something bigger than just me.

"Maybe that's why we *do* work," I answered. "Not because two halves make a whole—we'd never get all our little pieces to fit together—but because no one else can really understand what it's like to *not* be whole."

"We do seem to have an odd sense of understanding," Arrow murmured.

I smirked. "Except when one of us is running like a pussy."

He scowled. "I already made it clear how I felt about pussy."

I chuckled.

I wanted to earn those heartbeats, the ones he said I made start up again. I hadn't done anything nearly enough to warrant them. I might already have them, but I could do better.

I *wanted* to do better. I wanted him to have more.

I took a breath. "Maybe my heart isn't as unavailable as you think."

His eyes flashed. Some of that danger, some of the challenge I saw when he went up against Lorhaven came out. "Don't say shit you don't mean."

I wasn't offended. He earned the right to protect himself. After all, he'd practically reached out, and I ran.

I sat up. Nerves bunched in my stomach and coiled at the base of my neck. I did it anyway, continuing what I wanted to do. I peeled off my leather jacket and let it fall on the floor behind me. Then I pushed up the sleeve on my left arm.

Even in the dark, I saw him perfectly. Maybe it was because my eyes were adjusted to the dim lighting. Or maybe it was because I was focused so completely.

"I wear this all the time," I told him, reaching for the thick leather bracelet always strapped around my wrist.

"I noticed."

I glanced up. "You ever notice the symbol?"

He nodded. "That's an infinity symbol, right?"

I made a sound of agreement and traced the outline of what I always thought looked like a horizontal eight. Beneath my fingertip, the silver metal was cold. "I thought I had my infinity figured out a long time ago. I thought Matt was my forever."

Arrow shifted uncomfortably, and I knew he probably didn't like to hear that. Fuck, it would make me crazy if he said it.

But it was my truth.

A truth I wouldn't ever deny. I couldn't give Matt my infinity, but this, this I could give.

I reached out without thinking and wrapped my hand around A's ankle. I felt him calm beneath my palm. The very air around us stilled.

"When he died that day, my entire life fell apart. I distanced myself from everyone. My family, my friends, my entire career. I couldn't bear the thought of another loss like that ever again. So I shut down, closed up, and I told myself even though Matt was gone, he would still be my infinity. It was the least he deserved after he died in my place."

"Sounds lonely," Arrow murmured.

"You'd know about that." I eased back, releasing his ankle, though I wanted to keep touching him. I flipped my arm over and reached for the buckle that held the bracelet on my wrist.

I could hear a pin drop as I undid it and let it fall into my lap. "You asked me once if I had a tattoo." I held up my wrist for him to see. "This is it."

Arrow cradled the back of my hand in his, cautiously drawing my wrist closer so he could see the simple black ink permanently etched into my skin.

"Coordinates?" he asked, glancing up, still holding my arm.

I nodded. "The exact coordinates where Matt died. I wear the infinity symbol around it as a promise to him and to me that I will never forget him or the sacrifice he made."

The pad of Arrow's thumb stroked over the tattoo. I shivered. It felt good to be touched.

"I understand." He began to withdraw. I caught his hand and linked my fingers through his.

"You don't," I said gently. "For five years I've asked myself why. Every single day, over and over again. It keeps me up at night. It wraps around my brain and creates this smog I can't always see through. *Why?* Why Matt and not me? Why did I live? Why did he die? What did I ever do in life to warrant such a punishment? The questions are endless, and I always told myself I would never know the answer."

Arrow gave my fingers a squeeze, offering me support, empathy. Offering comfort so I didn't have to be alone.

"Earlier this morning, which frankly feels like a lifetime ago…" I muttered.

He made a sound of agreement.

"I realized something. When you came rushing out of the bathroom like a lion protecting its den and planted yourself in front of me. When you challenged your own brother to protect me? I knew."

"Knew what?"

"You're my why. *The* why."

I felt the surprise jolt his body. His eyes grew wide, so wide I could see the white all around the edges of his chocolate irises.

"Everything was leading me here. To you. I didn't want to admit it. It feels in some part like a betrayal to Matt. But not saying it, withholding everything I feel, betrays you. I can't betray you, A. I just can't."

"What are you saying right now?" he asked, still cautious as hell.

"I'm saying, I think, you taught my heart how to beat again, too."

We stared at each other. The intensity in this control room was thick, so thick you could slice it with a knife.

I felt… free. At peace. More so than I had in five years. It was overwhelming, but it was welcome.

"I really want to kiss you right now," I admitted.

"You do?" His voice was raspy.

"Every time we're in a room together, it takes an effort not to touch you." And now after hearing everything he'd been through, it made refusing to touch him even harder.

I wanted to show him touch could be comforting, pleasurable, and bonding. I wanted to prove to him it wasn't something that hurt.

"I haven't been touched much, not until you."

"By anyone?" I inquired, my heart clenching.

He seemed embarrassed, shrinking down in the chair.

"It's okay." I confirmed gently.

"*Before*," he said meaningfully, and I nodded, letting him know I understood so he didn't have to say it. "There was the guy I used to meet up with at the warehouse party. I didn't even know his name. We would disappear into the stairwell together and fool around."

"Fool around?" I asked, wanting clarity.

"Kiss. Blow each other."

"Sex?" I asked.

He shook his head.

"Before no-name?" I asked.

"No one," he replied quietly. "Except the girls. They would blow me, and I would imagine other guys. I had sex a couple times with them, but I never liked it. I just did it…"

"To be normal?"

"Yeah." He scoffed. "But it only made me feel less normal."

"So you've never had sex… with a guy?" *You've never had anyone touch you with pure affection.*

"No. After what happened, I never wanted to." Bleakness shone in his eyes. "It hurt so fucking bad."

You've only ever known lust. Greed. Force.

I shoved down the groan that rumbled in the back of my throat. The shit he'd been through, I wished I could take it away. My body rocked forward like I planned to vault myself at him, to wrap him up and promise it would never be like that again.

I stopped myself. The last time I moved too fast, he panicked. He had to come to me.

"A," I rasped. I held out my hands. "Come here."

He thought about it before slowly pushing up out of the chair. I watched as he pushed it back; the wheels creaked and groaned, but they rolled away. I folded my legs under me so I was sitting old-school Indian style. My bracelet was still in my lap. I heard it fall between my thighs and hit the floor.

I didn't get up. I figured me being down here and him being up there might make him feel more secure.

I hadn't always taken these precautions with him, but that was before I knew. Now I did. Now I would take into consideration the things he'd been through. I'd have to teach him, through action, he was safe with me.

I held my hand out, and his slid into it. My stomach flipped when he stepped on each side of my hips and lowered until he was sitting in my lap.

His legs wrapped around my waist, his high-tops resting on the floor behind me. We were face to face, chest to chest. Because he sat in my lap, he was a little higher.

"Hey," I murmured and caressed his jaw.

"Hey."

I went slow so he could track my movement. I brought my hand up, curved it around the back of his neck, and tugged.

He let me lead his forehead down so it rested on top of my shoulder. Once it was there, my hand dragged down his back, rubbing, and tucked around him in a hug.

He sighed.

A sound I never knew could be so sweet.

Arrow's body relaxed, and I carefully wrapped my other arm around so I was holding him. It was the first time he'd been in my arms this way.

I prayed to God it wouldn't be the last.

I felt full right then, despite all the obstacles, all the devastating truths between us. They didn't seem so terrible when he was in my arms.

I held him for a while. I didn't track the time, but I noticed the more time passed, the more languid his body became. Even when my legs started to go to sleep, I ignored it because he felt so right.

Then he moved. His face slid from my shoulder and pressed into the crook of my neck. I whispered his name, stroking up his back. His arms encircled my back, hugging me.

My chest swelled to near bursting. Emotion so epic washed over me like a fucking tidal wave. I just tucked him closer and rode the storm, trying to shield him from the water.

"I'm sorry about Matt," he whispered against my neck. Desire stole some of my emotion. With every word he whispered, his lips brushed over my skin. "I wish I could take some of your pain away."

My voice cracked. "You are."

He sat back. Our faces were so close if I leaned forward just an inch, our noses would collide. Every breath he took, his chest rubbed against mine.

I reached up, pushing the ultra-blond hair out of his eye.

He leaned forward and caught my lips. I wanted to grab him and yank him close. I wanted to thrust my tongue deep in his mouth like I had before. I held back, letting him take the lead. My hands fell at my sides while his cupped my jaws and held.

He kissed me slowly but thoroughly. In some ways, it was like a first kiss because, honestly, no one had ever kissed me like this before. With need but with so much give. With innocence but knowledge. With love *and* fear.

I drank him in. I drank him in so deep I could feel him slosh around inside me.

When his tongue skirted out over my lips, I opened and let it twist around mine. His fingers tightened on my face and his body leaned farther into mine. I supported his weight and matched the pressure with my mouth.

He was killing me.

Killing. Me.

This was foreplay at its finest.

Foreplay at its most innocent yet most scorching.

Eventually, his hands slid down the sides of my neck, and his lips began to pull away. I groaned with protest but let him go. His eyes were heavy lidded, sort of shy, when they came up.

What a rare gem he was. A diamond still surrounded by coal, already put through so much pressure. A diamond already formed, just waiting for the soot to be rinsed away.

I smiled, swiped his lower lip with my thumb, and then licked what was left of our kiss off it. He kissed better than most men performed sex.

He slid back a little, and automatically my hands reached for him, tried to clutch him back. I looked up, thinking perhaps I shouldn't have.

But he smiled. "I'm not going anywhere."

His hand delved down between my legs, brushing against the front of my pants and my thighs. I bit down on my lip because, fuck, I wanted more. When he retreated, the bracelet was in his grip. He motioned for my wrist, and I held it out. Without a word, he buckled the bracelet back where it belonged and then covered it with his hand.

"Matt's part of you. This bracelet is part of you. That's okay."

"Please don't stay here tonight," I whispered, taking his face in my hands. "I don't want you here. It's cold, and it's not where I am."

"I don't know if I can—"

"You're safe with me, Arrow. I swear. I would never ever make you do anything you weren't ready for." I held out my hands, surrendering. "I won't even touch you unless you say it's okay. I'll take the couch in my suite tonight. You can take the bed."

His hands reached for mine. Our fingers threaded together.

"You really want me to come with you?" he asked.

"More than anything," I swore.

"All right, Hopp," he said with a small smile. *I love when he calls me that.* "I'll come with you."

Yes.

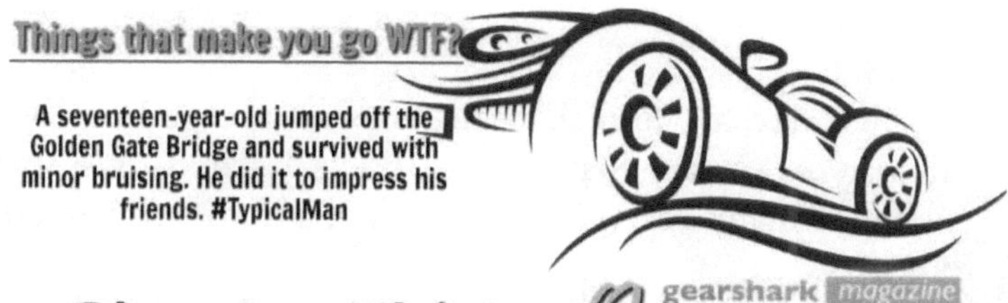

Chapter Thirty-One

Arrow

Sometimes people surprise you.

Sometimes you surprise yourself.

It usually doesn't happen on the same day, but today it did.

It almost felt like I'd lived a couple years in a single day. I woke up in a hangar, alone and resigned to it as always. But then coffee and donuts showed up, brought by a man I was so drawn to it was unnatural, yet it felt so right.

He kissed me.

He touched me.

Oh God, the way his fingers felt when he brushed the hair out of my eyes. It seemed obvious how he managed to get my heart so fast, so furiously.

It was ripe for the picking. Like a stray cat lost in the cold. Hungry, desperate, but also independent. The first sign of food, though, of comfort and warmth, independence becomes something that isn't as important.

Does the fact my heart was vulnerable mean anyone could have claimed it?

No.

Hell no.

Just like an animal, perhaps even a caged or lost one, my heart had instincts. Instincts learned over the course of many years, honed by pain, and mostly muted by sorrow.

But they were there all the same, and those instincts aroused when Hopper showed up on the other side of that fence. Something about him coaxed awake a sleeping part of me.

It wasn't his incredible good looks either. I barely noticed just how attractive his partly curly hair was, the scruff on his jaw, and the strength in his body. Okay, I noticed. I wasn't blind. But the way he looked was an afterthought.

The way he made me *feel* was everything.

Lorhaven was coming around. His support of my choices was as much a relief as it was a blessing.

And then we fought, Hopper and me. Not really fought so much as backed away and ran from each other, from the overwhelming way we were together.

I mourned when he left, but then he came back.

Hopper trusted me enough to tell me his truth, to explain the millions of tiny pieces his life shattered into. It hurt to hear, to know the way he suffered and punished himself.

It hurt because I empathized. I understood. Our pain was different, but it was both deep and crushing, a thief of the lives we once knew.

I did it.

I told him something I'd never spoken out loud before. Something no one else knew (except Jace). People knew I was beaten. It became pretty much common knowledge when Lorhaven almost killed those men. No one knew the worst of that night, and they likely never would.

Some pain was so deep, so painful, and so dark it was best it remained hidden. Forever.

Now I stood here staring down at a bed that wasn't mine.

He'd asked me to come, and I was a little embarrassed to admit I was almost beyond the point of denying him. Of denying myself.

Hopper's suite was standard for nice hotels. It was a two-room suite, the front room the one with a large couch, partial kitchen, television, and table with a few chairs. The bedroom was off from that, and in the center was a large king-size bed.

The walls were white just like the bedding, the furniture was dark, and the flat-screen hanging on the wall adjacent from the bed was huge.

Hopper's duffle was on a nearby counter, a large mirror hanging above it. A few T-shirts and a sock hung out of the unzipped top. My stomach turned over looking at it all because this was far more intimacy than I had ever known.

I was in his space, where he slept. Where he dressed. Where he retreated to at the end of an exhausting day. If I felt like this in a hotel room, what would it feel like to stand in the center of his apartment?

I glanced back at the down-covered bed. Nerves bundled in the base of my skull, and my fingers trembled slightly. He said I was safe with him, and I believed him.

But I wanted.

I wanted more of his hands, his lips. I wanted far more intimacy than I'd ever gotten from a dark stairwell at a crowded party.

I heard some sound in the other room, and I glanced around through the wide archway. Hopper tossed down his jacket and was standing in front of the thermostat, pressing a button repeatedly. Seconds later, the heat kicked on.

"You warm enough?" he asked, turning his head toward me.

"I'm fine." I assured him.

"It'll be warmer in a few."

I half smiled because he always seemed so concerned about how cold I was and where I lived. "You know…" I began, letting a little amusement poke through my words. "I do have a room at Lorhaven's place. I just never stay there. And I've never frozen at the hangar."

"You hungry?" he asked, choosing not to acknowledge my words.

"Starved," I replied. I hadn't eaten since the coffee and donuts.

He snatched his phone off the counter nearby and tapped the screen a few times. "You like pepperoni?"

"Who doesn't?"

He grunted. Then a few moments later, he tossed down the phone. "It'll be here soon."

I moved into the archway and watched Hopper from between both rooms. His back muscles worked when he opened the small fridge, leaned down, and came back with two longneck bottles of beer.

After removing both caps, he crossed the room and extended one to me. I took it and downed a sip.

"You mind if I take a shower before the pizza gets here?" he asked. "It's been a long fucking day." He sounded a little tired, and it made me nervous.

"Sure," I murmured and moved away. I went backward because he was in front of me and I didn't want to move past him.

I was waiting for the other shoe to drop. This was too normal. Us sitting around ordering pizza and drinking beer like we hadn't just poured out all our secrets wasn't the way it was supposed to be. Was it?

I was just waiting for something bad to happen, for Hopper to look around, see that I didn't fit in this room—in his world—and send me packing. I wasn't sure if what I told him fully penetrated yet, if he actually realized I was damaged goods.

How could he not be turned off by the fact I was raped?

"Hey," Hopper murmured, his voice much closer than I anticipated. I spun. He was right there, and my eyes widened. He didn't move back, though. Instead, he tapped the side of my head. "What's going on in here?"

I shrugged. "Nothing."

He made a sound. "I don't have to take a shower. Does it make you uncomfortable?"

"No." I promised. "Go ahead."

Hopper studied me for long moments, took a sip of the beer, then set it aside. He held out his hand for mine, then set it right beside his.

This was it.

"I want you here," he told me. "I'm not going to change my mind."

I blinked. He couldn't possibly have known what I'd been thinking.

His lips curled up. "What happened doesn't change the way I look at you. I still want you."

"You want me?" I echoed.

He nodded. "Yeah, I do. I want your time. Your smiles. The sound of your voice."

My chin dipped because I didn't want him to see how much his words affected me.

He tipped it back up. "Even the awkward moments we sometimes settle in."

"I don't understand why," I whispered, some of my naked doubt in my tone.

"I know," he murmured and stroked the back of his hand over my cheek. "But to me, you're so much more than just what happened that night."

I went forward, full on, and wrapped my arms around him. God, just the fact that I could reach out and hug him, hug someone who held my heart, was amazing to me. And more so?

He hugged me back. My body melted into his like butter. His arms tightened, and I sighed.

After a few, he pulled back, grabbed his beer, and headed toward the bathroom right off the bedroom. "I'll be out in a few." He promised before latching the door behind him.

I went out to the other room, turned on the flat-screen, found some old action flick, and then settled back with my beer. A few minutes later, there was a knock on the hotel door. I was surprised when I saw the delivery guy standing there with two large pizzas, because that had been hella fast.

I paid and set the boxes down, restraining myself from inhaling half of it before Hopp even appeared. That would just be rude.

Not long after, I heard the shower shut off and him moving around in the bedroom.

Have you ever heard any of those songs on the radio about wanting to watch a person when they didn't know you were watching?

No, not stalker songs.

You know, the songs that give someone a glimpse at the person they love at their most natural?

Fine, it's a terrible analogy. I'm not poetic. Fuck, I barely knew how to function when someone else was in the room with me.

The point is the pull to see him was irresistible. It felt like a string tied taut around my ribcage was being reeled in Hopper's direction. I stepped into the archway, the fresh scent of soap and balmy air wafting toward me. My eyes bounced off the bed, looked for him. Found him.

My feet halted. Actually, every part of me did. It was as if someone hit pause on just me and I stopped, frozen, unable to think or speak.

He was standing beside the foot of the bed, a pair of jeans low on his waist. They were looser than the usual cargo pants he wore, but they still showed off his ass. His feet were bare. A hint of the boxers he wore peeked out from his waistband and gave way to skin. Smooth, tight skin.

He wasn't wearing a shirt.

It was on the bed beside him. His hand was on it like he'd been about to shrug it on.

My mouth ran dry. It was the most skin I'd seen, and yeah, I'd imagined what he looked like beneath those snug shirts he wore. Hopper's body was a lot more filled out than mine. He looked strong and capable. The muscles in his back, arms, and waist were well defined.

Even his neck looked strong, and it was accentuated by the wet strands on his head that curled up and glistened with water.

He must have sensed me, because he spun and our eyes locked. I knew I likely looked like a deer caught in a pair of headlights. I felt stupid, and I told myself to knock it the fuck off. But I couldn't help it.

He made me curious.

"Arrow?" Hopper questioned.

"Pizza's here," I croaked. I couldn't stop looking at him. I couldn't stop wondering.

He frowned, but I barely noticed. "I tried to hurry so I could pay."

My feet started moving. I felt like a calf who just started walking on wobbly legs. I could literally feel myself breathe, the air whooshing in and out of my lungs. My heart thudded, excitement and anxiety pumping through my limbs.

His entire body swiveled around so we were standing face to face. I stopped with not much space left between us and swallowed thickly. I didn't want to say a word. Hell, I could barely think, let alone form a sentence. I longed for the… confidence, the familiarity to just reach out and take what I wanted.

I was unsure. I had to ask.

I knew what it was to not be asked.

"Can I touch you?" I didn't even recognize my own whisper.

My God, my stomach was flipping like it wasn't a stomach anymore, but a tilt-a-whirl with a broken switch.

"You don't ever have to ask," he said, low.

My fingers curled into my palms as I stood there and stared. I watched his Adam's apple bob and a stray droplet of water slide down his neck.

Finally, I brushed the tips of my fingers across his collarbone. It was a feather-light touch, barely there. He stood stock still, and I was pretty sure he even held his breath.

It wasn't enough, though, that whisper of a caress. My hand turned bolder. My palm flattened over his chest, pressing against his heart. I felt it beating rapidly, so rapidly my eyes flew up to his.

"It's okay." He promised, and then my hands started to move.

I dragged my palms out across his shoulders, down his upper arms, and curled around the rounded muscle of his bicep. I liked his chest better, though, that wide expanse of skin, the warmth he radiated, and how alive he felt.

Both my palms pressed back to his chest and then slid down until his rock-hard nipples poked their center. I circled around his pecs and then came right back to the center. Using my fingers, I tugged lightly at the erect pebbles, and his eyes slid closed, his throat working.

After that, my hands continued down, following the lean lines of his waist and moving in to explore the ripples of his abs.

I noticed the hairs on his arms raised; beneath were thousands of tiny bumps racing over his skin. Gooseflesh. My touch was exciting him.

I left his waist and went back up, letting one hand delve into the wet, clingy curls at his neck. They were slippery and cool but curled around my fingers instantly. My heart constricted.

Leaving my hand in his hair, I slipped the other around his waist, fingered the dip in the small of his back, and stepped up to him. My fingers were trembling. Fuck, my entire body shuddered with mini quakes, but I ignored it.

Against his spine, my hand moved up and down as I inched closer and closer.

Eventually, I was so close our chests were touching. I couldn't help but wonder what it would be like if my shirt was gone and it was just our skin pressed together.

I didn't pull back, though. I wasn't about to give this up. Instead, I dropped my chin, resting it on his shoulder as I continued to stroke his back.

My eyes slipped closed. The hand in his hair kneaded his scalp, and his breathing hitched.

I felt his hand flexing at his side. I pulled back and searched his face. "What's wrong?"

"Nothing," he ground out. "I just want to touch you, too."

But he held back. He promised he wouldn't unless I told him he could.

"You can," I whispered.

The pale blue in his gaze warmed and bounced between my eyes. "You sure?"

I nodded.

The next thing I knew, I was pressed back against him, both his arms were around me, and he held me close. I shifted so one of my legs was between his, and both my hands pressed against his bare back.

He smelled good. He felt good. Even the sound of his silence was good.

I pulled back, dragged my hands around to his waist, and then traveled up his chest again. His hands settled on my sides and didn't move. I kissed him, tilting my head, licking over his lips, and kissing deep.

He kissed me back with the same amount of pressure and want. We made out until I was gripping his back and my lungs burned from the lack of air.

He pulled back first, sucking in a lungful of air. "Damn, A," he growled. "C'mon. Pizza."

I was still in a daze from his body. Down in my jeans, my dick was hard and throbbing. Need stronger than I think I'd ever felt hammered in me.

He wanted pizza? Now?

Hopper's fingers threaded through mine, and he tugged me toward the other room. When his free hand went for the shirt, I shook my head, and he abandoned it. I followed along after him, mostly looking at where we were connected.

Using one hand, he threw open the top box and handed me the first slice his hand closed around. When I reached for it with the hand he was holding, he made a sound and tightened his grip. So I held it with the other hand instead.

On the couch, we sat with the food, right beside each other, our clasped hands between our legs.

After a few quiet minutes of eating, Hopper glanced at me, lifting our tangled hands. "You're not shaking anymore."

I glanced down at our hands.

He was right.

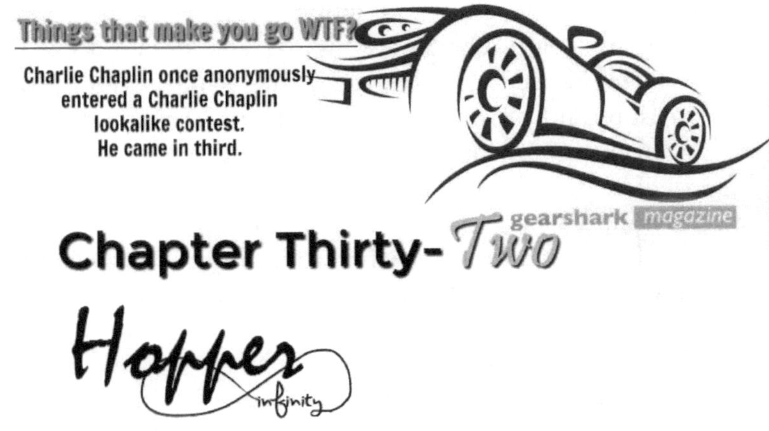

Chapter Thirty-Two

Hopper

A true lesson in patience = Arrow touching me.

It had been a while, a long while, since someone touched me like that. In a lot of ways, it might have been a first. He touched me like he was afraid of me but couldn't help himself. He explored my body like he never had with anyone before but wanted to over and over again.

Matt always had confidence; he was never afraid. When Matt and I were together, it was passion and lust. He knew where to touch to get the most pleasure, and he never hesitated to give it.

Arrow was different, which I was suddenly so grateful for. Different made me feel like I couldn't compare the two men, even when my mind tried to go there. Different didn't make me feel like I was trying to replace Matt, because that couldn't be done.

With Arrow, it felt like both of us were committed to learning each other completely, and though it was an odd thought, I felt I more naked with him than I'd ever been with anyone else. He was getting a part of me no

His shoulders moved like a weight just lifted, and he stepped up to me. "It's okay if you touch me."

I made a sound. "Yeah?"

He nodded.

I stepped around him and pulled back the blankets and sheets. The pillows fell around, but I didn't bother to mess with them.

"Which side you want?" I asked.

"The one closest to you."

I wondered how many more ways he was going to slay me tonight.

I slipped in first, holding up the blankets in invitation.

His forehead wrinkled. "You sleep in jeans?"

"Actually, I sleep naked. Figured that might be a little forward." I winked.

A small fire ignited in the air around us, and I suppressed a groan.

"Boxers?" he asked.

"Jeans are fine."

"It's like ninety million degrees in here." He scoffed. "You turned the heat up like we're a bunch of old grannies with no body heat."

I laughed out loud. "It is kinda hot in here."

"Kinda?" Arrow guffawed. "It's like the fucking Sahara."

"Hint taken," I muttered, got out of bed, and turned down the thermostat. I just wanted him to be warm. Warm and safe. It had somehow become the most important thing to me.

I walked around the mattress and stared at him from the other side. My hand went to the button on my jeans.

Arrow slipped into the bed and watched me.

I pulled down the jeans, hoping it wasn't a mistake, and then climbed into the bed wearing nothing but blue boxer briefs. He was sitting up, the covers at his waist, like he wasn't sure what to do.

I lay down, pulled a pillow beneath my head, and then extended my arm toward him. "Come here."

Arrow came across the bed. I felt his stare even in the dark lighting. He was shaking again. I felt the mattress beneath us vibrate. I didn't acknowledge it because it wasn't necessary.

I wrapped my arm around him, pulling him against my body. His cheek hit my shoulder and his pajama-clad leg pushed between my bare ones.

Keeping in mind he told me to touch him, my hand began lazily stroking up and down his back. Arrow settled a little farther along me, his arm draped over my middle, his fingers tucked between my side and the mattress.

Tenderness bloomed in my heart and burned my stomach. Such small things… just a single touch from him created so much feeling.

"I've never slept with someone before." He confided. "I've never shared a bed."

I pressed my lips to the top of his forehead and continued to stroke his back. After a few minutes, I said, "Do you like it?"

"You have no idea."

"I think I might," I whispered. Then because it was all or nothing, I told him what was on my mind. "I feel like I'm betraying him."

I felt his intake of breath. The muscles in his body tightened. I was prepared to pull him back if he tried to get up, but to my surprise, he didn't.

"I wish I could slay your demons," he said, quiet. "But some days, I can't even slay mine."

"You understand the fight, though."

"All too well." He agreed.

His understanding was all I really needed.

My hand moved away from his back, up to the damp strands of hair on his head. Since it was long on the side, I was able to pull my fingers through it.

"What was he like?" Arrow asked.

Remembering Matt was easy, but thinking of him always generated a twinge of pain. "Laidback, fun, a really good Ducati racer."

"Better than you?" As he spoke, he tapped my side with his finger.

I smiled in the dark. "No."

He chuckled. "You loved him, so that tells me all I need to know."

"I honestly thought I wouldn't love anyone again."

I heard him swallow. "And now?"

"Now I'm not so sure."

Arrow pulled his hand from beneath me, laid his fingers against my ribs, and began to lightly drag the tips over my side and chest.

I sighed. The thoughts in my head took a backseat to the way he made me feel.

"Do you think I'm damaged?" Arrow's voice cut through the quiet comfort of the room.

"No more damaged than I am."

His hand stopped caressing me, a simple touch I missed immediately. "Does…?" He fell silent.

"You can ask me anything." I promised.

"Does knowing what happened to me make me any less, uh, attractive to you?"

The back of my head lifted off the pillow so my chin could angle down. Arrow looked up, and I moved in, pressing my lips fully against his.

My lips were slow and languid, soft in pressure, but every inch of our mouths made contact. I tugged his lower lip into my mouth and sucked it. His small moan of pleasure tightened my balls.

I broke the kiss and shifted my body. Still keeping him against me, I rolled onto my side so we could face each other.

"I'm *so* attracted to you, and nothing is *ever* gonna change that," I whispered. "Even if you do look like Justin Bieber." I cracked.

He groaned and rolled his eyes. "Not you, too."

I grinned. "Confession?"

His eyes came back to my face, his head bobbing.

"After I saw you the first few times at Gamble Speedway, I went out and bought his CD."

Arrow burst out laughing. It was real and genuine. His smile was wide and his teeth flashed white.

"Every time I listen to that CD, I think of you," I admitted while running a finger up the center of his chest. "I probably know about ninety percent of those songs word for word now."

His heart filled his eyes. Honestly, it was the most beautiful heart I'd ever seen. What was it about the broken and damaged? The ones that rise from the wreckage to walk or sometimes even stumble away?

Being a survivor made every moment, every kind word a little more meaningful, because they were the ones who knew what almost never was.

Arrow's palm flattened on my shoulder and pushed. I rolled onto my back, and he leaned over and swept his tongue in my mouth. The weight of his chest lying across mine, his arms wrapped around my naked torso, and the way his lips coerced mine into some kind of magic dance made me feel drunk and tingly.

Eventually, his lips released mine, and I sucked in a deep breath before he continued kissing. I let my head fall to the side so his teeth could scrape across my jaw and latch onto my earlobe. Little shivers of delight raced up my spine and my nipples tightened as he sucked and tugged at the delicate flesh.

Next, he slid down over my neck and suckled the skin there with enough pressure to make me moan. My hand pressed against his back and urged him closer. Urged him to suck deeper.

He did but pulled back too soon, drifting his lips over the top of my shoulder before laying his head back where it had been.

I felt his erection pressed against my hip. It took everything in me not to wiggle against it. I, too, rocked a massive boner, but I did my best to ignore it. I wasn't about to rush things with Arrow. Our hearts were moving fast enough all on their own.

Arrow's fingers flirted over my abs, and my muscles constricted. "I like touching you."

I made a sound. "I like being touched."

He continued the sweet torture with a feather-light hand, so I added some of my own by rubbing his back with long, slow strokes.

Surprisingly enough, my eyes grew heavy.

Having him in my arms and the consistent thud of his heart against my side made me the most comfortable I'd been in a very long time.

Five years, to be exact.

It also marked the first time in five years I'd slept the entire night.

Chapter Thirty-*Three*

Arrow

Everything I owned fit in the back of my Camaro.

There wasn't much. Most of it was shoes. I liked sneakers. Especially high-tops. I didn't need much, but the idea of driving toward more excited me.

The contract for NASCAR was in the passenger seat, but it was unsigned. After I woke up in Hopper's bed, still plastered against his body, and after we ordered room service (waffles and French toast), we made out again.

Kissing him was my most favorite thing I'd ever done. I lost myself every single time. It was a rush, yet it was more.

It was letting him have a part of me no one else had ever been given.

Sure, I kissed other people in the past, but how empty every single kiss had been. Kisses that made me lonelier. Kisses that left me reaching for a connection. Eventually, I began to realize I wasn't going to connect to anyone.

Until Hopper.

I digress. Making out wasn't really the point here.

But clearly, it's where my mind was.

We went to the hangar so I could sign the contract, but just as I was lowering the pen to the dotted line, Hopper put his hand over mine.

"Not yet," he said. "There's something I want to do first."

The first turned out to be packing up all my shit and driving across the state. I could barely concentrate on the road in front of me because of the matte-black Audi in my rearview mirror. It was kinda torture to have him so close, but not right there. All I could think about was us in the control tower. Us in his hotel room. Us in his bed.

The way it felt when he touched me.

No one had ever touched me like Hopper. I felt wanted when I was with him. It left me awestruck.

Halfway through the drive, my cell rang. I answered it without looking at the screen.

"Yeah?"

His voice filled my ear. "Take the next exit."

I glanced in the rearview. "Everything okay?"

"No."

I disconnected the call and hit the gas, swerved around some cars that were in my fucking way, and drifted around the curved exit ramp, straightening the wheel. There was a gas station on the right, so I pulled in, parked the car at the edge of the lot, and got out with the engine still running.

Hopper stopped right beside my car and did the same. He came around his hood, and I started toward him.

"What's wrong?" I demanded.

We met beside the headlight of the Audi, but he didn't slow. Instead, his hands grasped my face and pulled it in.

My blood pressure spiked at the way he attacked my mouth. No longer did the sound of passing traffic fill the air. I didn't hear the purring engines of our cars or the scuffle of people walking in and out of the store.

I drowned in the way he desperately kissed me. The way his tongue stabbed my mouth and searched for mine. Need roared in my limbs. I reached for him, jerked his hips into mine so our bodies were pressed together. My chest heaved and my fingertips were likely leaving marks where I clutched him, but I didn't stop.

"I really fucking needed that." He gasped and pressed his forehead to mine. Strands of his hair tickled my forehead, and my stomach jumped.

Reality filtered back in slowly. The first thing I noticed was the sound of Justin Bieber's music coming from the interior of the Audi.

My face split into a grin. *God, I fucking love him.*

The thought caught me off guard.

No. It fucking shocked me. *Terrified me.*

So much so I jolted backward and stared at Hopper.

His face changed, twisting into a look of concern. "A, what is it?"

It really isn't a shock. I knew it. I felt it. My heart surrendered to him almost from the minute I saw him outside that fence. It was fast, so fucking fast. But those who thought it was *too* fast didn't know me. They didn't know how soft my heart was.

It was why I needed so many locks and such a high fence. Why I let Lorhaven stand in front of me.

What was so shocking was how easily the thought came. How loving him had become so obvious my brain automatically acknowledged it.

Oh fuck, the power he had.

That's where the terror came in.

I was supposed to be taking back all the power I'd been robbed of. Not handing it over to someone new.

"Oh shit," Hopper said. "Was that too rough? I shouldn't have done that." He grabbed the front of my hoodie, giving me little shake.

The only thing that could snap me out of my internal meltdown was his. Hopper started backing away, and I could tell by the set of his jaw he was angry with himself. He thought he'd hurt me.

I grabbed his hand, tugging him back. "You should do it again."

His glacial stare widened. "Did I freak you out?"

"Again," I demanded.

My hair fell over one eye when he pulled me into him, but I left it there. My eyes closed as his lips claimed mine. He took the lead, just like the first time. I loved it. I loved the way he was so sure but so tender.

His mouth lifted, but before he pulled back, he pressed one last swift kiss against me.

"So I take it nothing was really wrong?" I lifted an eyebrow as I waited for my heart rate to return to normal.

"Oh, something was wrong. The amount of time that passed since the last time you kissed me."

I ducked my head and smiled. Sometimes I just didn't know what to do with the blatant affection he gave so readily. I'd never, not ever, had someone pull off a highway in the middle of a road trip just so he could kiss me.

How far we'd come in such a short amount of time.

"Do you feel better?" I asked, rubbing my thumb over his lower lip.

"For now." His fingers reached for mine, our palms pressing together when they tangled.

"What happened a minute ago? Where'd you go?" he asked.

I shrugged. "Nothing. I'm right here with you."

He stared at me one second longer, then nodded. I knew he probably didn't totally believe me, but that was something about us. We knew when not to push. We both understood that sometimes we had to confront the inner battle always waging inside.

Still holding hands, Hopper gestured to the gas pumps behind us. "You need to fill up?"

"Nah. We don't have much farther."

"Thank fuck," He muttered.

I gave his hand a squeeze. "See you when we get there?"

On the way back to his car, I held his hand until our outstretched arms no longer reached and our fingers pulled apart.

I pulled out behind him this time, meaning I was the one in the rearview. My eyes stayed firmly ahead because that's where he was.

Yeah, I could have confided how off-kilter my feelings for him knocked me. I could have showed him how hella scared I was now that my mind echoed in words exactly how I felt.

I didn't.

This wasn't his burden. And that was exactly it. I didn't want him to feel like loving him was anything but absolutely amazing.

Because I did love him. I learned a lot from people over the years about how *not* to treat someone you loved.

I might not be ready to tell him those three words, but I would always, no matter what, treat him as if I already had.

Chapter Thirty-*Four*

Hopper

I called ahead to make sure his apartment was ready.

It was the first of two stops today.

I was glad we had that time together before we drove down here. Time alone was going to be harder to come by after today. We had work to do, and I had a job that included managing more drivers besides Arrow.

Which was why I stopped him from signing the contract. I wanted to make a few things crystal clear beforehand.

"What floor do you live on?" Arrow asked when we stepped into headquarters, on the side where the staff apartments were.

"Third. Same as you."

He was surprised, just as I knew he would be. The doors to the elevator were closing when he said, "You already know what floor I'll live on?"

I shifted one of the very few boxes he'd brought into one arm and fished a set of keys out of my jeans. "I've already got your key."

His head drew back. "I haven't even signed yet."

"Just a detail," I answered. Truth was I had this place readied for him before I even knew for sure he was going to sign with NASCAR. It became increasingly important to me that Arrow have a place of his own, a real place and not some cot in a garage.

"The apartments here are already furnished. They're practically move-in ready, so any new Gamble team member can move in as soon as needed," I explained as the elevator glided to a stop. "So it didn't take much to have it ready."

"Is it just a coincidence my place is on the same floor as yours?"

I glanced at him as the doors opened, revealing a standard wide hallway with gray carpet and white walls. "What do you think?"

Arrow smiled, and I continued down the hall. The apartment on the other side of me was already occupied, but having him just down the hall was better than one floor up.

He was quiet as he followed me toward the glossy black door with the pewter identifier on the surface. "3E," I told him, stopping in front of his new front door.

He still said nothing. I glanced around, and he shrugged, sheepish. "I've never had my own place like this."

He was nervous.

"Well…" I scoffed. "Don't get too excited. This place ain't nothing fancy."

He chuckled, and I slid the key into the lock and pushed open the door.

The fresh smell of paint wafted out, which made me curious, but I stepped back and motioned for him to go in first. "Welcome home."

Arrow adjusted the boxes in his hands and slipped past.

I followed along closely but stopped to push the door shut with my foot.

Arrow walked into the center of the open-concept space and looked around, taking it all in. Off to my right was the island that separated the kitchen from the rest of the place. It was topped with gray-and-white marble, and I set the box in my arms on top of it.

"You said it wasn't anything fancy," Arrow said sardonically, gesturing to the room we stood in.

"Did I mention Joey and Lorhaven might have been here?"

I wasn't lying when I told him the apartments here were furnished, but they weren't that fancy. They were basically blank canvases with basic furntiure. They didn't boast the homey feeling most places had because they'd been designed to work for varying people and styles. It was up to the tennant to make them a little more comfortable or "lived in."

I'd lived in my place for a little over five years now, and it still looked as non-personal and cold as the day I'd walked in.

Not Arrow's place.

I'd taken a chance and called Joey yesterday. I was worried she might not pick up, but after Lorhaven admitted she missed me, I had to try.

I missed her, too.

She answered on the first ring. I thought it might be awkward, but it wasn't, and the biggest sense of relief filled me. She'd actually given me hell for taking so long to call, and then we talked about everything just like we never took a break.

When I told her I was bringing Arrow down and he was moving into 3E, she immediately volunteered to get the place ready. I figured she'd put some milk in the fridge, maybe some sheets and blankets on the bed.

That's not all she did.

I didn't know if that girl had been watching HGTV in her free time or if she was just a damn good decorator, but damn… this place looked like someone already lived here.

Not only that, but they were stylish as hell.

The most prominent wall in the place, which was off to my left across from the open kitchen, was recently painted a deep shade of red. The rest of the walls were left in their original white.

There was a brand-new flat-screen hung in the center of the wall, with a huge cabinet below it that looked like a scuffed-up gym locker in a shade of gray.

Lining the red wall on either side of the flat-screen were framed posters of cars, all in black and white.

The standard black leather sectional didn't appear so standard with red and gray pillows scattered around and a blanket that looked like a checkered flag draped over the back.

The customary glass-topped coffee table was gone, and in its place was a wooden tabletop in a distressed gray finish that sat on industrial-looking black wheels. The remote for the TV was the only thing on it, and beneath it was a large gray-and-white striped rug.

Over by the door we'd just come through, hooks lined the wall for coats and shit, but beneath it was a shelving unit with a bunch of open cubbies that I knew were meant for all his high-tops.

There were red metal barstools next to me at the island, and beyond it was the kitchen, which was pretty much average for these apartments, with white subway tile, gray-and-white marble counters, and stainless-steel appliances. The cabinets were black.

There was a new coffeemaker on the counter with a box of those pod things that went in it beside it. I knew without looking there were a few basic things in the cabinets, like some white plates, cups, and bowls, along with some silverware and a couple pots and pans.

Arrow wandered out of the living room and around the counter to look at the kitchen closer. In the center of the long U-shaped space was a rug in the same color and pattern as the living room. Something caught his eye, and he walked over to yank off a piece of paper pinned to the front of the fridge.

"Table's being delivered next week," he read and glanced behind him at the empty eat-in portion of the kitchen.

He set aside the note and opened the fridge. There was six-pack of beer in the center of a fully stocked fridge with a note that read: "Beer is from Jace."

"They did all this?" Arrow twisted around to look at me.

My chest swelled with gratefulness. Maybe I'd been a little too hard on his brother before… Nah. Scratch that. But it was clear Lorhaven did care about Arrow. Joey, too.

"Bedroom's through there." I pointed to the only room leading off of the kitchen and living room combo.

Instead of heading right for it, Arrow crossed to me, slipped his hand around mine, and smiled. "Thank you."

My eyebrows shot up. "I didn't do anything."

He made a sound. "We both know they wouldn't have done all this if you hadn't called my sister."

I looked into his eyes. "They would have. Maybe just not as fast."

"Thank you, Hopp."

Emotion clogged my throat and chest. "Let's go see what she did to the bedroom."

The walls were left white in the square bedroom, but there was a rug and padded bench at the foot of the wooden-framed bed. Above it on the wall were more black-and-white posters hung in frames. Chrome lamps sat on the bedside tables with a docking system for his phone. Across the room on the empty wall was a standard dresser with a single framed photo of Arrow and his brother on top.

The bed itself was king-size and made up with brand-new white-and-gray bedding. It basically looked like a cloud with a gray furry blanket over the bottom quarter. My favorite thing about it was the single red, rectangular pillow in the center with a big white arrow on the front.

The bathroom was off the bedroom and was done in the same gray-and-white finishes of the kitchen. It was stocked with new towels and a rug in front of the sink.

How the hell Joey and Lorhaven got all this done in a day was beyond me.

"So what do you think?" I asked when we were back out in the living room. "Will this place do?"

"Are you kidding?" he replied. "This place is too good for me."

"No," I intoned, went to him, and grabbed his face. My eyes bored into his. "You deserve this."

"Can I see your place?" he asked.

I didn't try to convince him of what he deserved. Over time, he would learn. Until then, I would keep reminding him.

"It's not near as nice as this." I grinned.

"I don't care."

I knew he didn't. It seemed material things weren't very important to Arrow. He was very used to living with next to nothing… and that included affection.

I hated to think what he would be like now if not for his brother. Unreachable likely. Possibly unsavable.

I glanced down. We were holding hands again. I had no idea who reached for whom or when.

"You're welcome at my place anytime you want." I promised. "I'm in 3A."

"You may get sick of me." He teased, but underneath, I knew he wasn't joking.

I made a rude noise. "I couldn't even drive across the state without stopping to get a fix of you."

Arrow tugged at the hand he was holding and licked his lips. "You need another?"

I groaned. "Always."

Without any warning, he pushed me up against the emtpy dining room wall and covered my body with his. He plastered against me and swooped in, our lips melting in a searing kiss.

There was something different about him this kiss. Something surer, something headier. He wasn't shaking. He didn't seem afraid.

Arrow was hungry, and it showed.

His hunger made mine more severe. As if it had been lurking, just waiting for the opportunity to come out and play. I didn't know if now was a good time, but I was too far gone to really think.

Arrow's hands slid up beneath my shirt, his fingers rubbing over my abs and chest. My nipples tightened so fast they actually hurt, and when his thumb flicked over it, I moaned.

He lifted his mouth, scorching me with the heat in his stare, and I nodded, assuring him everything was all right.

His hands left my chest, tugging at my jacket and shirt.

I pushed off the wall and allowed him to shove the coat down my arms, and it hit the floor with a slap. Arrow reached around me, grabbed a fistful of my shirt, and pulled. I lifted my arms to make it easier, and he tossed the shirt over his shoulder.

His eyes were like two bolts of lightning cracking over my skin. I felt scorched and electrified all at once.

"Hopp," he murmured, rubbing his palms over my pecs.

"Babe," I uttered as the back of my head hit the wall.

I felt his stare again, so I opened my eyes. He gazed at me with equal parts longing and surprise. I searched my mind, wondering what I'd done.

I'd called him babe.

It was like a suckerpunch to my gut. How easily that term of endearment slipped out. "I didn't realize—" I began, thinking he must not have liked it.

"Say it again," he demanded.

I liked his bossy side.

I shoved my fingers through his blond strands of hair. "I fucking love when you kiss me, babe."

With a growl, he swooped back in, but not in the direction I'd been expecting. Instead, his lips latched onto my painfully aroused nipple and sucked it deep into his mouth.

My hips arched off the wall and my eyes closed again. My breathing was heavy, and my fingers strained against the wall behind me.

He sucked and kissed, flicking his tongue over the hard pebble over and over again.

When he relented, I sighed, collapsing against the wall… but he only moved to the other.

The onslaught started all over again, and in my jeans, my dick was throbbing in a way that pained me. Fuck, I was so horny. It had been so long since anyone made me feel I was going to lose it right there in my pants.

I gripped the back of his head, wanting to pull him back because I seriously was afraid I was either going to blow right there or reverse the roles and shove him against the wall for a little sweet torture of his own.

Arrow released my nipple, and I shivered, but instead of obeying my hand, his tongue left a wet, warm trail down the center of my abs and circled around my navel.

My hips rocked toward him, and I bit on my lip, trying to control my urges.

"Babe," I said, reaching for him to pull him up. "You're making me crazy."

He straightened but stayed close. Flames flickered in his eyes, and his hand rubbed the front of my thigh.

My eyes snapped to his. I felt them widen when his fingers spider-crawled slowly toward my engorged cock.

"A," I said, shaky, and reached for his hand.

"I want to touch you, Hopp. You gonna let me?" As he spoke, the front of his hand brushed over my hard length.

I shuddered. With a deep breath, I said, "I don't expect this."

"I know." He agreed. "I want it."

I was powerless to deny him, especially since he was rubbing his palm over my dick now and I could already feel the tip weeping.

Our chests were pressed together. His lips slid over mine as his fingers fumbled with the buttons on my jeans. He lifted his lips as the button popped open, tilted his head in the opposite direction, and then fused us back together. The sound of my zipper sliding down filled the room, and both hands tucked beneath my boxers and the waistband, gliding over the smooth skin of my hips.

My breath hitched and my mouth fell away from the kiss. The back of my head bumped the wall, and I sucked in a deep breath. My legs were trembling. Fuck, everything was trembling.

Inch by inch, Arrow peeled down my jeans and boxers. I waited anxiously for my cock to be bared to him. It seemed like it took a million years when really it was probably less than a minute.

Arrow moved down my body as he lowered my pants. He kissed sporadically down my chest and then hit his knees before me. I jolted when his teeth scraped over my hipbone, and then with one final tug, my pants and boxers were around my ankles.

My cock had sprung free. It was so swollen it jutted right out toward the man responsible for making me so excited.

Maybe if I wasn't so turned on, I would have had enough sense to be cautious of Arrow and more concerned about the physical place he was taking us to right then.

I stared down my body to where he kneeled and watched as he wrapped his big hand around my hard-as-hell cock and slid toward the base.

I muttered a few words that didn't make sense, and my head fell back again.

Arrow squeezed the base gently and used his other hand to gently cup my sack. My tongue slid over the roof of my mouth as he simultaneously massaged my balls and slowly jacked my rod.

He had the perfect size hands. They wrapped around me fully and delivered bliss I hadn't known in what felt like forever.

"Hopp," he murmured, running his thumb over the tip of my cock.

I opened my eyes and stared down at him. Just seeing him kneel in front of my body, with his thumb spreading the silky moisture weeping out, made me weak in the knees.

"This okay?"

I barked a laugh. "Fuck yes."

His dark eyes pinned mine, holding me captive even though I really wanted to close them and melt farther into the wall. As we watched each other, his tongue jutted out, wetting his lips, and then he lowered his mouth to where he held my dick.

I couldn't look away. There was something about his stare that made it impossible. Arrow's pouty lips parted slowly, achingly, and the head of my dick slipped between them.

I made a sound. His eyes flared, but he still held my gaze.

The intensity he emanated was overwhelming. He owned me. He fucking owned me, and nothing would change it.

He took my cock deep, and the silky feel of the inside of his mouth enveloped me. My body shuddered and my hands gripped at the flat wall.

The hand wrapped around the base of my rod twisted lightly, creating a tingly sensation in my balls, and they tightened against my body instantly. He pulled back, dragged his lips over my length, then sucked my head with extra pressure before releasing to lick across it.

"Jesus Christ," I swore.

A small smile played on his face, and he broke eye contact and went back for me. On impulse, I made a sound, slid my hands beneath his arms, and pulled.

His eyes flashed, and I saw the worry in his face.

"You didn't do anything wrong. Just the opposite. I just don't want you on your knees before me. I want you over me."

Before I could move, I had to kick off my shoes and pants. Once I was completely naked, I let him lead me back to the bedroom.

The room was dim because all the blinds were closed. Arrow wrapped his hands around my waist and backed me toward the bed. He glanced at the mattress and then at me.

I thought I saw a hint of wariness.

"Whatever you want." I assured him softly, hopefully conveying this didn't have to go any further.

"I want your dick in my mouth," he replied and pushed me gently back onto the bed.

I wasn't about to argue with that.

On the bed, he straddled me. The weight of his body was heaven. Both his hands wrapped around my dick and slowly worked my rod before he bent his head.

"Wait," I rasped.

He glanced up.

"Take off your shirt."

Arrow reached behind him and pulled off his hoodie and T-shirt in one movement and threw them on the floor.

My eyes swept over his tattoos, down the lean sinew of his muscles, and satisfaction bloomed in my chest. I lifted my hand and pressed it against his pec, feeling the way his heart thundered.

Without another word, he moved down my body and took my cock in his mouth again. This time he didn't play. He didn't stare into my eyes with desire. He sucked the shit out of me.

His mouth applied just the right amount of pleasure; his throat took the perfect amount of length. He knew when to suck harder and when to pull back so the heated, sensitive skin stretched over my dick would glide over the slick, smooth inside of his cheeks.

When I would start to shudder a little too much, he'd pull back, jack me with his hand, and lavish attention on my balls and inner thighs.

My hips rocked against his lips. I couldn't help it. It was like my body had a mind of its own beneath his ministrations. Just when I started to grow frustrated with need, he slipped down over my cock again, grabbed my hips with his palms, and began to direct them. Even though he was on top, I was essentially fucking his mouth. On his order, I controlled how fast I pumped between his lips and how deep my cock went.

I moaned and he moaned back. The sound vibrated the tip of my dick, and I gasped.

"I'm going," I bit out, thinking to pull back, but instead, I shoved deeper into his mouth.

Arrow released my hips, wrapped both his arms around my ass, and held me deep.

He groaned again.

It pushed me over the edge.

A yell ripped out of my throat. My hands fisted in the blanket beneath me, and my hips bucked up. My dick pumped out an intense orgasm, and with every twitch, the head rubbed the back of his throat.

I'm not gonna be shy here. I made a lot of fucking noise.

The sounds that ripped out of me as he drank down my cum would probably have embarrassed me if I wasn't half out of my fucking mind.

When it was done, my body quivered lightly and my hips fell toward the mattress. Arrow was still wrapped around my ass, holding me close. My dick wasn't buried in his throat anymore, but he hadn't completely released it either.

Instead, he milked the tip of my head with his lips, using soft, light strokes and a little coaxing with his tongue.

I collapsed against the bed, heaved a great sigh, and threw my hands over my face.

Arrow withdrew from my core, and I felt him climb up the bed and settle beside me.

"Was that okay?" he asked, unsure.

Oh God, his vulnerability would be my undoing. How any man that fucking good at head could ever doubt it was one of the mysteries of the world.

I spread apart two fingers so I could stare at him through the crack. "Where the fuck did you learn to suck a dick like that?"

Spots of red bloomed on his high cheekbones.

He was fucking blushing.

Oh my God, I love him.

The thought made me peel my hands from my face. I wasn't expecting that. I wasn't sure what to do with it. Guilt came with it, but it was overpowered.

Overpowered by the waiting eyes staring down at me.

"I've blown someone before… more than once," he stammered.

I pushed up onto my elbows. "Like that?" I demanded.

The blush on his cheeks deepened, and he shook his head. "I just wanted to show you the way you make me feel."

"Kiss me," I demanded. "I want to taste myself on your tongue."

His eyes flared, and he lowered. He did taste like me. Slightly salty and smooth. The fact that I still mingled in his mouth turned me on all over again.

Arrow wrapped an arm over my waist and pushed a little closer as we kissed. His rock-hard dick pressed against my hip.

I broke the kiss and looked into his face.

"What about you?" I asked. "Will you let me do that to you?"

Desire filled his features. He hesitated, then nodded.

I shook my head. "Gonna have to hear you say it, babe."

His mouth tilted up. He really fucking liked the pet name. I was going to have to keep it.

"I want you to blow me."

Moving far slower than my body urged me to, I sat up beside him. His eyes were filled with desire and a little bit of wariness.

Instead of going right for his dick, I ran my fingers through his hair and kissed his forehead. Even though I relished the thought of him under me, I wasn't sure if he would feel out of control that way, so I gestured toward the headboard and all the pillows filling the space.

"Sit up," I instructed, and he did. Just before he leaned against the wooden frame, I used a couple pillows and pushed them behind his back.

Once he was sitting, I settled beside him, running my hand over his smooth chest. "I really fucking like the ink." I confided.

"That's good 'cause it's permanent."

I chuckled and traced over the arrow on his neck with my forefinger. "Since the first day I saw this one," I began, "all I wanted to do was kiss where the arrow led." My finger slid down and settled in the hollow spot behind his collarbone. "Right here."

His throat worked and his head tilted to the side, giving me great access to the teasing spot.

I dipped my head and licked over the collarbone, kissing lightly over the raised part. Then my tongue slid behind it and delved into the small of his neck. I sighed and licked into the spot a little deeper, pressing my lips against his skin.

His breathing hitched, and I wrapped my arm around the other side of his neck and cradled him gently as I kissed and sucked. Eventually, I moved on, licking up the arrow and delving the tip of my tongue into his ear.

Beside me, his body went languid, like putty in my hands. That above everything else was the most heady thing to me. He was granting me trust, letting go enough to feel pleasure at my hands. It made me want to do right by him, make sure this was so good hesitation would be an afterthought the next time I reached out.

I took my sweet-ass time kissing every inch of him I could reach without climbing on him. My lips and hands moved in tandem to make his skin buzz with pleasure.

When I finally reached for his jeans, his head fell back against the headboard and his hip rotated out, inviting more. I worked the jeans and boxers down his long legs, barely able to contain my pleasure at the first sight of his dick.

It was thick and long, the skin was taut and the head slightly swollen. The balls at the base were already drawn against his body, and I smiled because it meant he was good and ready for me to grab him by the stick.

"If you want me to stop, just say so," I whispered, wrapping my hand around his base.

Breath hissed between his teeth. "I want you to start."

I stretched out alongside him, partially lying across his lap, and dropped my mouth deep around him with one bold move.

He moaned softly, and I began to work his dick with my mouth and tongue. I sucked and licked and used my hands to give him the most pleasure I could conceive.

The thing about being a man, working another man's rod?

I knew the right buttons to push, or at least where most of them were. And I paid close attention to Arrow. Every sound he made, every intake of breath, and every quiver of muscle. He liked when I took him deep, but he also liked when I wrapped my lips around his head and sucked hard.

I knew I was doing a good job when his hand fisted in my hair and held my head.

When Arrow's hand fell away from my head and his body began to strain, I knew he was ready to let go. So with one hand I cupped his balls, and with the other I held the base of his cock firmly in place. I wrapped his tip and the sensitive ring below it between my lips, brushed my tongue over his salty tip, and sucked.

His hips shot off the bed, and his dick pulsed inside my mouth. His release was hot across my tongue, and I swallowed it down just as he had for me.

When his body fell back onto the pillows, I lifted my head and glanced up.

His chest heaved, and he looked at me in wonder.

I only smiled, moved up the bed beside him, tossed a couple pillows around, and then pulled him down so his cheek was on my chest. I wrapped him in both arms and felt his lips brush over my pec.

"I think I'm gonna like living here."

I laughed out loud.
I sure as fuck was gonna love it.

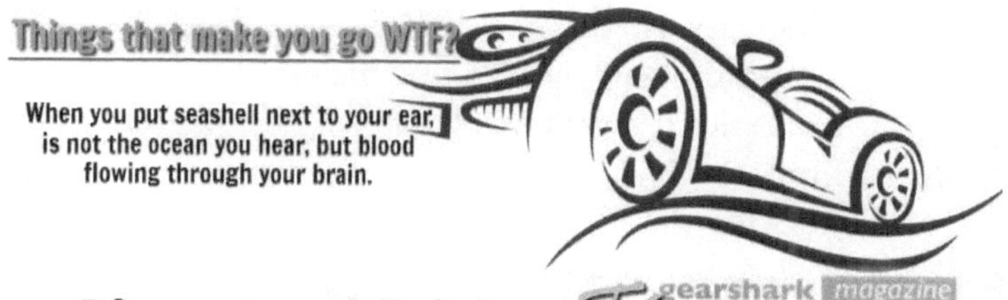

Chapter Thirty-Five

Arrow

The interior of Hopp's Audi was fucking sweet.

All leather. All black with touches of chrome. He looked sexy as hell behind the wheel, too.

Yeah, my mind was kinda stuck on sexy after the blowjob experience we had at my new apartment.

Seriously, it was like I was living in a fairy tale for real. Not only did I have a brand-new apartment that was nice as shit (thank you, Joey and Lor), but Hopper and I were getting closer despite all the baggage we both dragged behind us.

He was good to me. Patient. Gentle. Understanding.

Maybe it wasn't "manly" to need those things. God knew I beat myself up over not being "manly" enough on an almost daily basis.

But the fact still remained—I needed those things.

Suddenly, I was gifted them. Gradually, I accepted them as true.

Funny how when you start to get the things you need most, the less and less you beat yourself up for needing them.

Besides, I was still man enough.

I sucked the shit right out of his dick.

Or should I say cum? I sucked the orgasm right out of him.

Who's the man?

Oh shit, happiness was unfolding inside me. Was that was this was? That feeling of overwhelming change wasn't as paralyzing as I thought it would be.

Instead, I found myself walking toward it. Quicker and quicker each day.

Had I ever been truly happy?

Maybe when I was a child, before the age of ten.

That was a long fucking time ago, before life reared its ugly head.

I glanced across the car at the man driving. His hand was wrapped in mine, lying in my lap. I loved holding his hand. It made me feel connected, part of something. Like I wasn't just out floating in the universe without a lifeline.

It still scared me. I was so afraid of his rejection. Of being turned away once I let him all the way in.

But I had to try.

I owed myself at least that much. He couldn't hurt me like I'd been hurt in the past. I was older, wiser… better able to protect myself.

No one would hurt me like that again. Not my father, not strangers in a car.

I didn't have to lock myself away to guarantee it. I deserved happiness. More than that, I *wanted* it.

We pulled up to Gamble Estate, and it wasn't until we were pulling through the gate I looked at Hopp. "You made me get out of bed to come here?"

His teeth flashed white against the dark interior. "As much as I loved being in that bed with you…" He lifted our linked hands and kissed the back of mine. "I'm trying to take things slow."

I laughed.

He rolled his eyes. "Fine, less than breakneck speed."

I appreciated his commitment to making sure he didn't freak me out. I hated it was necessary. I wished I could tell myself, *It was three years ago; it doesn't matter anymore.*

But it did.

It might until I broke through the ceiling of fear and gave myself to Hopp completely. As much as I enjoyed the blowjobs and as much as I loved running my hands all over his body, I wasn't sure I was ready for sex yet.

My one and only experience was forced. It was the worst pain I'd ever known, and every time I thought about trying it again, my stomach seized with nerves.

"I'm sorry I can't give you everything right now," I whispered, the weight of my past suddenly crushing me.

His hand jolted in mine, but he said nothing as he pulled the Audi into a parking spot in front of the giant white mansion.

Hopper cut the engine and turned to face me in the dark. "I'm pretty sure you already have."

My stomach flipped. He always said the right thing. I shook my head slowly. "There's more."

"Well then, it will just be a bonus."

Someday I would give him everything. Someday when I was absolutely sure he wanted it all.

"You finally gonna tell me what we're doing here?" I asked, gesturing toward the huge-ass house.

"You ready to sign?" he asked.

My forehead wrinkled. "You made me wait to sign until we were here with Gamble?"

"There's a few things I want to go over with him first. A few things I want to make clear."

"I thought it was all in the contract?"

He nodded. "It is, the legal stuff. It's a solid contract. This stuff is personal."

With that, he got out of the Audi and left me sitting there to wonder. After a second, I flung open my door and stepped out. Hopper was there, reaching for my hand, and we walked, linked together, toward the huge front door.

Snow was once again falling, but it was light and lazy. The air was so cold when I breathed out you could see my breath in great white puffs. The second we stepped onto the porch by the front door, it opened and the housekeeper stood there, bathed in the light from the room behind her.

Hopper stopped, glanced at me, and then moved forward. "Actually, we'll just need a minute." Then he pulled the door shut right in her surprised face.

I lifted an eyebrow, amused. "Care to explain?"

"I should have explained before we left. Or in the car when you asked just now." He blew out a breath. "I'm nervous."

I shifted closer to him, feeling the hesitancy in his words. The wind blew, and I shifted again, putting my back to it so it acted as a buffer against the cold for Hopper. "Nervous about what?"

"Us."

My stomach dropped. "Is there an us?" The words turned white when I spoke them and floated between us for a few infinite seconds.

He shuffled on his feet, stuffed his hands in his jacket, and glanced up and then away. "I want there to be."

"You do?" I asked, surprised.

"I really fucking do." He relented, his eyes lifting to mine. Their icy tone was so piercing, way more than the frigid temps outside. "I came here tonight to basically tell Gamble that. Our personal life isn't really his business, but it will affect our business."

He came here tonight to tell Gamble there was an us?

Whoa.

Because I didn't say anything, Hopper rambled on. The nerves in his voice, the way he would pause and then speak rapidly, was totally endearing. "I don't really make it public knowledge that I'm gay. Not because I'm ashamed or anything. But because I don't want people to know me. I don't want people to figure out how I used to be. I like the anonimity I have here." He glanced up. I watched him, totally enthralled by his sudden outpour.

"I'm gonna be your manager, along with the rest of the team. But I'm not just your manager. You're more to me than that. I'm not going to pretend otherwise. Not even at work. I won't have people saying I give you preferential treatment. I won't have people hounding us because we're gay. But I won't step away from you either. I... can't."

My chest was tight, and I was pretty sure it was because I was holding my breath. "What are you saying?" I wheezed, shifting again to block him from the wind.

He stepped close, so close our feet bumped. We stared into each other's eyes while my stomach fluttered uncontrollably. "I'm saying I want there to be an us, and I want people to know about it."

I opened my mouth, but he bulldozed on.

"I don't want to hide the way I know I look at you. I don't want to revert to just staring when I think no one else can see. I want to hold your hand *all the time*, not just when we're alone. I refuse to make you a secret, Arrow. I'm not saying I'm going to shout our relationship to the world, and I know this is fast. It probably qualifies for the breakneck speed mentioned in the car, but this has to be ironed out before you sign that paper."

I started to say something, but once again his nervous rambling continued, this time as he wrung his hands.

"This isn't me trying to force you into something you aren't ready for. Fuck, I'm scared as shit right now. I still want to take things at our pace. I don't want to freak you out… but yeah, I also want to put a label on it."

"Hopper," I commanded. His eyes snapped up.

"Y-yeah?"

I lunged forward and kissed him hard. I tried to lick up the aftertaste of all the beautiful words he'd just vomitted all over my high-tops. I pulled back but wrapped my arms around him and tugged him into my chest. His nose was cold against my neck, and I hugged him harder.

My head turned just enough so when I spoke, my lips brushed against his head. "Yes."

A shudder moved through him, and I hugged him even tighter.

"Yes?" His voice was muffled against my neck.

I pulled him back, looking into his face. "Yes, I want there to be an us."

Relief washed over his features, and I hid a smile. Poor guy, he was just as hard on himself as I was on me. "You're sure? The press is gonna get ahold of this. It might become a circus."

"Are you prepared for that?" I frowned. "After the way they hounded you about Matt? What if someone realizes who you are?"

"I can't let that stop me from living my life anymore," he whispered.

I grabbed his hand. I knew exactly how he felt.

"We don't have to have this all figured out tonight, Hopp. Whatever comes, we can handle it, all right? And we agree to handle it together."

He nodded, the clouds in his eyes moving past. "Together."

Another brisk wind blew. I grimaced. "Maybe next time you want to talk about our relationship, you could do it before we're standing in below-freezing weather?"

Before he could reply, the front door pulled open again, but it wasn't the housekeeper standing in the light this time. It was Gamble.

"You two assholes need to get in here," he ordered. Then I noticed his eyes slip down to where our hands were clasped.

At the same time, our grips tightened.

"I figured that's what this was about," he grumbled. "Come on, then. I've been expecting this talk. I've already got measures in place."

He strode through the entryway and toward his study.

Hopper and I looked at each other.

He already knew? But we'd literally just decided.

"Dude," I whispered. "Is he phsycic?"

Hopper shrugged.

"I'm not heating the entire neighborhood!" Gamble bellowed from somewhere in the house.

We moved as a single unit through the door and shut it behind us.

Hopper looked a hella lot more relaxed than he had before. I guessed whatever "measures" Gamble was putting in place were exactly what Hopp was hoping for.

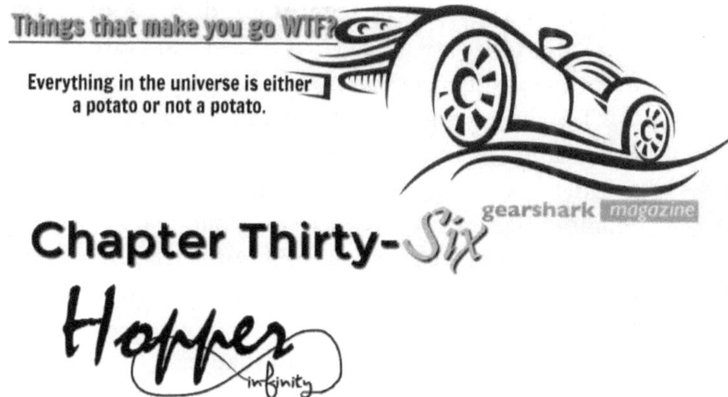

Chapter Thirty-*Six*

Hopper
infinity

And that, ladies and gentlemen, is how you get shit done.

Boo-yah!

I marched right into Gamble's office and told him exactly what I wanted:

1.) State-of-the-art cameras on every inch of the garages and indoor team practice areas.

2.) Someone on staff to review said footage on a weekly basis to guarantee there was no hazing or in-fighting happening on Gamble property.

3.) Acknowledgement that Arrow and I were together and it was not a conflict of interest.

4.) Permission to be at every race Arrow was in.

5.) Gamble's presence at a team meeting where I introduced Arrow as a new team member and blantantly acknowledged our relationship and the fact we were both gay. If anyone refused to work together in a professional manner because of our preferences, immediate dismissal.

6.) Explicit right to dismiss anyone from the race team and Gamble racing staff at any time due to hazing or engaging in hateful conduct of any kind. For Gamble to make it clear at previously mentioned meeting the power I have.

7.) For everyone on the team, including racers (including Arrow and myself), to sign nondisclosure agreements regarding any personal relationships they witnessed while on company time. Prohibition of sharing and trading racing practices and secrets with those outside Team Gamble.

Gamble agreed to all of my demands.

I mean, sure, he already seemed to know Arrow and I would walk into his house holding hands (seriously, maybe he *was* psychic) and was prepared for the "conflict of interest" talk. And yeah, he'd already called someone to install the cameras (I didn't know this), then told me he had to check with his laywers about the NDA, etc.

Point was ~~I~~ got what ~~I~~ wanted.

Scratch that.

We got what *we* wanted.

There was an us now. Arrow and me. We were still trying to feel our way, still working through all our jagged edges, but there was a label.

Usually people resisted putting labels on things, especially so early in a relationship. Arrow and I weren't most people. In fact, we were unique in a lot of ways. This label might be scary or stifling to most starting out, but for us, I think it was reassuring. It was something to hold on to. Something tangible in a world where practically everything had been ripped away once.

I didn't expect it to make sense to anyone, but I really didn't give a damn.

Once the details were hashed out, Arrow signed the contract. He was officially with NASCAR, and I was officially with someone who wasn't Matt.

It was difficult to move on from someone you thought was your infinity. Even in death, I planned to remain loyal to his memory. Sometimes I wondered if falling for Arrow meant I loved Matt any less. And sometimes I still told myself it wasn't fair I got to live when he didn't.

After the meeting with Gamble, I went to my apartment, alone. It felt like I'd been gone for years instead of just about a week. The entire place felt strange to me now—well, stranger than before. Less like home than it already had.

In fact, as I stood in the center of the undecorated living room and stared at the plain white walls and windows with cheap plastic blinds, I sort of felt I was standing in a prison.

A prison of my own design.

Matt wouldn't have wanted this for you.

You don't know what Matt would have wanted because he isn't here to ask.

I'd only been back a few hours, long enough to shower, change, and throw my dirty clothes at the washing machine so when I got around to actually doing laundry, I'd know where they were.

After the meeting with Gamble, which took quite a while, A and I grabbed some food, then came back here. I had shit to check on in my place, and he wanted to call his brother and Joey to thank them for turning the bland apartment into something far from bland.

Space was good for us. Guys like Arrow and me needed it.

The walls of this jail cell were closing in on me. I glanced more than once at my bed, but just as soon as I did, I would glance away. The thought of sleep, though I was tired as hell, was so unappealing.

I supposed the one night of reprieve, the one night of blissful sleep, was all I was going to get.

Just like always, my demons came calling. Dark thoughts, guilt, and warring viewpoints scrambled my brain and made my limbs restless.

I thought of the place I always walked to for a cup of coffee. It was familiar though unpleasant.

I didn't bother changing out of the sweats I put on after my shower. Instead, I shoved my feet in a pair of shoes, grabbed my keys, and left the apartment.

At the elevator, I didn't stop. My feet, my heart, had a mind all its own and directed me straight down the hall. It wasn't bad coffee, dark streets, or miles of walking I truly wanted.

My apartment no longer felt like a home because my home was with someone else.

Before I even got to the door, it flung open. My footsteps stuttered, and Arrow strode out into the hallway, no shirt, with a pair of too-large sweats riding dangerously low on his hips.

My blood spiked, and my stare settled on those sweats and what they almost weren't covering. My mouth tingled with the memory of his cock running across my tongue.

Arrow seemed intent on where he was charging to, which couldn't have been far because he wasn't wearing any shoes.

He stopped when he saw me standing just a foot away. Neither of us said a word; we just stared at each other, our eyes doing all the talking.

Slowly, Arrow backed down the hall, and I started forward again, following. In his apartment, he held open the door. I ducked under his outstretched arm and heard the latch click and the lock throw with delicious finality before I even turned around.

Arrow caught my hand on the way past and tugged me through the dimly lit place, straight into his bedroom.

The only light was from his phone screen, which was docked on the small side table.

The pillows were tossed around, and on one side, the blankets were drawn back as if he'd been getting ready to go to bed.

Still saying nothing, he turned, pulled the hoodie I was wearing over my head, and tossed it near our feet. I stepped out of my shoes, and Arrow shoved the sweatpants down my legs, leaving me only in a pair of red boxers.

My fingers delved into the waistband of his sweats, took a moment to caress the skin beneath, then pushed them toward the floor.

Taking my hand, he led me to the side with the blankets turned down. I slid between the sheets with an audible sigh. Arrow climbed in right after me, and I held out my arm. With him tucked so close, I almost supported all his weight. With the calming feel of his slow breathing against my neck, all was right in my world.

It didn't take a genius to figure out the reason my apartment no longer felt like home. Arrow wasn't in it. He was my home now, no matter how conflicted it sometimes made me.

With a deep sigh, he settled even closer. I tugged the blankets around us farther and closed my eyes.

Sleep ended up not being so hard to come by after all.

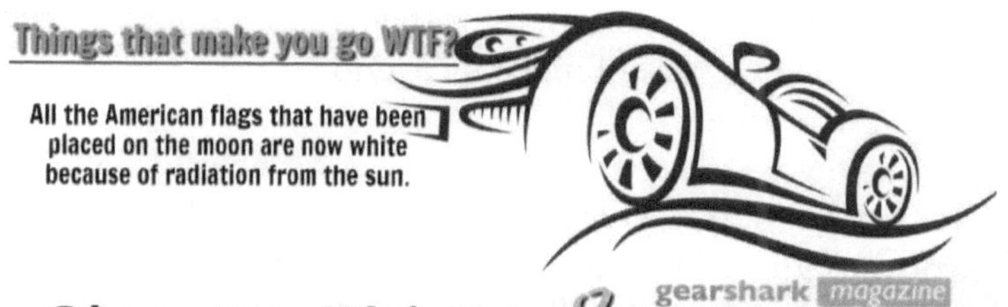

Chapter Thirty-*Seven*

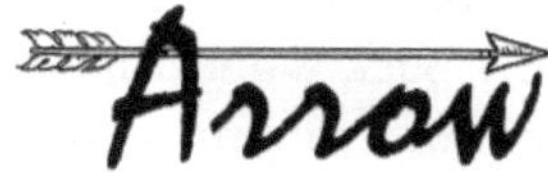

They changed my hair.

I agreed to it. Everything else in life was changing, so why not that, too? Besides, dying it blond all the time was getting kinda old. I had a feeling I was gonna have a lot more important things to do in the coming months.

And maybe if I changed it up, people would stop calling me the Biebs. I didn't want to be known as a celeb lookalike or Lorhaven's kid brother. I was my own man, and though I might have hidden from it for a long time, times were changing.

It wasn't just me anymore. There was Hopper. We were working toward an us, and it excited me as much as it blew my mind.

The morning of the *GearShark* interview, I woke up in my new place with Hopper wrapped around me. I lay there taking in his weight, the way it felt to be pressed into the mattress, and waited for panic to set in.

Since I moved in, there wasn't one night Hopp hadn't slept here. That first night, we went to our separate places, but it didn't last. We found each other in the hallway, both of us lost and searching for the thing we knew would make us found.

Each other.

Now we slept at my place because he said he liked it better here. This apartment was a little more comfortable compared to his, but it wasn't because of anything I did. I gave all that credit to Joey.

Usually we would crawl into bed and I would curl up into his side, my head on his shoulder. I liked the way his fingertips skimmed over my back when I lay on him. It was something I looked forward to almost from the minute we got out of bed in the morning, knowing later that night he'd repeat the action.

We didn't shift much in sleep. I fell alseep on him and mostly woke up that way.

Yet this time, at some point during the night, I'd shifted and he followed.

I was the one on my back, and Hopper was the one at my side, his leg flung over mine, partly lying across my chest, and his arm wrapped around my waist.

The panic didn't come.

I didn't feel trapped or pinned. I didn't feel an immediate urge to shove him off and reclaim all the personal space I thought I needed.

Turns out this morning I didn't need any personal space, not from Hopp.

I smiled to myself and reached for his tangled hair. Absentmindely, I began to stroke it, enjoying the softness of every strand and the way his chest felt as it rose and fell against mine with every breath he took.

It wasn't much later when I felt him wake. His body didn't stay as relaxed against mine, which was a dead giveaway. I continued playing with his hair until he looked up, balancing his chin on top of his hand on my chest.

"You okay?"

I nodded. "Feels good."

Hopper rose up and met my lips with a kiss. It was a slow wake-up kiss, involving a lot of tongue and lip rubbing. All our kisses were really good—the spark between us was undeniable—but this one was a little different.

It was better.

He was fully on top of me, elbows on either side of my head, our legs tangled together, our chests touching, as were our cocks.

Suddenly, I couldn't imagine not experiencing this. It seemed impossible something so delicious would ever give me anxiety.

As we kissed, I reached around, pulling Hopper closer against me.

He groaned and his hips thrust against mine.

I responded by doing the same, and we ended up settling into a rhythmic movement of rubbing our dicks together in sweet torture. Need suffused my skin and my body temperature rose about ten degrees. I felt an urge stronger than ever to be close to him, to feel him in ways I hadn't before.

Hopper lifted his mouth from mine, then dropped his face to the side of my neck to press hot, wet kisses against the sensitive skin.

I slid my hands down his back, beneath the waistband of his boxers, and cupped his ass. My fingers dug in, kneading the flesh as I lifted my hips to meet his.

Hopper raised his head and looked at me beneath half-lowered lids. Boldly, I rubbed his ass again, giving it a squeeze and then massaging deep. His eyes closed with pleasure, and I claimed his mouth again.

As we made out and basically humped each other, I grew a little braver. My fingertips starting sliding along his ass crack, delving between to rub and play.

Hopper's face dropped into the side of my neck again, but he pushed his butt up into my hands.

All at once, I rolled, pinned him beneath me, and started kissing down his chest.

He made a sound and spread his legs so I could settle between them. Blood hammered in my veins. Thought was near impossible; all I felt was an urge. An urge to be all over him at once, an urge to be *in* him.

"Babe," Hopper groaned. I hooked my fingers in the wasitband of his boxers, about to pull them down. "Hey." He pushed up to his elbows and glanced down. "Arrow."

I looked up.

"What's gotten into you?" he rasped, brushing his hand through the hair falling into my eyes.

"Do you like it?" I asked, suddenly self-conscious.

He chuckled. "Are you kidding? I love it."

My face broke into a lopsided smile, but then the need in my body took back over and I dipped my head.

Hopper pulled me back up. "Babe, we can't right now."

"What?" I blinked.

He grinned. "You have an interview in like thirty minutes."

"Fuck!" I spat, then buried my face in his abs.

My head bobbed with his laughter, and he rubbed my back. "If it wasn't such an important interview, I'd say fuck it and stay in bed."

I kissed his stomach right beside his navel. He groaned. "Something's different this morning," he murmured. "What is it?"

"I woke up with your weight on me, and I didn't freak."

"You're learning to trust me." His fingers brushed at my hair.

I shook my head. "I already do trust you. I just…" My voice faded away. It was almost impossible to explain.

I trusted Hopper, and I could count the number of people I trusted on one hand. I knew he wouldn't hurt me physically… but I was still apprehensive. Maybe it was the unknown. Maybe it was the broken pieces inside me, or maybe I was just scared.

Did it really matter about all the complicated feelings waging inside me just then? All I knew was after sleeping next to him for over a week, after kissing and touching, after daily blowjobs, I woke up feeling I was ready for more.

How much more?

I'd been trying to figure it out when he stopped me with the interview reminder.

Stupid work.

"You don't have to explain," Hopper said quietly, pushing up so he was sitting, leaning back against the headboard. I scooted forward, still between his legs. "I'm going at your pace here."

"I want more," I whispered.

"You can have whatever you want, babe." Heat sparked in his blue eyes. Then he grinned. "Just not right now."

"Bastard," I muttered playfully.

His face split into a grin, and I laughed.

He leaned forward, catching my face between his palms. "How about tonight?"

"That's very far away." I stuck out my lower lip.

He leaned forward and sucked it into his mouth just like I knew he would. "Tonight," he growled against my lips, then pulled back.

My stomach flipped with anticipation.

So now back to my hair. You're still wondering about that, aren't you? Thought I forgot?

I didn't.

I just get distracted very easily by a dark-haired, muscled man in my bed.

The *GearShark* interview was thankfully at Gamble Speedway. When we got down to the track, the crew was already there setting up. It looked just like the other interviews I'd been to that *GearShark* hosted. There was a full crew with lighting and photography. The photographer was already setting up in an area a short distance from the rest of the crew. There was a white background, some lights, and other props lying around.

Near where we walked in was a table filled with pastries, fruit, and a huge carafe of coffee with all the shit you might want to put in it.

My stomach growled loudly at the sight of the donuts, and Hopper snickered. "I should have known." He slapped me in the middle and went to get a plate of stuff for me to inhale.

The second he walked off, Lorhaven and Joey stepped into my line of vision. I smiled wide and started forward. Joey ran forward and hugged me, and I hugged her back a little tighter than normal, feeling her surprise.

After that, I offered my fist to Jace, and we bumped it out.

"You look really great," Joey observed, her eyes sweeping over me. "Happy."

I shrugged, a little embarassed but also kinda proud because I didn't think I'd ever actually looked happy before.

"You, too," I said, turning it around on her. "You both do."

Jace tossed his arm over Joey's shoulders, and she smiled. Her usually wild curly hair was sleek today, straight around her shoulders. They were both dressed in jeans and long-sleeved shirts. Lorhaven wore a leather jacket, and Joey was wearing one that actually looked kinda similar to my brother's.

"You guys are like matching and shit." I ribbed and wagged my finger between them.

Jace gave me the finger, and Joey elbowed him in the stomach.

"You ready for the interview today?" Jace asked, glancing toward the trailer where the reporter was talking to some people and writing what looked like notes.

"Sure," I said. In truth, I was a little nervous. I wasn't sure how personal she was going to go with the questions, and though Hopp and I were making no secret that we were involved, speaking out about it to a national magazine was something else.

"Just say what you're comfortable saying and notthing else. This is business. Just remember that," Lor counciled.

Hopper approached, and I automatically shifted so he was included in the group and there was a place right beside me. He held out a plate loaded with food while he sipped at a styrofoam cup in his other hand.

"Blueberry's my favorite," I announced, snagging it off the top and shoving a huge bite into my mouth.

"That's why I got it," Hopper replied.

"Thanks, Hopp." I grinned around the food, and he chuckled.

I polished it off in record time, and he handed me his coffee. I took a drink, handed it back, and then went for the bagel with cream cheese.

As I was chewing, I felt the overwhelming sensation I was being stared at. I turned to see Lorhaven and Joey looking between me and Hopp like we had twelve heads.

"What?" I grumped and shoved another bite into my mouth.

Lorhaven lifted an eyebrow. "Hopp?"

I shrugged. "You call Joey Josie," I pointed out.

Joey giggled, and Jace looked like he just swallowed a banana whole.

Hopper cleared his throat and patted me on the back. "They're ready for you." He pointed to two women who were waving me toward them.

I groaned. "I'm taking my bagel."

"You do that, babe," Hopper said indulgently.

Jace made a sound like he was choking, and everyone looked at him.

"Just go," Joey told me, beckoning me toward the women.

"I'm gonna go talk to Emily," Hopper said and disappeared.

I left my brother mumbling to Joey and went over toward the crew. Turned out they were there for makeup, wardrobe, and hair.

Yep, hair.

The second I stopped in front of the tall blond one, she started running her fingers through my hair like she had every right.

I drew back and shoved another bite of bagel in my mouth.

She seemed surprised I wasn't too thrilled with her hands on approach, then shrugged. "Have you considered a change? Maybe a cut and color."

I blinked. "Do we have time for that?"

"Won't take long. Your hair is short."

The other girl chimed in. "She's a whiz with hair. Let her do it!"

I squinted at the one trying to give me a makeover. "Like what?"

"Just shorten up the long side here so it's a little more shaped." She gestured as she explained. "That way its easier to style. It'll look great on the cover. And maybe take out some of the blond. It's a little too light."

I snorted and finished off the bagel.

"I'd just add in some lowlights, maybe some dark blond so the light pieces will pop a little more."

I considered it a second. "Yeah, okay."

Both women squealed like it was Christmas and ushered me into their lair.

Lair = a trailer where two women talked way too fucking much about hair and clothes and celebrities and treated me like their next project.

Halfway in, Hopper stepped inside, and I gave him a *help me* look.

"Everyone's ready," he announced, then noted the scissors and empty bowl of hair color. His eyes widened. "What the fuck are you doing to him?"

"Making him a little more cover worthy," the main stylist announced.

Hopper's face darkened. "He was already cover worthy."

"It's fine, Hopp," I said, trying to diffuse the anger suddenly masking his face. "It's just a little cut."

He crossed his arms over his chest. "You cool with this?"

"Why wouldn't he be?" the assistant stylist chirped. "It's going to look amazing."

I nodded, widening my eyes, and said, "Amazing."

Hopper laughed. "Fine, whatever. But the photgrapher and reporter are out here waiting."

"Give me ten!" the stylist insisted, then went to work furiously combing my hair to hold it out and snip it.

Hopper winked at me as he went out the door. It stirred up the desire I'd felt this morning.

About fifteen minutes later, I stepped in front of a mirror and saw the change I'd felt when I woke this morning. Just like she said, my hair was still blond; it just had some depth to it, and the long side wasn't as long, but the style was about the same.

I just looked more put together, maybe a little older… and, like Joey said this morning, happy.

I gave the clothes they asked me to put on a barely-there glance and then turned toward the door, wondering if Hopper would like the hair change.

He did.

I saw it in his eyes the second I came out of the trailer and walked to his side. Before we could say two words to each other, I was swept off by the photographer, where I was a complete *unnatural* in front of the camera.

Added to things I would never do in my lifetime: become a model.

Gah, hopefully the poor dude got a couple usable shots out of the five hundred thousand he took.

By the time that was done, I was almost grateful for the interview part because at least I got to sit down.

Before Emily could even ask her first question, I was flanked by my brother and Hopper. They towered nearby like they were security and I was wearing a giant diamond.

I almost told them to knock the shit off, but then I didn't. I couldn't be mad there were people who cared enough to stand around and look intimidating. I could still be my own man but have a little backup when needed.

The interview went pretty smooth. Her questions were mostly expected, with a few personal ones thrown in. I didn't back down from them. I answered with blunt truth while still guarding the man my heart beat for.

It was past lunch by the time everything wrapped. On one hand, I was exhausted from all the poking and prodding, physical and mental. But on the other, I was kinda grateful for all the activity. It made the day move faster.

That meant I was that much closer to tonight.

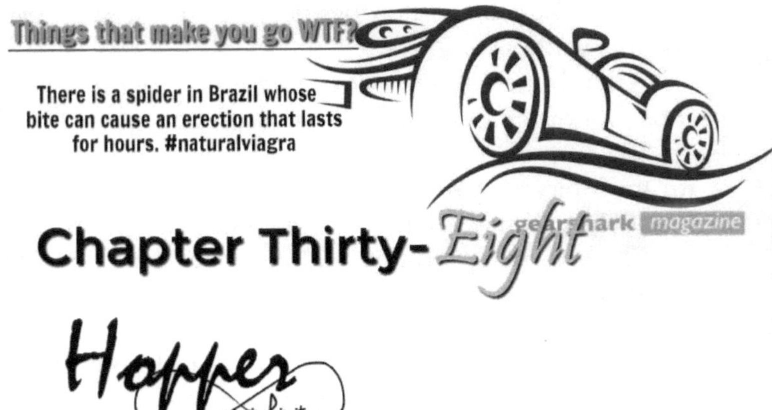

Chapter Thirty-*Eight*

Hopper

"You protected me today."

Arrow looked up from his second burger and paused in the middle of chewing. "Did you think I wouldn't?"

"No, I knew you would. I just…" *Was still surprised by it.*

The reporter didn't back down from any personal questions. In fact, she was sharp and picked up on our relationship before Arrow talked about it. What bothered me most were her questions about me, about my identity. I totally had an internal meltdown when she asked who I really was. I thought the jig was up, that maybe she recognized me from all the media coverage five years ago.

What a juicy story that would be: *The discovery of Jayson Hamilton, where he is now.*

Arrow didn't even entertain her, though. He shut her down almost instantly. He even directed the attention to his brother. When she came circling back, he flat out told her to forget it.

I knew eventually someone was going to realize who I really was, but it hadn't been today, and I had Arrow to thank for that. He kept his cool, not even hinting maybe there was more to my name than a choice.

He shielded me from it. Bought me some time. Bought us some time to continue putting our life together without the watchful, intrusive eye of the media.

"Earth to Hopp." Arrow snapped his fingers in front of me.

I blinked and looked up. "Hmm?"

After another massive bite of his burger, he set it aside on the coffee table beside him. "Are you having second thoughts about me telling the magazine we're together?"

He was sitting with his back against the arm, his legs stretched in front of him. I sat with my back against the cushions, feet propped on the coffee table. His feet were in my lap.

My hand wrapped around the foot closest to me and squeezed. "Not at all."

He smiled. "Me either."

"You bought us time today." I looked him straight in the eye. "Thank you."

"I'm always gonna protect you, Hopp. Protect us."

My hand ran inside the ankle of his pants and stroked his calf. "You still feeling like you were this morning?" I asked, my voice dropping.

"Oh yeah," he replied and rubbed the bottom of his foot over the center of my pants. "It's all I've been thinking about all day."

"Me, too." I groaned and rotated my hips.

Arrow pulled away. The weight of his legs left my lap to be replaced with his ass as he stradled me and we began to kiss.

Our mouths fused together so completely it was as if we were the same man. I didn't know how he he did it, but every time we kissed, I felt as if he were coaxing something from inside me, something I didn't even know I possessed.

His thick tongue licked over my lower lip, and I shuddered because it reminded me of the way he often licked my dick. Arrow scraped his teeth over the stubble on my jaw and kissed his way down my neck.

I swiveled my hips under him. My dick was completely hard, and the weight of his ass against it made me feel like I was on fire.

"Take off your shirt," Arrow growled, reaching between us and wrapping his hand around my cock.

I practically ripped off the shirt and threw it over the back of the couch. The leather of the sofa was shockingly cold against the overheated skin of my back.

Arrow slid down, nipping at my nipples while rubbing his palm over my cock. I threw my head back against the couch and closed my eyes, offering myself up for whatever he wanted to do to me. It was torture, you know, torture being so turned on by someone and having to move so slow.

I didn't regret it, not at all, but sometimes a man just wanted to feel someone moving inside him.

Arrow practically melted off me and slid down so he was on his knees between my legs. His fingers reached for my pants, and I lifted my ass so we could pull them down.

The second the air in the apartment brushed over my dick, I fell back against the couch and reached for it.

Arrow pushed my hand away, shoved my thighs wide, and slipped his lips over my rod with enthusiasm that made me ache.

I moaned and fisted both hands in his hair and started to pump into his mouth. His hands caressed my inner thighs and tight balls.

There was a slight sucking sound when he released me and looked up my body.

"Bed," he rasped and stood.

He offered his hand, and I took it. We went into the bedroom together, and I noticed he was still completely dressed.

I grabbed the front of the tank he'd worn for the cover shoot and pulled him closer. His fist closed around my still throbbing cock and jacked me.

My other hand joined the front of his shirt, impatiently I ripped the thin fabric right down the center. Arrow's eyes flared when I shoved the scraps off him and reached for his pants.

The second we were both naked, he gripped my dick and led me to the bed as if it were a leash and I were the dog.

I panted after him, caught a flash of his naked ass, and filled my hands with the flesh. He groaned but then turned, pressed our fronts completely together, reached around, and filled both his hands with my ass.

"You're killing me, A. I want you. I want you fucking bad."

"I want you, too," he murmured, kissing my shoulder, rubbing his dick against mine as his fingers delved into my crack. "I want to be inside you."

I moaned. "Please."

He pulled back slightly. "You'll let me?"

I grabbed his face. "Anything. I'll let you have anything."

His eyes flashed. "Tonight I want your ass."

I released him, yanked open the drawer on the nightstand, and pulled out a giant-ass bottle of lube, handing it to him. "We're gonna need this."

He stared at it, then looked up, shy. "This makes it not hurt?"

My heart turned over. It turned over and caved in. "You're not gonna hurt me, babe. I'm gonna cum so hard, and your name will be on my lips when I do."

The fact that I was his first made me dizzy with pleasure. His nerves didn't turn me off. The way he worried he might hurt me was endearing. He was going to be the perfect lover. I knew without even doing it yet. I knew because of the way he cared.

He tossed the lube on the bed and gently pushed me back. I turned, crawling up on the mattress, giving him a clear view of my bare ass.

His hand slid over it, and I groaned, pushing farther against the touch. He played for a while, touching, caressing, dipping his finger into my crack and across my taint.

When he pulled back, I practically collapsed on the mattress.

Our bodies pressed against each other. My heart pounded in my chest; my fingers shook and so did his.

When he reached for the lube, I nearly shouted with fucking glee. The first touch made me go lax against the sheets. Arrow pushed my legs wide, and I surrendered myself as he explored and slipped his fingers all along my taint and fingered the sensitive hole.

As he moved, I whispered how good he felt and let him know when he hit a spot I really fucking liked.

I knew he was nervous, but he grew bolder with every stroke. His hand locked around my cock as his finger probed my hole.

"Yeah, babe. Do it," I urged, growing wildly impatient.

He released my cock and pushed his finger inside.

"Move," I commanded, and he began to fuck me with his finger.

I writhed beneath him as he continued, slipping another finger inside me and then, soon, another.

"Do you like this?" Arrow whispered as he speared my body.

"Oh God, I fucking love it. I want more, babe. I want you."

Easily, he withdrew from my body and licked up the length of my throbbing cock. I felt more silky lube coat me, and I looked over my shoulder. Arrow was on his knees between my legs. The tattoos on his body were on full display, and the muscles in his stomach were contracted.

His long, thick dick stood straight out from his body like a fucking trophy, and I revelled in the fact that I was the only one who'd ever been with him this way.

On impulse, I spun around, took the lube from him, and poured it in my palm. I coated his cock thoroughly, jacking him, teasing him as I did.

He moaned, his body swayed, and his hands rested on my shoulders.

When he was good and saturated, I lay back and widened my thighs.

He stroked my dick as he positioned himself right at my entrance. The tip of his swollen head slid over the nerves, and I shuddered.

He paused. "Hopp?"

I cracked open my eyes. "Babe?"

"Do you want me to use a condom?"

I made a sound. "Fuck no. I want you. All of you. I want your skin against my skin."

He rocked against my ass. My chest rumbled with delight. A thought filtered through my sex-saturated brain. "If you want to use one, I'm cool with that, too."

"I don't want to," he said instantly.

"Come inside me, A." I beckoned.

He pushed in. There was a brief moment of resistance, but then my body adjusted around him, and it was like he was meant to be there.

"Holy fuck." Arrow moaned, dropping his hands on either side of my waist.

I chuckled, but it turned into a growl when he pushed in a little deeper.

"You're so fucking tight," he panted. "You feel so goddamn good."

I smiled, reaching down to grab his ass and pull him balls deep. He collapsed on my chest, and I held him to me. Between us, my dick twitched, and the need to bear down on him was intense.

After a second, Arrow pushed up, gazed down at my face, and started to move.

Oh, he felt amazing. The way he speared my body with the perfect amount of pressure. He moved fast and slow. He slid in deep but pulled out until it was just his tip, only to surge back in again.

His swollen, slick head slid across my prostate, and I nearly shot up off the bed. Arrow stilled, thinking he'd done something wrong, and pulled back. I grabbed his ass, shoving him deep, and rocked against him.

"That's the spot, A. Do it again."

He thrust in me again. And again. I fell back, opening my mouth, but no sound came out.

He started moving more furiously, pounding into me with greater force. All at once, he went deep, so deep I felt his sack against my ass, and his hand wrapped around my cock. It only took two pumps before I poured out all over my own abs, moaning his name as my body shuddered with pleasure.

Arrow held himself against my prostate, rocking against it every few seconds. I would shoot out more jizz, and he would use it to jerk me some more.

Eventually, I collapsed, completely bonelss and barely coherent, against the sheets.

I hadn't had sex in five years. Five long years.

I didn't remember it ever being this intense.

"Hopper?"

I gazed up, my vision slightly out of focus. Arrow released my cock and placed his palms on my thighs.

"You're perfect," I murmured. "Fucking perfect."

He began thrusting again, his breathing turning into short gasps. "I'm there," he rasped.

I shoved my ass down on him one final time as his hot liquid filled me up. He moaned and shuddered over me, and I worked my ass, milking every ounce of pleasure out of him I could.

After a few moments, he collapsed beside me with a great heave.

I rolled onto my side, folded him against me, and kissed his hairline.

"That was…" he said, still breathing hard. "I didn't know it could be like that."

"Fuck, I didn't either."

"Really?" he asked, his breath calming. "You liked it?"

I laughed. "You have to ask?"

He ducked his head into my chest, and I hugged him tighter. The self-conscious way he got sometimes only made me more determined to protect him, sheild him, to take care of him.

My chest was tight, my heart overfull… and yeah, I was fucking satisfied as hell.

"Hey, Arrow…" I began, and he lifted his face. Unable to stop myself, I kissed his lips. "I know I was your first, but I just want to make it clear I'm your only. No one else is allowed to have this. Have you."

He grinned and tucked his face back into my chest. "I can live with that."

My chin rested on top of his head, and I sighed. I knew we needed to go shower, but I was in no hurry to move. I was too satiated, too comfortable.

Instead, I began rubbing his back, stroking his skin, and running my fingers down his arm covered in tattoos.

A long sigh moved though him, and I kept stroking. My palm slid over his forearm, down to his wrist. I lifted it, leaned down, and kissed his palm, trailing my lips over the inside of his wrist.

The raised scars there bumped against my lips. I pulled back, gazed at them, and rubbed my thumb over the old wounds. He stiffened as I touched them, but didn't pull away.

I caressed them again, wanting to ask where he got them, but not wanting to intrude upon this moment.

"I tried to kill myself," he said, avoiding my stare. "It wasn't long after… I just didn't know how to cope."

I made an anguished sound, clutching him closer as part of me cried for him. God, I wished I'd been there. I wished there was something I could have done. The thought of him not being here today in my arms literally scared me.

"It was only that one time…" He went on. "I'm stronger now."

I pulled his wrist down, pressing a kiss to each of the puckered scars.

His breath hitched.

"I'm so glad you kept fighting. So glad you're still here," I whispered and kissed him again.

He whispered back, "Me, too."

Chapter Thirty-*Nine*

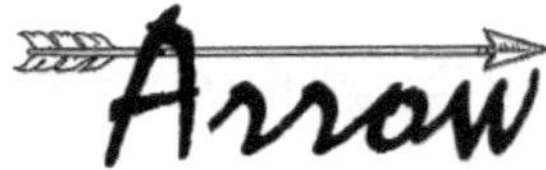

Arrow

The change in me felt permanent. Solidified in the couple weeks since the *GearShark* interview and since the night Hopp and I took things to a whole new level.

Things = we sexed it up.

Not that we were totally "sexed up" yet. Not in every way. There was still a little of that territory left unexplored, but I knew it was coming.

And I wasn't scared.

I anticipated it.

How could I not? The look on his face every time I entered him was almost euphoric. And while I knew I had the right equipment for the job, I wasn't exactly taking all the credit. I was still kinda new, in a lot of ways still a virgin learning my way. It was clear it felt good. Better than good.

Sure, TV and magazines and just about everything in today's world sang the praises of sex, but to see it firsthand was proof. I guess I needed proof.

Hopp might have been the only lover I'd ever had (and according to him would have), but I knew he was patient and caring. He moved slow when it would have been easy to go fast. He didn't push, but he showed me how to give pleasure. And even though at first, the idea of that was seriously embarassing, it really wasn't.

It was hard to be embarassed when someone was moaning because you were touching them in all the right places.

I wanted to experience it. I wanted in some ways to prove to myself and my body there was more than pain. I wanted to help push out that memory of the night in the alley. I wasn't stupid. I knew having sex with Hopper wouldn't make me forget or change the experience.

However, welcoming him inside me would mean rape wasn't my *only* experience.

I'd been in him more than once, and when I wasn't in him, we were blowing each other. His hands got a little more exploratory on my body, and I shook less.

We'd settled into a routine, not predicatble at all (because fast cars were never predictable), but one I loved. We spent our days at the track or in the team garage. He worked with all the drivers, and I worked with a few other people besides him. The team was shaping up. All of Gamble's drivers were good. Most of us were really young and kinda fresh, but in the end, it would probably work in his favor.

We were a clean slate for Gamble, moldable into the drivers he wanted to represent his brand. Most of us were getting sponsor offers; the logos on our cars were multiplying.

And best of all?

So far, no one gave me shit about being gay.

I wasn't dumb enough to think they all totally approved of my lifestyle. They didn't have to. But no one was an outright asshole about it. It was made crystal clear any of that shit wouldn't be tolerated. The big shake-up last year with Joey opened a lot of eyes and served as a giant warning to anyone who even thought about being a dick.

All the drivers and staff at the speedway got along for the most part, and I was hopeful, after several months of working and driving together, we'd all build a comraderie.

I guess I did enter NASCAR at the right time. Trent and Drew paved the way for gay drivers, Joey shined a spotlight on hazing and discrimination, and GearShark consistently refused to shy away from the issues that seemed to surround our sport, making it easier for guys like me.

Hopp and I didn't flaunt our relationship. Everyone knew about it, but we didn't go skipping through the offices, holding hands and singing love songs. We touched each other, obviously, but not in inappropriate ways, and Hopper was fair with all the drivers and didn't treat me any different.

On the track anyway.

After work was another story. He pretty much stayed at my apartment. I never slept alone. We ate together, played video games together, and washed our laundry together.

Sometimes I would look at him and fear would strike my heart.

What would I do if I had to go back to being alone?

I was alone a lot longer than Hopp and I had been together, but the impact he had on my life and soul made me sometimes wonder what life had been like before him.

I can't go back there.

I won't.

The kickoff to my first NASCAR season was rapidly approaching. Before the races officially counted, there were some fun ones on the calendar. The fans loved these for a few reasons:

1.) It gave them a chance to scope out new talent preseason.

2.) The races were more laidback, and some of them had a charity component.

And…

3.) They were fun.

The drivers loved the warmup, working out any bugs they might have before the season began. And of course, the money.

Some of these races had some big fucking cash prizes.

Like the one today, my first race as a Gamble driver. My first time on the track with my new car (which was fucking sweet) and people in the stands.

One million dollars was up for grabs. That would be a sweet-ass payday. I didn't necessarily hurt for money. I earned a pretty fat paycheck now, with bonuses as strong possibilities. I knew the more I won, the more I made.

But this check would be even sweeter because the cash meant even greater independence. In recent years, Jace pretty much supported me. At first, I didn't want to take his help; it felt like I was still being supported by our father, albeit indirectly.

Jace still used his trust fund, and I didn't blame him for it.

He knew, though, I couldn't live off what I thought of as blood money, and he started giving me a chunk of everything he earned off all the races he won.

I did the mechanic work on his cars and shit to make myself feel I was at least earning some of my keep.

I was grateful to my brother. Hell, without him I probably would be dead (literally), but I wanted—*needed*—to support myself.

Technically, I was doing that already, because I made more than enough to live on (I didn't need much), but still, who wouldn't want a cool mil?

"Babe, your phone keeps going off," Hopper said, coming into the bedroom. He was dressed for the race already, in a pair of dark jeans and a red T-shirt with the Gamble logo on it. (His NASCAR-approved firesafe suit would be put on over his clothes after he got to the track.) He wasn't wearing any shoes yet, which made me kinda smile because he must have walked to his apartment without any to get dressed before heading back over here.

No shoes, but already, the red baseball hat he liked so much was backward on his head. Dark waves curled up from beneath the edges, which turned me the hell on.

I tossed the towel I'd been rubbing over my wet hair on the bed and made a sound. "I'll check it in a few."

Hopper crossed the room and, without hesitation, slipped his arms around my bare waist. "You trying to make me feel worse I missed your shower?" He pressed a kiss to the top of my shoulder.

My stomach flipped. Even though he touched me a lot and had been for over a month now, it always felt like the first time.

"I'm sure I'll need another one tonight."

"Counting on it."

We met each other halfway, locking lips as if we hadn't just been in bed together all night. Hopper's hand delved into the waistband of my boxers and gripped my ass. I shifted closer, kissing a little deeper. His fingertips flirted with my ass crack, and I shivered a little.

Hopper lifted his mouth, brushing his lips across my jaw, then pulled away completely. I groaned.

He chuckled. "Later."

With a sigh, I went to my half-empty dresser and grabbed a pair of black jeans and a red shirt similar to the one Hopper wore.

"You ready for today?" he asked, watching me get dressed.

I shrugged. "Ready as I'll ever be."

"Hey." He stepped close again. Instantly, I stopped what I was doing and turned to him. "You're a damn good driver. Just as good, if not better, than anyone else on the team. You have an edge because you trained so much with your brother and Drew."

"You've helped, too," I added.

"And I'll be there today if you need anything. All you gotta do is say the word."

"Word," I echoed.

His lips curved up. "I gotta head down to the track. I want to have all my shit done before I put on the headset to spot you."

I nodded. "I'll be down in a few. Just gonna get dressed and shit."

He gave me a swift kiss and retreated to the doorway. "Don't forget to check your noisy-ass phone!" he called.

When he was gone, I threw on the rest of my clothes and blasted my hair with the blowdryer. I was used to the darker blond and cut now. When I looked in the mirror, it wasn't someone new. It was just me.

Out in the kitchen, I made a cup of coffee using the fancy brew machine Joey gave me. As it was pouring into the mug, I reached for my phone, which was where I left it when I grabbed some cereal this morning.

There were three missed calls and a text.

One call was from Lor. One was from a number I didn't recognize, and the other…

My father.

I tossed the phone down, reached for the steaming coffee, and took a big swig. I wasn't a huge fan of coffee really. I just drank the shit because it gave me energy and because I liked the way it burned the back of my throat when I swallowed.

Look. We all know I wasn't free of issues. Drinking coffee because I liked it to burn my throat was the least of them.

After the first big gulp of the brew, I sipped it a little less savagely, leaned against the counter, and regarded my phone.

What the fuck was he calling for?

Sure, he'd called quite a few times before I moved down here, and every single time, I ignored the calls. Hell, I should have changed my number like I'd planned, but Hopper walked into my life and trivial things like my phone number just didn't seem so important anymore.

Besides, he'd stopped calling. I figured he'd given up because I never answered. Guess he wasn't as good at taking a hint as I hoped.

Why now?

The coffee mug hit the counter with a thud. *Who the fuck cares?* I had more important shit to think about today besides my douche of a father and whatever agenda he was running.

I snatched the phone, deleted the three missed calls, and then pulled up the text, which was from Lor.

Where are you?

I took one last swig of the coffee, then set the mug in the sink. On my way out of the apartment, I typed out a reply.

On my way down to the track. See you in a few.

I took the elevator down to the ground level, bypassed the entrance to the parking garage where my Camaro was parked, and stepped out of the building onto a wide concrete sidewalk. I could already hear the revving engines, the low rumbling of cars out in the parking lot by the main entrance, and the general excitement of today's race.

I was a little earlier than I needed to be, but hey, being early wasn't a bad thing. It would just give me more time to get in the headspace to hopefully win.

Or at least place.

I shoved my phone in the back pocket of my jeans and headed toward the track. Living at racetrack definitely had some advantages.

A familiar white Lotus turned the corner up ahead, and I stopped walking. Lor pulled up to the curb and rolled down his window.

"Don't you know how to return a phone call?" he barked.

"Might want to reach around and pull the wedgie out of your ass, Lor. It's making you grouchy."

He made a sound.

I made one back. "I just texted you. I was on my way to find you now."

"Get in. I'll drive you over." He motioned to the passenger side.

"What's wrong?" I asked, totally picking up on his weird-ass vibe. Jace was a douche and he bitched at me all the time, but this was different. Something was wrong.

"Is Joey okay?" Another bad thought trampled over my chest. "Hopper?"

"Hopper and Josie are fine." He promised. "Hopper's over there barking orders like he runs the place."

"He does," I pointed out.

Lorhaven rolled his eyes. "Whatever."

I smiled. He was warming up to Hopp. He just hated to admit it.

He noticed me smiling and gave me the finger. Then he sobered up. "You love him, don't you?"

I chewed my lower lip, then nodded. "I haven't told him," I said, low.

He sighed, almost resigned. "You're happy. He's been good for you. Good *to* you."

"You have no idea," I whispered.

"I'll still kill him," Jace warned.

I rolled my eyes, but deep down, I really appreciated how much he cared. It meant a lot to me, and having Jace's blessing was something I really wanted.

"C'mon." He motioned.

I got in the Lotus, and he peeled away from the curb and around the corner. The staff entrance came into sight. I liked how my brother used the staff shit even though he wasn't employed here. That was

Lorhaven, though. He did what he wanted, and in his mind, since I worked and lived here, this was his place, too.

Really, I wouldn't have it any other way.

"So what's going on?" I asked.

He glanced at me, and the tension in the car went off the charts. "Just so we're clear, I had no idea he was coming here. Once I realized, I told him to fucking leave."

My stomach twisted. "Who?"

Lorhaven swallowed and gripped the steering wheel like he was having a hard time containing his anger. There weren't many people that pissed off my brother this much.

Right before he drove through the staff entrance, I glanced up and gasped.

Lorhaven followed my stare, and a string of cuss words filled the car. He slammed on his brakes, and the tires squealed before the car jerked to a halt. The man on the sidewalk stepped forward like he'd been standing there just waiting for us to pull up.

It was like a horrible flashback or a bad case of déjà vu. Suddenly, I was transported back to what it was like to be Dylan. To feeling completely repressed, worthless, and scared.

"Is this what you wanted to tell me?" I uttered to Lorhaven, still staring.

"Guess it was too much to ask for him to fucking listen. Sorry bastard," Lor growled.

So much for giving up. So much for taking a hint. Guess that's why my father tried to call this morning.

He was here.

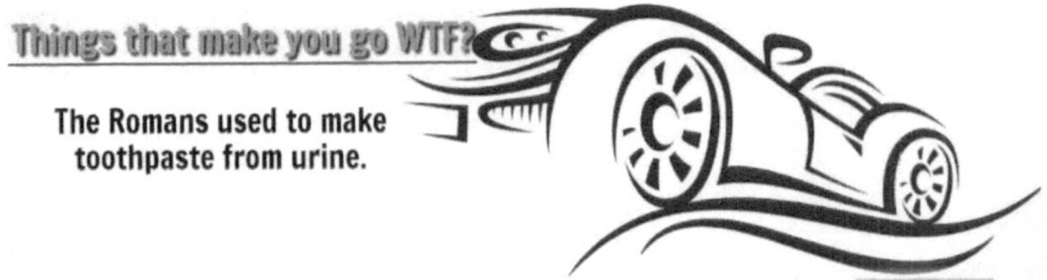

Chapter Forty

I was fucking busy. Getting a team of drivers ready to go, following protocol, blah, blah, blah, wasn't something that could be done in five seconds flat.

I didn't mind it really. I liked my job.

But something felt off.

I glanced at my cell, noting the time. *Later than I realized.*

Forgetting my clipboard and the people standing around, I craned my neck, sweeping around for the familiar blond head. He should have been here by now, but I didn't see him anywhere.

Where the hell is Arrow?

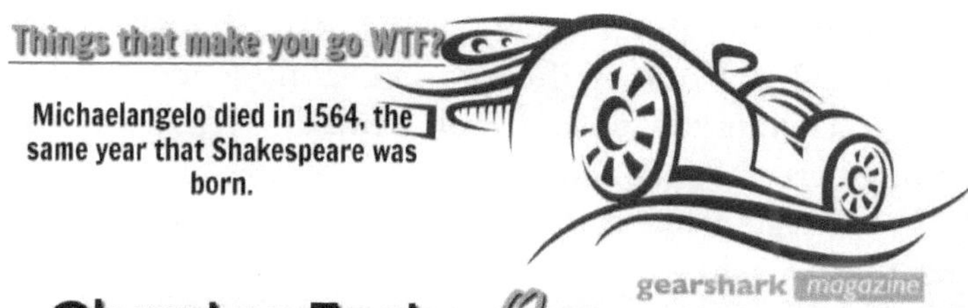

Chapter Forty-One

"What the hell is he doing here?" I said low, still staring through the window.

"I don't have a fucking clue. Didn't give him the chance to tell me. I just told him to leave," Lorhaven replied.

"Stay here," Lorhaven said when I didn't reply. "This time he'll do what the fuck I told him to do."

"Wait," I said suddenly out of the weird stillness that had overcome me and grabbed Jace's arm.

He glanced around, concern darkening his already deep stare. "You don't have to deal with this."

"Yeah, I do," I said. "This is my fight."

He started to argue, and I made a hard sound. "No, Lor. He's here for me. I've been dodging him for a long time now. I'm not running anymore."

"You have a race," Jace protested. "This isn't the time."

"Yeah?" I scoffed. "Add it to the long fucking list of shit I never had any say in."

My brother sucked in a breath. "Arrow."

I wasn't about to sit and debate any longer. Instead, I got out of the car with confidence I didn't feel and shut the door firmly behind. "What are you doing here?" I snapped.

Sullivan acted as if there wasn't a huge rift between us, like he didn't disown me several years past. "Dylan," he said, "so good to see you."

"My name is Arrow now, which I'm sure you know."

He inclined his head. "Yes, I had heard. I guess some habits are hard to break."

"That why you're here?" I intoned. "Have an itch to try and control someone?"

Behind us, the door on Lorhaven's side slammed shut. "I told you to fucking leave."

"And I told you I'm here to see Arrow," Sullivan said.

"He has a race. You have no right to show up here." Jace raged.

My father looked about the same. Same formal business suit. Same hair, same posture and demeanor. He stood in such a way it always appeared he was looking down on everyone else. All the old feelings of not being good enough and playing a part came rushing back.

"Well, we could have done this another time and place, but no one will return my phone calls."

Jace laughed bitterly. I knew it was the sound of him getting ready to tear into the old man.

I held out a hand to him, staring straight at my father. "What do you want?"

He seemed a little surprised at the direct, focused way I stared him down. The way I just told Jace to shut it with a single gesture and spoke for myself.

I might've had a lot of old feelings running wild inside me, but I wasn't the same.

"I read your interview with *GearShark*," Sullivan said.

My face twisted. "How? It's not on the stands yet." *I haven't even read it yet.*

"I have a connection at the magazine. They sent me an early copy."

Jace made a sound. "You bribing people at magazines now? That issue hasn't even gone to print."

Sullivan shrugged one shoulder. "I was proud. I wanted to be the first to read my son's big interview."

"You mean the son you disowned?" I said, cold.

"If you had answered any of the multiple calls I made or contacted me, as I asked your brother to do, you would know I wanted to apologize for that misfortunate understanding."

I made a choked sound. "Misfortunate understanding? You mean the fact that you paid some skank ten grand to have sex with me while you sat in another room and watched? That misunderstanding?"

Jace made an outraged sound. Oops, guess I didn't mention some of the details to him.

"Or maybe the misunderstanding when you took away my home, my money, my car, and tried to bribe me to be exactly what you wanted in order to earn it back."

"I've come to apologize, not to rehash it all," he said, hard. Guess the old man was starting to get frustrated. Maybe the picture I painted looked dirty, even to him.

"Saying sorry doesn't change anything," I intoned.

"I know that." Sullivan relented. "That's why I'm giving you back access to your trust fund, and I'd like to sponsor you in a major way with NASCAR. Perhaps you might like to do some endorsements for some of the companies I own as well."

Jace starting laughing. The sound was momentarily drowned out by a car driving through the staff entrance.

"Are you fucking kidding me?" Jace raged. "What the fuck is this? A bribe? Why now, Dad? Why show up at a race with all these pretty offers?"

"You wouldn't answer my calls, so I decided to come to watch your race. Try and make things right."

I tilted my head. "What's in it for you?"

Sullivan's eyes widened. "What?"

"What do you get out of this *new* relationship with the son you've had no use for?"

Jace leaned over. "Good one, bro."

"I don't get anything out of it but the ability to see my son succeed."

"No fucking way. Sullivan Lorhaven doesn't do anything unless it benefits him." Jace scoffed.

Sullivan started bitching at Jace, but I didn't hear his words. I just stood there as my brother and father argued, staring at the man who basically gave my life a one-way ticket into hell.

Except I got out.

And I wasn't fucking going back.

"You read my interview," I said.

Both men shut up and looked at me.

Sullivan cleared his throat. "Yes, I did. I was very impressed."

"Impressed by me or the fact that NASCAR is?"

"I beg your pardon?" He sniffed.

I straightened and regarded him in a way I hoped made him feel I was staring down at him. "You don't like me. In fact, I still disgust you. I can see it in your face."

"That is not true!" he spat.

"I'm in a relationship with another man," I announced. "We live together." Technically, we didn't, but he didn't need to know that.

"I'm aware," he said, distaste coating his tongue.

"Ah, that's right. The article," I mused. "Be careful, Sully. Your true colors are showing."

He started to argue once again, and I flashed a cold, hard look right at him. He shut up.

"I've been dodging your pathetic phone calls for almost a year. You never pushed. You never tried to see me. You just called so you could tell yourself you attempted to patch things up with me and I was the one who ruined it. It was just a way to assuage your conscience, but I have to admit I'm surprised you have one at all."

Lorhaven shifted closer and crossed his arms over his chest. I glanced at him, and he nodded in full support.

"But now, out of the blue, here you are. Just happens to be my first preseason race, right on the heels of a nationwide exclusive interview announcing I've signed with NASCAR. An interview you bribed someone to read early."

"What is your point?" Sullivan snapped.

"My point is you still despise me. My lifestyle still appalls you, but everyone else is accepting it. NASCAR signed me. I have big sponsors lined up, interviews booked. No one cares I'm gay. If anything, the fact that I'm out of the closet and willing to be one of the first openly gay drivers in the pros works in my favor."

Sullivan shifted uncomfortably.

"Strange world we live in, huh, *Dad?* Society is changing. Diversity is becoming key in marketing, business, and in getting big approval ratings from consumers. Way I see it, you want everyone to think we have a fantastic relationship. Sullivan Lorhaven, proud father of the first gay pro driver. You want your name on my car, on my suit. You want me to say how fucking great you are in all my interviews. Because if I tell people what you're really like, well, that's gonna hurt the name you've built."

"You sick son of a bitch," Lorhaven growled.

Sullivan shook his head sadly, but it was a lie. I saw the truth deep in his eyes. He couldn't hide it from me anymore. I saw who he really was. "I know I hurt you, Dy—Arrow. And for that I'm sorry. I made terrible mistakes. I'm here because I want to make up for them. I want to rebuild our relationship."

I laughed. "Go to hell."

Sullivan stepped toward me. Jace leapt forward, putting a restraining hand on him. "You said your piece. Arrow said no. Now leave."

My father stepped back. I could tell he was utterly surprised. He was expecting Dylan today. The kid who used to want so badly to have his approval, to be the son he wanted.

"C'mon," Jace said. "You have a race."

I shook off the sadness barreling toward me and headed for the car. Before I could get in, I felt a hand wrap around my wrist.

"Son."

I glanced around, snatching my arm out of his hold. "Don't touch me."

He drew back. "Just think about it." He implored. "I really do want to make it up to you. I'm proud of you, son. Of everything you've accomplished."

I shut my eyes. How many years had I longed to hear him say he was proud of me? So many I'd lost count. The thought to give him a second chance crept into my mind.

"A," Jace said from inside the car.

I blinked.

Sullivan nodded as if he knew what I was feeling. "Think about it."

I got in the car and slammed the door between us.

Jace sped away before I even settled back into the seat. "Hey."

I turned to look at my brother.

"That was fucking epic. Surprised the shit out of the old douche. You handled him well."

I grunted and glanced out the window. If it had been so epic and if I had done so well… why the fuck did I feel so shitty?

Chapter Forty-*Two*

Hopper

I was just about to go searching when I saw him.

I tucked away the phone pressed against my ear and started forward. Someone called my name, but I waved them off.

Arrow saw me heading his way; his footsteps stuttered. Something was wrong. I knew it instantly. Lorhaven was right beside him, but I didn't even glance at him. All my focus was on Arrow.

My steps quickened, and when I was close enough, I said, "What happened?"

Arrow seemed a little pale, though he stood tall. When he didn't answer, I glanced at Lorhaven. He was staring between us like he wasn't sure if he should say anything.

"Would you mind heading over to Arrow's pit? Light a fire under their asses and make sure they're doing their jobs," I asked.

Lorhaven nodded. "Sure." Before he left, he spoke to Arrow. "You need to me stay?"

"No."

Lorhaven gave me a short glance before heading in the direction of the pit. It was perfectly organized, and his crew was working hard. I'd already seen to it, but I wanted a minute with A.

"Babe?" I said softly, moving closer to his side.

He gestured with his head toward the locker room door, so I followed him inside. After he quickly made sure it was empty, he regarded me with more of a naked stare. The pain there, the way he appeared haunted, was oddly familiar.

I had worn the same look many times.

"My father is here," he said, slapping me with some unexpected shit.

"What?" I said, trying to get my brain to catch up.

A nodded. "Guess I should have answered my phone. Maybe I would've had a warning. Or warned him off."

My eyes widened. "Wait, he's here? Like at the track?"

"He was standing outside the staff entrance when Lor and I drove up."

I ran a hand over my face. My fingers smelled like oil and gasoline. "You talked to him?"

Arrow nodded miserably.

I crossed the room swiftly and yanked him against me. He ducked his face into my neck, and I pressed my cheek on top of his head. That fucker put him through the ringer. He damaged him beyond repair, and he showed up now? Just as Arrow was starting to discover he could have a life, one that made him happy?

White-hot rage started in my toes and moved up like flickering flames through my limbs until it reached my chest and muffled my breathing. I hadn't felt anger like this since Matt was killed. Since Matt was run off the road by jealous, selfish assholes.

The only difference between then and now was back then, I was also so broken with grief the anger came second.

Now?

I was just fucking pissed off.

"What did he say to you?" I demanded but rubbed his back carefully.

Arrow pulled back and sniffed. "Not much. I did most of the talking."

I tilted my head and waited to hear what else he would say. I didn't have to wait long.

"He fucking thinks he can just waltz back into my life and offer me a stack of money, a sponsorship, and a "new" relationship and I'll just pretend he didn't drive me into hell and drop me there."

I blinked. "He wants a relationship?"

Arrow laughed, hollow. "He wants to *use* me."

"Because you're with NASCAR now." I surmised, getting even more pissed.

"I told him to go to hell. He still hates me. He just has a use for me now."

My chest cracked. The misery beneath the anger in his words was unmistakable. I understood, because some pain was almost impossible to let go.

"Fuck him," I announced. "Fuck him and the subpar car he rode in on."

Arrow laughed.

I stepped close, grabbing the front of his T-shirt. "He hurt you. Abandoned you. He doesn't deserve you."

Arrow lifted his chin and stared into my eyes.

"That peckerhead took a lot from you in the past, but he can't touch your future. He can't touch you here and now. You told him to go to hell. You were the one in control today. Don't give him anymore time, babe. Focus on the here and now. Focus on me and the race."

He leaned in and kissed me fiercely. Our tongues battled it out, and he walked a few steps so I was pinned between him and the lockers. After a few moments of unbridled making out, he lifted his head.

"Thank you."

I smiled. "Don't thank me. I didn't do anything."

"You're here."

"And I'll be here after the race. And tomorrow. And the day after that."

He looked like he was about to say something, but across the room, the door cracked open and Lorhaven yelled in. "Get your asses out here!"

"You gonna be okay to drive today?" I asked, concerned. The last thing he needed was this shit in his head before he competed.

He nodded. "Yeah, I'm ready."

"Show 'em who's boss out there, babe." I smacked him on the ass.

"Spank it!" A joked.

"Don't tempt me," I murmured as we went toward the door. His chuckle floated behind him.

Outside, Lorhaven was waiting with a scowl on his face. "Took you assholes long enough."

"Sorry," Arrow muttered.

Lorhaven slapped him on the back. "It's cool, bro."

He gave me a probing stare, and I nodded. A look of relief washed over his features, and he flung an arm across Arrow's shoulders. "Your crew is looking pretty good," he said as we walked toward the pit.

"They know what they're doing, Jace."

"Well, I had to make sure. Not every day my little bro drives for a million bucks!"

As we passed a section of the stands on our way toward Pit Row, someone shouted Arrow's name.

It was another dude, so naturally, my instincts roared with jealousy.

"Arrow!" he called deep. *"Arrow!"*

"I know we said we were low key in public, babe, but I will low-key punch an asshole in the face if he's hitting on you," I growled and turned around.

Arrow and Jace weren't amused by my funny but all-too-true threat. In fact, they weren't even looking at me. Instead, they were both rigid and staring up at the stands.

I followed their eyes to a man in a full business suit, a coat, and red scarf. He was an older man… and frankly, I was surprised he had the balls to hit on my man right here.

"Good luck today, son!" the man yelled.

I jerked like he'd fired a gun.

"That's your dad?" I snapped.

"I'm rooting for you!" He waved and smiled.

The people around him were watching and curious.

Lorhaven gave him the finger. Arrow just turned and walked away.

I stood there a few seconds longer and stared with narrow focus on the asshole until he couldn't ignore me any longer. Our eyes met.

He knew who I was. He knew it instantly, because he could likely feel the hate rolling in great tidal waves right off me.

His eyes flashed. All the fake friendliness and excitement for his son's first race dropped to reveal his true sentiments.

He hated me, too. He hated the fact I was dating his son.

That's okay.

I hated him a hell of a lot more.

I put my back to him, refusing to give him a single second more of my attention, and jogged to catch up to Arrow and Hopper. I slipped right up to A's side and slid my hand into his. He gripped onto my fingers, and I held tight.

In the pit, no one reacted to us holding hands; they never did. It wasn't the first time we did, and it wouldn't be the last. I was serious when I held that staff meeting about being tolerant and accepting. Arrow already had enough intolerance and bigotry for three gay men in his lifetime, and I was seriously putting my foot down about this shit.

It wouldn't happen. Not now. Not ever.

Could I stop people from feeling the way they did? Nope. Could I keep them away from Arrow and the life we had?

I could fucking try.

He needed to live in a world where it was okay to be himself. My most important goal was to create as much of that around us as possible.

The start of the race was closing in on us, and I had some last-minute manager shit to handle, so I left A with Lor, Joey, Drew, and Trent, promising to be back in plenty of time for us all to take position.

I was glad all his family was here. He needed all the support he could get today. As I headed back over to him, I watched how all four people surrounded Arrow, how they closed ranks around him to keep out anything negative. They looked like a mini gang standing there in the matching ugly-ass fire suits.

I miss that.

I miss family.

I had a big family once. I pushed them all away. I was starting to think maybe it was time to reach out. It would be nice to have that relationship back. To have people who were always there. I wondered if they would still speak to me or if they had written me off by now.

I took a moment to imagine what it would be like to bring Arrow back home. What it would be like to visit Seattle with him and show him all my old haunts. The familiar ache when I thought of home surfaced, but instead of letting it shut me down, I embraced it. I allowed myself to feel the loss of Matt and my entire family

My parents would love Arrow. My sisters would want to do his hair, and my nieces and nephews would probably try and copy his grungy style right down to the high-tops he wore. There would be a loud family dinner with too much food, and they'd probably tease him about looking like Justin Bieber.

Not only would I get my family back, but he would get one as well. I wanted that for him. For me.

He looked through the people circling him and saw me heading his way and smiled. My chest squeezed, and I smiled back.

I was looking at my future. My true infinity.

Even though in my head it hurt to recognize, my heart whispered it unapologetically.

Something—*someone*—had never felt so right.

The group parted, and I stepped beside Arrow. From the side, my headset was being handed to me, and I glanced up at Trent.

He smiled. It was like he knew. He knew what I was thinking.

"You're a part of us now, too," he said quietly.

I took the headset and put it over my hat. "Thanks," I said, because I didn't know what else to say. "All right!" I called. "Positions!"

Everyone backed off but didn't go far. The pit was going to be pretty full this race.

Arrow was gazing off in the direction of the stands, where the man I would now to refer to as The Fucker was last seen.

I grabbed his chin and pulled his face around. "Don't think about him right now. Right now, it's the race. Divided attention is dangerous."

His eyes locked on mine. "I'm here."

"You sure?" I asked.

He nodded. "Let's do this!"

And just like that, the race was on.

Chapter Forty-Three

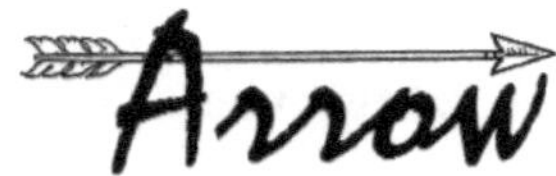

Laps flew by.

The faster I went, the more of a blur everything around me became. I relished the feeling. The freedom.

Maybe I felt a little out of control. Maybe that was why I drove a little less cautiously than usual, but it was working. I wasn't far behind the car in first place.

We had several more laps to go, so it was possible I could move up a few more places.

That was goal. Show everyone watching, everyone who ever thought I couldn't do this that I not only could, but I would.

Screw you, Sullivan.

In a sick way, I wanted to win, not just for me, but to stick it to him. Make him regret he never saw my value before other people he considered worthy did.

"Babe, you are magic on the track today." Hopper's voice filled my ear.

I grinned while keeping my eyes on the road. Everything was a blur, but his voice was crystal clear.

I gave a loud, *"Whoop,"* and he laughed.

"Someone's coming up on your right. They've been waiting to make a move. They want around you."

"Got it," I answered and slid over just enough to keep them back.

"Nice," he said, and I could tell he was already calculating. "After the next curve, on the straightaway, punch it. It's a good time to try and pass up a couple. Close in on the front of the pack."

"I'll start before I'm out of the curve so it's not expected," I said, already running through the maneuver in my head.

"That could work."

"Of course it will," I said, confident.

His warm chuckle filled my head.

"I like your voice in my ear."

"I'm thinking that may not be all I've got in you later tonight."

I groaned. "Don't distract me."

"Right," he murmured. "All right, get yourself into a position. Coming up to the curve. Watch your back right end. That guy's still hungry."

I settled into the seat, ready to try and lap some cars.

"Hey, A," Hopper said. "Hold off on the pass. The car several ahead looks like its tire is gonna go."

It did look a little wonky. That was the consequence of pushing to stay in the lead and not stopping in the pit.

"He's pretty far up and on the other side. I can lap a couple cars and still stay off his ass."

"Just hang back a minute," Hopper repeated.

Impatience made my fingers shake. My knee bounced up and down rapidly. I wanted this lead. I wanted to shove a win down my father's throat. I wanted to prove to myself that despite him showing up, I could win anyway.

As much as I tried to keep him out, he was in my head. I shoved him back, only to have him reappear. The way he looked today, the words he said… I tried to remind myself I wasn't a teenager. He wasn't in charge of my life. I was my own man, and nothing he said had to affect me anymore.

As I drove, I glanced up into the crowd that was nothing but a streak of colors as I tore around the track. I imagined him sitting in the stands, telling everyone around him his son was driving today.

He pissed me off. How dare he come here? How dare he try and take away my first race?

I channeled the anger trying to consume me into my driving, into the gas pedal. "I'm going for it," I told Hopper.

In seconds, I whipped around the car in front of me and closed in on the next. I smiled to myself as the possibility of placing in this race became closer.

Up ahead, a loud sound exploded. I heard it over the engine, over the other cars around me, and even the crowd in the stands.

Through the windshield, I watched the car with a now-blown tire swerve erratically and take out the car in front of it. He flipped up into the air, soaring over the car he hit, and slammed onto the track to roll into the shoulder, leaving parts littering the pavement behind.

The car that had taken the first hit struggled to remain in control, and he began spinning. The car in front of me slammed into it, and then the car dogging my back right side appeared out of nowhere on the other side and sped around me like it was going to somehow maneuver through the wreckage.

"Brake!" Hopper yelled in my ear. "Fucking pileup! Get the hell away from it."

I backed off the gas, driving across the track, trying to avoid the mess.

But the mess followed.

The asshole driver behind me, who was now in front, hit a piece of debris, skittering out of control, and slammed into another wrecked car, spinning straight toward me.

Hopper was screaming in my ear, but I didn't hear what he was saying. Everything slowed into a painfully clear picture.

I swerved the wheel, trying to avoid what I knew was coming. My car groaned, trying to comply with my urgent demands.

The impact was instant, the sounds of shattering glass filled the cabin, and the smell of burning engines, rubber, and fuel wafted inside.

It went by in a blink. One minute I was on one side of the track; the next I was on the other, my car part of the pileup I was trying to avoid.

"Jesus Christ!" Hopper rasped, horror in his voice. "Brace yourself, Arrow. Fucking hold on."

I glanced up when he said those chilling words as another car tried to stop but failed and slammed right into my side.

My head rocked on my shoulders, the helmet banging against the interior safety bars, and my body screamed.

More sounds of groaning metal and more jostling vibrated the metal around me. My helmet smacked the bar again, and everything went quiet.

Chapter Forty-*Four*

Hopper

My heart stopped. *One beat. Two.*
Not again.
Not fucking again.

One minute everything was fine; the next I was witnessed firsthand my worst nightmare literally crashing my life.

"Arrow!" I roared as cars piled on top of one another and he somehow got caught in the jumble. It was a true clusterfuck out there, hard to tell where the wreckage began and where it ended. Still, some cars that had been far enough back to avoid it cruised on past. The ones ahead still circled the track. The crash was bad enough I knew a red flag was about to be thrown down, halting everyone on the track, involved in the crash or not.

"Arrow!" I demanded into the mic. I needed to hear his voice.

Just let me hear your voice.

Radio silence greeted me. My breathing hitched, and I started to wheeze. I stared out at the crash, where responders were already on their way.

I couldn't leave his life in someone else's hands. I couldn't stand here and wait.

I couldn't go back to that morgue.

I glanced around furiously. The need to run pulsed through my body. I needed to get there faster than my legs could go. He needed me now.

Then I saw it.

The motorcycle sitting nearby, likely one of the crew's. I didn't even think. I ran toward it, leapt on the seat, and fired it up. It rumbled beneath me in a way my body recognized as familiar but my brain didn't even register.

I tore off across the track, not stopping for any of the cars. I didn't even pay them any mind. I heard a few wheels squealing as I ripped over the ground, but I didn't look back. Not even when I saw the red flag come waving. I wasn't getting off this track. Not without Arrow. I stared straight ahead, trying to clear my blurring vision as I searched for him in the wreckage.

The bike hit some dirt and grass. Chunks flew up, and the back end tried to fishtail, but I forced the control, dodged some debris, and buzzed around a car that had already been abandoned.

Flashing lights and sirens were all around, and then the loud, intrusive sound of a firetruck cut through it all. I glanced up as it pulled to a stop right beside the worst of the pileup. I revved the bike and scanned the cars.

When I spotted the hood of Arrow's car, I skidded around another car and jerked the bike to a stop.

"We need the hose!" the fire crew yelled, and a rush of heat from the flames nearby hit me in the face. One of the cars was on fire. The shit around it was catching, moving down the line… right for Arrow's car.

"Please don't die," I prayed, leaping over the hood of a demolished vehicle.

"I'm not going anywhere." His voice crackled in my ear.

"Thank Christ, Arrow." My voice wobbled as I rushed forward.

His window was busted and the windshield was cracked. Inside the car, he was moving, struggling with something. I reached into the window, ignoring the jagged glass, and grabbed him.

"I'm fucking stuck," he said, tugging on the harness that was doing too good of a job keeping him in. "Call one of the responders to cut this thing off."

I glanced over, noting the flames still growing, and sweat broke out between my shoulder blades. I wasn't leaving his safety to anyone else.

Fuck that shit.

I reached into my fire suit and produced a pocket knife with a sharpened blade. The harness gave way to my blade, and despite my trembling hands, I cut through the restraint in seconds.

Arrow shoved it all off and started to hoist himself out the window. Impatient and half out of my mind, I practically climbed in the window, grabbed him beneath the shoulders, and hauled him out myself.

Before his feet even hit the pavement, I yelled. "Fire! Move!"

He started to scramble up to run, but I dragged him back, half carrying him from the wreck.

"Hopper!" Arrow demanded, but I kept going, kept dragging him. "Hopp!" he yelled again. "I'm okay. We're safe!"

I glanced up, realizing we were out on the grass, away from the fire, the crash, and all the danger. I gasped in relief and nearly stumbled. Arrow caught me and righted us both. I was wheezing again, my vision foggy and my heart about to burst from my chest.

"Hey," he said. I knew he spoke softly, but because our headsets were still on, his voice was right in my ear. "I'm okay. You're okay. Everything's okay."

A choked sound ripped from my throat, and the urge to barf right the fuck there was so strong I gagged. Arrow made a sound and ripped off the helmet he was wearing, then his gloves.

"You almost fucking died," I rasped. "I can't go through that again."

"Hopp." Arrow spoke firmly, the voice of reason amid the fucking meltdown inside me. His palms surrounded my face, pulling my gaze up so I could focus on his face.

He was sweaty and red, but he was whole and unhurt. A sob broke out of my chest.

"I'm right here," he said. "You helped get me out of the car. I'm safe."

I heard his words. I tried to digest them. God, I fucking tried. I was spiraling. I was splintering… I was getting lost again.

He shook me gently but hard enough to snap my attention back to his face.

"I love you, Hopp. Stay here. Stay here with me." He pressed his forehead to mine. "I love you."

Just like that, my world came rushing back. His face came into focus, and his words…

They saved me.

I lunged forward and kissed him hard and deep. He still held my face, but it turned more into a cradle. I wrapped my arms around his waist, pressing my hands against his upper back. I kissed him like he was oxygen, like he was the last meal I'd ever have. I kissed him not with just my lips and tongue, but with my heart and soul.

He loved me.

I pulled back just barely. His hands tightened on my face. "I love you," I said, then fused our lips together once more.

He groaned and wrapped both arms around my shoulders, holding me so tight it almost hurt. Goddamn, I reveled in his strength, in his touch, in the feel of his heart hammering against my chest.

He was alive. He was here. He was mine.

"Arrow!" someone yelled.

I clutched at him. He drew back slowly but kept my body close. I dropped my face into his shoulder because there was so much going on inside me I was afraid to look up.

"I'm okay," Arrow said over my head. "Just got caught in the pileup."

"You're not hurt at all?" It was Lorhaven. He'd come out here, too. Of course he would. He loved Arrow, too.

But not as much as me.

"No. I'm fine."

"You need to get looked at," he said. I felt him reach for A.

Without lifting my head, my arm shot out, catching Lorhaven by the wrist, the fabric of his fire suit under my fingers slightly rough. Arrow's body, and the arm beneath my hold, tensed. Slowly, I lifted my head, turning to glare at Lorhaven.

"Don't fucking touch him."

Lorhaven dropped his arm.

Arrow rubbed up my back with his palm and leaned so close his lips brushed my ear. "I love you."

A shiver ran up my spine. Those words were my lifeline right now. They were my entire world. They grounded me, but they also set me free.

"We need to get you off the track and check you out." One of the responders jogged over and gestured to his truck.

Arrow nodded. "Yeah, we're coming." He pulled back a little but linked our hands. "C'mon, Hopp. We gotta get off the field."

The three of us walked to the vehicle that would transport us to the pit. But before they did, they insisted Arrow be checked out by a few EMTs.

I hovered while they did everything they needed to do, and I asked more questions than Arrow. I was starting to come down off the panic, and my limbs felt heavy, my knees weak.

As Arrow was finishing up, Lorhaven called to me.

I blew out a breath and walked over, glancing back once or twice. I stopped in front of him, figuring he was going to ask me for an update on his brother.

He didn't say anything at first. Instead, he stuck out his hand between us.

I glanced between him and his hand, then finally surrendered mine. He shook my hand firmly, and I tried to return the pressure.

"Welcome to the family," he said.

"You changed your mind about me?" I asked.

He shook his head. "*You* changed my mind about you. You didn't even fucking think. You stole a bike and fucking drove like a bat out of hell through a bunch of wreckage. All to get to my brother."

"I can't lose him," I said, that fear punching me again.

"You won't. Welcome to the family."

"Thanks," I said. I knew this was a big moment. Hell, I'd thought Lorhaven would never accept me, and most days, I didn't even blame him for it. I couldn't fully bask in his sudden approval, though, because I was still trying make sense of everything that happened.

Arrow yelled, and I spun. He waved us to the vehicle so we could be taken back to the pit. I sat as close to him on the ride as I could, squeezing his fingers probably too tight, but he didn't complain.

Before we stepped into the pit, Arrow put his back toward the waiting crowd and blocked me from everything but him.

"I'm sorry I scared you," he said sincerely.

"You really fucking did," I admitted, shaky.

He made a sound. "I know, babe." He used the name I reserved for him. "I'm okay, though."

I nodded, and he took my hand as we were swallowed by the crew.

Thank fuck Arrow was okay. But after that crash, I wasn't sure I was.

Chapter Forty-*Five*

I'd seen Hopper like this before.

I didn't like it, but I understood it. It seemed both of us were cursed with the past today. The baggage we usually dragged around was dragging us instead.

First me with my father and the reminders I couldn't shake. Then Hopper watching me crash while he stood by feeling powerless.

I knew about pain and closing myself off. I knew about a lot of shit. But trying to understand what Hopp went through today was something I didn't know. I could imagine. Fuck, the mere thought of anything happening to him made me sick.

But experiencing it?

Finally moving on after over five years and then watching something similar again?

It made what I experienced with my father feel like something that wasn't even important.

It seemed to take forever for us to break away from the track. There was so much shit that went with racing besides driving a car. Eventually, I got pissed enough and tired enough of watching Hopper fight it all back so he could appear "normal" and partly dragged him home.

We left Lorhaven, Joey, Trent, and Drew to deal with it all, something they were more than capable of doing.

I opened the door to the apartment and practically ran in. The second Hopper crossed the threshold, I shut the door and locked it behind us. He pulled the hat off his head and tossed it across the room, and I kicked off my shoes.

I grabbed two longnecks out of the fridge, popped the tops, and took one over to where he stood by the window.

He drank half the bottle, then leaned his head against the glass and shut his eyes. "The morgue is the most silent place I've ever been. It's devoid of life, even the people who are still breathing."

"Hopper," I whispered. A severe ache bloomed in the center of my chest.

"I was unconscious for a little while after. But when I woke up, I went there. The last time I ever saw Matt was when he was lying in the morgue."

I took his beer and set both aside. Without any hesitation, I moved up behind him, wrapped my arms around his middle, and pressed my chest along his back. My chin rested against his shoulder, and for long moments, we just stood there, not saying a word.

"I got on a bike today. Didn't even think twice and didn't even realize what I'd done 'til later. The last time I'd been on a bike was when I tried to save Matt. This time, I was trying to save you."

"Don't do this to yourself, Hopper," I practically begged, even though I knew it wouldn't stop him. I knew all too well how easy it was to torture yourself.

"I keep seeing the crash. How your car went into one and then another T-boned you."

"It was my fault," I murmured, stroking his stomach. "I let myself get distracted. I let him get the best of me for a split second."

"You could have died."

"I didn't."

Hopper's back arched, pressing farther against my chest with his indrawn breath. He was shaking. "I don't think I can do this."

I stilled. "Do what?"

"Us."

Remember that beating I took a few years ago? That's sort of what this felt like.

I pulled back, paced away, then turned back. "You can't do this."

He pushed off the window and turned. His eyes were bleak and pale, his posture defeated. "I'd never live through something like that a second time. I—"

"I love you," I said, rough.

"I love you, too. It's why I can't." He sounded miserable, looked miserable.

I was miserable, too. It took me so long to get here. To find him. Now he just wanted me to give that up?

Maybe the old me would have run back to my place behind the fences with all the locks. Maybe I would have turned to Lorhaven and let him be the strong one.

I admit it was tempting. Tempting to be rejected, to retreat and lick my wounds.

No.

I wasn't that person anymore. I might still have those urges, but I was stronger than that. I was better. I was going to fight for what I wanted.

As someone once told me, I needed to "man up."

"I'm so fucking sorry," he said. "I should have realized this sooner. I should have known trying to be with someone who drove, who could potentially die every time he got on the track, would be a deal breaker."

"Did you know one hundred people die every year from choking on a pen?"

I caught him off guard. Some of the freak-out and misery left his eyes. He shook his head as if he wasn't sure he heard me right. "What?"

I nodded. "I read it online. It must be true."

He made a sound, a laugh and groan all rolled into one.

I held up my hand. "I could get hit by a bus, choke on a pen, fall and hit my head in the shower… There are a million ways I could die. Yeah, my job increases the risks, but I'm still vulnerable. Everyone is."

He squeezed his eyes closed and pinched the bridge of his nose between his thumb and forefinger. "I know that. I just… I can't do it again."

I finally opened up to someone, finally let my heart go… and he was trying to walk away with it. "So walking away from me and living alone will be easier?"

"Yes. No." He spun away. "Fuck!"

"I don't know how much love you had in your life before Matt, like with family and shit. And I'd honestly like to know about it, someday, if you'll let me. But I can tell you from the experience of not having much love, having love on conditions my *entire* life… It sucks.

It eats away at your self-worth. At your very core. I did okay, though. Know why? I didn't know any better."

He glanced around. His piercing eyes found mine.

"You showed me better. You showed me love, and now you want to just take it away?" My voice cracked, and I told myself to knock it the fuck off.

He stepped toward me but stopped. The instinct to shield me from pain, even pain he caused, was still his automatic reaction. Hopper didn't want this. He just didn't know what to do with all his pain and fear.

"I'll give it up," I announced.

His body jerked. "What?"

"I'll go to Gamble, ask to be released from my contract. I'll even sign a non-compete that keeps me from racing anywhere else. I'll get a job. I know a lot about cars. There's something I can do. Something that won't scare you every day of our lives."

A look of awe transformed his features. "You would give up racing?"

"For you? For us? In a heartbeat." I meant it, too. I loved racing, but I loved Hopper more.

His breathing hitched. "I can't ask you to do that. That's an asshole thing to do."

I flashed a smile. "You didn't ask. I decided. Guess that makes me the asshole."

He lunged forward, wrapping his arms around me tight. "You are not an asshole."

"Hey," I said soft, pulling back enough to grab his hand and press it against my chest. "Feel that?"

His eyes went soft. "Yeah."

"Be a shame to waste something as exclusive as my heart. You're the only one who's ever gonna have it."

Hopper's hand slid up, curving around the back of my neck, and he leaned in inch by inch. Our lips met timidly at first. He kissed over mine softly, barely there, as if he were trying to savor the moment.

Eventually, the kiss grew deeper, our lips hungrier. The tension and adrenaline of the day started draining away and left us both tired, but never more awake.

In that moment, it seemed to me the thing to do when the true fragility of life reared its ugly head was not to push away the time you had left, but embrace it.

As we kissed, I pulled his shirt up and broke apart long enough to pull it over his head and toss it aside. I ran my palms over his chest, cupped his pecs, and dragged my fingertips down the center of his abs.

His hands explored beneath my shirt, rubbing everywhere he could reach. I shifted so one of his thighs was between mine and sucked his lip into my mouth. He groaned as I nibbled at the full flesh, and he began tugging at my clothes.

My shirt joined his somewhere on the floor, and I pushed him lightly back toward the bedroom. The blinds were still drawn, so most of the daylight was kept out. It was cooler in here because of the lack of light and movement in the space.

At the side of the bed, my fingers reached for the button on his jeans, popping it open and guiding the fly down. He was already hard, already straining against his clothes. I wanted him so badly my hands shook and my eyes were blind to everything else.

Hopper ripped his mouth from mine and started sucking down my neck, leaving a hot trail of moisture. I groaned and shoved his pants over his hips.

He lifted his head, his blue eyes half closed as he gazed at me. "I really do fucking love you."

"I love you, too, Hopp," I murmured.

He gripped my chin with one hand, turned my face to the side, and then used his free hand to trace down the arrow tattoo on my neck. The thick, slightly rough texture of his tongue glided across the same place, and then his lips latched onto that spot he always said taunted him. I angled my head away, giving him all the access he desired, delving my hands into the wild curls at the back of his head and pushed him just a little bit closer.

He sucked hard. It twinged with pain but bloomed into pleasure. My ball sack tingled and my ass clenched.

As he sucked and licked, I reached around, filled his ass with my palm, and squeezed. His hips pumped closer. Between us, his hard dick rubbed against me. I gave his ass a squeeze, then let my fingers delve into the crack. He jolted a little, lifting his mouth in surprise, but when my fingertip brushed over the sensitive nerves, he moaned and started sucking my neck again.

Sex with him was addicting, but never so much as it was now. I couldn't even think straight; all I could do was feel. When I released the back of his head, he lifted his mouth, puffy and red.

He held my gaze as he reached for my pants, unbuckled them, and pushed them to the floor. The second we were both standing before each other, completely naked, Hopper reached between us, grabbed our dicks in his one hand, and started jacking us at the same time.

I swayed a little on my feet, then reached down to wrap my hand around his. Our lips fused together again; our tongues fucked each other's mouths while we both stroked each other..

Silky liquid wept out of the tips, and I used it to enhance the pleasure and slip my hand up and down

Hopper's rod. He did the same with me, and soon we couldn't keep up the kiss because we were stroking each other so hard we were both gasping for breath.

I pulled back first. His dick sprang away from his body and pointed at me. I licked my lips, pushing him back onto the bed. He spread out on his back, hands at his sides. I climbed between his legs and lowered my mouth.

I sucked him deep all the way until my mouth hit his balls. I clamped my lips tight and slowly dragged back, releasing him little by little.

The head of his cock glistened with my spit and his precum when I finally let him go. He reached for me, but I shook my head and sucked one of his balls into my mouth, then moved to the other. As I played with his sack, my fingers dragged down his taint, then circled around the puckered hole, and he shuddered.

I leaned over to latch onto his inner thigh and sucked deep. A breath hissed between his teeth, and I gently probed at his hole.

"Jesus," he murmured, and I smiled.

I lifted my head and crawled up his body to straddle his waist. I reached behind me grabbed his throbbing dick and laid it against my crack.

His eyes shot open and stared at me. I smiled and continued to slide it along my slit. Gently, I started rocking against his body, and he wrapped a hand around my cock, which was hard and begging. Using his thumb, he spread the leaking fluid all over my head and then gave the tip a squeeze. I shuddered and leaned forward to suck one of his nipples into my mouth.

Hopper's fingers clung to my back as I sucked, then moved to the other. His hips pumped upward, and

I rocked against him. His hands slid down, cupping my ass cheeks, and I wiggled against his palms.

He looked at me; I felt the question in his gaze. I wiggled my ass again. "Touch me."

His fingers delved between my crack, slowly, exploring everything. It wasn't the first time he'd touched me there, but he always made sure I was okay with it, and he never got too bold.

This time when his finger grazed the sensitive hole, I groaned and pushed back against him. He paused, then stroked the area again. I was draped over his chest. My cock was hard between us, so I moved, rubbing it against his chest, and he stroked again.

I growled and whispered his name.

"What do you want, babe?" he whispered.

I sat up, and he pulled his hand away and wrapped it around my cock instead. I leaned over to the bedside table and pulled open the drawer.

Hopper's lips closed around my dick unexpectedly, and I shuddered and looked beneath me. He was deep-throating me, sucking hard, and my knees were starting to shake.

Quickly, I reached in the drawer and pulled out what I needed, a big-ass bottle of clear lube. Hopp introduced me to the stuff, and I always used more than I should when I entered him because I knew what it felt like when a body wasn't ready.

He sucked me deep again, and I jerked back. He glanced up at me, question in his eyes. I held the bottle out to him, and his eyes rounded into saucers.

"You don't have to do this to keep me," he vowed, caressing my cheek. "I'm not going anywhere. I promise."

"I never would have let you go." I kissed him. "You have my heart. It's time you got the rest of me."

"I…" His voice fell away. I saw the debate in his features. He didn't want to hurt me or bring up pain. "It's already been a shitty fucking day."

I held out the lube again. "So make it better."

He moaned.

I climbed off his lap and lay beside him, spreading my legs just enough for him to fit. He took the lube, laid it aside, and moved between my legs.

"You sure you want me on top?" he murmured, picking up my hand and kissing the palm.

"I'm sure."

With a sigh, he stretched his long, muscled body over mine. He was wider, stronger than me, but instead of feeling I was at a disadvantage, I felt protected and secure. There was something to be said about only seeing the man you loved above you and nothing else.

I stroked his back, and he dipped his head. We kissed languidly and rubbed our dicks together. Slowly, he moved down my body to draw each nipple into his mouth and suck them into hardened, sensitive pebbles.

As he kissed my chest, his hand moved down to cup my balls, then stroke my inner thigh. By the time he made it down to my waist, I was panting. We weren't new to foreplay. Fuck, I felt like every moment since he showed up at the fence was some form of foreplay between us, but I was starting to grow impatient.

He chuckled like he knew and sucked my cock, working it over with his tongue and mouth until I strained against him.

He pulled back, licked across my sack, and then dragged his tongue down my taint. I shivered with pleasure, but when his wide hands pushed my legs wider and settled on my thighs, the nerves broke in.

He didn't move fast, though. He put his head down and stroked me with his tongue some more. The nerves around the area began to tingle, and I squirmed. One hand left me, reaching for the bottle of lube, and I lay still, listening to it open and the soft movements of Hopp pouring it out on his hand.

I jerked a little when he rubbed it all along my taint and crack. It was slippery and smooth. It felt… good.

"I'll go slow, babe, and I'll stop anytime you want." He promised, his voice husky.

I nodded and waited, I admit, nervously for the first penetration.

After adding even more lube, I felt his finger at my entrance. Instead of jamming right in as I expected, he caressed and made me want it. As he worked, he leaned up and drew my cock into his mouth and sucked.

I groaned, and his finger sank in.

My eyes opened when I realized what he'd done, but he kept sucking my cock and his finger pumped slowly.

Oh my God… I shuddered.

"Babe?" His finger stilled inside me.

"It's fucking good," I rasped.

He chuckled and went back to working my hole, stretching it. Teasing it.

At one point, he even penetrated me with his tongue.

I started moaning, gripping the sheets, and spread my legs farther when the third finger slid in.

"No pain?" he asked, adding even more lube.

"Just want," I panted and wiggled against his fingers.

"Almost there, babe," he crooned and started fucking me with his fingers. I grabbed my dick and started rubbing it.

He pushed my hand away, and I groaned.

After what felt like endless, blissful torture, he withdrew. Before climbing up my body, he coated me with even more lube and then began covering himself.

I watched with half-closed eyes, then tried to push up to help stroke his dick. I didn't get very far before I fell back, all my muscles weak.

He laughed, coming over me with his palms on either side of my head. "You make me feel the same way," he whispered and kissed me soft.

His body positioned between my legs, and suddenly, I grew nervous.

He must have felt the change, because he settled against me, delicious weight on my body. "I'll stop right now," he vowed. "This is far enough for one day. I'll suck—"

"Inside me, Hopp," I said and lifted my hips.

He studied my eyes, trying to find even one shred of doubt. I didn't doubt him or this decision. Sure, I was a little afraid, but it wasn't because of him.

"I love you," I whispered.

His eyes melted. "I love you, too, babe."

He kissed me, and then I felt the round tip of his cock against my ass.

I watched him pull back, positioning himself right at my entrance. He looked up, and I nodded. Gently, slowly, he pushed inside.

I tensed at first, feeling that overwhelming sense of pressure.

"That only lasts a second," he vowed and pushed in a little deeper.

Oh, he was big. I was tight, but I felt my body stretch to accommodate him. We were both slick with lube, and he glided into me with ease. The feeling of pressure faded, and I sighed.

He smiled softly and pushed a little deeper. My eyes shot open, my mouth forming a little O. He chuckled, but I noted the way his arms shook.

"Is it okay?" I asked, suddenly worried maybe there was something wrong with me. Maybe the past had broken something.

"Are you fucking kidding me?" He groaned and lowered to his elbows. "You are fucking perfect, Arrow." He stroked and his eyes slid closed. "It literally doesn't get better than you."

His praise made me feel brave and hot all over. I shoved my ass down on him, and we both groaned.

"Oh fuck," I growled and wiggled.

"That's the spot," he murmured and pushed deeper. His cock rubbed over a place that created chills over my entire body. He found my G-spot. And now my feet were fucking tingling.

"I need to move, babe," he murmured.

"Do it."

Before he did, he kissed my cheek, brushing his lips over my ears. "Love you."

He started to move, to pull out and push in. He wasn't rough. He moved with care, but he used enough force and pressure that my eyes rolled back in my head.

Holy fuck, I had no clue. Not one clue this would ever feel this good. I mean, sure, I knew he liked it when I was inside him… but *dayum*.

He grunted, pushed deep, and hit my prostate. At the same time, his hand wrapped around my dick, and he started to pump me. I was weeping all over my abs, and he thrust in me again.

I caught my breath. He squeezed my head and began rhythmically pumping my cock and into my ass.

"I'm go—" I exploded all over his hand and my own stomach before I could even warn him.

It went on and on. I shuddered and jerked. My body lifted off the mattress, and I pulled a pillow over my face to muffle the sound of my loud moans.

Just when I thought it was over, he would pump in me again, brush that G-spot, and more release would shoot out.

"That's it, babe," he crooned. "I want it all."

Oh, he had it all.

He had everything.

Finally, I collapsed against the mattress, completely spent. I opened my eyes, lifted the pillow and his face filled my vision, smiling. "How was it?"

"We're not done yet," I panted and pushed against his still throbbing cock.

He groaned and thrust in me, pulled out, and thrust again. His hands ran up my chest, and I grabbed one of his hands, linking it with mine.

"I'm so close," he murmured, his voice hoarse. I felt his body pull back.

I squeezed his hand. "Don't even fucking think about it, Hopp. In me."

He grabbed my other hand so both ours were clasped and pushed them over my head, pinning me. I saw him glance down to make sure I was okay, but I would never not be okay with him.

We held hands while he thrust in me twice more.

I felt the jerking of his swollen head inside me, the sound of his release pronounced with a shout. I kissed his shoulder and chest while he shuddered and emptied inside me.

It was the single most epic physical experience of my life.

The walls this man broke down to be able to get this far. To be able to get inside me. The trust something like this required… I didn't think I'd ever be capable.

I was wrong.

He made it possible.

Hopper was still supporting his weight, afraid to give it all for me to support. I untangled our hands, wrapped my arms around his waist, and pulled him completely against me. He turned his head into my neck and sighed.

I rubbed his back, blissfully pressed into the mattress.

Eventually, he pulled back, glancing between my chest and his, then down between my legs.

I nodded and started to push up.

"Hey," he murmured and pushed me back. I looked up.

"Did I hurt you? Was it okay?"

I smiled so wide all my teeth flashed. "It was everything." I promised. "I loved it."

Relief relaxed his features. "You're going to be a little sore for a while. If it's too much…" He cleared his throat. "If it reminds you of other…"

I made a sound and shook my head. "Nothing about that reminds me of what happened to me. Nothing. There could never be any type of comparison."

"I was really fucking worried," he admitted.

I smiled. "I know. You were very thorough and very patient."

His eyes turned downcast. "I'm sorry I freaked out earlier."

"I did my own share of freaking."

"It was a bad day," he whispered.

"We're gonna have those, Hopp. We'll get through them. *Together.*"

He swallowed and nodded. "Together."

"Can you forgive me for trying to run?"

"What do you think?" I scoffed while nodding enthusiastically.

He laughed. "C'mon, shower. I'll wash your back."

The shower was long and hot. We made out like we hadn't just had sex and washed each other like it was foreplay. After we were both towel-dried and still naked, we climbed back in bed together. I curled up against Hopper's side.

It was pretty much unspoken we wouldn't be leaving each other's side the rest of the day. "I'm thinking pizza and movies," I said, brushing my hand over his abs.

"We need a TV in the bedroom," he observed.

"You need to bring some clothes over from your place," I added.

"You don't like me hanging out naked?"

I grunted. "Fucking love it. But you ain't answering the door for the pizza man with all your equipment on display."

"Hmm, give the guy a little dick and the jealousy begins."

"I'm pretty sure your dick ain't little," I muttered and reached beneath the blankets to grab it.

He began doing that thing I loved. The thing I anticipated most during the day (although it might be replaced with his cock inside me now). His fingers danced along my spine, and I let my eyes close.

I spent a long time being uncomfortable every minute of the day.

It was such a luxury, such a big thing to be so comfortable so often now.

"You know you can't give up racing," he said after a while.

I opened my eyes and stared across the room. "Yes, I can."

"I won't lie. I'm gonna be scared when you get on the track. Every single time. But I know you can do this. I want it for you. I won't hold you back because I'm scared. It's like you said. All of life is a risk. Not just your job."

"I do have a really good spotter that watches my back." I poked him in the side.

He growled. "Not good enough. Look what happened today."

"Today was my fault. I got distracted for one second. It won't happen again. I won't let it happen."

"Today wasn't anyone's fault. You would have avoided the pileup if that other car hadn't shoved you into it. It was an accident."

I lifted my head and smiled at him. "Look at you being all calm about this. I thought you might try and blame yourself."

"I thought about it," he muttered.

I know he did. And part of him still probably blamed himself; he was just trying to beat it back.

"I can't believe he had the fucking balls to show up today," I muttered.

"That guy is a real piece of work." Hopper agreed. "I wanted to deck him when I saw him."

I stiffened and looked up. "I don't want you around him. Not ever. He hurts everything he touches, and it won't be you. I'll fucking kill him first."

Hopper's muscles contracted. "Whoa, babe. It's okay."

"I mean it, Hopp. Stay away from him." Fuck, just the thought of my father pulling even one-tenth of the shit on Hopp he ever did to me made me crazy.

I felt the tension radiate from his body. "If he comes at you and I'm standing there, I won't just look the other way."

"He won't. He's not going to be around."

"You sure about that?" he asked skeptically. "He seemed awfully gung-ho about waving to his son from the stands."

I muttered a string of colorful curses that might or might not have included the words hairy goat balls, and Hopper laughed.

"I like it." He patted my bare ass. "Very creative."

"I'm sure," I said after I enjoyed his hand against my ass for a moment. "I'll make sure he stays gone."

"How are you going to do that?"

"By making it clear he won't get what he wants." I decided. "It seemed that damn *GearShark* interview was what brought him here."

"I can't believe the pecker read it before you did."

"Money talks," I muttered but jumped out of bed despite Hopper's attempts at towing me back. I walked out of the room to find my phone, curious about something.

When I came back into the room, Hopper wagged his eyebrows at me. "You got a nice ass."

I grinned and climbed back into bed.

"I wonder if the article is in my email," I said, pulling up the screen. "I haven't looked at it in a few days because we were so busy prepping for today."

Hopper sat up, propped some pillows against the headboard, and flung his arm out. I settled beside him, and his arm draped over my shoulders, his fingers absently playing with my nipple. He made a sound as I began sifting through the emails.

Seriously. I did not sign up for a newsletter about hemorrhoid cream. Where these vultures got my email, I had no clue.

Nasty.

Hopper's finger ran over the spot where my neck and shoulder met. "I left a bruise," he noted. "I was too rough."

"Nah, I liked it."

He leaned down and kissed the spot. My heart constricted.

"Here it is," I said and clicked on the email. I shifted as it opened and laid my head against his shoulder.

"*Arrow,*" I began reading the email from Emily out loud.

"*On behalf of GearShark Magazine, I would like to thank you for taking the time to be our cover star for the upcoming issue. Apologies on the delay of getting this proof of our interview to you. There were some setbacks. Professionally speaking, I am authorized to tell you that we made some minor emittances from the copy but otherwise stayed absolutely true to your words. We apologize for the minor inconvenience but hope you find the article to be a fantastic read. The issue will be going to print in the next few days and will be on the stands just after your first preseason race but in plenty of time to announce your signing with NASCAR before your first season begins.*

"If you require any changes, please contact me immediately. Otherwise, thank you again, and GearShark hopes to see more of you in the future!

"Sincerely,

"Emily Metcalf

"PS: Personally speaking (which I'm not supposed to do), I just want to let you know I empathize with who you grew up with. Living under that can't have been easy, and I am deeply sorry some of that truth won't see the light of day in this interview.

"For your convenience, I have left in the few passages being removed from your article due to some... circumstances... but have put them in BOLD lettering so you know exactly what is being removed and will not appear in the issue. Also attached is the cover."

My father was a real piece of shit. Obviously, he threw a big stink to the powers that be at *GearShark* and probably threatened a lawsuit.

I wondered exactly what I said that riled him up so badly.

I went to click on the attached article, but Hopper stopped me. "I wanna see the cover first. Give me the goods, babe."

I groaned but clicked the attached image. "I don't want to be seeing my skinny ass on camera."

"Your ass is not skinny," Hopper intoned.

The image appeared onscreen, and I stared at it, honestly not that impressed. In my opinion, I didn't make a very good model.

"That's fucking hot!" Hopper exclaimed and grabbed my phone from my hands. He sat forward a little and studied the image. "You look sexy as hell," he murmured. "I love the tats. Maybe I'm the one that should be jealous."

I grabbed the phone back and glanced at the aqua-colored text and the big picture of me before closing it out. "No one will ever take your place."

He pulled me back into his side and pressed his lips to my forehead. The stubble on his chin tickled my skin. "Love you, babe."

"Love you," I replied. Every time he said that, it felt like a massive gift.

Like it was Christmas morning every day and his words were the one thing I'd been waiting for all year.

"All right," he said, turning serious. "Pull this article up. Let's see what pissed off the old man."

I clicked the attachment and waited for all the words to load.

ARROW AMBROSE

prestened by

gearshark magazine

written by Emily Metcalf

© GearShark Magazine

The biggest shakeup in NASCAR history was almost a year ago, yet the racing world still buzzes about it. The ramifications are still being felt by the entire industry. Especially over at Team Gamble, the center of NASCAR's earthquake. The revelations last season about the terrible hazing and sexual harassment of none other than Joey Gamble, former pro racer and daughter of Ron Gamble himself, lead to a massive dismissal of nearly all of Gamble drivers (and even some staff).

Not long after, Gamble started rebuilding his team, combing the driving world for racers that were up-and-coming but also fairly fresh. He's put together a team critics and fans alike are frothing at the mouth to watch perform this season.

Will his brand-new team be as talented as the ones who came before? Will they be better behaved? More importantly, who will be his frontrunner? Which driver is the industry watching closest?

All of that remains to be seen. Except for one question. The who. It is a well-known fact that Gamble began courting driver Arrow Ambrose shortly after his daughter crossed over to the NRR. Unlike most drivers, Arrow didn't jump on board right away. In fact, he seemed to veer onto a different road altogether, the one leading toward the NRR, where his brother, Lorhaven, is one of the biggest names (next to Drew Forrester of course).

It seemed like a natural road to take, really. Why not join the family in a no-rules racing division?

But he didn't sign with the NRR either, and sources tell us Arrow had a deal on the table with Gamble for that division as well.

Two contracts, one big sponsor, and a choice between two major racing divisions? Here at GearShark, we think that qualifies Arrow Ambrose as the most fascinating driver of this year. It also definitely makes him Gamble's frontrunner.

So which division did Arrow choose? Which contract did he sign, and how exactly did the kid who bears a striking resemblance to a certain music heavyweight make a choice?

A choice that is going to surprise you. It did me. It also piqued my interest. Who exactly is Arrow Ambrose, and are all those rumors I've been hearing about his painful past and sexual orientation true?

I sat down with Arrow himself, at the center of all the action (Gamble Speedway), to bring you the hottest story of the year about who is sure to be NASCAR's next huge sensation.

Buckle your seat belts. The ride starts now.

GS: I have to tell you I haven't looked forward to an interview so much in a long time.

AA: <smiles> I won't tell my brother. He gets jealous easy.

GS: What's it like being the kid brother of such a well-respected racer?

AA: I'm not a kid. Haven't been for a long time.

GS: Noted.

AA: And having Lor for a brother is cool. He's taught me everything I know.

GS: I see you brought him with you today, along with another team member.

AA: *<nods>* My manager, Hopper.

GS: *<I'd like to note at this time there is a definite vibe to this interview, a feeling of protection that circles Arrow like a bubble. Lorhaven and his manager, Hopper, tower over where Arrow sits, eyes active and even throwing warning glances at me every few seconds. I have to admit it makes me even more curious.>* Doesn't Hopper work on the NASCAR side of Team Gamble?

AA: Yes.

GS: So it's true, then, that you have recently signed with NASCAR, and this is the first interview you're giving as a pro racecar driver.

AA: You heard it here first. I'm officially signed with NASCAR and am being sponsored by Gamble, among other companies who will be announced shortly. *<Looks over his shoulder at Hopper, who nods in agreement.>*

GS: Congratulations! That is very exciting. I have to say, though, I'm surprised. I think almost everyone, myself included, expected you to sign with the NRR. It seemed like a natural fit for you. Why veer onto a road less traveled?

AA: Because if I signed with NRR, I'd always be staring at my brother's taillights. *<grins>*

GS: *<There is something impossibly endearing and sneakily sexy about this guy.>* You don't think you would ever be able to beat him?

L: <*speaks up from behind Arrow*> Hell no.

AA: I think I could give him a run for his money, but that's not really what I meant. You said it yourself. I'm Lorhaven's kid brother. If I went into the NRR, I would be slapped with that label, and it would never come off. I'm my own man. I have my own goals.

GS: What kind of goals?

AA: To make a name for myself on the track. To have a life based off what I want and no one else. To win races.

GS: Why NASCAR? From what I hear, you auditioned months ago. You had an offer on the table since then. You didn't sign. Why now? What changed?

AA: I changed. I decided that reaching for what I wanted might not be as impossible as it seemed. And I'm a thoughtful guy, I wanted to think about what I was doing before I did it.

GS: I have to ask. Is one of the major reasons you waffled about signing with NASCAR because of recent events involving hazing and discrimination and your sexual orientation?

AA: You mean because I'm gay?

GS: <*I like a blunt man.*> Are you?

AA: Yes, I am. And yeah, it factored into the decision, but not as heavily as you might think.

GS: So you aren't worried the same thing will happen to you that happened to Joey Gamble?

AA: Honestly? No. I sure as hell don't expect everyone to accept me, but the new Team Gamble is full of professionals.

GS: Describe to me your first day at the track, the day you were introduced to everyone.

AA: There was a big meeting. I can't tell you everything that went down. <*Leans close conspiratorially*>

Trade secrets you know. *<winks>* But I can tell you my sexuality was addressed. It's not a secret, and everyone on the team knows. So far, it hasn't been a problem. Everyone is cool, and those drivers know their shit. Keep an eye out for Gamble drivers this season. We're gonna dominate.

GS: Oh, we're definitely watching. So you aren't worried about your own teammates giving you a hard time, but what about the rest of NASCAR?

AA: I can handle it. I've been through a lot worse.

GS: Speaking of, there's a lot of mystery and speculation around your past. You just implied it hasn't always been so great. Care to elaborate?

AA: I've known I'm gay since high school, maybe even before that. When I came out to my parents at the age of seventeen, I knew there would be a lot of shock, maybe even some anger. **But it was a lot worse than that.**

GS: Worse how?

AA: My father disowned me. Actually, at first, he told me to just stop, like I was a leaky faucet that just needed adjusting. When that didn't work, he took everything away and kicked me out.

GS: What did you do?

AA: I went to my brother. He took me in, helped me start my life over again. *<Clears throat. Shifts uncomfortably.>*

GS: Is there something else?

AA: I was attacked and beaten up for being gay.

GS: *<Gasps>* That's terrible. I'm so sorry.

AA: It made me who I am today.

GS: And who are you?

AA: A guy who just wants to leave the past in the rearview and drive ahead.

GS: Do you ever speak to your father?

AA: No, and I'd like to keep it that way.

GS: Do you think being the first openly gay driver in NASCAR is going to open the door, not just in racing, but all sports, to those who maybe have been afraid to be who they really are?

AA: I hope so, but I don't think someone should come out or reveal anything so personal unless they are absolutely ready. That isn't something that happens overnight. And look, I might be the first openly gay driver in NASCAR, but I'm not the first in the industry. Drew Forrester and Trent Mask get more credit than me for paving the way. If it weren't for them, I might not have had the balls to be sitting here today.

H: *<This is Hopper, Arrow's manager… but as I look at him now, I'm wondering if he isn't more. And just who is the manager with only one name?>* Not true. You would totally be here.

GS: How long did it take you?

AA: *<Smiles>* I'm still working on it.

GS: Are you currently dating or in a relationship?

AA: *<Shifts and glances behind him. Hopper, who is still standing there like a bulldog with a bad attitude, nods once.>* Yes, I'm currently seeing someone.

GS: Anyone we know?

AA: Hopper, the manager for Team Gamble.

GS: So the vibes I'm picking up aren't all in my head.

AA: *<Slowly smiles>* Depends on what vibes you're talking about.

GS: *<Did I mention the tattoos on his neck and down his arms are very distracting? In a good way.>* I'm assuming everyone at Gamble knows about your relationship?

AA: We aren't hiding it.

GS: How long have you and Hopper been seeing each other?

AA: A while.

GS: That's very vague.

AA: That's very personal.

GS: Are you in love with him?

AA: How about we get back to racing?

GS: I've been wondering… Why do you have a different last name than your brother?

AA: Because I changed mine.

GS: Is this also because of your father?

AA: Yes. I don't want anything of his, even his name.

GS: What about your mother?

AA: She's very supportive of me. We have a good relationship.

GS: Tell me the one thing you are most excited about in NASCAR?

AA: <*smiles*> The car of course.

GS: I have to say I think you're a brave man. Brave and confident for stepping into a brand-new racing team, right into the hot seat, on the tails of something that would scare away most gay men.

AA: Like I said, I've been through worse. And I'm used to fear.

GS: Okay, I have to ask. I'm curious, so I know our readers will be. Tell us something about Hopper. He's been with Team Gamble for a while, but no one seems to know anything about him.

AA: He drinks his coffee black.

GS: I was hoping for something a little more… riveting. Who is Hopper, and why does he only go by one name?

AA: Some people only need one name. Like my brother.

GS: You're not going to give me the goods, are you?

AA: *<Lifts his hands in a 'what can you do' gesture.>* Not a chance.

GS: All right. Let's shift gears. Can you sing? *<I had to ask, you guys. Just look at him on the cover! I know you want to know, too.>*

AA: *<laughs>* Not at all.

GS: But you can drive.

AA: Most definitely. Keep a close eye on the track this season. I'll be the car that's nothing but a blur.

Arrow Ambrose, the new NASCAR driver who is openly gay, in a relationship with not only another man, but a fellow Gamble employee. Ron Gamble must have a very lax company dating policy.

Or maybe he just knows real love when he sees it.

Arrow might have sidestepped my questions like the pro he is, but energy doesn't lie and neither do the looks I saw passing between him and his manager, Hopper.

We at GearShark want to offer an official congratulatory welcome to Arrow for signing on with NASCAR and changing the face of pro driving potentially forever.

Because whether he believes it or not, this guy is breaking down barriers. This might be the first we've seen of Arrow, but it most definitely won't be the last.

You won't see him on the track, though, because as he said, he'll be nothing but a blur.

Good thing you have GearShark to keep you up to date on all things racing, including its newest hottest commodity.

Chapter Forty-*Six*

Hopper

I almost lost someone I loved because holding on to them was sometimes even scarier that letting go.

I'd learned something since Arrow stepped into my life.

The difference between life and death.

There wasn't one, not really.

Death was when life ceased. When something or someone you loved was permanently taken away. Part of them remained in life, though, didn't they? In a heart, in a memory... even in something as simple as a tattoo.

Life *is* death when you allow it swallow you whole. You can be dead while your heart still beats.

Life and death were permanently intertwined.

They weren't separate, even when they felt that way. Death was part of life. Therefore, even gone, Matt still lived on inside me. And even though I was still alive, I lived as though I were dead.

Until Arrow.

Until he reached into my chest and gave my heart a squeeze.

I didn't know what I ever did to find real, true love, not once, but twice in my life. But I did, and because of it, I was more grateful than ever.

I might always feel a little guilty for loving Arrow so fiercely after Matt. Deep down, I understood loving A didn't mean I loved Matt any less.

If anything, Matt taught me how to love so when Arrow came along, so shattered and shy, I knew how to love him back to life.

I might not have been able to save Matt that day, but in a sense, I saved Arrow, just as Arrow saved me.

It wouldn't ever be easy for him and me, but nothing worthwhile ever was.

I grabbed up the boxes and bag filled with clothes and shoes, glancing around my empty, impersonal space I'd mistakenly thought of as home far too long. I walked out of the place without a second thought, without a single glance back.

I hefted it all quietly, barely noticing the weight, and pushed into the apartment with the giant red wall. His high-tops were scattered on the floor, my hat was in the corner, and there were pizza boxes on the counter.

This was home.

This was where I belonged.

All this time I'd been saying all or nothing… Well, I think it finally clicked.

Arrow was my all, and without him, I had absolutely nothing.

I dumped all my shit in the half-empty dresser and scattered some stuff across the bathroom counter, smiling.

On my way to the door, I put the three measly pair of shoes I owned in the cubbies next to Arrow's twenty-five.

Nothing's ever felt so right.

At the door, I glanced around with a grin on my face before locking up and heading out. I was already looking forward to coming home later.

But first, I had somewhere to be.

Chapter Forty-*Seven*

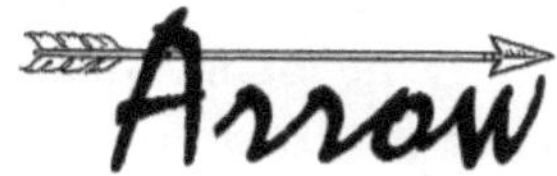

I hit the nail on the head.

Fucking bull's-eye when I called my father out. I had no idea I'd gotten as close to the truth as I had.

Sure, I knew he wanted to use me. I knew his little trip to see his "son" wasn't about me at all. It was about him. Everything was always about him.

After I read that article, I knew exactly. Exactly what he was trying to avoid and exactly what I said that bothered him so much.

What a douche.

A class-A, award-winning douchebag.

Frankly, my mother was lucky she got the fuck away from him. I was, too. Funny how I never really thought about my situation before as lucky, but in some aspects, I was.

Some aspects = I got out from under my father's giant bigoted thumb.

He hadn't bribed someone at *GearShark* to read my article early because he was just booming with fatherly pride; he was covering his bases, protecting himself.

Everything I said about him in the interview was stricken. I never called him by name. All I ever referred to him as was "my father." Hell, we didn't even have the same last name.

It didn't matter, though. He knew what I knew.

It wouldn't take long for the press to figure out who my unnamed father was. I was Jace's brother after all, and he would lead everyone's eyes right to ol' Sully.

What bothered me most was he knew what he did to me was wrong. He knew the way he behaved and treated me was disgusting. He didn't feel bad about it, not one bit. What he felt bad about was that the whole world might discover exactly who he was.

Wait. That wasn't what bothered me most. It was close, but something else nudged it out of the top spot. Hopper.

What my father pulled today affected me. No matter how hard I tried and how I stood against him, inside, a part of me still caved. He fucked with my head, which took a piece of my mind off the track.

It took a piece away from Hopper.

I would allow nothing, and I mean *nothing*, to come between Hopper and me. I would allow nothing to compromise the safety net we were building between each other.

Sullivan had to go.

Permanently.

And no, that didn't mean I was plotting his murder. Geez, you guys, get your head out of the gutter.

Besides, I wouldn't ruin my life to take out someone as shitty as Sullivan. He wasn't worth the sacrifice.

Nerves bunched so densely I felt I had a rock sinking in my stomach, pushing it down and putting pressure on my intestines beneath it (yikes, that was graphic). He made me feel that way though—graphic. Shocked to the point I wanted to look away.

It was disgusting he was my father, that his blood flowed through my veins.

Even though I felt so violently nervous and, yeah, intimidated by him, I marched on anyway. I was doing this for Hopper. More importantly, I was doing this for me.

I wasn't going to live like a shadow anymore. Just when I started to step out, he showed up again to try and knock me back into place. Fuck him. This was my life, and he got no say.

I didn't walk away from the strip club that night years ago just to slink away and live in isolation. No. I threw his conditions, his bribes, and his money right in his face so I wouldn't have to be someone I wasn't.

I hadn't done a very good job living up to that.

I was disappointed in myself. I felt as if I'd just woken from a very long dream, opened my eyes, and realized what my reality was.

A quick call to Jace and I knew exactly where Sullivan was staying. I could have guessed it would be the nicest hotel in town. But calling only made it easier to find the room number. Jace was concerned. He wanted to speed over and meet me.

I told him no.

This was something I had to do on my own. Sullivan was going to see I could stand tall on my own two feet, and I didn't need anyone to back me up because I was strong enough.

I took the elevator up to the penthouse (cue eyeroll). The entire way, I stared at myself in the mirrored doors. I was dressed in a pair of faded, ripped jeans and a hoodie Hopper left at my place a few days ago. It smelled like him, something I really loved, and at the risk of sounding corny, whenever I wore it, I felt he was wrapped around me no matter where I was.

I had on bright-red high-tops because my father hated ripped-up jeans and "clunky" shoes. My hair was a little wild because I'd just spent hours in bed with Hopp.

Just thinking about it made my dick stir. I was ready to go again. I was gonna keep that guy up all night long.

The elevator slid to a stop. Before the doors opened, I ran my hand through my hair nervously, trying to tame its messy style.

"Fuck it," I said, striding out into the small hallway and beating confidently on the door.

A few seconds went by, and I pictured my father peering through the peephole at me. I thought about covering it up just to be a dick, but in the end, I just stood there and waited.

"Arrow?" he said when the door was open.

"I'm here to talk," I announced. Without waiting, I slammed my hand on the door and pushed it open to stride into his suite.

There was a wall of windows overlooking the landscape. It was nearly dark, but not quite. It was probably a hella nice view when all the lights were on outside. But I wasn't here to enjoy the view.

I spun around, pinning him with a stare. "You're leaving."

He made a sound like he was weary of my tantrum and went over to the wet bar for a drink. The action made me sneer. So did the fact that he was dressed in pajamas that made him look like Hugh Hefner.

"You've already made it clear you want me to leave."

"I'm not talking about just tonight. I mean forever. This is the last time we will ever see each other."

He paused, halfway lifting the glass to his mouth. "That seems a little extreme considering you are my son."

"I'm not. You gave up that right the day you disowned me. No. You gave up that right long before that. Lorhaven has been more of a father to me than you ever have."

He slammed the crystal down and turned to look at me. "How dare you?"

"How dare I?" I raised an eyebrow and advanced. "How dare *you?*"

"Perhaps we should talk about this another time, maybe after you've had time to, uh, decompress after your accident."

I snorted. "You think that accident has anything to do with me wanting you out of my life? Maybe it does." I nodded. "It's my final straw. It's the last time you will ever have any power over my mind."

"You'll want my sponsorship, my support," he intoned.

I laughed. Then I laughed some more. "Are you fucking kidding? I wouldn't touch anything with your name on it with a ten-foot pole."

"You've grown some balls since I saw you last," he observed. It was almost as if he thought it was cute.

I stalked across the room, channeling all the anger I'd ever felt at his hands, all the humiliation, the pain. I remembered how it felt that night in the hangar after I was beaten and raped, how hopeless, and I recalled the blood I'd spilled from my own body just trying to end it all.

Whatever he saw in my eyes made his face pale. He stepped back, but I kept coming. Every step he took, I advanced. Eventually, he came up against the bar.

I smiled like the Cheshire Cat and moved in. I slammed my hands on either side of him; they slapped against the stone. He jerked like it was him I'd stuck.

I leaned in close, close enough for him to get a real good look at how very deeply I loathed him.

"I'm not scared of you," I whispered darkly. "I might have been once, but not anymore. It's you who should be afraid."

"Leave now," he commanded, but it ended up sounding weak.

His hands flattened on my shoulders and pushed. I didn't budge, looking down to where he touched me and then back up, lifting an eyebrow.

He dropped his hands.

"Oh, I'm leaving, but not until you listen, and you better listen good. I am not fucking repeating myself."

He swallowed.

"You listening?"

He nodded.

"I know damn well you had all mention of you wiped out of my interview. All mention of any kind of mistreatment I suffered at the hands of the man who was supposed to take care of me. Even though I didn't mention you by name, even though I didn't call your bitch-ass out like I should have, you still had it wiped."

"People would have figured it out," he snapped.

I grinned widely, but from the look in his eyes, I knew I succeeded at making it look anything but friendly.

"All you care about is people knowing what kind of sick, depraved man you really are. You thought you could waltz back into my life hand me some cash and your stamp of approval and you'd own me. Tell me, *Dad*," I spewed quietly. "Are you surprised your throwaway son is the one with the pro contract? That I'm the one who would do your *prestigious* name the most good?"

"I made a mistake," he said miserably, as if he really were sorry.

"Yes. You did. And now you can live with it."

I shoved away, causing him to flinch, and strode toward the door. Just when I practically heard his sigh of relief that I was leaving, I turned and smiled again.

"Here's what's going to happen." I held up my fingers to tick them off as I spoke. "You're going to pack your shit, change out of those ridiculous pajamas, and leave. Now. You'll go back to your pathetic existence and sit in your towering glass building and pretend you really do own the world. You won't call. You won't text. You won't write. You won't check up on me. Or bribe people to find out what I'm doing. You won't claim me as your son."

He rose to his full height and lifted his chin. The stubborn, cruel Sullivan was coming out to play. Good. "You don't control me. I do what I want, when I want. You can't stop me."

"Oh, I can. And I will. If you don't disappear out of my life, I'm gonna destroy you and everything you hold precious."

He scoffed, and I took one step toward him.

He jerked back.

"Shut the fuck up and listen," I snapped.

He nodded dumbly.

"I will call up the biggest news outlet and magazine in this country, and I will go live with an exclusive tell-all interview. You know what live means, Sullivan? It means you won't be able to pay anyone to cut out the parts you don't like. You won't know when or how. You won't see me coming. One day, you'll walk into work, and all the people who usually scurry away or bow at your feet will look at you with disgust and horror. They'll whisper behind your back. The secretary you love to screw on your desk and get your little dick sucked off by? She won't touch you. No woman that you don't pay will ever again."

"You wouldn't dare." He seethed.

"Fucking try me. You pushed the wrong buttons, old man. You went for the one thing that's off-limits to you. As of right this second, we don't know each other. If you see me on the street, turn and walk the other way. Leave Hopper alone. You don't talk to him, look at him, or acknowledge him. All the rules for me extend to him."

"You're doing all this for a man who takes it in the ass?" he snarled.

"No," I said, not even offended he was so disgusting. "I'm doing it for *love*. And I'm doing it because I finally realize I am so much better than you ever tried to make me."

He began to sputter. The color still hadn't returned to his face.

I turned to walk away.

"You won't get away with this. If you out me to the press, I will ruin your life."

I smiled. "No. You won't. You don't have that power over me, and you never will again."

He frowned.

"If you want everyone to know every sick detail of every sick thing you've done to me, go ahead. I'll spill it. It won't matter. The only one it will hurt is you, because the people in my life, they'll love me regardless."

"No one loves you, you little bastard!" he screamed after me as I pulled open the door.

I heard his slippers slapping against the floor as he raced after me. I turned to see him raising a fist. I caught it in my hand and squeezed. He looked between me and our hands, his eyes nearly popping out of his head.

I reared back, ready to bury my fist right in his face.

Then I didn't. I dropped it. I let go of his hand and I stepped away. "You're nothing to me. Not even worth the energy of a fucking punch."

He stared at me in shock as I hit the button for the elevator. It opened immediately, and I stepped inside, folded my hands in front of me, and stood straight and tall.

Sullivan stared at me as the doors slowly slid shut.

I saw the defeat in his eyes. The shock. Maybe even a hint of regret.

When the doors secured, I was left staring at myself in the glass once more.

I smiled.

Chapter Forty-*Eight*

Hopper

When I got home, the apartment was still empty. Arrow was still not home.

Worry curled through my stomach, and I pulled out my phone and shot off a text.

Where are you?

The second it sent, the front door opened and Arrow's blond head appeared. He was wearing my hoodie. He looked better in it than I did. Seconds later, his phone when off in his hand.

"That was me," I said. My face split into a smile because he was here and he was sexy.

"You need something?" he asked, immediately concerned.

"Just you."

He smiled and crossed the room, kissing me deeply, and when we pulled back, he rubbed at my lower lip.

"What've you been up to?" he asked, looking around, seeing my shoes next to his and turning back ninja fast.

"Hope you don't mind… I moved in."

"Seriously?"

I nodded. "My underwear and pants are in the bedroom. You know, so I don't have to answer the door naked."

He leapt at me. Like for reals leapt off the ground into my arms. I laughed and caught him. His legs wrapped around my waist, and he made a *whoop* sound.

"You're skinny, babe. But you aren't *that* skinny." I joked.

"I'm hungry." He complained.

I pulled his head down and kissed him. As we kissed, his cock grew against my stomach and aroused my own desire. But I banked it for now and walked with him still in my arms to the sofa, where I sat down with him in my lap.

"How was it?" I asked, nervous, but not quite as much now that he was in my arms and smiling.

"He's not going to be a problem ever again," he replied confidently. Confidence was a good look on him.

"Want to talk about it?" I asked, completely ready to listen.

Arrow shook his head. "No."

I nodded. Confronting his father was something he did for him, not for anyone else. And I didn't need to know what happened, because the most important thing was Arrow felt free of him.

"I'm proud of you," I told him, rubbing my hands up his back.

Sometimes he looked at me with awe in his eyes. I didn't think I'd ever get used to it, and I doubted he would ever stop. "I love you."

I was a lucky man.

I reached up to cover his heart with my palm, wanting to feel the strength of his heartbeat.

He winced.

Immediately, I pulled back. "What's wrong?" I demanded. "Motherfucker, if that peckerhead touched you…" I started to get up.

Arrow laughed, then pushed me back down. "He didn't touch me." He promised. "Calm down."

I sagged back against the seat, and he settled again in my lap. I slapped a hand to my forehead and dragged it down my face.

"Hey," he said, alarmed. "What's this?"

Gingerly, he lifted my arm up, looking at the white bandage wrapped around my wrist. "Where's your bracelet?" he demanded.

"In the bedroom." I gestured to the room with my head. He surrendered my arm, and I peeled up the tape around the bandage. "I did more than just move in while you were gone."

He lifted an eyebrow.

Slowly, I unwrapped the bandage and turned my wrist for him to see.

His breath caught. His fingers hovered over area, his eyes entranced.

"You got a new tattoo?" he whispered.

"Like it?" I asked.

He looked up, then back down. A smile so happy it actually hurt my heart bloomed on his face. "Are you fucking kidding me?" He glanced up. "You did this for me?"

I cupped his face. "For us."

He gazed down at the design again.

"I hope it's okay I put it under the coordinates."

"It's perfect," he murmured, his voice watery and low. Still staring down, he traced the design in the air above it, knowing it was still to tender to touch.

It was an infinity sign with an arrow right through the center. It represented him and me and how he shot right into my life and handed me forever.

He pulled his hand back but still stared down. Seconds later, a drop of moisture fell on the design. I tipped his head up; he tried to stop me, but I prevailed.

A single tear tracked down his cheek.

I brushed it away with my thumb.

He sniffled and pulled back, reaching for the hem of his shirts. "I didn't just go see my father," he admitted and peeled the clothes over his head.

There was a bandage very similar to mine over his heart.

I sucked in a breath. "Are you freaking kidding?"

He shook his head slowly. I fingered the edge of the bandage and glanced up for permission. He nodded, his eyes still slightly wet.

I peeled away the bandage, and it fell, fluttering between our bodies.

"Arrow," I half groaned.

"Guess we had the same idea," he mused.

He had the exact same tattoo over his heart, just a little bigger because it was on his chest.

I touched the edges, just out of reach of the tenderness.

"You're my infinity, Hopp," he vowed. "I don't care where life takes me as long as you come, too."

I wrapped my arms around his back and dove into the couch, sliding him beneath me. My mouth landed on his instantly, and we kissed like it was the first time. His lips were warm and soft, his tongue promised pleasure to come, and when he started smiling in the middle of our kiss, my heart expanded to a size I never thought possible.

"I love you," I growled against his smile. "I fucking love you forever."

And I did.

Our love was infinite.

Author's Note

If you made it here, you deserve a cookie. Warm from the oven.

I was supposed to release this book in July. It is now December, and I'm just writing THE END. I knew this book would be challenging. I mean, all of them are. But I really had no idea how much it would take to write.

#Blur was incredibly hard to just sit down and "pound out." I would write some. Then I would need a day or two to almost digest it. To think about it. I spent a lot of time just thinking about this book, trying to understand these two characters. Trying to get it right.

I don't know if I will ever fully understand them, because I've never experienced what they have. Perhaps that's why this was so hard. I try to write with truth, with emotion, and with a certain type of empathy. Not only was the subject matter in this book very challenging and dark, but I felt an overwhelming desire to "get it right." Arrow claimed my heart a long time ago, back when he first appeared in *#Junkie*. I didn't know a lot about him then, but I understood he was broken.

I wanted to tell his story. I wanted to give him a happily ever after, but good Lord, getting there was a task! It wasn't easy to get him there. And Hopper… he surprised you, didn't he? Me, too. He's real and raw. And that hair of his… Does anyone else just want to push your hands through it?

No? Just me?

I'm delirious. This book has drained me.

(I still want to touch his hair.)

I wish I could sit here and write an epic author's note, pour out exactly what I went through with this book. How it was a fight at times, how it was awkward at times, and how sometimes I would have butterflies in my stomach when I wrote. Alas, I am exhausted. Even so, I don't think I can fully explain what it was like to write this book. I'm hoping the words speak for themselves. I hope you *feel* everything I tried to say. I also hope you find this story to be everything you wanted it to be and a book fitting of the *GearShark* series.

I have to say the *GearShark* series is something I am very proud of. It really challenged me as a writer. It pushed me way out of my comfort zone. I'm tired, I'm a little brain fried, but the end result is something I wouldn't change for anything.

I want to thank you for reading this far, for hanging in there as I told Hopper and Arrow's story. I think it might be a little different than all of us were expecting (longer, too!), but I truly hope it's one you enjoyed.

See you next book!

XOXO,

Cambria

Cambria Hebert is an award-winning, bestselling novelist of more than thirty books. She went to college for a bachelor's degree, couldn't pick a major, and ended up with a degree in cosmetology. So rest assured her characters will always have good hair.

Besides writing, Cambria loves a caramel latte, staying up late, sleeping in, and watching movies. She considers math human torture and has an irrational fear of birds (including chickens). You can often find her painting her toenails (because she bites her fingernails) or walking her Chihuahuas (the real rulers of the house).

Cambria has written within the young adult and new adult genres, penning many paranormal and contemporary titles. She has also written romantic suspense, science fiction, and, most recently, male/male romance. Her favorite genre to read and write is contemporary romance. A few of her most recognized titles are: *The Hashtag Series*, *GearShark Series*, *Text*, *Torch*, and *Tattoo*.

Recent awards include: Author of the Year, Best Contemporary Series (*The Hashtag Series*), Best Contemporary Book of the Year, Best Book Trailer of the Year, Best Contemporary Lead, and Best Contemporary Book Cover of the Year. In addition, her most recognized title, *#Nerd,* was listed at Buzzfeed.com as a top fifty summer romance read.

Cambria Hebert owns and operates Cambria Hebert Books, LLC.

You can find out more about Cambria and her titles by visiting and following her here:

Website: http://www.cambriahebert.com
Email: cambriahebert@rocketmail.com
Facebook: http://smarturl.co/CambriaHebertFanpage
Twitter: https://twitter.com/cambriahebert
Instagram: @cambriahebert

Sign up for her newsletter: http://eepurl.com/bUL5_5

Join her fan club:
https://www.facebook.com/groups/1535723103367408/